I0600169

Bound In Nightmares

V.V. Webb

Copyright © 2024 by V.V. Webb

All rights reserved.

No part of this publication may be reproduced, distributed, or transmitted in any form or by any means, including photocopying, recording, or other electronic or mechanical methods, without the prior written permission of the publisher, except as permitted by U.S. copyright law. For permission requests, contact [include publisher/author contact info].

The story, all names, characters, and incidents portrayed in this production are fictitious. No identification with actual persons (living or deceased), places, buildings, and products is intended or should be inferred.

Book Cover by V.V. Webb and Rachelle L

2nd Edition, 2024

CONTENTS

AUTHOR'S NOTE

Dear Beautiful Readers,

Writing this book was, in many ways, very healing for me. While I had to open some old wounds to create certain parts of this story, I can tell you all that it was well worth it. Like going and getting surgery to remove an old rock from your knee that had healed beneath the skin (a childhood friend I knew had this issue, it was *not* cool).

However, as fulfilling as this was for me, I must warn each of you readers – this is not a 'light' read. This is *dark romance*. There are many triggers, several of which are *not* romance related. Now, for those of you that enjoy having the ground ripped from beneath your feet, continue on past the next page and delve in. But for those of you that like reading trigger warnings like shopping lists, flip that page and read away.

But whichever of these kinds of readers you are, please understand that there are things that will almost *certainly* be triggering. Not to sound redundant, but your mental health matters (it truly does – more than anything else in your worlds). And I have hope that by the end of the book, many of you will be able to see beyond the dark stuff to a bigger picture. Because there *is* an overlaying message here (do you feel like you're in high school again, being told by your English teacher to interpret the mind of someone they have never met?).

Anywho,

My piece has been said.

So, turn one page,

Or two,

That's up to you –

But, either way, enjoy your ride into this world of nightmares.

Trigger Warnings

- Dubcon

- Noncon

- Suicidal Thoughts

- Self-Harm (**on page**)

- Suicide (**on page**)

- Stalking

- Claustrophobia

- Bondage

- Kidnapping

- Torture

- Abuse

- Violence

- Murder

If you or someone you know is struggling with depression, thoughts of suicide or self-harm, please do not hesitate to contact a *trusted* connection or your local emergency assistance line. ***<u>You are important</u>***, no matter who or where you are.

DEDICATION

To those of you that wish you could make a nightmare turn into a sexy fantasy, this one is for you.

Chapter 1

***

I ran through a black forest, trees rising from the frost coated soil; their limbs seemingly reached towards me with their leafless claws. Roots appeared at random in an attempt to trip me, to make me fall and tumble to the unforgiving ground. My breath was ragged, the frozen air coating my lungs in icy fire. I knew someone was chasing me, though I didn't know why. My long hair flew into my face, but I didn't have time to tie it back. I had to keep moving. Electricity crackled through me, a pure shot of fear making my arms and legs pump faster than they ever had before.

Suddenly, I heard a low laugh. I felt the vibrations deep in my bones and knew it was over. He was here. A flash of color on my left sent me crashing to the ground. The laughter grew louder, relishing in my torment. I tried to lurch to my feet, but a heavy weight pressed painfully into my spine. Cold fingers gripped my hair as my head was jerked off the ground.

"Tsk, tsk, tsk. You didn't really think you could outrun me, did you?"
A growling voice whispered in my ear. "You're *mine* now, Evalyn. You're
in *my* world. There is nowhere for you to run," the voice chuckled
quietly. "Now, where shall we begin?"

Despite the cold, heat flashed through me.

***

I woke with a start, sweat coating my skin, gasping desperately, trying to
suck air into my lungs. I raked my trembling fingers through my hair,
but abruptly stopped as I realized this only served as a reminder of the
dream. So, I lowered my hands to my face instead. I felt flushed, my body
confused and exhausted. I glanced at the clock, noting the time. Half
past three. I sigh and rub my eyes again, knowing I won't be going back
to sleep any time soon.

I berated myself for not being a normal person that sleeps through the
night. Any time I move or sleep in a new environment, these dreams take
over me. It's just a mental reaction to change, my subconscious trying to
process everything. According to a therapist I'd had, at least. Hopefully,
this would be my last move for a while. At 29, I finally bit the bullet
on buying, mostly so I didn't have to rent in this ridiculous economy
anymore. I had been waiting, hoping, that I'd eventually be able to do
this with a partner, but as my list of failed relationships grew, I realized it
was a dumb reason to wait on buying a house. At first glance, the house
I purchased was...daunting. The messy landscaping and rotting porch
on the outside combined with the outdated and dirty interior was more
than enough to scare most away.

But I was able to see what it *could* be, which is why I was able to take
this lovely place off the market. Renovations would need to be made, but

the charm and coziness of the house was undeniable. While the yard was overgrown, it could be molded. The bay windows and vaulted ceilings were beautiful, combined with the open floorplan on the first floor. The roof had a few peaks at different heights, adding a hint of grandeur to the outside. Trees lined the yard, thin in the front but thick in the back. Internally, I'd made a mullet joke the first time I'd thought of it like that. A long driveway wove in front of the house, and enough trees covered the property to ensure a certain level of privacy – although not a forest, by any means. It was perfect, far enough from people to be comfortable, but close enough for easy access to the conveniences of a suburban area.

I was thankful to have found this quiet property where I could focus on writing my screenplays. Some days it was arduous work, but others my creativity could spill in rivulets on the page – or keyboard. I hoped that a house like this would do wonders for my creativity.

I sighed, walking to the bathroom that was in dire need of a renovation. I had already spoken to some contractors that would be stopping by in the next few days to look over the different areas of the house that needed some modern touches. I didn't have an endless stream of money, but I had saved more than enough over the years to be comfortable with paying for a few beneficial projects. Selling screenplays wasn't the most lucrative at times, so I saved as much as I could as the years drifted by. Luckily for me, the last screenplay I wrote paid out nicely with horror movies in high demand.

As I reached the bathroom, I peeled off my favorite over-sized sleeping shirt and turned on the water to full heat. My favorite way to get rid of a lingering nightmare was burning them out of my system via boiling water. Steam filled the bathroom after a few moments and I stepped under the spray, flinching at the heat but embracing the pain. I stood there for longer than necessary, letting the warmth seep into my pores and turn my pale skin red. When I noticed the temperature slowly dropping, I quickly rushed through the washing process, then stepped out of the shower and wrapped myself in the fluffiest robe I had. I wanted to hold onto the heat as long as I could. The robe was the last step of my recipe to erasing a nightmare.

I walked through the house towards the kitchen, turning the lights on as I went. Since I had an early start to my day, I might as well put some use to it, I thought. Cleaning was my number one priority right now and since the kitchen was one of my favorite spaces to occupy, I decided it had high priority cleaning status. I began the slow process of cleaning the dusty cabinets, bleaching the counters and scrubbing the floors. With music in my ears and my head focused on getting rid of grime, my mind had little else to latch onto. Yet, as I cleaned, I caught my thoughts drifting in the direction of the dream. Rather than focusing on the intense fear that had been clinging to me as I ran through the dead woods, however, I was thinking about the grip on my hair, the heavy weight on my back, and the heat that coursed through my veins.

Any time these thoughts drifted into my mind, I quickly berated myself for being so goddamn horny that even a nightmare's touch left me feeling hot and bothered. With work, moving and a general sense of disinterest in the men I had tried dating, finding a way to fulfill my needs was mildly challenging. Don't get me wrong, it wasn't hard to find a sexual partner with the amount of hook-up apps that clouded social media. But I was bored of them. The percentage of men I had found this way that *actually* gave me some pleasure was painfully low. So, instead of wasting time on so many disappointments and vapid connections, I told myself it was time for me. I would do what *I* wanted to do when *I* wanted to do it.

I had an idea of the kind of man I was holding out for, but it wasn't as easy as it should be to find him. It had been nearly a year since my last sexual encounter, if you could even call it that. At thirty-one, you would think a man would know how to use his dick for more than pissing. *Psych!* I rolled my eyes, annoyed at myself for my line of thinking. I blamed it on the time of night – or morning.

So, I shot a quick text over to my best friend – someone I knew would give me the pep talk I needed. While it was unlikely she was awake, at least I could vent this shit out of my system.

> I think I'm going crazy, cuz I just had a wet nightmare. Yeah. It is what you think it is. Remind me why I'm not letting any men near my vaj?

I put my phone back on the counter, feeling an internal cringe reading that message. Even with that thought, I knew Elly wouldn't judge me for anything. Elly was the bright sun in my life – we'd been roommates for years, but she'd found herself an amazing partner and had moved in with him. I was intensely happy for her – she deserved the best of the best. And she was the reason why I was still okay being single. I wanted so badly to find what she had. I blew out a breath. Soon. Or someday. Whatever works.

As I was aggressively scrubbing one particularly stubborn mark on the counter, I heard my phone ping.

> Because you deserve better. Girl why the *fuck* are you up so late?

> I'm cleaning the kitchen since my nightmare interrupted my beauty sleep. Duh.

Well, if you're having "wet nightmares" as you called it, maybe it's time to get a new B.O.B.?

You're breaking my heart here, Elly. And why are YOU up so late?

I needed some water and saw your text. Wanna talk about the nightmare?

Same shit as always. I run, I fall, I'm caught.

Buuuuuut this time you were "wet"?

He pulled my hair while he pinned me down -_-

Really?

Hey, don't kink-shame me bitch.

I would never. Just surprised that's *all* it took to get you bothered. Lol.

It's been a year, okay? And hair pulling is sexy. ☹

You're right. Now get your ass back in bed bitch. Tyvm. ☺ <3

I laughed, clicking my screen back off. Elly, also known as Elleanor Briggs, was, hands down, the best person to cheer me up. After reading her message telling me to get back to bed, I realized how tired I actually was. I quickly put the cleaning supplies back to where I had found them, the scent of bleach burning in my nose, and dragged myself back to my room, turning lights off. I crawled back under the covers, allowing myself two and a half hours of sleep since it was already almost 5am. It was easier drifting off than I was expecting, but right as I was about to be greeted by sweet nothingness, I thought I felt a tingle of awareness – I wasn't alone. In that moment, however, I was too tired to be bothered, and let my mind slip into a dreamless sleep.

***

A week later, I found myself sitting at a coffee shop with Elly. Both of us were coffee addicts, and as the remodeling of the kitchen was starting today, we decided to come here. I cradled a steaming hot cappuccino between my palms and stared out at the red and orange trees lining the street. Fall was upon us, and I couldn't be more excited. Nothing like an onslaught of horror films and Halloween decorations to drive my creativity while I worked.

"So, any more of your wet dreams? Or nightmares?" Elly asked abruptly, causing me to whip my head towards her. She had the devil's grin on her face, her red hair framing her rosy cheeks and making her blue-grey eyes glow with mischief. I let an incredulous look slide over my features, though I knew Elly well enough to expect nothing less – in public or no.

"No, actually. All quiet up here," I tapped a finger on my temple. "Too quiet, honestly. I'm stuck on one of my creations. Writer's block is a bitch." I roll my eyes as I take a sip from the steaming mug.

"Well, why don't you come over tonight and we can watch a horror movie? It's spooky season, which means most of the good ones will be easy to find on one of the thousand streaming services we share. Plus, I can cook us our favorite dinner?" Elly waggled her eyebrows at me, encouraging me to say yes.

"I won't be getting anything done at home the way my head is, so why not? What's the man up to tonight?" I carefully took a sip from my much too hot coffee.

"He's working a late shift, so it's just you and me until he gets home," she replies.

I nod. "I'll bring the wine," I say with a grin.

While I can cook, and love to, nothing can outmatch Elly's food. My mouth was already watering thinking about eating dinner tonight.

As we finished our coffee, we discussed movies and wine, then decided to go on a walk down Main Street. It was quiet since it was a Monday morning, but that's exactly the way we liked it. We stopped in the little shops and mostly just looked at the goods, only buying a few things here and there – namely some books. After, we parted ways and agreed to meet at 6, and I made my way home.

The remodeling in the kitchen was well underway when I got home, so I busied myself upstairs, attempting to clean the room I would be using for an office. Most of my office things were tucked away in boxes due to not wanting to put everything out before it was remodeled. The office was scheduled for work next week, so, for now, any work I did was on my laptop. After giving up on cleaning before renovations, I sat on my bed and typed a few things on the computer, then changed my mind and then changed it again. My creativity was currently drier than a desert, and I knew I needed to do something to get the juices flowing again. I already had a few requests for more scripts, and I knew if I didn't provide, I would fade away like anyone else in this industry. I could get hired to write a script for a movie with ideas already in place, but I enjoyed the pressure of creating something new – or relatively new, at least. But if this dry spell kept up for much longer, I may have to accept one of the requests as a temporary measure. I didn't feel like it would come down to that, though. Stress sometimes halted my creative process, and between buying a house and the nightmare that was still plaguing my mind, I had more than enough stress to deter me.

After mindlessly writing and rewriting the same sentence several times, I gave up for the time being. My mind had been dragged once more in the direction of a particular nightmare. What might have happened next? Instead of shutting these thoughts down like I had been all week, I opened my browser and pulled up some music. Once the music was playing, I slipped my hand into the nightstand drawer and pulled out my favorite toy. I was aching, and while I knew it was risky with the contractors downstairs working on the kitchen, they were loud enough I wasn't too worried. I tugged off my shorts and flipped the vibrator on, wincing at the noise, but knowing it was nearly impossible for it to be heard. It was a quiet but intense little guy, and with my music and their banging, it was basically silent.

In the week since moving in, my sexual frustration had grown. I had been denying myself, ashamed of where the desires had stemmed from, but would wake up in the morning more flustered and frustrated than when I had gone to bed. I wasn't even having dreams, as far as I could remember. But each morning, I would wake up flushed, nipples hard, and wetness coating my thighs. Today was the worst yet – every thought had somehow drifted towards the dream since coming home from coffee and shopping. The nightmare was the cause, but it was mine. What was wrong with me?

At the first touch, I felt a low moan trying to crawl up my throat. I quickly covered my mouth, biting down on a knuckle. The sharp pain only helped me melt more into the feeling. Heat pulsed through my body, and I felt every vibration driving my core tighter and tighter. I imagined a mouth, teasing and sucking on my clit. My toes were curled, and my thighs were clenched. I could almost feel the head between my thighs, hair curled in my fingers. I rubbed against the vibrator, finding a rhythm that left my body tingling, pushing me to that sweet spot between full body tension and a sense of weightlessness. I was lost in the sensations and visions of a man worshipping me, pleasing me. Vaguely, I noticed the banging had stopped momentarily, but the music was still playing, so I continued. Had the banging stopped before I reached this point, I probably would have angrily foregone my idea to get off while there were people in my house. But now? I was mad with lust and so close to the peak I knew it would kill me to stop. I bit my knuckle harder as I came to the edge, suppressing the gasps trying to escape. Finally, I felt the first wave of the orgasm cresting over me, but before it could crash down, the music stopped. I gasped, my orgasm disappearing in a puff of smoke as I scrambled to turn the vibrator off, leaving me writhing on the bed, my hand covering my mouth as I tried to hold any sounds in. I was angry, pissed that I had made it to that point and couldn't even get the orgasm I deserved. My own pleasure had been cut off, and with how frustrated I had been, I wanted to scream.

I remembered the workers downstairs and cringed, praying to all things dark and unholy that they hadn't heard me. I opened my door silently and peaked my head out, listening. I was met by silence. I frowned, wondering why it was so quiet. I walked to my window and parted the silver curtains. The sight that met me had me sighing in relief. The workers were outside, apparently eating lunch. As relieved as I was, I couldn't help but feel a little angry at the fact I had destroyed my own orgasm in an attempt to stay quiet when they wouldn't have heard me in the first place. I closed my eyes for a brief moment, then went back to my poor attempts at moving forward in my screen write.

As it happened the first time, I seemingly was stuck on a single sentence in the writing. I skimmed over the outline again, knowing the direction I wanted to take the story, but feeling like somehow it didn't make sense. But if I changed this now, I would be causing a butterfly affect over the rest of the story. While that wasn't always a bad thing, I didn't know if it was the best move in my currently "dry" state. So, I abandoned the thought and wrote several sections of dialogue from different perspectives to see if one of them stuck – none of them did.

Several hours of frustration later, it was finally time to get ready and leave – leading me to thank all things dark and unholy for Elly providing this beautiful distraction. I quickly dressed and nearly tripped down the stairs in my rush to leave the creativity-deprived room. The workers had left earlier, so I didn't have to worry about being social, thankfully. I stopped and grabbed our favorite wine – a dark red with rich flavors such as coco, blueberry, and coffee. It might stain your teeth after one glass, but it was a unique concoction that I couldn't resist. Finally, I arrived at my best friend's house and entered like it was my own.

We put on a paranormal horror movie as we stuffed our faces with the delicious Indian dish she had created. We were giggling and laughing after two glasses of wine each, commenting on the character's stupidity of always making the wrong decisions. But that's what was fun about horror movies – they allowed us, as viewers, to live through them as they acted on their intrusive thoughts. It was one of the many reasons why I was so interested in writing horror. Additionally, I loved creating something dark that lured people into the shadows, just to send them running away in fear. I focused mainly on psychological thrillers, creating an evil yet somehow alluring entity that waited until the right moment to show its true colors. Sometimes my work turned out beautiful, and other times I laughed at the lack of character development that I didn't notice until it was too late. But that was simply the life of a writer.

Shortly after our second movie concluded, Tyler came home, and I took my leave. Tyler was the husband and love of my best friend's life, a tall, brown hair and brown eyed man with a gentle heart. While Tyler was nice and I adored him for how he much he loved my best friend, it was late, and I knew that Elly would like some time with him for herself before they called it a night. I said my goodbyes and left for my new home, taking the second bottle of wine for myself. I pulled up the drive and noticed a small light in my bedroom. I frowned, chastising myself for forgetting to turn all the lights off.

I walked inside and popped the cork off the second bottle, pouring a deep glass of wine and making my way up the stairs. When I got to my room, I realized my antique glass lamp was on. I must have left it on this morning before I even left for coffee and hadn't noticed it was still on because of the daylight. The lamp was something I had found in a small store several years ago and had developed an intense attachment to since. It was a unique glass creation in the form of a tree lit from within, with tiny glass leaves sprouting from the branches. The only color on the entire piece were the bright red apples that hung from the branches from small hooks. It sat on a wooden base that was carved with leaf designs. I decided to keep it on while I finished my glass, curled up in my favorite reading chair and opened a book that had been left on the seat.

I finished my glass of wine, and then another, starting to feel a lot tipsier than I probably should on a weeknight. But fuck it – it's not like I didn't control my own work schedule. When I knew I wasn't properly processing the words anymore, I shut the book and decided to get ready for bed. After tugging on my oversized t-shirt, I walked to my bed and flipped the lights off. I crawled under the covers and shut my eyes, feeling warm and happy. As my subconscious slowly took over, I felt the same presence as before. But, before I could really register it, sleep took over.

CHAPTER 2

***

I was sitting on the couch of my living room. Except, not exactly my living room. My living room didn't have this couch, or the same wallpaper. The house looked newer with the fresh wood floors and new furniture, but the yellow and blush colored floral wallpaper was out of date, and so was the furniture. The latter had a unique wooden design, an almost gothic appeal to it, aside from the yellow floral pattern of the cushions. I stood, taking in my surroundings. This must have been the house right after it was built, I thought to myself. But that wouldn't make sense – I had never seen the house before I was on the market to purchase it. I shrugged, walking toward the stairs leading to my bedroom. I heard a creak of wood above me and tilted my head to listen. Then, steps. Sure, steady, and confident steps. I frowned, wondering who it was. I made my way up the stairs, just like one of the idiots from my stories. I didn't think this was real, so no harm could be done. But that didn't mean I wasn't scared. My stomach was bound in knots so tight I wanted to throw up.

It felt irrational, almost, to be this scared. But something inside me was screaming to stop and turn around. I reached the top step. My heart thumped erratically. The steps were coming from the room to the left – my bedroom. I frowned, wondering who, or what, the fuck was walking around my room as though they owned the place. The steps stopped as I reached for the handle.

The door creaked open, revealing the back of a man. He was impossibly tall, and his head was facing the window opposite of me but tilted as though confirming he heard my entry. He had a broad frame, appearing strong but not overly muscular. I wouldn't be able to take him down without a weapon, I knew that. He was clad in a black suit that clung to his frame, and a fedora on the top of his head. A *fucking fedora*.

"Who are you?" I asked.

"Who are *you*?" Was his only response. His voice was like melted dark chocolate, smooth but with a bit of a rasp to it. Death lingered underneath, too, like a constant threat and promise of pain.

I ignored the sliver of heat that ran through me. "You're in my house. I'm not Alice and this isn't fucking Wonderland, so who are you?"

"You're in *my* house. Who are you?" he parroted mockingly. His voice caused shivers to trickle down my spine.

A crackle of anger sparked through me. "Alright, don't answer. I don't care. But you need to leave." I forced the words out firmly, not letting my fear show. Every cell in my body was raging at my stupidity of approaching this man. My spine was ramrod straight, even though he hadn't even turned to look at me. I had a chance to run right now, if I was smart enough. I wasn't.

As if hearing my thoughts, he turned towards me slowly. Darkness cloaked him like a mysterious lover. Black hair fell around a face shadowed by the fedora. He looked like he had just stepped out of a movie from the 1940s, and while I would've liked to call his fedora stupid and not scary at all, I couldn't lie to myself. I was paralyzed in fear. This man, this *creature*, elicited a fear so potent I could taste it on my tongue. He stood casually, one hand tucked in his pocket, and the other hanging at his side. Nothing about him felt casual, however. Visually, I couldn't say he looked like a monster, but instinctively I knew. This man would kill someone just for shits and giggles. As he faced me, I realized that somehow, he looked even larger from the front. My heart was pounding in my chest, and I struggled to keep my breathing under control.

"I can't," he said. I felt like I had been slapped out of my reverie.

Damnit, Evalyn Wright, get your shit together, I thought. "Why not? The door is right there," I said with more venom than I felt. My hand gestured to the door behind me.

He didn't answer, and instead took a slow step towards me, then another. I knew it wasn't to leave. His eyes, though I couldn't see them, were watching me intently. I felt frozen. He looked like a lethal predator, a jaguar slinking towards its prey, and, while his posture was still casual and unbothered, I knew *I* was his prey. Like before, his steps were slow and confident. I backed up with each of his steps forward. Suddenly, I bumped into the door and felt it latch shut. Shit. I thought the door had been wide open after I entered, but it must have started to close on its own. I would have noticed, but my eyes were glued to the man in front of me, and I was too terrified to look away. Now I had mere feet between me and this nameless man, and I knew he would be able to stop me if I made any moves to open the door. My fingers inched towards the handle, trying to seem composed. I could feel the energy radiating off his form, even at such a distance. He was like a tsunami of darkness about to collide into me.

Another step.

Another.

Finally, he was only inches from me, his chest nearly grazing mine. My fingers had yet to find the doorknob, and I was caged. The breaths I had been trying to keep under control were now ragged. My fear was laid out in the open, but there was something else, too. Heat was pooling low in my body, rivaling the gut-wrenching fear in my stomach. His presence was overwhelming, and every inch of my body felt like it was gravitating towards his darkness. Knowing this made me want to scream. What was so wrong with me that in this situation, one so saturated with fear and danger, everything could be twisted into something that awakened my carnal desires? I forced myself to stop thinking about my traitorous body. I could worry about that *after* I wasn't in immediate danger.

As soon as that thought came, it was swept away as his powerful presence moved the last little distance forward, his body now flush against mine. He towered over me, and I had to tilt my chin up to look at him. The fedora could no longer fully hide his gaze. Shadows still lurked around him, but I could make out a straight nose, a sharp jaw, and a cutting gaze. Even through the shadows, I could see his eyes. They were dark and light all at once. His eyes were as sharp as a blade and the color of glowing steel. He smelled of lavender and mint and shadows. I was enraptured with his beauty. His full lips were set in a smirk, as though he knew the exact effect he had on me. It pissed me off. My head cleared slightly.

"Step away from me." My voice was firm, even though I felt like a wilting flower on the inside.

"Or else what?" He asked quietly. His voice made me want to melt and shiver all at the same time. My nipples tightened in response, and the look on his face indicated he somehow knew. His question lingered in the air between us, both a threat and a challenge. I struggled to find an answer. It was like my tongue was stuck to the roof of my mouth and my words had dried up like vapor on the wind.

He tilted his head, and suddenly, as though my mind was wiped clean of whatever spell he had on me, I saw my opportunity. My knee jerked up on its own accord, right between his legs. It was a solid hit, and he stepped back with a grunt. As he bent over, I slammed a fist against his face. It wasn't a strong hit or even a practiced one, but at least I knew how to avoid breaking my thumb. I knew he would recover in seconds from the annoying smirk still tugging at his lips and the low laugh emanating from his form. So, I lunged for the handle and ripped the door open. I slipped through, sprinting down the steps, nearly falling on my face. His laughter echoed in the house around me as I made my escape. Finally, I reached the front door and opened it.

My heart thudded to a painful stop as I saw what was in front of me, or rather, whom. There he stood on my porch, face hidden beneath his stupid fucking fedora, his evil smirk a seemingly fixed object glued to his face. A drop of blood rested on his lower lip, and I watched, mesmerized, as his tongue darted out to lick it. Not possible. This isn't real. He couldn't be here, at the front door. He was in my bedroom only seconds ago.

"That was a good hit, Little Eve." I felt as if I had been punched in the gut at hearing him offer me a nickname. Nickname or no, it was too similar to deny the reality of it. That's when I understood. This wasn't real. It was a dream. Something I knew at the start but had forgotten amid his presence. I slammed the door in his face, his grin disappearing behind the wood.

"Wake up, wake up, wake up," I chanted to myself. I tugged on my hair, pulling hard enough for pricks of pain to spread across my scalp. "I want to wake up. *Please* let me wake up, *please.*"

A fist slammed against the door, and I jolted awake.

***

I bolted up in the bed, clutching my chest. I was shaking and sweating, my head throbbing from the wine.

"Fuck *me*," I whispered in the dark. The nightmare lingered, the man's twisted grin a burned image in my mind. It wasn't real. I shook myself. I got nightmares after moving, but I had never had one like that. I could *smell* him, for fuck's sake. I'd been able to feel his body, as well as his aura, which rivalled most of the evil characters I created in my stories. If it wasn't for the fact that I wanted to forget the dream entirely, I might have made him into one of my antagonists.

I hadn't been this scared in years. The worst part was that the fear had stemmed from the man rather than the dream itself. I felt powerless and weak against that creature, something I thought I had left behind ages ago. It was a feeling only my father had ever been able to pull out of me. I shook my head, curling into a ball and wanting nothing more than to shake off the fear that was sticking to me like a poison. I reminded myself, once again, that it wasn't real. And remembering my father wasn't going to help any either.

I had a troubled history, with a father that was so deranged he justified each horror he put my mother and I through. But they were twisted and coated in evil. He would talk about whispers guiding him, reminding him that the world was sick, and he had to purge us of our sins. We were only freed after he died.

I shut my thoughts down. *No. I'm not going back there*, I reminded myself. It was a challenge to bring myself into the present when my mind wanted to stay glued in the past. But trauma defines someone in one of two ways – it controls them with fear, or it strengthens their spine with titanium. I chose the latter. Nothing would break me; nothing *could* break me if I survived what I had already been through. There were still some things that I couldn't help but fear, such as small, dark spaces. But that was a part of growth. I wasn't ready to face that part of me, yet.

I blinked my eyes open against the pounding headache and centered myself into the present. A light was shining out of the corner of my eye. I turned my head and blinked, realizing the glass tree was lit again. I frowned, trying to remember if, in my alcohol infused haze, I left it on overnight again. I could have sworn I flipped the switch off. But after the dream I had, I couldn't help but feel a small relief that a light was on, and I hadn't even had to leave my bed. It was childish of me, but I didn't care. A dark room left a lot to the imagination, and any small bit of light could help.

I groaned as I crawled out of bed to take a shower, stripping my shirt off. However, as I did, I felt a cold chill rush down my spine. Without thinking, my hands flew to my chest, covering my suddenly hard nipples. I couldn't explain the feeling, but I almost felt as though I was being watched. The feeling left the hairs on my neck standing on end and a tremble in my hands. Again, fear curled in the lower pit of my stomach. Not as strong as before, but still there. The numbness of alcohol was nowhere to be found in this moment. I peeked around the room, looking for any signs of disturbance, any shadow that could shroud someone, finding none. I realized I was expecting to find the man from my nightmare watching, so I chalked up my hesitation to the nightmare and continued on.

With the water on full heat, I stepped under the spray and melted into the liquid fire. I closed my eyes and let the water cascade over me, soothing and loosening my knotted muscles. My skin was reddening, and my eyes were drooping once again. As the water began to drop in temperature, I was nearly brought to tears. I wanted to stay here, under the steady rhythm of the water as it beat into my tired muscles. I groaned in frustration, telling myself I was going to figure out how to get an unlimited supply of hot water to this shower so I could soak until I was nothing more than a shriveled-up sack of blood and bones. Or perhaps I could invest in a hot tub with jets. Those were certainly nice and soothing.

I finished my shower, dried off, and wrapped myself in my robe once again. I grabbed my book from the reading chair and curled up on my bed. I found the last section I had actually read and picked up from there. Within minutes, I felt my eyelids getting heavy. I continued to shake myself awake, not wanting to fall asleep just yet, but knowing I couldn't stay up all night like this. After struggling for a while longer, I curled the book to my chest and let my eyes drift shut.

CHAPTER 3

Unknown

I watched from the edges of her sleep, feeling a mixture of frustration and desire. She could be like all the rest, too weak to keep going. But she seemed different. She held a flame inside her. Would my presence in her life extinguish that flame? Or would it ignite her? I wanted to ruin her, to drown her. But I also wanted to see how hot her fire could burn. Her sleeping form looked peaceful beneath the soft light of her apple tree. How fitting. Little Eve, naïve and helpless, waiting to be corrupted by a devil. Her breasts rose and fell with each breath, her long, dark hair fanning across her pillow. Her eyes were shut, but I remembered how they had been full of green fire as she gazed up at me in the dream. Her full, soft lips looked delicious, slightly parted. I wanted to know what they would taste like, what they would look like wrapped around my cock and her long hair wrapped around my fist. Her face was the picture of an innocent seductress – I wanted to tarnish her. I had been entranced by the way her pale skin had flushed, and her eyes glowed with desire right before she snapped out of it and fought me.

Watching her fight herself against self-gratification had been amusing, if not a little concerning. She didn't come off as someone to refrain from pleasing herself. I wanted to own every moment of her pleasure, every gasp and moan of ecstasy, but seeing her torture herself was beautiful. She would be stunning when she came, but anything she had ever experienced before was nothing in comparison to what I could do for her. What I *would* do for her. I wanted her under me, bound and helpless, not even able to take a breath without my permission.

She was certainly the most beautiful of all the women that I had haunted, and the first that I felt a true addiction to the moment I laid eyes on her. Everything about her pulled me in, more so even than *her* – the other woman. At the thought of the other woman, my fists clenched, and fury twisted my insides, followed by a hollow pain. Shaking my head, I turned my attention to my sweet Little Eve. Something was different about her. My hopes rose briefly, but I quickly stamped them out. Only time would tell the truth.

I drifted closer to her subconscious, contemplating another dive into her dreams but stopped myself, knowing I could ruin everything if I rushed this. Breaking the barrier currently between us might make everything stop before it even starts. It was a shame, really. I wanted to peel away her defensive layers until she had no way to hide from me. I craved to be inside her, mind and body. But I held myself back. Slipping behind someone's mental defenses was a fickle thing and took time and patience. So instead, I stood there and watched her dreams slip by peacefully.

CHAPTER 4

I woke, sprawled on top of the covers, still wrapped in my robe. My book had slid off to the side, thankfully undamaged. I rubbed my head, wishing I had taken time to drink more water before drifting off. As I rose to grab a glass of water, I realized I had, once again, left my tree light on. I flipped it off and made my way downstairs. I realized the kitchen wasn't the best place to be with the remodeling only halfway complete. The time on my phone read 8:21am, which meant the workers would likely be arriving any minute. Sure enough, as soon as the thought crossed my mind, I heard a vehicle coming down the driveway.

Forgetting about water, I sprinted back upstairs and threw on a pair of jeans and a sweatshirt, along with a pair of black boots. As I tied my hair up into a ponytail, I heard a knock at the door and rushed back downstairs to open it. It was the head of the construction crew that was waiting, with the rest of the crew unloading their tools.

"Good morning, ma'am. We're gonna get started in a few minutes, and I think we should be done with the kitchen by this evening. If you're alright with it, we might stay a little late to wrap things up in case we don't finish by 5:30?" The crew leader, Dave, was a nice, older gentleman with a good crew. They were certainly efficient and thorough. Before starting the kitchen yesterday, the man had shown me a mockup of what the kitchen should look like, and I couldn't be more excited.

"Absolutely. I'll be upstairs doing some work if you need anything."

"Sounds good. We should have the downstairs finished by the end of the week, and hopefully the upstairs will be finished next week. There's a chance it could take longer, but I know it's not easy living in a house that's half constructed."

"You're fine, don't worry about it. I don't mind waiting since I know the outcome is going to be worth it!" I tried to sound chipper, even with my headache and parched throat.

"Thank you, ma'am." He nodded to me and then made his way to the kitchen.

After they started, I decided to make a stop at the store only a few miles up the road to grab a gallon of water and an energy drink. I didn't want to bother them constantly by trying to get water, and I was the first to admit that tap water was *not* my thing. I was glancing down at my phone, reading a text from Elly about a funny interaction she had with one of her clients when I bumped into a firm chest.

I stumbled backwards, nearly dropping the gallon of water and my phone. "Oh, I'm so sorry!"

The man looked down at me. I thought I saw anger cross his features for a split second before smoothing out into a smile. "Hey, no harm no fowl." His tone was friendly and warm.

"Oh, well, thanks." I moved to step around him, but his tall frame stepped in my way. I chuckled awkwardly.

"No problem. If you wanted to make it up to me, though, you could let me grab you a coffee?" He had a full smile on his face, and while it seemed charming, something about this man bothered me. He had a nice face with a strong jaw and bright blue eyes. His hair was brown and carefully styled, his teeth white and straight. He wore a dress shirt and slacks with a watch on one wrist that screamed rich.

As I opened my mouth to reject his offer, I practically heard Elly telling me that I wasn't going to find the right guy by sitting in my room all the time. I blew out a nervous breath.

"Um, sure. I can do that." I tried forcing some enthusiasm into my tone, but it didn't work well.

Instead of acting insulted at my apparent lack of excitement, he smiled wider and said, "Great! Are you free now?"

Internally I cringed at the thought of going out now, on a *date* with no preparation. "I, um, have some work I have to get done at my house, but we could do it later?"

He didn't miss a beat. "Sure. How about dinner then? 7pm? At the Italian restaurant off Poppy Street? I could always give you a ride if you like?"

I forced my lips into a smile. This guy was determined, apparently. "That's fine, I can meet you there." I wasn't going to let this stranger know where I lived, no matter how nice he tried to be.

"I have no problem giving you a ride," he hinted.

"That's alright, really." I moved to step around him again. Definitely *not* giving him my address. Ever.

"I didn't get your name," he said.

"I didn't get yours, either," I replied smartly.

His smile dropped a millimeter. "My name is Luke. And you are?"

"Evalyn," I said.

"That's a lovely name. Nice to meet you." I fought the urge to roll my eyes.

"Nice to meet you, too. Anyways, um, I have to go. But I'll be there at 7." *Maybe,* I thought internally. I forced another smile on my face.

"Great, see you then!" He smiled again, finally stepping out of my way.

It wasn't that he specifically did anything wrong, but something about him rubbed me the wrong way. But maybe tonight's dinner would change that. After grabbing what I needed, I made my way to my car and saw him walking to his own a few cars down. He didn't have anything in his hands, which I thought was odd. I shrugged it off, thinking that maybe he hadn't found what he was looking for, or maybe he had dropped his cart off or something. The cynical, horror story writer wanted to see it differently, but I had to remember that my life wasn't one of my stories.

When I got home, I dove into my project, slipping headphones on, feeling a different level of focus than I had in the past week. Whether from my experience at the store or my nightmare from last night, the words seemed to be pouring out of me, slowly creating a trap to lure viewers in, only to be shoved off the edge of a cliff into a spiraling abyss of fear.

As I wrote, I felt the nightmare tugging at my mind, but I kept brushing it off while I drove myself into a deeper focus. Music played in my ears and the world disappeared around me until it was just me and my creation. I felt like I was in a trance, my own creativity controlling my mind and body. This is where I felt true bliss – lost in my work in a bubble of my own creation.

A loud pounding on my bedroom door knocked me out of my reverie, and I jumped. *Holy shit.* If I got scared *one* more time, I was going to send in a resignation to the horror movie community for being more scared of real life than their treasured movies that I wrote scripts for.

I pulled my headphones off and walked to the door. I opened it and glanced at the concerned look on Dave's face.

"Are you alright, Ms. Wright? I tried calling your phone, but you didn't answer. When I came up here and called your name, you still didn't answer right away." He asked.

Understanding washed over me. My phone was muted so I could focus on work, and with headphones on, I couldn't hear a quiet knock. "Yes, I'm so sorry. I had my headphones on and was hyper-focused on my work. I'm so sorry for worrying you." I truly felt terrible for scaring this sweet man, and hoped he didn't think I was insane.

His face smoothed into a smile. "That's completely fine, my wife is the same when she's readin' a book at home. Just glad you're okay. Wanted to let you know we finished up the kitchen, so we'll be movin' on to the livin' area tomorrow."

"Oh, that's awesome! I can't wait to see it." I glanced at the time and flinched. My phone read 6:11pm. This happened sometimes, where I would work and lose myself so deeply, I forgot about anything else, even forgetting to use the bathroom.

"Well, we're headin' out. Take a look at the kitchen, and if you notice anything you wanna change, just let me know tomorrow and I'll take a look at it."

I nodded. "Thanks again. I'll see you tomorrow!" I said.

As soon as he left, I remembered the stupid date that was in less than an hour. I would call to cancel, but I didn't get his number. Standing him up also briefly crossed my mind, as it had earlier, but I also knew I wasn't that type of person. I sighed and started to get ready, relieving my very angry bladder before anything else. Elly would laugh at me and be angry all at the same time for being so invested in my work that I forgot about myself. I picked out a nice pair of jeans and grabbed one of my favorite sweaters, letting my hair down and finger combing my natural waves. I put light makeup on and donned my boots before leaving.

I drove to the restaurant, arriving just before 7, wondering if I was supposed to meet him inside or outside. I really, *really* hated first dates. Before I could decide whether to try and go inside to grab a table and wait for him or sit outside and hope he wasn't already there, he appeared to my right.

"Hey, you made it!" Luke said with that giant smile plastered on his face. He wore another dress shirt and slacks with the same watch and perfectly styled hair from this morning.

I forced a small smile to my lips. "Yeah, I'm here."

"Great, let's head inside and see if we can snag a table." Internally I found myself rolling my eyes again. As if it would be hard to find a table at this mid-tier restaurant on a Tuesday night.

Biting down my remarks, I followed him in. I was almost certain there wouldn't be another date, but at least I could tell Elly I tried. *Shit, Elly,* I thought. I forgot to let her know I was going out tonight. It was an agreement we made years ago – neither of us would go out with a stranger without letting the other know first. I typed out a quick text explaining what I was doing and added an apology for not letting her know sooner. When I put my phone away, I realized Luke was staring at me with a slight frown on his face.

"Setting up an escape plan?" He laughed at his own joke.

"Should I be looking for one?" I shot back.

An offended look slid over his features, but as he went to reply, the host arrived to seat us. Silently I thanked whoever was kind enough to spare me his reply. We sat down at a booth and our waitress came over promptly to take our drink orders. I ordered a glass of white wine as a silent celebration for the work I had accomplished today, and he ordered a draft beer.

Once the waitress took our drink orders, he looked back to me. I couldn't put my finger on it, but something just genuinely felt...off about this guy.

"So, tell me about yourself, Evalyn."

How original, I thought. I blamed Elly for forcing me through this painful situation. While she technically had no real part in this, I didn't want to take the blame for my poor choices. "Not much to know. I'm 29, I write, I cook, and I spend time with my best friend."

"And is this 'best friend' the person you texted earlier?"

A strange ripple of unease rippled through me. *He's just trying to get to know me,* I reminded myself.

"Yeah, that's the one." I replied. I felt uncomfortable but didn't want it to show. Though I wasn't sure the tight smiles and short comments were helping my case.

The waitress returned with our drinks and asked if we were ready to order.

"We'll take an order of the bruschetta," Luke asked without even consulting me. I would be upset, but it was something Elly and I got every time we visited the restaurant. The waitress smiled and went on her way with our, well, *his* order.

"So, you're 29 and not married? Or did you go through a divorce?" He asked abruptly.

For what felt like the fifth time already, I bit back my first response and cleared my throat. I met his blue gaze. "No, I've never been married. How about *you*, Luke?"

His smile stretched wider somehow. "Me? I work at an accounting firm. Family business, and all that." So, he had money from his mommy and daddy, *check*. "I spend most of my time there and travelling." Money is all that matters to him, *check*. His tone became more reserved. "I had a wife, but she passed away a year ago. You're the first girl that's caught my eye since then," he said. As he finished his sentence, he looked up at me through his lashes.

I knew I should feel some sort of sympathy for this man, but something still felt off. *Jesus Christ, Evalyn. He isn't a monster*, I thought to myself. I mean, we bumped into each other at the grocery store, and he wanted me to believe I was the "first girl" that caught his eye? But maybe he believed it. Or maybe he was just a player.

"I'm sorry to hear that," was my only reply.

"Sorry for what? That was a year ago now. You know what they say, 'time heals all wounds' and all that." His smile was back.

Never mind, I thought to myself. *He* definitely *has something wrong with him*. "If you say so," I said. I still couldn't figure out why I was so put off by this man, but I now knew for a fact I would go out of my way to never see this man again after tonight.

"I forgot to mention my age," he said almost expectantly. Almost like he was hoping I would ask. What was with this guy?

"You did."

Seemingly annoyed by my lack of curiosity, he said "I'm 32. I hope that's not too old for you." He laughed at himself again. Was that even a real joke?

"Nope."

He started browsing the menu, and I took that chance to look at my own. A few blissful moments of silence went by before the waitress came back with the bruschetta and asked for our orders. I settled on something I'd had before and knew I liked. Luke spouted off something and handed her the menus, sending her on her way. I almost wanted to beg her to stay so I could feel less uncomfortable.

Instead of going in for the food, Luke stared at me expectantly. "Are you going to eat?"

While I was hungry, I wasn't going to eat while this man just stared me down. "What if I don't even like bruschetta?"

He laughed. "Well, of course you do! How could you not?" While his words were light and easy, it rubbed me wrong that he felt so confident in his knowledge of me.

"Some people don't like tomatoes," I said.

"You ordered a pasta with tomatoes, come on. Just eat," he tried persuading.

"I don't like bruschetta," I said, lying through my teeth. At this point, I just wanted to wipe the confidence off this fucker's face. "I'm just going to wait for the entrée to come out."

A flash of anger passed over his face but was gone so fast I could have imagined it. "Your loss," he said with less enthusiasm than before.

To my dismay, he waved the waitress over. She came, glancing at the untouched food. "Is something wrong with the bruschetta?" She asked with concern.

I opened my mouth to assure her that of course everything was fine, but Luke cut me off. "No, nothing is wrong with the bruschetta. Evalyn here just apparently doesn't like it. I don't want it, either. Would you mind taking it away?" He asked with a smile, as if this was completely normal behavior.

The waitress looked confused. *Same, girl*, I thought. "Uh, sure. I still have to put it on your ticket, though."

"I'm sure you can fix that, can't you?" Luke smiled up at her, expecting this woman to just give in.

Before she had to respond, I cut in. "You can just put it on a separate ticket, and I will take care of it," I gave her an apologetic look and smiled softly.

"Are you sure?" She asked.

"*No*, Evalyn. We aren't paying for this. Period." Luke wasn't smiling anymore. His jaw was set, and barely concealed anger hid under the surface.

I ignored him and looked at the waitress. "Actually, why don't you just go ahead and put my meal on the separate ticket, as well. And if you can pack it up, that would be great." I shot a determined look towards Luke. I can't believe I went out with this asshole. *Guts are better than brains*, I told myself. I should have followed my instinct instead of giving this entitled idiot a chance to redeem himself.

The waitress nodded, sharing a sympathetic look before heading to the kitchen.

"Evalyn, I said no." I glanced back at Luke who was still staring at me with frustration.

"And I don't care. I'm done. Next time you ask someone on a date, maybe be less of a dick," I said with venom. "And while you're at it, take responsibility for your choices. You *chose* the bruschetta, I didn't. You had no right to try bullying the waitress into taking it off the ticket."

"I got the bruschetta for *you*. You're just too stubborn to eat it."

I scoffed. "You got it for me? Without asking me if I wanted it? Bullshit."

He went silent. "Fine. Tonight didn't go as planned, but I'll make it up to you next time."

This time I burst out into full blown laughter. "You think there's going to be a next time? No, *absolutely* not." I stood, grabbing my phone and purse. He stood as well. As I started towards the exit, he blocked my path. "What is it with you and standing in my way?" I asked.

"Don't be rude, Evalyn. I'm trying to apologize and telling you I'll make it up to you."

I scoffed again. This had to be some type of fever dream. "No. The answer is no. And that was a piss-poor apology if you ask me. Now get the fuck out of my way." I steeled my spine and stared him dead in the eye.

He glanced at the rest of the customers whose attention was locked on us. He shook his head and then stepped out of my way. The waitress rushed over with my food, and I handed her a bill that would cover my food and a hefty tip. She looked at me with gratitude. "That was a badass move," she whispered to me. I felt a smile tug at my lips as I walked to the door.

As I stepped outside into the chilly air, I heard Luke's voice follow me. "I'll see you again, Evalyn." I pretended not to hear him as the door closed behind me, ignoring the chill racing through me that had nothing to do with the temperature outside.

CHAPTER 5

I drove home with my heart thundering in my chest. After making my way inside the house, I made sure to lock my doors and windows before changing my clothes and diving into my food.

While eating, I called Elly and gave her the rundown of my nightmarish experience. She seemed as shaken as I was and told me to keep an eye out in case he tried popping up again. I knew that had I actually asked Elly about this date when I felt like something was off, she would have encouraged me *not* to go. For all her pestering about getting me to explore and date, she cared about my safety above anything else. It took several minutes to convince her that I was fine and all I wanted was to curl up and read my book before bed before she finally let me go.

Trying to shake off that very weird and awful experience, I finished my food and finally took a moment to look at the freshly finished kitchen as I cleaned up after myself. It was gorgeous and better than I could have imagined. The counters were black granite, the cabinets sanded down and repainted to a dark grey. I still had to replace the out-of-date appliances, but I had them scheduled for install the middle of next week. The floor was white tile, and there was a unique backsplash of black, silver, and red glass. The lights were now modern and elegant, rather than something from the 70s. It was a nice-sized kitchen, and the remodeling had changed the cut of the counters and added an island that was much needed for extra counter space.

As I admired the kitchen, I prepared some chamomile tea, one of my favorite drinks when I felt high-strung. Once the steaming mug was warming my hands, I made the trek upstairs to my cozy reading chair. I was so drained that I couldn't even bring myself to feel surprised when my tree light was on. So, I sat in my chair, reading my book and settling into my happy place.

The tea warmed my body, relaxing my tense nerves and leaving me feeling slow and lethargic. After finishing the tea, my eyes were drooping. Before I could fall asleep in my chair, I decided to put my book away and curled under the covers on my bed instead. Slowly, I drifted off to sleep.

***

I found myself in my childhood home. It was cluttered and messy, reeking of mold and mildew. The house was bitterly cold, instantly numbing my fingers. My breath fogged in front of me, and shivers wracked my body. Not only from the cold, but fear. Fear was a poison here, oozing from every crevice and corner. I felt frozen, rooted to the spot in the middle of the room. I was in the living room, the room where many punishments had occurred, and many tears had been shed. Screams still echoed against the walls, and I could almost feel the remnants of my father's presence sticking to the floorboards and walls like a putrid sap.

Move, I told myself. I had to get out. This was just a dream, and I just had to move so I could escape it. But it was like my skin and bones had been turned to stone, and only my organs were still alive. My breath rasped harshly, my heart thundering in my chest so fast I thought it might burst. Any second, my father could appear. And he would hurt me, all over again. He would torture me and try to cut out the pieces that didn't suit his vision of what I was supposed to be. He would smother me until I didn't exist anymore, only his shadow.

It was the thought of disappearing into myself again that ripped me from the trance. My jaw unlatched, mouth opening wide. A scream erupted from my soul, not in fear, but anger. *Fuck* this. I wasn't going to sit around and wait for shit to take a turn for the worse. I wasn't a helpless child anymore. I could handle anything I decided to, and I sure as shit wasn't going to let this get the better of me.

My scream ricocheted around the room, the sound exploding like a bomb, dissolving everything it touched. The walls peeled away like scraps of burnt paper, the floor crumbling like sand. The scent of mildew and mold burned up and was replaced by the scent of lavender and mint and darkness.

I gazed at my new surroundings, a black marble floor, black walls, black furniture. The only light came from two soft yellow bulbs, seated in elegant silver fixtures. I was gasping for breath, my body trembling violently in the aftershock of my nightmare. Was I awake, then? I didn't think so, but I wasn't *there* anymore, and nothing could be worse than that place.

As soon as that thought crossed my mind, a shadow shifted in the corner of the room, taking the shape of a man. My heartrate picked up again. Was it my father? The relief I had felt only moments ago disappeared like puffs of wind; my courage nonexistent. He couldn't be here. It wasn't possible. My breath came out in ragged gasps, and I knew I was seconds away from shattering entirely. I stepped backwards, wanting to run, but meeting a solid wall instead. Tears gathered in my eyes, but I refused to let them fall. The man in the shadows followed my movement, stepping forward. Stepping into the light.

Relief swept over me, and I felt a sort of emotional whiplash. I wasn't certain my heart could take anymore. A traitorous tear slipped from my eye. The monster from my dreams had to be better than my father, the memories. Even in the dim lighting, I could see the same smirk pulling at his lips from before. Relief and fear twisted in my gut. This man was still irrationally terrifying, even though he wasn't as scary as my father. I could easily say this man from my dreams was the second most terrifying man in my life – and he wasn't even real.

Closer and closer he stepped, his long, confident strides eating up the distance in seconds. I had nowhere to go, nowhere to run. I couldn't see any doors. *Trapped*. He stopped when he was only inches from me, then reached a hand towards my face, I flinched and started to turn my head away, but his hand whipped out, blindingly fast, and gripped my face between long fingers. His touch was harsh and biting. I couldn't move if I wanted to. *Fear, fear, fear* pulsed through me. I had no doubts this man could probably break my jaw without a second's thought, so I let my hands hang uselessly at my sides.

With his other hand, he reached out a finger and swept a tear off my cheek. "Why are you crying? We haven't even started." He tsked. Though a smirk still played on his full lips, his eyes looked like they held a controlled rage. Tonight, he wasn't in the 1940's gangster outfit. Instead, he was clad in a black long-sleeve shirt and black jeans. He wasn't wearing that stupid fedora, but the lack of it only made him seem more terrifying.

"What do you want from me?" I asked, my words coming out funny with the way his hand was gripping my face.

He tilted his head at me. "What do I want? Currently, I want to teach you a lesson." His voice had a hypnotic affect, but the pain in my face was enough to keep me grounded.

"And what lesson would that be?" I ground out. Anger was slowly burning up my fear. I had let fear control me as a child, and I made a promise to myself that I wouldn't let it control me as an adult. I didn't care what boogeyman came crawling; I would get away without losing myself.

"That you're mine, Little Eve. Mine, until the day you die."

Anger blackened the edges of my vision. "I belong to *no one*," I hissed through his grip on my jaw.

"If you're so eager to get away, we can make that happen. Are you ready to die, Little Eve?" He leaned in as he spoke, his minty breath washing over me, raising goosebumps on my flesh.

"Fuck you," I hissed.

He tsked. "I think you should rethink your words when you're in such a...compromising position," he said with that same goddamn smirk on his face. His eyes lowered, roaming over my body. His knee slid between my legs and his grin widened. I glanced down as well as I could with his hand gripping my face and nearly choked. I was wearing a silk slip that had lace details and landed a few inches above my knees. It was dark red, the color of blood. I felt a chill over my body, and my nipples hardened. I knew they would be visible through this piss-poor excuse for clothing.

"What the fuck?" I whispered. His hand shifted moving down to the column of my throat, squeezing slightly.

"Do you like it? I picked it out myself," he chuckled darkly. "If you ask me, I quite like it." As he spoke, he slid his other hand up my arm and over my right shoulder. "It's perfect, actually." His finger began pushing the thin strap down, slowly, teasingly.

"Stop," I hissed. His grip tightened on my neck.

He tilted his head and looked at me with those silver eyes. "No." His finger continued until the strap dropped off my shoulder and down my arm, revealing more of my chest than before.

My hands lifted on their own accord, trying to fix the strap so my breast didn't fall out. But before I could lift the strap more than an inch, he pressed into me, tightening his hold on both my neck and arm. I could feel blood rushing into my head and my breathing became labored.

With each change and increase in intensity, his face stayed the same. His features were still relaxed and calm, as if it was completely normal to choke someone and start taking off their clothes – without consent. His hands felt impossibly strong, as if nothing less than the force of a mountain would be able to break his hold. It felt like with the barest twitch of his wrist, my neck could snap like it was a mere twig. Fury built in my chest. I didn't care if I was in danger. I didn't care if I was physically powerless. Half of this was a mind game, and I wasn't about to crack under pressure.

"Get your hands off of me, prick." My words rasped, but the venom was still evident.

He stared at me silently, looking over my face. He looked al-most...pleased. "Do you feel like you're in control here, Little Eve? To me, you look open and ready for whatever I want to do to you. I could *fuck* you, right here, and you wouldn't be able to do a single thing to stop me." My heart thudded in my chest. "I can touch you how I want," he said, moving his hand from my arm to my collarbone. "Where I want." His finger trailed down towards my breast leisurely. "When I want." His finger was at the top of the slip that was being held up by my right breast. I felt frozen, and my fury was twisting with something else, something heated and carnal. His finger slipped under the cloth, letting it slide past my breast. His eyes glowed with hunger as he took in the sight. As if he was entranced, he drew the tip of his finger over my chest, slowly circling my hardened nipple. Fire shot through me from my nipple to my core, and that feeling alone had me wanting to scream in anger. He had no right to touch me like this – like he owned me. He had no right to make me feel whatever the fuck I was feeling right now.

It felt like I was a flame, and he was dousing me in gasoline. Red danced in my vision and my hand swung up to hit him in the face. Faster than I could blink, his large hand was wrapped around my wrist. He squeezed it so tightly I thought it would snap. A groan slipped out of me. "It was cute last night, but I find myself bored of it tonight. I was in the middle of worshipping your perfect tits." His face remained calm, his grin still set in place, but rage flashed in his eyes.

I tried to tug my hand out of his grip, but I may as well be trying to bend iron. It made me realize how inconsequential my blow must have been last night. He *let* me hit him last night. The thought only enraged me further. "Is this a fucking *game* to you?" I rasped. His hand hadn't budged from my throat, and it hadn't loosened any, either. I wasn't sure where my sanity had gone, but between the fresh wound of seeing the old house again and now this, I didn't give a fuck what happened.

"You're not just a game to me, darling. I can promise you that," he said in a low voice.

"This isn't even fucking real," I hissed. "Wake the fuck up Evalyn."

His dark laugh filled the room. He released my neck, and I sucked in a full breath. Rather than releasing me entirely, however, he grasped my other hand and lifted both above my head, repositioning them in one hand. I struggled, trying to kick and butt away from him, to rip my hands from his hold. In a flash, his hand was back on my neck, choking me harder than before. This time I *couldn't* breathe, and I felt the blood rushing back to my face. I realized in that moment how gentle he had been before. He pressed harder into me, pushing me back into the wall until I couldn't move a single inch. His body was solid muscle, revealing how powerless I truly was against him.

"Does this not feel real, *Evalyn*?" His voice was mocking as he brought his face down to mine. "Does this feel like it's all fake to you, Little Eve?" He whispered in my ear. Suddenly, my earlobe was caught between his teeth. "Can you not feel me?" His hot breath washed over my neck. There was electricity arcing down my spine, straight to my core. I was powerless, suffocating, and, to my absolute humiliation, wet. Another tear slipped down my cheek.

"Cat got your tongue?" He asked sadistically. His tongue darted out and licked the tear running down my face.

Spots crowded my vision, and I felt like I would fall unconscious any moment. Except I was sleeping. How could I fall unconscious if I already was? He was right – I felt him, as though he was actually here with me. I had even smelled him earlier, back when I could breathe. But how? I knew I needed to wake up. I was trapped in this hell, and escape felt impossible.

Suddenly, he relaxed his hold on my neck. I coughed and gasped, drawing air into my oxygen-deprived lungs. His hold on my wrists didn't change, and his hand didn't leave my neck. He just stood there, pressing me into the wall and watching me choke on air.

"I own you, Little Eve. And no one is allowed to come near this fucking body. *No one*." Another tear slipped down my cheek. The fight left my body, even though rage still simmered under the surface. But how could I fight this man? I was powerless against his strength – a flower caught in the ripping winds of a hurricane.

"Are you going to rape me?" I spit out after regaining my breath. I couldn't help the bitterness that tainted my voice.

He laughed darkly. "No. What fun would that be? That's too easy. No, I won't fuck you. Not yet." He leaned back in and whispered in my ear, "In the end, you'll crave it just as much as I do." His breath on my neck sent shivers running through me.

"That won't ever happen," I growled.

He stepped away the tiniest bit, moving his hand from my neck down my body to my legs, between my thighs. I began struggling again, knowing it was useless but unable to stop myself. His fingers dropped past the hem of the slip and then trailed back up, higher and higher. Humiliation washed over me as I felt his fingers meet the wetness that was dripping down my thighs. Before he even reached my pussy, he drew his fingers back and raised them, glistening, in front of my face. His smile was that of a cat that caught the canary. "We'll see about that," he whispered. To my dismay, he brought his fingers to his mouth, covered in my arousal, and sucked on them. He growled in appreciation. His fingers left his mouth. "I think your soaking cunt says otherwise."

I felt sick, betrayed by my own body. Shame twisted through me. "Please let me wake up," I begged. I didn't care anymore if I sounded pathetic or weak. I just wanted to leave.

He looked down at me. "That's all you had to ask, Little Eve. Until tomorrow, darling." His grin widened, hunger darkening his gaze. He released me from his hold, and the world turned black. I woke.

CHAPTER 6

I woke, heart pounding in my chest and my eyes wet with tears. It had felt so *real*. The nightmare had started off so horrifying, then blended into some type of erotic nightmare. I'd had my share of nightmares in my life, but in the past several years, the only nightmares that plagued me were when I moved to a new home. Which, this was still a new home to me, but these nightmares felt...different. Too realistic. My nightmares before had been bogged down by running from something, or someone. It was always an unidentifiable figure, and it certainly wasn't something that felt tangible.

I wondered if this was what people meant when they talked about a sleep paralysis demon. But from what I had heard, a sleep paralysis demon was something that caused literal paralysis (hence the name). I was pinned, not paralyzed, sleeping deeply, not waking up or falling asleep. I supposed I could rule that out. But what character from a nightmare could be so tangible? Even my childhood home had felt painfully realistic. It wasn't fuzzy or inaccurate the way my dreams tended to be when reliving the bad times in my life.

I curled in my bed on my side, tears pouring freely. I didn't cry often, but the dream had sliced me open, cutting through all the scar tissue from my childhood, and burying new fears in with the old ones. I felt vulnerable, exposed, and trapped. It might have something to do with the way I had been deprived of any modem of control in the second half of the nightmare, or the way my body had decided to betray me in a dream – a nightmare. What was wrong with me?

I wanted to text Elly, but I was worried I would wake her up or that I would give her something else to stress about in her life. The more awake I became, the more I realized this character from my dreams must be some strange manifestation of trauma. It wasn't real, it was something from before. As I considered this, my breathing came easier, and the tears slowed. The vice around my chest loosened, and I became more aware of my real surroundings. I wasn't in that doorless black room anymore. I was in my room, in my house. There was a door several feet from my bed and a window on the far wall. Once again, my lamp was on. A sense of relief washed over me, glad to not be trapped in total darkness after waking, even if it was a bit unsettling. I began to categorize each of the items in my room to center myself. I sat up in bed and ran my fingers through my hair. If I was turning nightmares into hot fantasies, maybe I really did need to get laid.

I recalled the date from earlier that night and changed my mind. Nope. I wasn't that desperate. If those were the kind of men I was meeting right now, I would gladly stay celibate for another thousand years. I had my toys, and that had to be enough for now.

I pulled myself out of bed and began my ritual of showering to wash away the horrors. I wanted to roll my eyes at the fact that late-night showers seemed to be a common occurrence for me right now. I peeled off my shirt – thanking whoever was listening that it wasn't that blood-red slip. I took my time in the shower, soaking in the burning droplets beating down on my skin. When the water finally started dropping in temperature, I sighed and pulled myself out of the shower and wrapped myself in my robe.

Returning to my room, I sat on my bed and grabbed my phone. I decided to text Elly, simply to ask if she wanted to grab coffee in the morning since I knew I was *definitely* going to need it. And it would give me a chance to rant to her about the nightmares that plagued me. While I didn't want to worry her, I told her everything and I hoped that with talking, I might feel better. She would probably ask why the fuck I was up at 3am on a Wednesday again, but I also knew she would understand. Clicking off my phone screen, I curled up in bed and debated going to sleep. I wasn't sure I wanted to, but I was exhausted. All I could hope was that I didn't fall back into the nightmares.

The next morning, I met with Elly at the same coffee shop as before. I had a blissfully dreamless sleep after going back to bed last night, but I was still exhausted. Luckily, Elly was more than happy to meet with me before returning home for her job. She was a photographer, and most of her time was spent on editing her photos from whatever wedding or photo shoot she had done the previous weekend.

"So, I take it you didn't sleep great last night, huh?" She asked me.

"I had another nightmare." I sighed.

"The one where you're getting chased down by a creature that turns you on?" Elly giggled.

"No. This one, and the one the night before, they're different."

Elly frowned at me. "You had another nightmare, too? How come you didn't talk to me?"

"I'm sorry," I offered genuinely. "By the time I woke up I got distracted. Then I bumped into Luke where he pushed a date on me and then got lost in my script," I babbled, feeling guilty for forgetting to confide in my friend.

"You don't have to apologize. I get it," she assured me. "What are these 'different' nightmares?"

"Last night, I saw my old house," I said. I was nervous to mention the man from my nightmares for some reason. Elly would never judge me, I knew that, but I was still ashamed of myself. "I thought my dad was going to appear, but he didn't."

Elly's eyes widened. "Oh, I'm so sorry. How long has it been since one of those nightmares?"

"Years, I think."

"And what about the night before?" She asked. I internally shriveled.

"Well. There was a man. A terrifying, horrible man," I start.

"You think it's your father?" Elly asked.

My face burned. For more than one reason, I was thankful that it was *not* my father. "Uh, no. A different man. He doesn't look like anyone I know. He's tall and terrifying in a way I don't know how to describe. He just makes me scared," I explain. Elly looks at me expectantly. "He was in my dream last night, too. After the house."

"Did he do anything?"

My face burned hotter. "He said he owned me. Threatened me. He even asked if I was ready to die," I whispered.

Elly raised a brow at me. "And you're blushing because you liked it?"

"*No*," I said sharply. "I was terrified. But my body...I don't know. I feel like I'm going crazy...." I trailed off.

"You're not crazy, you're horny. It sounds like you conjured a devil to steal your soul and provide erotic fantasies." A grin played on her lips.

"But I was terrified. And he was doing things even when I didn't want him to. And he was so tangible, I could feel him; I could even *smell* him."

I was frustrated, not at her reaction, but at the fact that when I recalled the dream, I couldn't exactly say anything was overly horrifying about it. Yes, it was nonconsensual. No, that isn't okay. But my body was into it, even if my mind was enveloped in horror. But why?

"I don't know, Ev. I'm sorry it was scary for you. It sounds like it should have been a fun time. Maybe it's still part of the move, and things will cool down soon," she offered hopefully.

I sighed with her. "I hope so. I need good sleep. At least I have coffee. Plus, I think my nightmares are giving me horror fuel," I joked.

"There's a silver lining," she laughed. "How are renovations going?"

I appreciated the change in topic. As much as I wanted to rehash and dissect the dreams to understand them, I needed something else to latch on to. "They're going good. They're starting on my living room, which will be nice so I can actually get furniture in there and use it." I had decided to wait on buying most of the furniture until the renovations were done. I brought my bed from my old rental, which I obviously needed, as well as my reading chair. Other than that, the house remained relatively naked. I had the furniture picked out, so buying it wouldn't be too difficult.

"I can't wait to come over to see it!" Elly exclaimed. She had been to the house when I first moved in, but since it was in a bit of a disarray currently, it was easier to go elsewhere.

I felt excitement pumping through me. I had the perfect image of what I wanted the house to look like, and it was all coming together. Based on what the contractor and I had discussed this morning, he thought he could have the house completed in less than a month. He said that for the most part, the house was in great shape, but installing new floors and fixtures was the more time-consuming aspect of the job. Luckily, I wasn't in a rush, although I was struggling to not let my excitement lead to impatience.

Elly and I chatted about the renovations and her work, the wedding she had been to last week, and the details of her edits. Photography was a bit lost on me, but seeing the before and after with her photos was all I needed to understand. She was passionate and amazing at capturing details that the normal eye would likely miss. We planned our yearly fall photo shoot, where we dressed up and took photos together that she would then take and post on her website. They always turned out fabulous and I had several prints stored away in a box that would eventually get unpacked when the remodeling was completed.

"I don't have any clients next weekend and the weather is supposed to be nice, if you want to do our photos then?" She asked.

"That sounds great. I can't wait! What should I wear?"

"I'm thinking 'Witches Rise Again' for the theme. We can do makeup like we were killed and then wear some creepy dresses. Just wear something you don't mind getting dirty." I nodded, thinking about what the options were. I had an old black dress that might work for the shoot, but I wasn't sure I knew where I last saw it. Moving was a bitch.

"Let me dig through my things and I'll send you pictures of what I have in mind," I said.

"Sounds good to me." Elly glanced down at her phone and frowned. "My customer from the weekend is hounding me about sample photos. I need to go home and start working on them. Sorry Ev." With that, Elly disappeared from the coffee shop. I stayed, sipping on my drink and letting my thoughts wander. I found myself back in the black room with the nameless man. Even after being awake, I could still feel how his body had pressed against mine, his hand around my throat, his breath washing over me. He was terrifying in a way that didn't really make sense. And the fact I was able to feel aroused in the midst of that fear also surprised me.

Sometimes fear comes with pleasure – in the right scenario. The same way pain can be an enhancement to a sexual experience. But this wasn't the "right" scenario for me to feel that way. He didn't lure me in with sweet words and soft gestures. He simply...activated me. It wasn't looks alone, although he definitely had that going for him. Perhaps it was the mystery of this man. Some dark fantasy that lurked in my mind was now antagonizing me, both horrifying and alluring.

I shook my head. Whatever. It was a dream, and eventually they would stop, just like the rest. I finished my coffee and left the shop. As I got in my car, I thought I saw Luke across the street, but when I whipped my head back around to look again, no one was there. *Great*, I thought to myself. Now I was seeing a crazy person that wasn't there. It was like my mind was determined to bring one of my horror stories to my actual life, of which I was very much unappreciative. Still, I caught myself checking my rearview mirror a few times on the drive home to make sure no one was following me. Of course, no one was.

I made my way inside, the construction in the living room loud enough to drive any more of my wild thoughts out of my head. I went upstairs and began digging through my belongings, trying to find clothes for the photoshoot as well as organize my things. Renovations were limiting my ability to really start unpacking how I wanted, but I had one spare room that I wasn't going to be renovating other than to replace the floor to match the rest of the house, so I started there. It was going to be a storage room, but I still wanted it organized. In the room was an old table with drawers that I had decided to keep after the move and several boxes of clothes and random belongings I brought from my previous rental.

I found the kitchen boxes and began making trips with them to the new kitchen, unpacking and cleaning them before putting the dishes and small appliances away. By the time I had emptied my boxes, I realized I still had room in the kitchen for more, a fact I couldn't be happier about since in my last rental I had barely enough space to fit all the kitchen supplies into.

Making my way back to the room, I debated on what I wanted to do with the rest of the items. I began moving boxes around, sectioning them by room. Suddenly, I knocked my hip into the table as I slid one of the boxes to its appropriate spot. Cursing, I clutched my throbbing hip and glared at the table. One of the drawers had opened an inch from the impact, and I could see there was still something in it. Still nursing my wound, I opened the drawer fully and took a peek at the contents. It didn't look like anything special. There were several pens, an old newspaper, and a few random items one would expect to find in a junk drawer. I pulled the newspaper out, wondering how old it was. I flipped it open, seeing an article about stocks on the front page. It was a paper from seven years ago. I browsed the articles, nothing out of the ordinary catching my eye. Why was anyone saving this paper? Then, on the last page, a picture stood out to me.

It was a picture of my house, a woman standing in front, smiling widely. The photo caption read "Suzanne Elliot, months before suicide." There was an attached article, named "Elliot Family Speaks on Daughter's Suicide." I began reading through the article.

"A month ago, Suzanne Elliot, 23 years old, was found dead in her bathroom. The family lived off Pyke Street. Her mother, Jeanine Elliot, was the one who made the terrible discovery. Her father, Bruce Elliot, was not home at the time. Both parents state their complete shock and horror at the loss. 'We had no idea. We knew she was a little more tired than

*usual, but we thought that was from college exams,' stated Mr. Elliot. 'She
was always so happy and sweet. I'm not sure we will ever know what really
happened.' The Elliots have since been speaking on suicide and how it isn't
always accompanied with obvious signs. 'Through our loss, we just hope
there are some other parents out there that don't have to go through what
we did. Sometimes you never know what someone has going on inside their
head,' Mrs. Elliot shared. Suzanne Elliot's parents will be speaking at the
local high school during Suicide Prevention Awareness Month, September
21st of this year. Everyone is welcome to attend the event, where multiple
speakers and presentations will be offered."*

I blinked, reading the article several times. So, a girl had committed
suicide in this exact house; the house that I bought. I sighed, twisting
the ring on my index finger. It wasn't that I was afraid of ghosts. More
so, I was saddened by the thought of what she must have been going
through. I knew what it felt like. I wouldn't pretend I knew her situation
specifically, but I felt like I could understand her pain. I had experienced
that pain myself.

I shook my head, removing myself from that line of thinking. That
had been years ago, and I wasn't going to let my mind drag me back there
again. Not after all this time had passed.

My therapist used to remind me that staying in the "here and now"
was the best thing I could do to heal. But here I was, having nightmares
and reliving some of the worst times of my life. At least I hadn't had a
nightmare about That Night. I twisted the ring on my finger again as I
glanced back at the article.

Not knowing what else to do, I put the newspaper back in the drawer
it had come from and continued on with my previous project. Thoughts
of that article drifted through my mind as I organized, and before long,
I was finished with the room. I returned to my room and opened my

laptop. I should be working on work, but I instead found myself typing "Suzanne Elliot" into the search bar.

Several articles popped up, titles ranging from "Devastating Loss," to "Devastating Suicide," to "Devastating Mystery." Really, could no one think of a better word than "devastating"? Sighing, I closed the browser and opened my project. My eyelids were drooping, and my brain was as dry as the Sahara Desert. All the creativity I had felt yesterday was nothing but dust. Thinking about the girl who had committed suicide in this house, in my bathroom, was opening old wounds I didn't want to think about. I rubbed my arm subconsciously. I didn't want to fall into the hole again. I rubbed my eyes and let out another one of my endless sighs. I shut the laptop, knowing that progress wasn't going to be made today.

Instead, I made my way down to the living room to peak at the progress. They weren't doing much aside from replacing the floors and repainting the walls. The walls were currently covered in a yellow wallpaper that was a bit of an eyesore. Well, not just a bit. Seeing past the terrible decorations and older appliances was something of a challenge when I purchased the house. But I knew that it would be my own place soon enough, sans the painful, ancient style. While I didn't want it overly modern, new furniture and floors could add a beautiful affect, along with new paint.

The workers were currently prying the existing floors up. The wallpaper had already been removed, but a few strips still clung to the wall. One of the remaining pieces caught my eye. It was eerily similar to the yellow and blush wallpaper from my first dream, although it was faded and torn. Could it be the same?

I snapped myself out of it. No, what was probably happening was that I saw something similar and immediately wanted to believe that it was the same. But similar doesn't mean the same, and dreams were dreams.

"Did you have a question, ma'am?" One of the workers asked. The voice startled me, and I jerked my finger away from the peeling of wallpaper I had been staring at to look at the speaker. It was a younger man; one I hadn't spoken to before. He held a mallet and a crowbar, crouched down to the floor.

"Oh, not really. I had just noticed there was a different wallpaper underneath. Don't people normally remove the old wallpaper before they put the new one on?"

He stood up, and I noticed how tall he was. "Yeah, normally they would. But whoever put the second wallpaper on might have not done it before. We see it a lot, but it doesn't affect anything, so you don't have to worry. Your walls will look good as new!"

"I guess that makes sense. Thank you!" He seemed nice, and I was glad I had chosen this company to do the renovations. While being "nice" wasn't necessarily a prerequisite for having good work done, it was comforting to know I could feel comfortable (for the most part) in my own home.

"Anything else you need?" He asked. He had a small smile on his face. He had long brown hair, pulled back into a bun. His skin was tanned and his form muscular, likely from his labor job and possibly some gym time. He was attractive and had a flirtatious look in his blue eyes.

I smiled brightly back at him. "I'm alright for now, I think." While I felt like he was interested in me, I wasn't brave enough to assume. I began to turn away.

"Well, if you want any more lessons on this kind of stuff, you know where to find me," his teeth flashed. It wasn't the best joke, but I chuckled anyways.

"Of course. If you need anything either, just holler." I made my way back upstairs.

CHAPTER 7

T he rest of the day seemed to be uneventful, but I couldn't shake the odd occurrences of the day. From the rehashing my nightmares in the coffee shop with Elly to finding the article of a dead girl to thinking I was seeing the wallpaper from my dreams in the real house, the day had been mentally draining. I had made slight progress on my current project, but far from enough. I knew it would get finished, but with the way my mind seemed to have been so distractable lately, I wasn't sure when.

The contractors had left for the evening, and I was cooking some pasta in the kitchen when a paper fluttered in the corner of my eye. My head whipped to the side, noticing a small note on the counter for the first time. A phone number was written on it in a masculine scrawl, followed by a name and short note.

(217)602-5830 ~ Ethan

In case you have any more wallpaper concerns ;)

I laughed to myself. Well, I guess my question had been answered already. Though I wasn't certain I should be getting involved with one of the contractors, whether he was nice or not. I whipped out my phone, snapped a picture and sent it to Elly.

> A contractor left this behind for me…thoughts?

Is he cute?

> Very…

And your hesitation is?

> They're still working on my house. If things get weird that would be awful, ya know?

OOOOR, and just hear me out, it goes great and nothing is awkward. Also, what's with the wallpaper comment?

> Whoever owned the house before me didn't remove the wallpaper before throwing another one on. I was asking about it.

My thumb hovered over the "send" button as I debated telling her about the weird recognition I'd had with the wallpaper and my dreams. After a single twist of the ring on my finger, I typed out a few more words.

> I thought it looked similar to the wallpaper I had in one of my dreams, but I think I must be losing my mind, lol

Oh? That's freaky as fuck. I'm sure it's a coincidence though?

That's what I was thinking. Some weird psychology thing, idk. Oh, another weird thing today happened.

What's up?

I found this article in the house today. It was about a girl who lived here. She committed suicide...

Oh my god...that's so sad...are you okay? I know that stuff is kinda hard to take in sometimes.

Yeah, I'm fine. It just really caught me off guard. It's awful. I'm just glad I'm not in that place anymore.

You're right. You're not.

Still weird to know someone so young died here, though.

Yeah, I agree. Wonder what happened to her family?

They moved on to help with suicide prevention awareness, apparently.

Well that's good!

Yeah. Definitely. Well, I'm gonna finish my pasta and debate on sending this text ;)

DO IT!!!!! But also, if you need anything, let me know <3

I sighed, clicking my screen off and returning to my pasta while glancing at the note on the counter. I was surprised I hadn't noticed it before when I was prepping the food, but the way my head had been today, I couldn't say I was overly surprised. I went back to twisting my ring back and forth, feeling uncertain about sending the message. Some of it stemmed from the dream last night, but it was just that – a dream. Why was I so worried?

I bit my lip while I plated the pasta and poured a glass of wine. I took a large sip and swirled it over my tongue while debating. Finally, I scoffed at myself and took another sip while reaching for my phone. I typed out a quick message to the number then locked the screen again.

I was halfway through my food before a text chimed on my phone. Without a second thought, I snatched my phone off the counter.

> Hey, wasn't sure for a minute if you were going to message. I hope it isn't weird for me to leave my number.

> No, you're totally fine. I only just found the paper a bit ago while cooking.

> Okay, awesome. What did you make for dinner?

> I made some pasta with pesto sauce. Nothing too crazy lol

The conversation continued on in a way that was entertaining enough to keep me engaged. After finishing dinner and another glass of wine, I decided to call it a night and lay down. Ethan was sweet, offering a simple "goodnight, Evalyn" before I flipped the lights off and set my phone down for the night. As I closed my eyes, my mind wandered. I thought about the intensity of the dream last night and briefly wondered if someone as sweet and gentle as Ethan seemed to be could ever be rough. The thought caused me to giggle, but then my eyes snapped open as I realized I was actually considering the dream last night to be a fantasy.

"Oh, my *fucking* god, Evalyn. Get your shit together. Ethan is nice and probably great in bed," I hissed to myself. I rolled my eyes and twisted the ring on my finger some more. Closing my eyes again, I felt anxiety prick at my nerves as I wondered if the nightmares would return. I forced myself to breathe and stay calm. If I fell asleep while peaceful, I would likely have less stressful dreams. I focused on the typical meditation techniques of visualizing energy flowing through each part of my body, warming and calming me. I relaxed further and further and *further*....

***

I opened my eyes to soft moonlight peaking through the thin branches of the willow tree above me. The soil beneath me was unbelievably soft, and I could hear water flowing nearby, likely from a stream. The branches over my head swayed in a gentle breeze, and the air that brushed against my skin was warm. I glanced down, noticing I was wearing a loose camisole and matching shorts. I wasn't sure I had ever been more comfortable in my entire life. I sighed happily, relaxing further into the soil. I wasn't worried about getting dirty, which was odd, but I was too relaxed to think much on it.

I stared at the tree above me for some time, just embracing the perfection around me. A leaf drifted towards my face, tumbling and spiraling from the branches above me. I went to reach my hand out to catch it, but my arm wouldn't move. For a brief moment, I thought it was that I was simply too relaxed. But, as I glanced down, I realized it wasn't that. Terror shattered the peacefulness around me as I stared, horrified, at my body, slowly being swallowed by the earth. I began trying to wrench my body from the soil that had been soft only moments ago, but now scraped and cut into my flesh. I wanted to scream, but I couldn't gather enough air as the earth tightened painfully around my chest. Slowly, the soil covered my mouth and nose, choking me. Panic shot through my body, but I couldn't move a single muscle to react.

Suddenly, the earth released me, and I went into a freefall. A solid surface slammed against my back, making me wince as I gasped for air. I had fallen further into the earth. Darkness surrounded me. The moon was gone, as was the tree, the breeze, and the sound of water. I couldn't see anything in front of me, so I reached my hand out gingerly, trying to feel the earth I knew was in front of me. Instead, my hand brushed against a smooth surface. The surface was mere inches from my face, and as I stretched out my arms, I realized it was only inches from my sides.

My breath began to rasp painfully through my lungs, tears springing from my eyes and dripping down my face. It was a coffin. *A fucking coffin.* I choked on sobs, beginning to desperately pound against the walls surrounding me. My sobs turned to screams, the skin on my hands splitting as I pounded against the wood in desperation. Nothing moved. I was fucking buried alive. I continued screaming until my voice was hoarse and blood dripped from my hands to my forearms.

I began to quietly sob, tears still pouring down my face. I curled in on myself as much as possible in this tight space. Panic swirled through my veins, but I closed my eyes and tried to breathe. My nose was stuffy from the crying, so I focused on breathing through my mouth, fighting the gasping sobs. My body trembled and shook, convulsing as I fought the fear, but I focused on each muscle.

As my mind began to calm, I realized this had to be another dream. The last I remember, I was in my bed, focusing on breathing and relaxing. My breath hitched in my chest again, but I forced myself to stop.

In and out, Evalyn. In one, two, three, four; out one, two, three, four, I chanted to myself. The terror wouldn't dissipate, but I could at least force my body to relax and give something for my mind to latch onto. I kept my eyes closed, breathing in and out, in and out. Finally, even though I felt the fear still latching onto my soul, I leveled my breathing and opened my eyes. Shock and relief raced through me as I realized I wasn't in the coffin anymore. However, as I took in the black marble and familiar light fixtures, dread filled my stomach. I was back. I stumbled to my feet clumsily.

"Well, you didn't act like you wanted to die just then," a voice whispered against my ear. *His* voice. I shrieked, lurching forward, but didn't make it far until steel arms wound around my body, pinning me to a marble chest. "After your behavior tonight, I thought you wanted to attend your funeral," the velvet voice whispered. I felt his fingers brushing against my arm, a stark contrast to his vice-like grip on my body.

"Let me go," I whispered. My voice was hoarse from screaming, and I felt as though the fear from earlier had sucked the life from my body, but somehow my voice stayed level.

"Tsk, tsk, tsk. I thought we had been over this already, Little Eve. You're *mine.* Why did you disobey me?" One of his hands slid up my body to the column of my throat, tilting my head back against his shoulder, his silver eyes clashing against mine.

"This isn't real," I whispered, my grasp on the calm I sought loosening. His grip tightened on my throat at the last word, making it come out in a rasp.

"Again, I thought we'd been over this already. Do I need to do another demonstration?" He asked. The hand that wasn't grasping my throat loosened its hold to move down my arm, grabbing a swollen, bloodied hand. He slowly brought it to his lips, kissing each cut, smearing blood on his mouth. Then, his tongue darted out to lick the crimson. A guttural groan came from his lips, an animalistic sound of pure ecstasy. He followed suit with my other hand, again kissing each wound. I was too stunned and exhausted to fight. With his touches, the pain faded to a dull throb as I lost myself in the pools of silver in his eyes.

"I will say, my sweet little Eve, I was very impressed with your ability to calm down. That is a first for me," he whispered as he leaned his head down to my neck, burying his face in my hair. "It was so beautiful, I almost couldn't watch," he groaned. His arm had returned to its original position, his other hand still grasping my neck.

I knew, logically, I should be fighting. But for some reason, my head was floating several feet from my shoulders and my body felt languid and heavy. Perhaps it was some sort of spell he had cast on me, or the shock, but I felt the fear melting away like snow in the rain. In this moment, I didn't want to fight. He might be terrifying, or majorly fucked up, but nothing mattered. Not in this moment.

I didn't particularly want to be there, but anything was better than that fucking coffin. Small spaces, especially those that had no easy exit, were a major weakness of mine. Memories from before writhed through my head, fighting to see the surface. I couldn't go back there, though. So, I focused on where I was. Anything was better than there.

"No fighting tonight, hm?" He asked, dragging a long finger along my jugular. Another tear slipped from my eye. How could I admit my temporary surrender? So, I stayed silent, ungrounded, not having the energy to formulate words. *Anything is better than there.*

His brow furrowed, shadowing his molten silver eyes. He stepped back, coming to stand in front of me. His hands moved to my shoulders, forcing me to step backwards until my back hit a solid surface. His head bent down to stare directly into my eyes. Through it all, I did nothing. He guided me and I followed, muscles limp and accommodating.

A frown pinched his full lips, disapproval and disappointment leaking from him. His eyes swirled faster, irritation simmering beneath the surface. "No. You're not allowed to give up yet. You're different from the rest." His voice sounded from somewhere around me, rather than seeming to come from his mouth, hushed and almost...sad. He brought a hand up, lightly smacking my cheek. "Hey, get it together. I'm not fucking done with you," he hissed, raising his voice, lip lifted in a snarl.

I blinked up at him, still not fully feeling grounded in my body. *Anything is better than there.* Then, another slap, harder. "Focus, dammit," he said, giving my shoulders a rough shake. I flinched at his words more than I had the slap.

"What do you want from me?" I finally asked. Each word trembled as it slipped from my lips. *Anything is better than there.*

"And she speaks," he said. His expression became colder. "I want to play with a human, not a puppet. You have more fire than that, don't you?"

The words landed solid blows, bringing me further and further down to my body again. My heart ached for a reason I couldn't pinpoint. "Just let me go." My voice sounded hollow, even to my own ears.

He shook me again, harder this time. "*Enough*. You can't give up yet!" He growled in my face. One of his hands moved to grip my hair painfully. A whimper escaped my throat at the rough touch. "Fight me!" He hissed.

I raised a hand to push against his arm weakly, but his grip didn't loosen. "You can do better than that, Little Eve," he encouraged tauntingly.

Finally, something inside me snapped. Maybe it was hearing the nickname, like I was some naïve, innocent creature. My veins began to boil with rage and fury snapped against my skin like electricity. "Fuck. *You*," I snarled. I dug my nails into the skin on his wrist and pulled. He growled against the pain, blood welling where my nails had cut, but still refused to let go. My knee launched up to land a solid hit on his dick, but faster than I could process, he was standing just out of reach, hand no longer wound in my long tresses.

"There she is. Good. I don't like playing with boring dolls." He stepped back into me, his heat warming my chest. He tilted his head down to me in a challenge. I stood, fists at my side, trembling in anger. "You're not allowed to give up like that, do you understand? No matter what anyone does to you or puts you through, you are never allowed to let your fire go out like that." He gripped my face, fingers digging into my cheeks painfully. "Do you fucking understand, Evalyn?"

In response, I spit in his face. He lifted a hand to wipe it, chuckling. "Good girl," he growled. He leaned in, silver eyes glowing brightly, and kissed me on the forehead. Everything went black.

***

I lurched upright in bed, heart thundering in my chest, body still shaking with fury. I looked at my hands, noting there was no blood or swelling, and then drove my fingers through my hair, sighing.

"Fuck!" I yelled, yanking the hair at my roots. I glanced over, noticing the light gleaming in the darkness. I raised my hand to flip it off, then decided otherwise. I couldn't really explain why, but I knew I didn't want to. I didn't even have the energy to shower how I normally do after a nightmare. I felt drained. And I wasn't sure I could even say I was scared anymore. Angry? Yes. And, though I didn't want to admit it, having that final line of approval before waking up had calmed me more than it should have. I sighed, flopping back against my pillows, not even bothering to check the time. This time, when I closed my eyes, nothing waited for me.

CHAPTER 8

"I'm sincerely fucked in the head, Elly." I stared down at my latte as I sat across from my friend who had her face inches from her laptop screen, looking at photos.

She hummed in agreement. "You're only noticing this now, Ev?" She raised an eyebrow, still with her eyes focused on the computer screen. I knew she was going to be like this since she had mentioned her deadline for edits was today. But, like the bad influence I was, I lured her out with promises of coffee and pastries.

"I feel like I'm losing my mind. Every night is a new nightmare. It's weird. I don't understand why I keep having them."

"You've spent a lot of time at the house, renovations are stressful, and you have yet to get some good dick," Elly listed off, shrugging her shoulders. Her eyes briefly flicked to mine. "Oh! What about that Ethan guy?" She asked.

"Oh, I messaged him last night. He was engaging enough to keep the conversation going, which was cool. But I'm not really feeling the whole 'romantic' thing, especially after last night. And I'm probably going to see him at the house today, too."

Elly rolled her eyes, finally offering me her full attention. "Don't go sending him packing because you had a nightmare. Just see where it leads. I'm not saying that your nightmare isn't important or doesn't have some meaning that you should try to understand, I'm just saying that you shouldn't let that determine what you do in your waking life. Plus, don't forget that your nightmare was almost certainly related to that information you found out about the house yesterday." She gave me a pointed look.

I opened my mouth, then closed it again. She wasn't wrong, not by a long shot. But I still didn't feel like I had it in me at this point. "You're right. I'm over-analyzing." I ran a hand through my hair.

She grinned. "I'm just here to keep your sanity intact – if that's even possible." She laughed at her joke as I playfully smacked her arm. "Sadly, I think I need to return to my cave in order to edit these photos properly. And you need to go home to your hot construction worker before you chicken out again." She slid her laptop closed and I nodded at her, feeling a pang in my chest at the short interaction, even if I understood why.

Leaving out the fact that I didn't know if I would actually engage with Ethan, I said, "No worries, Elly. Thanks for grabbing coffee with me. I know I've been extra needy this past week."

"You're not needy, just losing your marbles," she nudged me with her elbow. "Alright, well don't forget to share updates about this boy." She waggled her eyebrows at me before standing up to leave.

"Alright, alright I will. Now go back to your cave," I said. With that, she walked off, leaving me alone with my half-finished latte. I spent a few minutes scrolling on my phone, trying to keep my mind occupied until I was ready to leave. Finally, with the last of my drink gone, I decided to grab my bag and leave.

As I stood, I glanced around and realized I saw a familiar blond head. My heart rate picked up in my chest, seeing him standing across the street, arms crossed and stance casual as he leaned against a building. Quickly, I pulled out my phone and called Elly.

"I just saw you, bitch, what's up?" She said with a laugh in her voice.

"Elly, I have a problem." My voice was hollow.

Instantly, Elly sobered up. "Talk to me, what's going on?"

"It's Luke," I whispered. His eyes glittered from across the street, a small grin on his face. The hair on my neck stood up.

"What? Did he call you or something?" She asked.

"No. He's standing across the street, Elly."

"What the fuck? I'm turning around right now."

"No, don't. I'm about to head home anyways, but I want to be on the phone, so just hang with me for a sec, okay?" My confidence was nonexistent, but I knew I had to be less approachable if I was on the phone. Right?

"Okay, I'm here for you, Evalyn. Don't worry," Elly's voice remained cool and collected, but I could still tell she was worried. I made it to my car parked on the edge of the street, hands shaking as I slid into the driver's seat. I clicked the locks closed as soon as the door was shut.

"I'm in the car, but can you stay on the phone with me?" I asked.

"Of course, Ev. Is he still staring at you?" I glanced over my shoulder in the direction where Luke had been, finding empty space. I glanced around rapidly, trying to locate where he went. When I found nothing, I sighed in relief, the tension leaving my body. My hands gripped the steering wheel and my phone, and I leaned back and rested my head against the seat.

"Evalyn?" Elly's voice came from the speaker on my phone.

"Yeah, yeah. I'm here. Sorry. He's gone. Maybe I panicked a little too much." I winced at myself, frustrated with how easily I had been able to get worked up.

"You're fine, and, if I'm being honest, I'd rather you were over-cautious than under-cautious. I'm glad you're on high alert after that creep basically threatened you the other night." Elly's voice soothed my nerves, making me feel less wimpy for being frightened.

"Thank you." I whispered. "I don't mean to bother, but can you hang on the phone with me 'till I get home?" I was still feeling rattled, even though I knew I was safe.

"Of course. I wasn't going to hang up until I knew you were in your house, anyways."

"And this, my dear, is why you are the best friend a girl could ever ask for." I turned on the car, setting my phone down and waiting for the call to sync with the Bluetooth. I checked the road before sliding out of my parallel parking spot, making small talk with Elly as I made my way home. It wasn't a long drive, by any means, but it was a good ten minutes before I rolled up onto my driveway. I sighed happily, seeing the trees lining the pavement, leading up to the cozy house with the beautiful windows and small porch. The house needed a fresh coat of paint, but the columns on the porch were well made and the landscape held a lot of potential for bushes and flowers. Still, I was more focused on the improvement of the interior rather than the exterior. My comfort came first.

I stepped into the house, confirming my safety to Elly before ending the call. It looked like they were almost done with the living room, and it sounded as though half of the workers were now upstairs, working on the office area. It was Thursday, and it seemed that they were splitting a smaller group to complete the downstairs while the larger group began the upstairs renovations. They were nearly two days ahead of schedule, which excited me immensely.

Within a couple minutes of me wandering around the lower level of the house, admiring the gorgeous new floors and revamped walls, Dave found me. "Good mornin', ma'am! I have some good news – we're ahead of schedule, so we'll be outta your hair sooner rather than later."

"I saw," I said, smiling in excitement. "It looks absolutely beautiful; you guys are doing great work."

"Thank you, ma'am. Now, since it's your personal space and all, I wanted to talk about your bedroom and bathroom. I don't wanna go bargin' in and disrupting your space, so I wanted to ask how you wanted to go about it." His thoughtfulness was refreshing and made me even more happy I had chosen him for the job.

"Of course. Thank you so much for asking. How long do you think it will take? For the bathroom and bedroom, I mean."

"Well, I'd say that if we start on Monday, we'd probably be done in that space by Wednesday, Thursday at the latest. We work fast and all, but tearing up the floors, repainting, and gutting the bathroom is gonna take a bit of time. Would that be okay?" He asked.

"Of course. I'll take the weekend to clean up my bedroom and bathroom, so you don't have to worry about all my stuff getting in your way."

"Okay, perfect. Since we are only replacing the floors and painting in the office upstairs, we should actually be done with all that by the end of tomorrow. I'll let ya know if we need to stay a bit late. The renovations are going quicker than expected partly 'cause the floors an all are in better shape than we figured they'd be. You've got a good house here, Miss Evalyn."

I smiled at his compliment, feeling even more relieved with the purchase decision with his words of encouragement. While I could see the potential the house had when I purchased it, as well as confirmation from the inspections, it was nice to hear from a professional working on the house that the structure of the house was better off than they had expected.

"Thank you so much, Dave. I'm glad to hear it. This weekend I'll make sure to get everything situated and I'll spend some time at my friend's house so I'm not stepping on your toes here."

"Alrighty then, ma'am. Well, I'm gonna get back to work and keep this crew on pace." He chuckled a bit, heading off to observe the living room as I made my way upstairs. I glanced towards the office, seeing the workers cleaning out the area and setting up their equipment. While I still had a few rooms to go, it was hard to believe how quickly everything was coming together. I had expected renovations on the entire house to take at least a month, not a measly two weeks. I wasn't complaining, however. The quicker it was done, the quicker I could truly settle in.

I slipped into my bedroom, popping my headphones on and diving into my work, thankful I hadn't seen Ethan. There was too much happening for me to handle that kind of interaction right now. I decided that while I may not be able to get all the juiciest, goriest scenes out with my brain running on creative fumes, I could at least generate structure and a plan for what would come next. I figured it would look something like:

Character is chased by antagonist.
Insert gore scene
Camera pans away, antagonist leaves scene.
Character two enters screen, discovers the remains of character one.

While it wasn't that overwhelmingly impressive, at least I could then modify and add to what I had planned when the creative juices were flowing.

The day slipped by, and by the time the workers had wrapped up for the day, I decided to settle in and watch a movie. I almost wished I'd already had my couch and living room furniture delivered early so I could enjoy my movie in the newly renovated area. I instead settled for watching the movie on my laptop screen while reclining against the pillows on my bed. Next week, when everything was finished, I would get back into my nightly yoga, but, for now, I would take the lazy break.

I threw on Tim Burton's Sweeny Todd and hummed along to the songs as they played, feeling tiredness settling over me. I hadn't ended up talking to Ethan at all today, which didn't bother me as much as it should have. He might be a bit more confused, but after the run-in with Luke, it hadn't even crossed my mind. I was sure I would see him tomorrow, and when that happened, I would just explain that today had been a weird day.

Before I could fall too deeply into my pillows, I paused the movie to make some chamomile tea, leaving the room dark as I tiptoed my way through the room. As I heated the water, I took a moment to appreciate the beautiful kitchen once again. I scooped the tea leaves from the canister and into the infuser and poured the hot water over it. I grabbed the cup, making my way towards the stairs, glancing outside. What I saw made my blood run cold.

My heart thudded in my chest as my bones froze in place, seeing the car at the end of the driveway. The car's headlights were on but faced parallel to the road. It was far enough away that I couldn't make out much aside from the lights and that it was an SUV. My phone was upstairs, but I didn't particularly want to take my eyes off of the vehicle to go grab it. I quietly stepped towards the front door as if whoever was in the car all the way at the end of the long driveway could hear me and checked to see that the deadbolt was in place.

Suddenly, the car reversed, backing into my driveway. My heart leapt up my throat and panic squeezed my organs in a firm grasp. I held my breath, not knowing what direction to take. Did I take my eyes off the car to go get my phone and dial the police? Or did I wait to see what this person was doing? Before I could panic too much, the car lurched forward and headed in the opposite direction they had been facing when parked.

The air in my chest whooshed from my lungs, and I rested my head against the door. *Jesus Christ, Evalyn. They were just using your driveway to turn around. They must have been lost,* I chastised myself. These nightmares definitely had me on edge with how jumpy I was being. I clutched my tea as though it was my lifeline while I made my way upstairs to the bedroom. When I entered my bedroom, I paused. The tree light was on. My trembling frame calmed a little at the sight, which didn't particularly make much sense, but it felt comforting. It made me feel like I wasn't alone, and in the best way possible. If this house was haunted and that was the reason the light was always on, I couldn't help but be glad this was the ghost I was stuck with. The light was always on when I was most scared or frightened, and that, in and of itself, was a huge comfort.

Sighing, I climbed back into bed, sipping my tea and humming along as Sweeny Todd slashed his way through the dirty elites of London and Mrs. Lovett made meat pies out of his revenge. Before the movie had finished, my eyes drifted shut and I fell into a peaceful abyss, nothing waiting for me on the other side of the veil tonight.

CHAPTER 9

S omehow, my dreams were quiet over the next two nights. The dreams I had came and went, slipping from my memory and spiraling out of reach. I thought I felt a familiar presence there, but even that didn't feel solid. I couldn't say I wasn't happy I was no longer falling back into a new horror every time I closed my eyes, but the dreams I had felt disorienting, even if I wasn't able to remember what they were.

Saturday, I called Elly to see if she was fine with me crashing at her house for a few days while the workers remodeled the bedroom and bathroom. Of course, she agreed, promising good food as long as I brought the wine. After settling on our plans, I started staring at my project once more.

I gnawed on my lip and spun my ring round and round, deliberating. After several minutes of nothing, I growled, frustrated, and opened a new project. There had been an idea itching at my brain today, and decided to stop trying to force one when there was another begging to be let out. I was hoping that starting this would clear some of the blockage on my other story.

However, as I began writing out the synopsis of what I wanted the project to be, I felt myself melting into the work, feeling settled and excited with my creation thus far. It was different than the normal psychological thrillers I dove into, because this time, the story was centered around paranormal events. This story was almost certainly inspired by my experiences in the house since moving in, but the fun part about these kinds of creations is that I could take the idea and mold it and twist it into whatever creation I wanted.

The story spoke of an individual moving into a house, strange occurrences happening, and nightmares. Horrible nightmares that kept the character on edge. I wanted the end of the story to lead to the character losing their mind – not being able to tell if they were awake or asleep anymore. I wanted the audience to question it, too.

So, I continued to write, twisting ideas around in my head, trying to find the most believable path for the character to follow in order to lull the viewers in. Anyone could write a story. But it was the *way* it was written that mattered. The more believable, the better. And not believable as in someone believes it could actually happen (although that is a bonus), but believable in the way that someone understands all the things that are going on. World building plays a large part, but character growth is the other.

In stories like mine, a slow deterioration of the mind was best, followed by the rapid deterioration after the truth ended as the snake bite that the character didn't see coming. My headphones played music as I wrote, leading me into an almost meditative state. The thoughts came into my mind, then flew from my fingers onto the keyboard. The day slid by, turning into evening, and still, I wrote.

Finally, when my stomach twisted in hunger, growling for the tenth time, I stopped. I had created several potential outlines, all with different scenarios on the best way to make the character fall down the rabbit hole of insanity. Satisfaction filled my bones at the creation, even if I wasn't practiced in writing paranormal horrors. However, with the number of paranormal horrors I had seen in movies along with my strong knowledge of movie writing, I felt confident. I was excited to share it with Elly to get her opinion.

I closed the laptop and made my way downstairs, browsing the fridge and freezer for dinner. I spun my ring as I deliberated, nothing really standing out to me. Finally, I opened a food delivery app and ordered a burrito from a local restaurant. While waiting for the order, I decided to head upstairs and begin moving some things around so the workers wouldn't have as much difficulty while trying to renovate.

In the short couple weeks I had been in the house, somehow both the bathroom and bedroom were messier than I figured they should be. I began putting things back in boxes to temporarily place in another room, sweeping and cleaning so they wouldn't have to. While the house wasn't fully furnished, I did have my bed and reading chair, both of which sat in my bedroom. I could move the reading chair relatively easily, but moving the bed was a different story. I decided to go ahead and move the bedside table as well, carefully unplugging the antique lamp and setting it safely in the other room where it couldn't be accidentally broken. The little red apples shook on their hooks as I set it in a box filled with newspaper and towels for safekeeping.

A pang hit my chest as I put it away, knowing it was only for a few days, yet knowing I was going to miss waking up with it on. *What the fuck is wrong with you, Evalyn?* I thought to myself. The light being turned on and off basically indicated the house was haunted. But even though I knew this, somehow that little tree had become a beacon of hope when I woke up in distress.

After the side table and lamp was put away, I swallowed the burrito in a few bites before laying down in bed and resting my headphones on my ears, closing my eyes and letting myself relax. Exhaustion pulled at my body, but my mind still swirled on the tendrils of creativity that had hooked into me with the new story idea. But as the minutes ticked by, I slowly lost myself into the dark abyss of sleep.

***

I opened my eyes, finding myself in a now familiar black room, smelling mint and lavender. The lights on the walls were on, the dim glow spreading glittering light onto the black marble floor. I saw a form sitting in one of the black chairs in the room, facing away from me. Nervousness for what was to come slithered through me, and I glanced down at my attire, seeing a familiar oversized t-shirt hanging from my frame. Relief tugged at me, thankful that I at least had the comfort of my own clothes.

I glanced around, trying to subtly find an exit, hoping to leave before he noticed me. As my eyes flicked from wall to wall, I realized there was no obvious exit. I held my breath, trying to think past the fear. When my eyes returned to the man sitting in the chair once again, I stumbled back, a gasp slipping from my lips while terror became a viper, twisting into my organs. His face was turned in my direction, clearly aware of my presence.

"No need for that tonight, Little Eve," he whispered. My brows furrowed in confusion. "Your fear, I mean. I'm too tired for it."

His words left me even more confused. He gestured to an empty chair a few feet from him. I felt my head shaking in a clear "no." A frown twisted his lips.

"Sit. Please. I already told you I'm not here for your fear tonight." His velvet voice was laced with tension, but there was an undercurrent of exhaustion to it, as well.

My legs shook as I took tentative steps towards him. My fear was still there, but I would rather not anger this nightmare creature when he claimed to be wanting peace tonight. It felt like an uneasy truce, but I would take what I could get. Finally, I reached the chair sitting adjacent from him and stiffly sat down.

He sighed softly, taking a sip from a glass in his hand that I hadn't noticed before. "Thank you," he said. My brain was frozen, confusion sticking to the gears and cogs of my thoughts.

"What do you want from me?" I asked. My voice was firm, though inside I trembled. This was almost more terrifying than when he intentionally tried to terrify me.

"Tonight? I just want company." He wore black trousers and a black button up, looking as refined as ever sitting in the black velvet chair and sipping what looked like whiskey.

"Why?" My brows felt like they were glued together, not understanding what was happening.

His swirling silver eyes flicked to mine. "Everyone needs company sometimes," was his only reply.

I realized that now may be a good time to ask questions, to understand where he came from and why I had created this nightmare. "What's your name?" I asked.

His eyes stared into mine, his dark hair dripping over his face. He truly was beautiful, with a strong jaw, lean body, and eyes that could cut through the soul. "My name is Daemon. Took you long enough to ask," he said sardonically.

"Daemon. Fitting. So, what, you're a demon?" I would have imagined my creative head could have come up with something more original.

His eyes narrowed at me before he leaned his head back against the chair, reclining into a relaxed position and staring at the ceiling. His lips touched the rim of glass as he sipped on a honey-colored liquid. My eyes refused to look away from the graceful bow of his lip, followed by the soft movement of his throat as he swallowed. "Something like that."

"Why are you here?" I asked.

A grin tilted his mouth upward. "In your mind, or in this room?" There was a humorous undercurrent to his low voice.

My world felt like it was being tilted sideways with how normal this conversation felt, aside from the fact it was all happening in my head. "Both."

"Well, as far as why I'm in your head, you came to me, just like all those before you. And as for why I'm here in this room..." he trailed off as though trying to find the right words. "Well, I simply have nowhere else to be." While his tone was light as he said this, bitterness twisted the words.

I stared at him, glancing at the column of his throat and down to his chest where the top two buttons of his shirt were open, displaying a hint of black ink against his skin. I swallowed. "There were others before me?" I asked, distracted, as my eyes tried to determine what tattoos were hidden beneath his dark attire.

"Would you like me to remove my shirt?" He asked, ignoring my question. My eyes whipped to his face, realizing he was staring at me. Red flushed my cheeks and shame coursed through my veins. I wanted to pull my eyes away from his silver ones, but I wasn't sure how. I felt as though my whole being was being pulled into them, a vortex of sin and beauty.

I coughed, loosening the words from my throat. "No. I just saw the tattoo, that's all," I said.

His teeth flashed through his grin. He looked like he was enjoying every moment of this. "Your face is as red as an apple, Little Eve. I wonder if the rest of you can turn that red," he thought out loud.

I flinched, anger rising in my chest. *There it is,* I thought. *Hold on to the anger.* "You'll never find out," I hissed.

His eyes narrowed on mine, rising to the challenge. The flame of anger sputtered out, fear lacing its way back through my ribcage. *Why did I set him off? Just when I was finally getting some answers. For fuck's sake, Evalyn.* "Well, well, well. Little Eve seems to want to play after all," he said. His head tilted to the side, eyes scaling my body, as if he was imagining the very thing I had claimed he would never see. The anger returned, humiliation throwing gasoline on the embers. Who gave a fuck about answers when it involved placating this monster?

"I don't want to play, I want you out of my *head*, dumbass," I hissed.

His eyes flashed and he let out a low laugh. He suddenly stood, taking two steps in my direction, towering over me. I moved to stand, but before I could move a muscle, his hands wrapped around my wrists, holding me to the chair. I wasn't sure where the glass had gone, but I didn't have a moment to think on it. I yanked on my hands, trying futilely to escape. All of his bright white teeth were on display as he smiled at me, inches from my face, causing my heart to beat rapidly in my chest.

"But being in your head is so much *fun,*" he said, laughter in his voice. "I told you I was tired, but I don't mind playing a bit." His hands left my wrists, but when I glanced down, another wave of horror ripped through me. Black leather restraints had replaced his hands, pinning them effectively to the chair. I struggled, yanking desperately in an attempt to free myself.

Daemon kneeled in front of me, so large that even in this position we were eye to eye. I moved to kick him, but I realized my ankles were also frozen in place, tied against the legs of the chair. He chuckled, his dark laugh filling the dim room. "You should have admitted what we both know to be true. The hunger in your eyes was obvious. This could have been a whole different kind of fun." He placed his hands on my calves, softly massaging as his eyes stared into mine.

My breath wheezed through my lips, not knowing how to get out of this predicament that I could have avoided had I just placed a leash on my anger. But the anger was bubbling up, mixing with the fear in a dark concoction of emotions. His hands moved up towards my knees, still slowly massaging the muscles while his eyes never left mine. He wasn't hurting me, but he was forcing me to be vulnerable, and that pissed me off. In each interaction with Daemon, I felt like the anger began to overwhelm the fear, bit by bit.

"What the fuck is wrong with you?" I hissed.

"I could ask the same of you, Little Eve. Why are you so attracted to the monster from your nightmare?"

"I'm *not*," I snarled. The voice in the back of my head disagreed, but that wasn't the point right now.

Daemon's eyes narrowed again. Like this, he looked terrifying. He was a beautiful monster, pulling me in and making me want to run away at the same time. Fear crawled up my throat, trying to swallow the anger. His hands made their way past my knees, his fingers now massaging my naked thighs.

Beyond the fear and anger, traitorous pleasure snaked its way through me at the touch, at being forced to take the touch, at not being in control of what he touched. Humiliation washed over me, and I gritted my teeth. His touch softened, his fingers merely tickling the sensitive flesh of my upper thighs. My breaths were rapid, and my eyes flicked to his hands as they began pushing up my long shirt.

I wanted to scream at him to stop, but some small part of me didn't let the words leave my lips. It felt like that would feed whatever his sick mind was hungering for. And an even smaller part of me recognized I wanted this, whatever this was. I quickly squashed that thought down, letting the anger twist and writhe in my chest instead.

Daemon's fingers slipped higher and higher, pushing the shirt past the apex of my thighs, exposing my naked sex. My legs were slightly parted from the restraints, and I did my best to push them together to hide myself. My cheeks heated, and I knew my face was probably glowing in the darkness of the room.

"Naughty, naughty Little Eve. Coming in your own clothes and still not wearing underwear? It's almost like you were expecting this tonight." My eyes flicked back to his, which were bright and glowing with lust. To my horror, he leaned forward, bringing his nose closer to my pussy, and took a deep inhale. "So sweet," he whispered. "I've been thinking about this taste since I licked you from my fingers." His tongue slipped past his lips and licked my upper thigh, torturously close to my core.

My hips tilted towards his lips, my body completely acting on its own. His lips spread wide in a victorious smile before slowly leaning down to kiss my right thigh, then the left. His hands began trailing up my waist, raising my shirt higher and higher. His fingers brushed against my ribs, making goosebumps flair across my skin. I was a slave to my own body. I could feel the wetness starting to drip out of me. My anger had evaporated in a puff of smoke, taken over by a different kind of heat flowing through my body. My breath was coming in rapid gasps, fear twisting with dark lust. His fingers brushed the bottom of my breasts, the sensation causing my nipples to harden.

He laid kisses on my upper thighs, lips trailing higher, tongue darting out to taste my skin. His hands pushed my shirt above my breasts, and his lips brushed against my hips, then my lower stomach, following the path his fingers had taken. My breath came out faster, rasping through my lungs. His breath heated the skin of my stomach as his fingers grazed the skin above my chest in small circles.

His lips moved up my ribcage, then to the valley of my breasts. His tongue licked a trail up my sternum, pausing briefly. "Your heart is thundering so beautifully," he said huskily, sending another wave of goosebumps across my skin. Briefly, shame flashed through me, and I started struggling again, but then his mouth was on my nipple, causing a surprised moan to escape. My eyes flashed down, transfixed on the sight of him licking and sucking on the hardened bud. Ragged breaths knifed through my chest. Fire licked down my belly, straight to my core, causing me to unintentionally rub my thighs together to relieve the needy sensation there.

Then, his teeth turned vicious, biting down hard, causing me to cry out. He released the nipple, laving it with his tongue to soothe the sting. A breathy moan slipped from my lips. Before I had a moment to bring myself out of the sensations, his mouth moved to the other side, providing the same attention to the other nipple. As he offered the other side his attention, one of his hands slid further up my chest, wrapping his long, strong fingers around my throat, my t-shirt bunched up around his wrist.

I wasn't sure I could feel more powerless than I did in that moment. His other hand trailed back down my body, light caresses stimulating the nerves in my skin, leaving my body trembling. Down, down, down, his hand trailed until it reached the apex of my thighs. My thighs opened and relaxed on their own accord as his hand dipped lower, grazing my mound. My breathy pants turned into low moans as I waited for him to touch me where I wanted it most. Right as his fingers grazed my clit, his teeth bit down on my nipple, ripping a hoarse cry from my lips. As he released the nipple and began to soothe it, his finger began circling my clit. But the touch was too slow, too soft.

My head was floating, my body only existing in the sensations Daemon was creating with his fingers and mouth. My skin was on fire, my pussy aching with need as he stimulated me just enough to melt my brain, but not enough to push me further. His mouth left my nipple, kissing his way back down my chest, his finger still teasing my clit slowly. His hand on my throat tightened, not enough to restrict breathing, but enough to spike the blood pressure in my head. His mouth passed my belly button, his head dipping lower. He kissed and softly licked the skin just above my pussy, slowly dipping lower and lower. Too slowly.

His finger suddenly left my clit, and I felt a protest rising, but before I could complain, his mouth latched onto it instead. It wasn't the gentle touch that his finger had been administering, but rather a demanding, forceful attention. Moans were now pouring from my lips and his hand around my throat tightened just slightly, enough to cause the animalistic sounds flying past my lips to be distorted. His free hand moved to my hip, yanking me forcefully, roughly further towards the edge of the seat, tilting my hips up further so he had better access to my dripping pussy. He growled against my tender flesh, and I could sense he was rapidly losing control.

In the back of my mind, I realized my ankles were no longer pinned down to the chair, one leg now draped around his shoulder, his free hand gripping and spreading my thighs, the other one trapped beneath the arm grasping my neck. His tongue flattened against my clit, massaging and teasing better than anything I had ever felt before. He groaned in pleasure as he feasted, his hair tickling my thighs with his movements.

"So fucking sweet – the sweetest cunt I've ever tasted," he rasped between licks. My head was stuck in a foggy haze of lust and need as I watched him pleasure me. His hand released my thigh as he pulled his head back, away from my pussy. Before I could register what was happening, his hand came down, smacking my clit. I screeched in shock, but instantly the sharp pain transitioned to fiery pleasure. His mouth fell onto me again, sucking and soothing the overstimulated bud. His fingers dipped down, suddenly filling me up, curling to massage the textured flesh inside while sucking on my clit. His fingers moved with the ease of an expert, tongue moving in tandem.

I felt pressure building in my lower stomach, tension coiling up, preparing for a powerful release. His teeth grazed my swollen clit, adding to the flames consuming me. His hand tightened around my neck even further, causing my breath to stutter and my moans to sound more strained. I was reaching the edge, and I knew I was about to be tossed off into a sea of pleasure that I had never experienced before. I had never felt this much at once before. It was as though every nerve was tingling, every sensation electrifying me, driving me towards insanity. He controlled every piece of my body in this moment, playing with me like a puppet, drawing the moans and sighs of pleasure from my trembling body.

Just as I was about to tumble off the edge, he withdrew. I shrieked in fury, sounding like a deranged animal. His eyes lifted to mine, heavy and shining with hunger, his lips, covered in my wetness, tilted in a satisfied smirk. He licked his lips and sucked on the fingers that had just been about to push me off the cliff into a sea of uncontrollable pleasure. He appeared as though he had no care in the world, the only indication of his lust burned in his silver eyes. Anger boiled in my veins, and I felt my face twist in a feral snarl.

"Tsk, tsk, tsk. Someone's not happy. I'll be glad to finish what I left off, but I need something from you first." I fought once more against the restraints, the flames of pleasure now morphing into an inferno of rage.

"Fuck you," I hissed.

"Well, we can do that, too. But I want you to admit something." His grip loosened from around my throat, a shit-eating grin on his lips. "Admit that you want me, that your body is *begging* for me. Admit that you *belong* to me. Just look at how your pretty cunt is crying for me." His eyes flashed down to my pussy, hunger darkening his eyes.

Reality slammed down on my head, the weight crashing into me like a ton of bricks. I stared at my body, paralyzed in horror at how close I had come to orgasming for this man. My eyes watered in shame, my anger causing a new kind of tremor to wrack my body. "I want to wake up, now." I hissed, voice trembling.

Disappointment and frustration shadowed his eyes before they turned icy and cold. "Have it your way, then." He stood and stepped back, and the world around me went up in smoke.

CHAPTER 10

I sat up in bed, fury roiling through me at my stupid pleasure saturated brain. What the fuck was wrong with me? If all I had to do was say "I want to wake up," in order to leave, why did I wait so long? Each time I felt more and more compelled to unravel Daemon, fear controlling me less. I had wanted to understand him – a *fictitious* monster. And then promptly let him drag me into the depths of pleasure and lost all sense. I couldn't help but feel anger that this figment of my imagination was trying so hard to break my mind.

But the wetness still dripping between my thighs and the burning need in my core forced me to admit there was a part of me that actually enjoyed this. I could even admit I was angry I had been left high and dry. At the same time, I was glad he hadn't finished – I knew I would be wrought with shame at letting that temporary lust to consume and control me. But admitting this attraction to the monster of my nightmares felt too real, too damning. I felt like admitting that would mean something more than just giving in to a wet dream. I wasn't sure why. Part of me blamed it on the hyper-realistic sensations and colors, even *smells,* within my dreams.

It all felt too real for me to give in. But that didn't mean that when I was awake, I believed it *was* real. I felt like I might *actually* be losing my mind. Perhaps moving into a house completely alone was somehow different than living in an apartment alone. And maybe that sense of loneliness was what was causing these vivid nightmares. Or maybe I truly was being haunted. At that thought, I laughed at myself. I believed that ghosts were real, but being able to control my dreams was more than just haunting – that was mind control. I didn't believe there were any ghosts with that power.

My eyes flicked over to where my lamp typically sat, disappointment leaking into my veins when I remembered it was boxed away in the other room. Sighing, I rubbed my face and flopped back against my pillows. The wetness between my thighs was still there, the throbbing in my core drawing my attention. Biting my lip, I debated on finishing what had been started in my dream. On one hand, doing that felt like I was admitting my desire for this man in my dreams. On the other, I was coiled and ready for release.

"I never thought a dream could control whether I chose to orgasm," I whispered in the darkness. I shook my head at my thoughts, trailing one hand slowly down my stomach to my aching pussy. My other hand slipped beneath my shirt to toy with my nipple, stimulating the nerves, causing a gasp to pass through my lips. My fingers toyed with my clit, occasionally slipping into my cunt. My eyes closed, and I imagined it was someone else's fingers teasing me, someone else torturing me.

No, not *someone else*. Him. Daemon. I almost stopped at this realization, but liquid fire was pulsing through me, and thinking about stopping now seemed torturous. I couldn't stop. I picked up the pace on my clit, imagining it as his tongue, flicking and teasing the sensitive nub. The hand on my breast moved to my neck, squeezing as I imagined it was his. My body was writhing on the bed, flames consuming every inch of me as I teased and played with myself. Still, it was nothing as potent as my dream had been. I pushed that thought away and continued.

I quickly reached the ledge, pressure building and setting my nerves on fire. "Fuck, fuck, fuck, *fuck*," I moaned. "Oh my god," I whispered as I imagined his eyes latching onto mine as I spoke these words, imagined how they would drive him wild. I imagined his lips lifting in a self-satisfied smirk, knowing exactly what he was doing to me.

Tighter and tighter I coiled, ready to explode. *Admit that you want me*. Remembering the words was like being doused with a bucket of ice water. All desire to finish what I'd started disappeared at the realization I was about to get off thinking about *him*. In the moment, it was easy to let my thoughts wander, but now that I was distracted, I couldn't forget. With a huff, I threw myself back down onto the bed, pulling the covers up to my shoulders and shutting my eyes, forcing myself back to sleep.

In the morning, I checked my email, finding a message from yesterday confirming that my new kitchen appliances would be delivered and installed tomorrow, and my living room furniture would follow the next day. I had yet to decide on a desk for the office, but as it wasn't finished yet I wasn't worried about it.

After drinking a cup of coffee, I lounged in the chair I had moved from my room and settled in to read. I had already messaged Elleanor and confirmed I would be heading to her place in the late afternoon as well as finished moving what I was capable of moving. For a few hours, I simply lost myself in my book and the fantasy world that it built around me. The story wove beautifully, twisting romance and magic together in a unique world that I could practically feel around me as I dove deeper into the book.

Out of nowhere, ripping me from the trance the book had put me in, my phone rang. I jumped dropping my book where it landed with a page bent the wrong way. "Fuck," I hissed. My books were my prized possessions, and I did my best to take ultimate care of them.

I grabbed my phone and answered the call. "Yes?"

"Whoa, who peed in your Cheerios this morning?" Came Elly's voice from the speaker.

"Sorry, I was reading and dropped my book." An understanding "Ah" came through the phone. Elly knew how much I loved my books.

"Sorry, Ev," she said.

"No biggie," I said as I tried smoothing out the page as best as I could with my phone smashed between my shoulder and jaw. "What's up?" I asked.

"I was just worried about you. Hadn't heard from you in a bit and it's 3, so I thought you'd be heading over soon."

"Oh, shit, really?" Time really had disappeared as I lost myself in the pages of the novel.

"No, no, it's totally fine. I'm actually glad you haven't left yet. Our photoshoot is next weekend, and I figured we could spend the next couple days designing our outfits and such. If you can find something you think fits the whole 'Salem Witches Rise Again' theme, grab it and bring it over. We can do some crafty shit, too, now that all my edits are done for that antsy customer. She was happy, but man she wanted things to be done within a day, and that's just not how that works." Elly ranted for another minute about the needy customer as I "hm'd" and "no way'd" while she talked to show I was engaged. I was rummaging through boxes, looking for a very specific black dress that had chiffon sleeves that buttoned at the wrists and a chiffon skirt. The top was boned with silver designs sprawling across the top, and the back was laced with ribbon.

Elly had mentioned not being worried about messing up the outfit, but I couldn't resist the witchy feel this dress gave me. Still though, I searched for another, more simple skirt and blouse that I had little connection to as far as clothing went.

After packing the items in the bag that I was going to be bringing for the next few days, I also snagged the essentials – toiletries and normal clothes. I also packed my makeup kit as I figured we would likely practice a bit on that as well. After finishing getting my things ready, I told Elly I would be heading over in the next few minutes and ended the call.

A strange feeling skittered through my chest – I almost felt like I should be saying goodbye to the house or something. No, not the house. Whatever was inside the house. But, with that thought, my mind whipped back to this morning to the light flicking on. Friendly ghost or no, it was weird.

When I reached Elly's house, we talked a bit as I got my things settled into the guest room of their house. Well, not so much a guest room as it was a storage room with a futon in it. Still, it felt cozy and clean, the items being stored in the room neatly organized and structured. While Elly made dinner, I ran and grabbed some wine from the grocery store.

As I arrived back, I noticed an SUV behind me, pausing across the street from Elly's house. My nerves went on high alert as I glanced at the vehicle without appearing to be too interested. Within seconds, the vehicle continued driving along the neighborhood street, pulling into a driveway several houses away. For a moment, it reminded me of the vehicle from the end of my driveway the other night. I quickly shook that thought off. The person just now may have been looking at house numbers, trying to locate the right one. I was being overly paranoid. I walked in with the wine as Elly pulled the pan off the burner, the aromas of basil, thyme, rosemary, and roasted garlic flooding my senses and causing my mouth to water.

"Smells delicious, Elly. As always, of course." It was my usual response when she cooked.

"Just wait till you taste it," she said with a wink. This had been her follow up line since I first said the phrase, and I couldn't help but smile at the number of memories we had compiled together with those two sentences. There was nothing that would ever compare, even if it was plain, repetitive wording.

But then my thoughts drifted, as they had been doing much too often these days. Briefly, I heard Daemon's name in my head, whispering about how sweet I tasted and how he had been waiting to taste me again. I felt my core tightening in anticipation, screaming at me for release since I had been left high and dry – well, soaking, actually, and I had yet to satisfy that animalistic craving inside me. I sighed, knowing my urges would have to wait, even as they burned through me and every thought in my head.

I shook myself, realizing I had just been fantasizing about Daemon in a positive way, a lustful way, without any negative additives. I shook my head at myself. I might be into a few minor kinks, but demon fucking was *not* one of them. If he even *was* a demon. Although, since it was my dream, I supposed I could just leave it at demon since it wasn't even real. I chastised myself. What the fuck was going on? Why was I daydreaming about this man/demon/thing from my nightmares when instead I should be running in fear? Or, at the very least, trying to find ways to avoid the nightmares, rather than getting pulled in by them? What about just trying to find a normal guy?

I shoved that thought away – I no longer cowered and shook in fear. That wasn't to say that I didn't feel fear. I definitely did. But I fought the urge to succumb to it. Turned it into a wall of anger and indifference. Nothing could hurt me or scare me more than what I had experienced before.

"Yoo-hoo? Ev? You with me?" Elly called to me, snapping me from my trance.

"Yeah, yeah sorry. Just went down a train of thought that took a few turns." I responded.

"I figured. You were doing that 'staring into nothingness' dissociating thing. Has sleeping gotten any better, by the way?"

"Oh, fine. Yeah, I'm fine." As I said the words, however, I could feel my face heat as shame and embarrassment coursed through my veins.

Elly called my bluff with a raised eyebrow and a twist of her lips. "Right. And that's why you're as bright as a ruby right now, huh? More wet dreams? *Oh*, did you sleep with Ethan and not tell me?" Her voice was excited, but also held a hefty amount of accusation in her tone.

I shook my head vigorously. "No, I haven't had time or the desire to meet with another person after that dickwad, Luke."

"Ah, so the 'wet nightmares' are taking over then, I see."

I ran my hands through my hair. "I don't know what's wrong with me, Elly. I'm so fucked up it isn't even funny. I mean I am literally scared shitless, full of rage, and controlled by this...this *lust*, all at the same fucking time. I know people get off on the fear and shit, but this is a literal nightmare – not just some roleplay." My voice was quiet as I reached the end, shame coating every word with a sour taste.

"Honey, those kinks and whatnot come from dreams – if your imagination can't take you to the point of feeling like the fantasy is real, then what's the point of the roleplay at all? I mean, do you at least have a...safe word, or...whatever?" She paused. "No, what the fuck am I thinking? It's a fucking nightmare, not real life. But, Ev, if you ever try this shit in real life, you better have a safe word on hand. If I find out you didn't, I'll personally beat your ass." Elly looked at me pointedly. She was a tiny woman, though not much shorter than me, and had a thin but curvy figure. But I always believed her fiery personality was too big for her body.

"Actually, Elly. Weirdly enough, I think I sort of have a safe word type thing. I just have to say that I want to wake up. Which makes sense, I guess, if you think about it."

"Oh, right. That would make sense, I guess. So – have you used that right when the nightmare starts happening?" She cocked her head at me in curiosity, her red hair falling over her shoulder.

"Uh, no. Which is part of why I'm so ashamed." The words stuck in my throat even though I had never kept a single secret from Elly since the day we bonded. There was a reason I called her my twin flame.

She nodded contemplatively. "And why do you think that is?"

"Because I'm trying to understand where this character *comes* from. Why did I create him?" The little voice in my head pushed me to continue. "And, as weird as this sounds, I feel this weird attraction thing, I don't know." A flash of red-hot embarrassment swept over me again.

"I think you're craving a little more adventure in your life with a man. Maybe he started more nightmarish, but maybe your mind has turned him into more of a freaky, kinky desire. I can't tell you what the dream means, Ev, but I can tell you that it is just a *dream*. Let's just relax tonight and maybe you'll get some real rest." She squeezed my hand and smiled at me comfortingly.

After eating too much food with one too many glasses of wine, we separated. Tyler had finally made it home after a long day of work and Elly wanted to make sure he ate and got some sleep. I found my way to the cozy little futon that was laden with blankets and pillows. I slipped my phone on the charger and cuddled into the soft textures around me, letting my mind relax and hoping my nightmares wouldn't chase me here.

CHAPTER 11

***

I woke, finding myself in my house. But, once again, it wasn't "my house." It felt as though it had just been recently built, and the décor was outdated. I was in my room upstairs, pacing and rubbing my temples.

"Shut up, shut up, shut up!" I hissed at myself. Except, these words weren't my words, and my voice wasn't my voice. I wanted to look around, to see what else was different, but it was as though I was trapped in this body that felt like mine but wasn't mine. I was simply existing in the shell while someone else controlled the body.

Upon realizing this, I began to feel emotions that didn't belong to me. Fear, anger, pain. None of those emotions belonged to me, although I was almost surprised at that fact. I felt like I was watching rather than experiencing, in this moment. I could see, feel, and smell what was around me, but it was muted and dulled. It didn't belong to me.

The me that wasn't truly me was wringing her hands, seemingly fighting with herself about something. Agony was slamming itself against the film separating me from her, screaming for me to experience it fully with her – this other me. Dread filled my chest. I wasn't sure why, but I felt it like bricks being laid down on me, one by one.

Other Me took a shaking step towards the closet. "No, stop. I don't want this!" She whispered. "Stop, stop, *stop!*" I felt the tears pouring down the face that was and wasn't mine. Her hand wrapped around the doorknob of the closet, knuckles white and arm trembling. She began outright sobbing, and I felt my chest heaving with each shuddering breath she took.

I tried, once again, to move, to do something, but there was nothing I could do. I was caged, and no amount of trying would let me help this Other Me. I was forced to watch as she reached for a long blue scarf hanging from a hook near the door. I felt like I was going to puke. No. This couldn't be happening. No, no, no. This wasn't real, it wasn't really happening, it was just a dream.

But no matter the awareness of the dream, I couldn't wake up. I could only watch through the eyes that weren't my eyes. My trembling hands knotted the scarf around the metal beam above my head. The world began to blur as my feet stepped up onto a box. My hands shook violently as the scarf came around my neck.

"I don't want this. I don't want this, I don't want this, *please*, I don't –." The words stopped as the feet that were not my feet no longer touched the floor, the hands that weren't my hands fell to my sides, and emotions that weren't my emotions evaporated in a puff of smoke. The world disappeared with a crack.

***

I jolted upright on the futon, hand clasping my neck. I was gasping, tears pouring down my face as I felt like my heart was being ripped in two. Out of habit, I glanced over to where my light would normally sit and felt a sinking feeling when it wasn't there. I rubbed my face, wiping the tears and sniffling as I tried to piece my thoughts together.

Nausea turned in my gut, and within the next few seconds, I found myself lurching off the futon towards the restroom. I heaved into the toilet, the dinner from the night before spewing from my lips. I was still sobbing, hardly able to breathe between the vomit and my dripping nose.

Why had it felt so fucking real? Why were all my dreams recently so real? What had changed? For as long as I could remember, it was always the singular dream of running through the forest that felt that realistic – the smells, sounds, and the feel of the forest beneath my feet. But those dreams had only been when I moved. Beyond that, I didn't have any other dreams that were quite so realistic.

I could still feel the scarf around my throat. I could feel the trembling hands. I could hear the cries to make it stop. If the other me had been so adamant about not wanting to follow through, why did she? She felt terror, and nothing about that situation felt like the mindset or words of someone who was in that mindset. It was like her body had its own mind.

I couldn't tell if this was some kind of sign, or a trigger from my past. But why was it always about the house? A part of me felt like I shouldn't have bought the house – maybe I wouldn't be experiencing all these terrors. My body convulsed over the toilet again, pushing more bile up my throat.

I heard a soft knock on the door. "Ev?" I heard Elly call quietly.

I spat into the toilet and pushed the handle, flushing down the vomit. "I'm alright, Elly. I'm sorry if I woke you," I said weakly. I opened the door to my friend, concern painted over her features.

"Are you okay? Do you need anything?"

"No, no. I'm fine. Just a bad dream, that's all." I said hoarsely. I could tell my face was still wet with tears.

"A dream made you throw up? Was it the same demon dude you've been dreaming of?" Her voice was filled with worry, squeezing my heart and sending more tears tumbling down my face. But, in the same moment, I realized that Daemon hadn't been there. Not a single trace of him.

I felt a sense of loss, but quickly shook myself. No, it was a *good* thing that he hadn't been in that dream. Or if he didn't come back to any dreams. But the little voice in the back of my head said that wasn't what I really wanted.

"No, actually. He wasn't there at all. It...it was at the house, but he wasn't there. It was *me,* Elly." My voice cracked on her name.

Her eyes widened even further. "What do you mean, 'you'?" She said in a hushed voice, as if she was scared of the answer.

"I-" The words stuck in my throat. I gagged once more but swallowed it down. "I went to the closet. There was a...a blue scarf." I took a shuddering breath, trying to stop myself from hyperventilating.

"Oh, Ev, I'm so sorry," Elly whispered, tears pouring down her face. She pulled me into a hug, letting me sob into her shoulder. Elly knew why I was so affected by this. She knew my past, my history, and the weight of the burdens that came with it. She knew who I had been, where I had been, and why I had been in those places. Places I didn't want to think about anymore.

"I promise, I'm not...I'm not thinking that way," I said between gasping sobs.

"I know, I know you aren't. You're okay, it's not real. It was just a dream. Just a dream," she whispered, as though also convincing herself.

For a while, she just held me there and whispered comforting words to me. My tears slowed and my breathing evened out. "Is it alright if I take a shower and brush my teeth? It...helps." I grimaced.

"Of course you can, Ev. Whatever makes you feel better." She left me alone after one final glance of concern in my direction. I went to my overnight bag and grabbed what I needed for the shower, then turned the spray to its hottest setting. I stepped in, the water scalding me and instantly turning my skin red. I let it flow over me and imagined the last vestiges of the dream following the water down the drain. I closed my eyes and rubbed my face, sobbing into my hands.

As my thoughts slowly trailed away from the nightmare, they traveled towards a different nightmare. A tall, handsome nightmare with eyes that burned bright silver. I knew it was fucked, but I would gladly take that dream over this one. There was something about him that I was drawn to, something I had been in denial about, but now knew it was true. I remembered my last dream of him, his lips and hands on my skin, whispered words of worship. Lust dripping from between my thighs and him tasting it.

I felt heat pooling between my legs, the unsatisfied ache returning with a raging force. I looked down at my body, bright red from the heat of the water – reminding me of how he had wondered if the rest of me would turn as red as my face. My hand slipped down the valley between my breasts, down my stomach, down to the wetness between my thighs. I bit my lip, holding in the sounds that wanted to escape. One hand grasped my breast, kneading it and teasing the nipple. I roughly pinched it, imagining his teeth on the sensitive flesh once more.

My finger teased my clit, and I tried to mimic the way his hand had felt. Flames poured through my body, and I added pressure. The number of times I had been prevented from orgasming were building into an inferno, driving me towards the edge faster than ever. My lungs were deprived of air as I tried to hold in the sounds. My hips ground into my hand, finger slipping inside. I placed a foot on the edge of the tub for better access, imagining Daemon knelt between my thighs, worshipping and pleasuring me.

I closed my eyes, imagining how his dark hair had fallen down his forehead, his blazing eyes glued to mine. I could practically hear his voice, telling me how sweet I was. I reached the edge, about to tip over, still imagining him between my thighs as I closed my eyes. Finally, *finally*, I tumbled over the cliff as I imagined Daemon speaking to me, the waves of the orgasm rolling through me, electrifying my body and making my knees shake. I could barely stand, and as the orgasm faded, I collapsed on the edge of the tub, shutting the water off.

My chest was heaving, trying to catch my breath, heart slamming against my ribs. "Fuck," I whispered. I had gotten off to the images of Daemon. I don't think that the saying "man of my dreams" was supposed to be *literal*. I giggled at my bad joke, feeling bubbly and light. Somehow it was the complete opposite of how the shower had started.

At that thought, the smile fell from my lips and the world crashed back down. My stomach turned as I realized what just happened. I felt like the character from my new story idea. Crazy, irrational, falling off the edge of insanity. How could I flip the switch so quickly? *You wanted comfort. It was just a dream, you don't have to be guilty*, I thought to myself. I sighed, running my hands through my wet hair.

As I argued with myself back and forth, I brushed my teeth and slipped my oversized t-shirt back on. I'd talk to Elly about it tomorrow...maybe. We had planned to get ready for the photoshoot this weekend over coffee. I planned on showing her the outfits I'd chosen as well as put together some little props and such that could double as Halloween decorations for my house. Since it should be finished this week, I was excited to add some creepy accents throughout the house. Not that I really needed to be creeped out more. But my nightmares were different than the decorations I had in mind – much gorier and less psychologically traumatizing.

I dried my hair off a bit more before returning to the room and plopping back down onto the futon. I glanced at my phone to check the time and saw it was a little past three in the morning. I sighed and laid back, trying to ease my mind into a peaceful sleep. My mind continued to race, so I played some soft music on my phone and, finally, my mind floated off into the abyss of sleep.

CHAPTER 12

The following morning, Elly and I made coffee and sat at her dining room table. Her finger traced a path around the rim of the cup, the steam from the coffee spiraling around her fingers languidly. She looked just about as tired as I felt, and I knew it was partly my fault.

"I'm sorry I woke you up last night," I said, breaking the silence.

Elly shook her head. "Ev, I'm more worried about you. I know you've had rough patches before and all, but this seems different. Is there something I can do to help?" She asked. Everything she was saying was kind, so kind – but I couldn't help feeling guilty for the fact that I was worrying her at all.

"I'm okay, really. I'm sorry I'm worrying you. Last night's dream was the worst I've had, so don't go thinking I wake up and vomit constantly. That's a first for me." I ran my fingers through my hair.

"Did the shower help, at least?" Elly asked. My cheeks heated, and I looked down at my hands, twisting my ring back and forth. Elly's assessing gaze slid over me, and an eyebrow raised questioningly. "I take that as a yes," she said.

"It's not what you think, I promise." I said quickly.

"I'm not sure what exactly I think, so feel free to elaborate." A small grin graced her full lips, and I shriveled inside.

"I know it's thoroughly fucked up-" I started.

Elly cut me off. "You keep saying that as if I'm going to judge you. Which I never have. And I sure as hell won't start now. So. Stop pussy footing around and just spit it out." It wasn't often that Elly would put me in my place like that, but I couldn't blame her. It seemed like every other sentence coming from my mouth was "I'm so fucked up" or "this is so fucked up" or whatever other ways I can use "fucked up."

So, I sighed heavily. "Well, you know how the 'demon' thing from my other nightmare kinda turns me on?"

"Yeah, but didn't you say he wasn't in the nightmare you had last night?"

"No, no, he wasn't. Thankfully. But also, I think my brain just wanted to revert to something that was less scary, I guess. So, I was thinking about the last dream I had with him which can barely be considered a nightmare at this point, but that's not the point. I guess, somehow, I feel drawn to him, and I think part of it is the mysteriousness of him, and the other part is like...he's hot. But admitting that seems too crazy, even for me, so when I'm in the dream, I just don't." I took a deep breath, knowing I was rambling but feeling unable to stop the thoughts from pouring, unfiltered, out of my mouth. "I wouldn't necessarily say he's a comforting figure, but I think I've gotten used to having a fucked-up dream and then it turns into something less horrifying and more controllable with Daemon. So, last night, in a weird ass way, I guess I missed him and finally let myself be vulnerable to the fact that there's a part of me that's attracted to him." I finished my train of thought and sighed, closing my eyes briefly at the amount of word vomit I had unleashed upon Elly.

I glanced at her, surprised to find she just seemed deep in thought about what I had just said. I wasn't sure what I had expected, but the fact she was actively listening and considering what I was talking about lifted an invisible weight off my chest. I somehow felt less...humiliated.

"Ev, that makes sense to me. I mean, everyone always talks about choosing the 'lesser evil' and whatnot. I don't see why it wouldn't apply here. I do think it's kind of wild that you won't just admit the attraction to him in the dream, but maybe that's another kinky thing – like you want to pretend you don't want it, but you actually do. And as far as looking for comfort? Hun, after the nightmare you had there is nothing wrong with that. And maybe, somehow, this Daemon character is a little comforting because he *is* a constant, a reprieve from the scary stuff. Not saying you can control him...but I think you know what I mean." Elly trailed off, still looking contemplative but also looking at me in a way that I knew she wasn't being judgy.

As Elly took a sip of her coffee, her phone pinged. She glanced down and made an ugly face. "Bad news?" I asked her.

"You know how we were supposed to do our little photoshoot this weekend?" Elly had a guilty look on her face.

"Do we need to reschedule?"

She blew out a frustrated breath. "Not this weekend, but the next one, I promise. I just had someone message me about doing a last-minute photoshoot for an engagement and they promised to pay extra. I'd turn them down, but you know how I am."

"You're fine. We can still prep for the photos and everything and decide on props and outfits. I brought a couple dresses. And I'm not sure what day the photoshoot is, but we could possibly go to the haunted mansion in the town over, if you want." I offered. While the photoshoot would only take one day, I knew Elly would be spending the next on just peeling through the photos and picking out the best ones. But generally, night times were free which meant we could raise hell in another way.

"Ooh, I like where your head is, Ev. We can definitely make time for a run through the 'Purgatory House.' I heard they've added some extra cool stuff this year." She thought for a moment after typing a quick reply back to the customer. "Alright, I scheduled the shoot for late morning into the evening on Saturday, so we can do Friday night without regrets," Elly said excitedly.

The Purgatory House was the best haunted mansion in the area. While it was about a thirty-minute drive, it was so good that Elly and I made it a mission to go every year. The Purgatory House focused specifically on horrors that involve the strange state between life and death. Last year there was a wall with arms that reached out, as though begging to be freed. On occasion, one would latch on and send one of us squealing away. Who knew what would happen this year? We talked for a while about the haunted mansion trip and discussed what we might see and whether or not we should dress up at all.

Afterwards, Elly did some work on her laptop, and I decided to pull out mine and see whether I could continue on with the original story, or if I was going to work on the new concept. After last night, I couldn't help but feel drawn emotionally towards the new concept, and so I popped in my headphones and continued mapping out the story and the best options to develop the story.

I thought of stories like the theory of infinite dimensions. You can have this little kernel of an idea, and each little step can change the outcome of the ending in a huge way – sometimes in a good way and sometimes in a bad way. So, for me, story mapping was how I chose the biggest, cataclysmic moments of the story to test out different endings. I knew I was getting close to choosing one, and a part of me worried I may finish this script before finishing the one I was originally working on. But a script was a script, and while this one was different from my usual style, I knew that it was going to be good.

Elly finished her work a couple hours later, and we decided to get to work on photoshoot ideas. We would definitely have to purchase a few things, but since Elly was a photographer, she typically had extra props laying around for different shoots. She gathered some of the extra fake flowers she had, and we began putting them into bouquets, crowns, and even removed the petals on some of them so we could toss them. While Elly was digging through her props, she found an athame from a previous Halloween.

I showed her my two dresses, and she immediately got to thinking. "We could easily get some dirt and all that on the dress, as if you've just crawled out of the ground. And maybe some fake blood. If you're okay with it, we can rip it up, too." She was holding up the simple black dress, looking at it as though imagining what it would look like behind the lens of the camera.

She turned to look at the nicer one. "First of all, I can't believe you never showed me this. Second, this is gorgeous, and I will make sure we get some photos in with this dress. Maybe like to portray the witch has 'returned to power' or whatnot." She ran her hands over the fabric, the black chiffon flaring out softly at the waist, the top made of chiffon and boning. Dangling silver pendants dropped from the waist, making a slight tinkling noise when they touched each other. It had fabric that spilled over the shoulders and down to the floor, a slit in the skirt, and a plunging neckline. The mesh didn't hide much, but I knew I would be wearing pasties and something under the skirt area that wouldn't take too much away from the seductiveness of the dress but would still keep what I didn't want seen out of sight.

I wasn't even sure why I had purchased it in the first place, but when I saw it, I just purchased it without a second thought. It was gorgeous, in my size, and felt magical. While I knew there was no real "magic" to it, I knew there would be a time, eventually, when I could wear it. And what better time than for a witchy Halloween shoot? Elly sometimes called me an "impulse buyer," but I would always say that right back to her. The number of things she had purchased on a whim because she was immediately magnetized towards it or the idea was just about even with mine.

We planned everything out a bit more, but we still hadn't decided where, exactly, we should do the shoot. We knew we wanted it to be woodsy, somewhere with a wilder environment. She had mentioned a couple parks, but we both knew they would likely be busy at this time of the year with the colorful foliage and comfortable temperatures. We both agreed to look around since we still had some time since Elly was going to be busy this weekend.

Tyler got home a bit later, having worked an early shift. As he went to shower, Elly drifted off to the kitchen to begin dinner, and I trailed after her in case she needed any help. It was unlikely she would, but I loved watching her cook because of how much she loved to cook. She would buzz around the kitchen in a way that most might see as chaotic, but I knew she had a method to her madness. Tonight, it seemed, we would be having some chicken with her famous zucchini salad.

"You know, I've been thinking," Elly started. "I've known you for years. And I haven't ever seen you with nightmares this bad." She seemed hesitant to continue. "Maybe, well, maybe there's something to the house you bought. I'm not trying to sound superstitious or anything," she rushed out. "I just think that it's strange." She stared at the chicken sizzling in the pan, avoiding eye contact.

I was surprised at the abrupt conversation, but it seemed like she had been thinking about this for some time, and only just now decided to bring it up. "I get it. I mean I feel like there is something to the house, but why would I have a worse nightmare last night, while I was here instead of at the house, if that's the case?"

Elly blew out a breath. "I don't know. But I just have this nagging feeling that your nightmares are something more than surface level dreams."

"Why haven't you brought it up before?" I asked. It wasn't accusatory, but if she had been feeling like this for a while, I couldn't understand why she hadn't brought it up yet.

"I didn't really think about it in depth until last night. I saw how bad it was, Ev. Now, I don't know what happened in the dream specifically, but I haven't ever seen anyone *throw up* from a nightmare before. When I went back to bed after making sure you were okay, I just couldn't stop thinking about it. Then, I remembered how you've always said they felt so real, like you could feel, smell, and hear everything going on like it was happening in real life." Elly turned the chicken over. "I just feel like it seems odd that the most realistic nightmares of your life only started up when you moved into that house. And don't go thinking I've forgotten how you felt like you'd seen the wallpaper before."

I would almost agree with her, but there was another time, many years ago, when I had a dream that was just as realistic as these had been. That one hadn't turned out well. I shook myself out of those thoughts. "I don't know, Elly. Maybe it is something more. I mean, I've noticed some weird stuff happening, but if it was a ghost or spirit or whatever, it definitely doesn't seem vengeful." I paused and realized how strange that had come off. I wasn't an expert on the supernatural. I believed in it, but I wasn't even sure if I could consider myself as having an intermediate level of understanding in the supernatural. "Never mind," I said. "That came off stupid." I laughed quietly, twisting the ring on my finger.

Elly opened her mouth to say something, but, at that moment, Tyler walked into the kitchen, grabbing Elly around the waist and kissing her cheek. She laughed and pushed him off playfully, but the warmth in her eyes was palpable. My heart clenched, seeing what they had. I wanted that, too.

Daemon's face popped into my head, and I choked down a hysteric laugh at myself. The man was a figment of my imagination. Jesus, I wasn't six years old anymore – imaginary friends were not normal for a twenty-nine-year-old. On top of that, hadn't I just hated him last week? What was going on with my head? I felt like giving into my urge last night had clicked something in me, as if I may as well have told him I wanted him.

As Elly finished dinner and we all sat down at the table, she looked at me pointedly. "When the renovations are done, I have to see the new house. Why don't we get ready there on Friday before Purgatory House?"

I knew exactly where her mind was going, and I internally cringed. She probably was hoping to get an answer to her question on whether or not the house was the source of the problem. And, of course, I was going to have to show her the house at some point anyways. "Sure, Elly. That sounds great." I put a smile on my face as I gave her a look back that said, "I know exactly what you're up to."

For the rest of the night, Elly and Tyler watched something on the TV and I found myself drawn back to the new script. Time floated by as I worked, and when I finally realized the right path I wanted to take, I felt a wave of excitement. I went to share the idea with Elly, but when I got to the living room where she had been sitting with her husband, neither of them were there. The TV was off, and the living room was dark. I glanced at the time on my phone, realizing it was nearly midnight. "Shit," I whispered to myself. I hadn't meant to stay up so late.

A light caught my eye from outside. Chills crept up my spine, and I felt my head turning to the window in the living room, facing the front of the house. An SUV was parked by the curb. My heart thudded to a stop, then picked up to a dangerous pace. I had brushed off the first two sightings as paranoia and coincidence, but this time, I felt certain that this SUV was following me.

My first thought was of Luke, who had seemed like the type of guy that might stalk girls that didn't eat up the bullshit he served on a golden platter and drink the side of douche poured into a crystal glass. But I remembered Luke had a sporty car, not an SUV. And I couldn't imagine him driving an SUV like this – old, worn down, and basically the opposite of everything that Luke had flaunted around. Still, I couldn't rule him out. I checked the locks and made sure they were latched securely before returning to the room with the futon and trying to calm my mind enough to sleep. I'd tell Elly about this tomorrow. No need to make her stressed right now. Plus, I could still be acting paranoid after everything I had been experiencing lately. I breathed, trying to calm my racing heart and remove the tension that was winding its way around my chest.

Slowly, I felt the tension draining my body. It wasn't likely that whoever was in that SUV would be coming in this house tonight. Why come in Elly's house when they hadn't come into my house when I was alone? I curled on my side, knowing that my best friend and her husband were down the hallway, and I wasn't alone. Thinking about this, I considered it might be a good idea to get security set up around the house. I could probably get that done Thursday if I called tomorrow. I could at least get a camera attached to the door if they couldn't do it immediately.

With each thought, I convinced myself I was safe, I was okay, and I wasn't going to be the girl that lets people catch her off guard. I was going to be prepared, install cameras, and make sure there was an alarm system set in place in case someone tried to break in. My mind began to fall into the space between sleep and awareness, sinking lower and lower until I reached blissful darkness.

CHAPTER 13

I was in my house once more, but it was different still. Different than that of my previous dreams, different than that of the dream from last night. I was standing in the hallway, staring at photos of a family dressed in clothes that might be found in the '80s. My vision blurred, and my hand reached to touch the picture. That's when I realized that once again, I was not in control of this body. I was simply experiencing what this person was experiencing, except, this time, I felt closer somehow. More connected. Pain filtered through the film that separated my mind and that of the body I was being hosted in.

"Please, I don't want to do this. Don't make me do this," our voice said. I could feel the muscles protesting as they fought against a force that was making us step away. Back, back, back. Then our feet were forced further down the hall. Past our bedroom door. Towards the string that hung down from the ceiling.

The muscles in the arm of the body I resided in fought the pressure urging it up, up, up to grab the string. "Stop," we whispered. "Please don't make me do this," we cried. We fought our hands as they yanked the cord down, freeing the stairs that led to the attic. Our foot shook as it took the first step up. And the next. Every cell in our body was fighting each movement. But whatever was driving us was too great. Inside, I felt us screaming in fear, frustration, and desperation.

The feet finally met the top of the stairs. "No. I can't. I don't want this. Let me go," we were sobbing, tears and snot rolling down our face. Our body shuddered, taking another step, then another. Towards the window that led to the back garden. How I knew this, I could only imagine was her memories filtering into mine. I had never been in the attic, and I didn't have a garden. Our muscles were protesting each movement, and I wished more than anything to be in control. To stop this for her. For *us*. I didn't want this.

"I'll do *anything*," we sobbed. "Anything at all. I can't do this." But our feet kept moving, hands reaching for the latch on the window. As the body I couldn't control reached the now open window, I could see the great iron spikes below. The body that was not mine was breathing rapidly, beginning to hyperventilate. "No, not like this. *No!*" We wailed. For a moment, it felt like we gained some control. We stepped back from the window, unclasped a necklace from around our neck. It was a white pearl necklace, and we dropped it to the ground, right as the whatever was in control took over. Stepping back to the window, sobs wracking our frame, fear writhing within us, we stepped to the ledge. Then, we fell.

***

I woke up, a scream crawling up my throat. I grabbed at my stomach, my chest, everywhere I had known the spikes had touched. I was sobbing, gasping for air, and all I could think was *get to the toilet*. I stumbled, falling, then crawled, dragging myself to the porcelain bowl. I heaved, body trembling violently as I retched and retched, stomach convulsing even as there was nothing left to upheave. I finally stopped, collapsing in on myself, hugging my knees to my chest, rocking back and forth.

That wasn't suicide. It looked like suicide, but it wasn't. But maybe it was. Thoughts tumbled and swirled in my head, nothing making sense and everything feeling as though it was falling apart. I couldn't do this. Whatever this was, whatever I had been cursed with, I wanted it to stop. As the tears slowed, numbness took over. My body still shook, but my mind just stopped. I vaguely heard my name being called, but I just sat on the floor, next to the toilet where my vomit still floated. Tears still rolled down my face, but I felt empty. I was receding into myself again.

I hardly felt the hand on my back, rubbing and soothing. My name once again reached my ears, but I felt so far away. I felt like I was still not in *my* body, but hers. I felt her fear still. Her pain. The way her muscles fought every movement. I still felt the way the iron spikes had pierced the flesh of our stomach, our chest. The agony that accompanied it. There was nothing I could have done, no part of that that I was in control of.

I hazily heard the water turn on, the curtain being pulled, and someone tugging me up and over to the shower. I didn't fight. I just allowed the movement. I collapsed in the bottom of the tub, the sensation of hot water jolting me back into my body. Elly's face floated in front of me, tears of concern dripping down her cheeks. She was rubbing my arms, my back, brushing my now wet hair out of my face.

"It's okay, it's okay Ev. You're okay. Everything is going to be okay. Just breathe, just breathe," I heard her say. She kept repeating it as though she was also trying to convince herself. For a moment, her hand left my body to flush the toilet, and immediately returned back to my hair, stroking my head softly.

My body shook with silent sobs once more, but I didn't know how to stop. "Hotter," I managed to whisper.

"It'll be too hot, Ev." Her voice was filled with concern.

"Please," I choked. My sobs were no longer silent. I heard a wild keening coming from my throat as I sat, dripping, in the tub. At my plea, she turned the heat up until it was scalding against my skin, burning everywhere it touched. I gasped for air, letting the water drain away the blood that wasn't there, the memories that weren't mine. Each drop that scalded my skin felt like atonement for my dream, washing away the sickness that had come from it.

Eventually, my breathing slowed, sobs no longer convulsing through me. The shower continued pouring its near acidic water onto me. "I'm sorry," was all I could say.

"No, Ev, it's okay. I'm here." Her voice was soft and comforting. Calming. Grounding. And that's exactly what Elly did for me. She grounded me.

After another few minutes, I reached and turned the faucet off, my giant t-shirt dripping wet as it hadn't been removed before the shower. I slowly stripped it away from my body, the soaking cloth clinging to my skin. I grabbed the towel that Elly offered, wrapping myself in its softness. I felt so drained, so tired. I stumbled back to the bedroom with the futon, sniffling as I sat down. Elly sat with me, holding my hand.

"Do you have another sleep shirt, Evalyn?" She asked softly, like she was talking to a terrified animal. Which, I guess I was in that moment.

"Maybe. In my bag," I whispered. She reached over and brought the bag towards us, opening it to peer inside and look for the oversized shirts she knew I slept in. After finding it, she pulled it out and handed it to me. I dropped the towel and slipped the shirt over my head. Then I curled up against the pillows and wrapped a blanket around me.

"Do you want me to stay?" Elly asked.

Fear still lingered, and I didn't want to be alone. Not right now. As real as the dream from last night had felt, this one felt even more real. I felt even more integrated, as though I was more connected to this one than the last, where I had been almost more detached. So, I simply nodded my head in agreement, and felt the dip of the futon as she settled in beside me. She held my hand, continuing to ground me, as I drifted back off to sleep.

When I next woke, Elly was missing from the futon. I could hear movement in the kitchen and a sweet smell floated into the room, so I assumed she was likely making some breakfast. The ache from last night's dream was still heavy in my chest, and I was relieved that I hadn't had anymore dreams. I was also more than thankful for Elly being there to pull me from the darkness I had so quickly fallen into.

I rose from the futon, mouth tasting like a creature had died and was currently rotting there. I realized that in my haze last night, I hadn't brushed my teeth. Not that I had been functional. After the dream, I had practically been a corpse, and the morbid irony in that wasn't lost on me. Elly had been the one to carry me through the fog I had been drifting in.

I went to the bathroom, quickly brushing my teeth before heading to the kitchen, where Elly was flipping pancakes on the stove. She glanced at me and shared a soft smile.

"Hey, Ev," she said quietly, like she was trying to gauge whether I was present or not.

"Um, thanks for last night, Elly. I'm so sorry you had to see that. Again." I trailed off, shame coursing through me.

"No, you don't have to be sorry. I'm just glad I was here to try and help. You know I'm here for you any time. If...if you have a dream that bad and you're alone, try to call me if you can. I'd rather know in the moment rather than the next day."

I rubbed my eyes, trying to push away the memories of last night. It was now Tuesday, and I figured I would stop by the house today to make sure everything was going smoothly. The thought triggered a different memory of last night. "Elly, after everything, now might not be a great time, but I've seen this SUV three times now. The first time was at the end of my driveway – I thought it was just someone using the driveway to turn it around. Then I thought I saw it when I was driving here Sunday night, but I just figured it was a different one, since it drove past the house and pulled into a driveway. But last night after I was done writing, I went to the living room and saw it out front." I took a deep breath. "I think someone has been stalking me. I thought maybe Luke, but I can't imagine him driving that SUV. But I figured I can't rule him out, either." I closed my eyes, waiting for Elly's response. I wanted to believe that she had a solution.

"Ev, what the *hell*?" I glanced at her, and she looked just as lost as I felt. "First thing we're doing is getting some fucking security at your house." She slapped a pancake onto a plate aggressively. "Did you get the make and model of the vehicle? Did you see anyone *in* the car?"

My brows drew together. As I tried to recall the details, I realized all I could remember was that it was an SUV. The same SUV each time, but the details were murky, like I was staring through swamp water to revisit my memories. "I didn't get any of that, I'm sorry. I'm trying to remember, but it's all so fuzzy. I think I'm just tired," I whispered, feeling both deranged and exhausted.

Elly set a cup of steaming coffee in front of me, where I leaned against the kitchen island. "It's okay. You're going through a lot right now, and we'll figure it out. I'm here for you, you know that, right?" She asked.

"Of course. Who else could I trust to feed me the best food in the world?" I joked. I walked around the island. "Decompression hug?" I asked.

She wrapped her arms around me, holding me tight and sighing. "Decompression hug," she agreed. It was a label I had put on certain hugs that were specifically meant to help make us feel like the world was going to be right side up again.

While Elly and I were best friends, we didn't go out of our way to hug each other the way some friends did. It wasn't necessarily rare, but it wasn't common for us. Elly and I were simply comfortable with each other. There was no concern if she saw me naked (she had, many times, including last night), no worries if there wasn't a conversation constantly going, no judgement even in our wildest stories and thoughts. Elly and I simply existed together, like two flames burning side by side.

And when one of us needed it, we were immediately there for the other. Like right now, I needed a hug, someone to hold the crumbling pieces of me together because I felt like I wasn't strong enough to do it alone. I took a shuddering breath, trying to let the negative thoughts and emotions float away from me, breathing in fresh, clean air filled with positive energy and light.

We pulled away from each other. "Thanks, Elly."

"Of course, Ev," She turned around and sat a massive plate of pancakes down on the center of the island and placed a plate next to my cup of coffee one straight across. After pulling out the toppings we liked on our pancakes, we stood and ate at the island, chatting about lighter things.

As we were cleaning up the kitchen from breakfast, I turned to Elly. "I'm going to stop by the house today and see how things are going. Before I do that, though, I'm going to look into some security systems and figure out how fast one can be installed. I shouldn't be gone long, though."

"Sounds good to me. I'll help you research if you want me to. While you're out I'll do a little work, and then afterwards do you want to go to the Halloween store and see what we can find for decorations and props?"

I smiled at the beautiful simplicity of that request. Some normalcy would be nice, untainted by the stressors currently plaguing my life. "I'd love to," I said.

CHAPTER 14

After looking through a few websites, I found what seemed like a good option for a security system that wasn't overpriced but was still good quality. I called, and they confirmed that they would be able to stop by the house Thursday for installation. I was surprised they would be able to do it on such short notice, but the consultant on the phone ensured the comfort and safety of the customers was top priority. Doing these things on short notice was the norm for them.

After ending the call and setting up my information on their site and setting up autopay, I grabbed my keys and set off for my house. The trip was short, but I found myself glancing in the rearview mirror constantly, checking for a vehicle that wasn't there. Thankfully, I arrived at my house where there were no vehicles aside from the workers' and my own. I walked into the house, feeling warm and happy seeing how beautiful it all looked with the new updates.

The living room was painted a cream color with an accent wall of a black and red floral wallpaper. The furniture had been delivered earlier this morning and was dark grey, nearly black, and consisted of an 'L' shaped couch and plenty of pillows, a recliner, and a small coffee table of stained black wood. The light fixtures were modern and unique, hanging on short chains from the ceiling. The new floor was a dark wood, polished and shining beautifully.

I moved towards the kitchen, an excited squeal coming from my throat as I saw all the new, beautiful appliances. A new stove, dishwasher, microwave, and fridge. The dark grey steel of the appliances meshed nicely with the black granite countertops and the dark grey cabinets. I planned on adding splashes of color by hanging lavender plants in the window and placing some unique glassware I had seen in some of the shops off of Main Street.

The house features were dark but elegant, and I was more than pleased with what I had seen so far. I heard the workers upstairs, and I made my way in their direction, hand running over the newly polished banister. I made my way into the office, which hadn't had much work done aside from replacing the flooring to match the rest of the house and repainting the walls as well as adding another accent wall with wallpaper.

As I stood admiring the newness of the house, I heard someone clear their throat behind me. I turned, seeing Dave, and smiled. "Everything looks absolutely amazing," I said in greeting.

"Well thank you, ma'am. I didn't hear ya walk in. Hope we aren't banging around too loud," he said apologetically.

I laughed softly. "I'm the one stepping on your toes in this situation. No need to apologize. How are things going?"

"Well, they're goin' well, but I hate to say that Ethan hurt his hand while workin' on the floors." He sighed. "He'll be fine, though, don't you worry. But a little birdie told me he had stars in his eyes over you," his eyes twinkled with mischief.

I felt a blush creeping into my cheeks. Avoiding the topic he had nudged the conversation towards, I said, "Well, I hope he wasn't hurt too badly. He seemed like a good worker."

Dave smiled at me. "Oh, he'll be back for the next job I think."

"Good to hear." I felt the awkward silence settling around us like an itchy blanket, and I cleared my throat. I wasn't the greatest with holding conversations. "Well, do you mind if I see how the room is coming along?"

"Of course, come on in," he said as he began leading the way to the room across the hall. Before we walked into the room, I glanced down the rest of the hall, seeing my mattress and bedframe leaning against the wall. As I glanced further, I felt bile slide up my throat when I saw the string hanging down for the attic. I quickly turned my head away and followed him into the room.

The carpet had been replaced with floors to match the rest of the house, and the walls were painted the same cream color from downstairs, but all four walls were going to have black floral appliques once the workers had finished. My gaze slid over to where my bed had been, then further to the other side of the room where the closet was. This time, I felt my stomach convulse, trying to purge the pancake and coffee breakfast from this morning. I ran quickly down the stairs to the bathroom there and heaved into the toilet.

I closed my eyes, trying to push away the memories of the dreams so I could at least act like a normal person. I forced a sense of calm to wash over me, and my stomach stopped trying to escape my body. I wasn't sure how long it would last, but I was thankful for it, nonetheless. I pulled myself together, flushing the toilet and rinsing my mouth, wishing I had a toothbrush on me. I made my way upstairs and back to the bedroom, where Dave glanced at me concernedly.

"I'm sorry, not sure where that came from," I lied, trying to make myself seem more normal than I felt inside.

"No need for an apology, ma'am. Sometimes the dust mixed with the staining chemicals can mess with a person's stomach. Can't say it hasn't happened to me before." I truly was thankful for Dave in this moment. In his own way, he was helping me not have to explain myself.

"That must be what it is," I replied.

"Well, I won't keep you in here too long if your stomach is a bit queasy, but I'll just quickly show you the bathroom." He paused. "Maybe, ah, cover your nose?" He offered.

Doing as he recommended, I followed him to the bathroom, feeling excitement at seeing the new tile flooring. The tub wasn't placed yet, but we had discussed doing a large claw-foot tub and a glass standing shower. The existing standalone sink would be replaced with a new sink and vanity. I smiled at Dave. "It looks lovely. I'm excited to see it finished. Do you still see it being done by tomorrow?" I asked.

"Oh, I'd say most likely. Might be a little late since we have to wait for some of the sealants to dry, but we should still be done. Is that alright with you?"

"Of course," I replied. "I want the house finished right, rather than rushed."

"Good to hear, ma'am. Some of our customers are real pushy about the deadlines and whatnot."

"I can imagine. But this is all getting done quicker than I'd even expected, so I'm most certainly not concerned."

"Alright good. Now let's get you on out of here before your stomach attacks you again," Dave said.

I nodded, making my way back into the hallway, ignoring both the closet and the attic. I felt a wave of exhaustion, knowing it was coming from the piss poor quality of sleep I'd been having. I just hoped I would get some real sleep tonight. I rubbed my eyes and grabbed my keys off the counter.

As I headed back to Elly's, I called her and asked if she wanted some coffee. She agreed, never being one to turn down a good coffee. As I stepped into the coffee shop, my nerves instantly went on alert. I quickly ordered the drinks, ready to head back to Elly's as soon as possible. As soon as the drinks were ready, I started towards my car. Across the street, I glimpsed someone with blond hair facing in my direction. Luke.

My stomach turned as he lifted his lips in a grin. I slipped into the car, splashing the iced coffee over my fingers. Without sparing a thought for my dripping fingers, I started the car and pulled out of the spot. My heart was pounding in fear, but I felt anger swallowing up all other emotions. I was tired of always feeling fear. I was exhausted, drained, and I just wanted to feel normal again.

I feared that Elly might be right about the house being part of the problems, but I refused to think much on it as I zoomed towards her house. I wasn't going to just up and leave the house. I would find a solution and get my life back in order. As far as Luke, he would have to be stupid to try anything more than his current creepy antics. For all he knew, I might have already reported his strange behavior to the police. I hadn't, and wouldn't, but he wouldn't know that.

I blew out a breath as I made it to Elly's house. As I pulled in, I noticed the SUV driving past the house. Certainty of who was driving it sat in my gut like a ton of bricks. It was Luke. While I knew that was the only sensible answer, I still felt confused. Luke had clearly *wanted* me to see him all those times when I was out. And he knew that I'd seen his sports car. So, what was the theatrics with the SUV? The puzzle pieces were there, and they looked like they fit, but something was still off. I spun the ring on my finger and chewed my lip as I thought about it. Sighing, I let it go for now and made my way into the house, making sure I looked around me for anything suspicious before exiting my car.

I walked into the house, checking behind me one last time before shutting the door. "Ev? What's wrong?" I jumped at Elly's voice.

"I'm sorry. I'm just on high alert right now. I saw Luke across from the coffee shop and then the van when I got here. I guess that confirms it's Luke, but I don't know..." I trailed off. I glanced down at my empty hands. "*Shit*," I hissed. "I forgot the coffee in the car. One second."

I raced outside and then back in once I had the coffees in hand. I handed Elly hers as she looked at me, seeming to try and find the right words.

"Alright, well. That's a lot to unpack. Um." She began.

"No, no. Elly, I just want to pretend that everything is normal right now even if it isn't. Let's just...go to the Halloween store like we said and then we can come back home and watch some cheesy movie and eat takeout. Is that okay?" I knew I sounded ridiculous, but I needed something *normal*. No nightmares, no throwing up, no stalkers. Just a girl and her best friend and Halloween activities.

Elly sighed. "Alright, let's go have some normal fun," she plastered a grin on her face and tugged me into the other room. I sipped my coffee as she got ready to leave, and realized I should probably send a message to Ethan and check in on him, even if dating was the last thing on my mind right now.

I pulled out my phone and realized I had missed a "Hello!" message from him on Sunday. I typed up a quick message telling him that I was sorry and hadn't seen the message and hoped he was alright since I had heard he had gotten hurt while working. I slid the phone back in my pocket as Elly came out of her room.

"Ready?" She asked.

"Yeah, let's go," I tried to sound upbeat, but I was still feeling weighed down by the events of the last couple hours. I tried shaking myself out of it, but it clung to me like a disease, clouding around me like a poisonous cloud of smoke. As we got in her car, though, and she turned on the music, I felt a little bit of the stress melting away.

On the drive, Elly told me a funny story about a family photo shoot they had done where the son had thrown deer shit at the dad, thinking it was some weird dog food (he was apparently the cutest 3-year-old ever). To put it mildly, the dad was not happy. When we arrived at the Halloween store, I chugged the last of my iced coffee and we headed in. Of course, right at the entrance was a jump scare machine – Elly and I just laughed at the lunging skeleton covered in moss, pointing its finger towards us accusingly and glaring with red eyes.

As we moved through the rest of the store, we played with several masks, some silly and some eerie. We grabbed a gallon of fake blood, because even though it was easy to make, it was easier to buy for a couple extra dollars. We found some skull props and bones that could be used in the photoshoot – Elly would edit them to look more realistic later. We decided to also grab a fake cauldron. When we were ready for the photo shoot, we could grab some dry ice and drop some colorful lights in the pot and create some wild photos. We wandered around the store a bit more before finalizing our purchases and then stopping by a craft store to purchase a few things that we could make ourselves.

Afterwards, we went back to Elly's and made a few things with the crafts and worked on figuring out how we wanted to go about mucking up the dresses. The simplicity of it all, along with spending time with Elly and listening to her wild stories while snacking on junky chips and dips, had finally put my mind at ease in a way it hadn't been in a while. I didn't feel my thoughts drifting down the dark hole it had been previously, caused by the nightmares of the past two nights. I didn't feel the tension from being followed by someone I had mistakenly gone on a date with. I felt...normal.

As the day turned towards the evening, Elly and I ordered from our favorite ramen place. Tyler had gotten home a short while ago and he mentioned taking a shower and then going out to watch some sports game over at his friends, meaning Elly and I were alone for the evening. When the food arrived, I opened my bento bowl of rice, spicy salmon, lettuce, and seaweed salad. Elly had gotten her favorite spicy beef udon dish, and we had both gotten our favorite boba milk teas. While the ramen at the restaurant was delicious, a lot of their other food was even more alluring.

As we ate our food, we turned on a cheesy horror movie and laughed at the predictable plot and mid-tier acting. We were both bundled beneath a blanket and curled into the cushions. Everything about this moment just felt...right. I felt my phone vibrate, and I pulled it from my pocket, seeing a message from Ethan.

> Hey, thanks for the well wishes. And you're fine – I'm sure with all the moving stuff things can get hectic. Glad to hear back from you. How are you?

> I'm good, just trying to get everything together with moving and all that. Hopefully your hand isn't too messed up!

> No, it's alright. Not to bring up blood and gore, but I somehow tried using the nail gone to make my hand a part of the floor. Apparently, I broke a couple bones in the process, but I should be making a full recovery.

That sounds super painful, hopefully you aren't feeling too much of it right now. And don't worry about the gore, I'm sort of used to it.

Elly cleared her throat, and I glanced over. Her eyebrow was raised at me, and she sent a pointed glance to the phone in my hand.

"Sorry, Ethan hurt his hand while doing the flooring, and I was just checking on him," I rushed out. I didn't want Elly to think this was romantic, because it wasn't. Maybe a few days ago I had thought it could be a possibility, but now it just didn't feel right. Between my head and life being a mess, it wasn't exactly the right time. And a tiny, annoying voice in the back of my head whispered that there was no thrill, either.

Elly went that direction anyways. "So, things are going well between you two then?"

I blew out a breath, twisting the ring on my finger. "It's not really like that. I thought so at first, but right now with everything going on, I'm a mess. I just want to figure out my head, first." I paused, not wanting to bring it up and ruin the normalcy of this moment, but I knew it was necessary. "Plus, with the stalker situation, I don't want to bring him into that."

Elly frowned but nodded in agreement. "Alright, I can't argue that one. Does he know? About you not being ready for a relationship, I mean." She asked.

"I mean, we never specifically declared it like that. But he also knows things are hectic for me right now, so I think he'll understand." I didn't mention that I had wondered whether Ethan could ever be more than a little rough in the bedroom. I glanced back at my phone, seeing another message.

Used to gore, huh? Watch a lot of horror movies? We could go see one, if you wanted.

I love horror movies. Maybe we can when things settle down a bit, but right now would be hard.

I felt guilty for not being clear in that I wasn't exactly interested anymore, but I set the phone down and directed my eyes back to the movie. I felt the phone buzz again almost immediately, but I ignored it this time, not wanting to overthink anything right now. After finishing two movies, Tyler returned home, seemingly bummed about his team losing. As someone that understood absolutely nothing when it came to sports, I didn't get it, but Elly seemed familiar with it. She went and talked to him quietly, trying to cheer him up. I took that as my cue to leave. It was getting late, anyways, and I was more than just a little tired. The constant nightmares had drained all my energy, leaving me perpetually lethargic.

I said goodnight to the two of them and made my way to the room, dropping onto the futon and plugging my phone in. I glanced at the message from Ethan without opening it, seeing that he had said it was alright and to just let him know when would be a good time to go. I clicked the screen off and laid back, closing my eyes and hoping tonight I would have normal dreams.

CHAPTER 15

***

I opened my eyes and found myself, once again, in my house. It looked similar to how it was when I first purchased it, but the bedroom was decorated differently. Clothes were scattered around, a backpack and schoolbooks flung across the bed. My hands were braced on my thighs, and I was breathing heavily. *Go to the drawer,* an unwarranted voice whispered in my mind. Fear thrummed through my chest, and each muscle in my body was tensed, fighting the urge that wasn't my own to go to the bedside table.

I fought the compulsion, but my body moved anyways. My hands were ripped from my thighs, leaving scratches on the bare skin from my nails. My right foot slid forward, then the left. My whole body was trembling, both from the strain in fighting whatever had control of my limbs as well as the fear that poisoned every cell in my body.

I knew what was going to happen, and I couldn't let it happen. Tears flowed down my cheeks freely, gasping sobs being wrenched from my chest. Still, my feet moved, dragging me closer to the bedside table. My unwilling hand reached out towards the drawer, practically vibrating in the effort to fight whatever controlled me.

No matter how I fought, I wrenched the draw open violently and slid my hand inside. *Grab the knife*, I heard in my head. My breaths came faster – I knew those weren't my thoughts. I didn't want to do this. No part of me wanted this, but I couldn't do anything to stop it. My fingers clasped around the knife.

Get in the tub. My muscles ached with the effort to not go. To keep fighting and hope that this would stop – that I could stop. Muscles screaming in protest, my feet lurched forwards. Each step dragged me closer to the bathroom. I could barely see beyond the tears, I could only feel the agony in my heart, the burning in my legs, the biting metal of the knife squeezed painfully in my palm.

The bathroom loomed in front of me, a promise of what was to come. *Get. In. The. Tub.* Each word pushed into my head was a sure strike to my chest, my feet moving with each hissed direction. I felt the cold edge of the tub brush against my legs.

My sobs were ringing in the room, cries for help seemingly unheard. My leg lifted over the side of the tub, then the other. The strength in my legs disappeared, and I collapsed, landing painfully on my tailbone. *Do it.* The voice slithered through my mind again. I knew what it wanted. I knew. But I couldn't stop myself from fighting with every little ounce of power I had. I was fighting against something so much greater than me – my strength was a drop in the ocean compared to the compulsion to follow the voice.

The knife flicked open, and my grip twisted the blade towards my wrist. *I'm so sorry*, I thought. I saw flashes of faces behind my eyes, those that would miss me the most. The ones I would miss the most – if there was something after this. Through my tears, I saw the blade pushing against the skin. Still, I fought. I felt the sharpness, the cut, the deepness of the wound. I felt the way my hand pulled back, making a line of red down my forearm. Red filled my vision, dripping, dripping, dripping. The fight left my body, and, as though I was a mere puppet, I switched the knife to the other hand, repeating the motion.

When the act was done, the knife clattered to the bottom of the tub, and I fell back against the edge of the tub. Beyond the pain, I just felt cold. Maybe the soul was what made us warm, I thought deliriously. Maybe that's why, when we died, we got so cold. I grew weaker, unable to feel much of anything anymore as the room around me darkened.

At last, I closed my eyes, embracing the darkness waiting for me.

***

I bolted upright on the futon. I clutched my wrists, trying to hold in the blood that was pouring from the cuts. But all I felt was skin. I glanced down, trying to see through the tears, but I couldn't see any red. Was I already dead? Did I have more time? I stumbled off the futon and out of the room, trying to hold my skin together, to stop the bleeding. *I have to stop the bleeding,* I thought. I reached the kitchen, grabbing the towels hanging from the oven and pressed them tightly against my arms. My stomach heaved, and I barely made it to the sink before feeling the vomit make its way up my throat. I gasped rapidly, head feeling light – I knew it had to be from the blood loss.

I stumbled, crying out, not knowing how to stop the inevitable. I kept clutching my arms, not knowing what to do. I heard Elly screech my name, concern and fear in her voice. Her arms wrapped around me, holding me up as my legs began to give out. *I'm going to die*, I thought. Elly had to know the truth.

"Elly, I fought it, I fought it I promise I swear I didn't want to do it but I had to do it, it wasn't my choice Elly I'm sorry, I'm sorry, I'm sorry," I chanted. My tongue was heavy, and the words came out like a chant, seconds withering away as I knew it would be my last breath soon.

"*Tell me what's wrong!*" Elly yelled. How could she not see? How could she not know?

"I'm bleeding and I can't stop it I can't stop it I can't stop it," I sobbed.

Elly shook my shoulders roughly. "Where are you bleeding, Evalyn? Tell me!"

"My arms my arms my arms *myarmsmyarmsmyarms*!" My voice raised to a shriek. Why couldn't she see?

Elly grabbed my face roughly. "*Look at me*," she hissed. My eyes sought her blue ones through the tears. She ripped the towels from my hands, and I shrieked again, not understanding how she could be so cruel. Did she want me to die?

Then she grabbed my wrists and lifted them, nearly shoving them in my face. "Evalyn, you're not bleeding. It was just a dream. See? You aren't bleeding," she cried.

I shook, not understanding. I know what I'd done, I'd been in the tub, I knew I had. And with that thought, reality crashed into me with the force of a tsunami. I didn't come in here from the tub. I came from the futon. I saw no red on my arms, just pale white scars.

Shock shoved me into a frozen state, no longer crying or thinking. Just emptiness. I trembled in Elly's arms as she moved to wrap them around me. I was shaking, feeling nothing at all yet everything at once. I was hollow yet overflowing with emotions. I couldn't do anything more than sit there, limp in my best friend's arms. She brushed her fingers through my hair, whispering things I couldn't understand. I wasn't in my body anymore. Numbness seeped through me, shutting down every emotion, every nerve, every thought. Down, down, down, I fell into the darkness.

I heard Elly saying something, then felt a different set of arms picking me up, carrying me as I lay limp. I vaguely registered the sound of water running, and the bright lights stinging my eyes. Only when I realized I was being carried into the tub did my panic return.

"*No!*" I screamed. I struggled against the arms around me, but they held me still. "Not the tub," I sobbed. "Not the tub, please not the tub."

The hands carrying me backed away from the tub, and almost immediately I fell back into the state of subconsciousness. The arms carried me to a different room, then a different bathroom. Panic rose for a moment until I saw the standing shower. The strong hands that had been carrying me gently set me down in the bottom of the shower.

Elly's voice returned, as well as her hands. She ran her hands over my hair then briefly stopped. Within a moment, I felt icy water pelting my skin. I jolted, some awareness beginning to return. The flow of water turned hot, then burning. My skin felt like it was on fire, but the sensations pulled me further and further from my trance. Tears leaked from my eyes once more and I collapsed against the wall of the shower. I brought my knees up to my chest and began to sob. This time, there was no barrier, nothing to separate me from the person in my dream. I *was* that person. The emotions, the thoughts – everything was mine. I felt the blade of the knife. I felt the blood leaving my body. And, above all, I heard the voice in my head. I couldn't fight the voice – I was too weak.

I felt Elly's hand grasping my arm, once again grounding me. I faced her, lifting my head from my knees and sniffling. "I'm so sorry," I said. I knew she didn't want me to apologize, but I needed to. I was sorry for scaring her, sorry for screaming at her, sorry for being crazy.

"No, honey, no. I'm sorry I couldn't do more," she replied, voice as soft as gentle rain.

"Do you think I should go to the hospital?" I whispered. The last thing I wanted to do was to go back to that place. To admit that I had fallen down so far.

"Do you want to go?" She asked.

"No," I sobbed. "But maybe I should. Elly, I'm so confused."

"You said you 'fought it.' What did that mean?"

"Something...something was controlling me. I couldn't fight it. I couldn't do it. I wasn't strong enough," I choked.

"Honey, that doesn't sound like suicide. We need to figure out what's going on, but I'm not sure the hospital is the right move, either." She sighed, reaching a hand to her face to wipe away her tears. "Do you need more time in here, or are you ready to get out?"

"I'm okay, I think." She helped me to my feet and I peeled off my soaking shirt once more. She wrapped me in a large towel and helped me to the futon once more. She searched my bag, finding nothing but a pair of gym shorts and a normal t-shirt, but she helped me slip them on, anyways. This time, without even asking, she laid down with me, clutching my hand as though she needed the comfort just as much as I did.

CHAPTER 16

T he next morning, Elly and I both slumped over our coffees, both exhausted. Three nights of disturbed sleep was catching up with us. While I'd had several nightmares over the past few weeks, none had felt as terrible as these three. I had no energy to do more than lift the cup to my lips occasionally, sipping the hot liquid that likely wouldn't be enough to make me feel remotely awake. When Tyler had left this morning, he had glanced at me with eyes full of concern. Shame filled me at the fact that he had seen me that way.

While I wasn't close with Tyler, I knew he was a good guy and didn't shy away from emotions. Elly constantly talked about his emotional intelligence – something she felt lucky to have found in a man. After last night, the fact that Tyler wasn't avoiding me like a rabid dog, I couldn't agree more.

My mind traced back over the last few nights. Of course, when I'd woken last night, I'd been delirious, lost somewhere between consciousness and unconsciousness. That would explain why I was so confused that it wasn't actually happening. But it didn't change the fact that each nightmare I'd had over the last few nights had felt sickeningly real. Even more real, in some aspects, than the other nightmares I'd had.

Then there was Daemon. Why hadn't he appeared in my dreams over the past few nights? Now that I wasn't as scared of him, did my subconscious take him away? It didn't make sense. Daemon had plagued each of my nightmares since I started having them – but the last three nights I had felt no trace of his presence. As terrible as it sounded, I missed him. At least the dreams where he was involved didn't end with me dying each time.

I sighed, twisting the ring on my finger as I stared down at my cup of coffee. I was so tired, but I wasn't sure that sleep was a better option. It was funny, almost, that when I started writing the new idea for a script, I had decided to make the main character so overwhelmed by the dreams that they couldn't tell the difference between the real world and the dream world. That's what last night had been like. Maybe I shouldn't spend as much time on that project, and, instead, return to the other project. But I had never been one to run away from the scary stuff. I had never been afraid to bleed onto the pages of my work, sharing my darkest moments with my brightest ones.

My eyes drooped as I continued to spin my ring and stare at the coffee, but I shook myself awake.

"We could take a nap day, if you want," Elly said.

"Part of me wants to, and the other part of me doesn't. I don't want to return to that place," I whispered. I cleared my throat. "But, if you want to nap, please do. I've kept you up the past few nights."

Elly nodded in understanding. "Why don't we just chill on the couch then, put on a cartoon or something, and if we fall asleep, great, and if not, no big deal?"

I smiled gratefully at her. "That sounds great."

We sat on the couch and watched old reruns of our favorite cartoons from when we were kids and as the day wore on, we only got up to make popcorn and then cuddle back into the couch. At some point, I must have dozed off, because the next thing I knew, my phone was buzzing against my thigh where it had apparently slid from beside me. My eyes groggily stared at the screen, and I realized it was Dave.

I cleared my throat, trying to wake myself up as I answered. "Hey, Dave. Everything alright?" I asked.

"Oh, yes ma'am. We just now finished, and I was just makin' sure everything was alright since it's so late now and all. But your bed is back in place an' all that, so you can feel free to head home whenever."

I peered at the time. It was 8:17pm. Holy shit. "Oh, I'm so sorry. The time slipped by me, I guess. I'll head right on over. Hopefully I didn't make you feel like you had to stay."

"No, ma'am. I was just going to hand of your key in person, since I'd rather it not fall into the wrong hands. I can either wait here or we can meet up tomorrow at some point." My heart clenched at Dave's words. He came off like a fatherly figure, careful and aware of risks that were out there. A part of me wanted to ask that he stayed till I got home so I could get inside and lock the doors without having to look over my shoulder the whole time.

"Oh, I can be home in fifteen or so minutes, if that's not too long. I don't want to keep you waiting, though," I said, hoping he couldn't hear the plea in my voice.

"No, that's not bad at all. I'll be right here when you get home, then." Relief swept over me.

We ended the call, and I raced to grab my things from Elly's, catching her up to speed on what was going on when I found her in the kitchen, making a cup of tea.

"I'm sorry for sleeping so long, hopefully you got a good nap in, too," I said.

"I only woke up a few minutes before you. You sure you'll be okay alone at the house tonight?" She asked.

"Yeah, I think I'll be fine." Somehow, I felt like I really meant it, like I was going to feel safe inside the house. "Plus, the security company should be coming by tomorrow morning. I'll have to be there for that."

Elly looked at me and nodded. "Alright. Well, if you have another dream, call me. I don't care what time it is. And I'll call you in the morning to make sure you're okay, too. I'm here for you, Ev. Whatever you need."

One of my favorite things about Elly was that she trusted me to make my own choices. She offered advice and help when she felt it was warranted, but for the most part she trusted me to do what was best for me. "Alright, I'll see you later then. Friday?" I asked.

"Yep, I'll come over Friday to see the new digs and to get ready for the Purgatory House. But if you need anything tomorrow, I don't have a lot going on, either."

"Sounds good, Elly. I have to go, though. Dave is being nice enough to wait for me until I get there. I'll let you know when I'm home safe, I promise." I said as I rushed towards the door.

I slipped out into the brisk night and into my car where I raced home, happy to still find Dave waiting for me. We chatted and he handed me the key I'd loaned him. We parted ways and I got inside, noticing he stayed to make sure I'd made it inside safely before pulling out of the driveway. I smiled, thankful for that small comfort.

Before heading upstairs to see the new room, I double checked that all the windows and doors were closed and locked. Finally, I made it to the hallway in front of my bedroom where the string to the attic dangled ominously ahead of me. I closed my eyes and took a breath, trying to clear out the memories. I made it into the room, having a similar moment when I saw the closet, but again, I breathed through it. Instead, I focused on the new floors, the walls that I planned to put the appliques on tomorrow, the new light fixtures, and my bed and nightstand all back in place.

Hardly noticing what I was doing, I went and grabbed the tree lamp and put it in its rightful place, brushing my finger against one of the hanging apples. I'd missed waking up to it on. Whether or not it was a ghost turning the light on, I didn't care. It comforted me and made me feel better. When the lamp was on, I finally went to the bathroom, steeling myself for the memories from my dream to hit me.

However, as I walked into the bathroom, I felt calm and steady. Something I hadn't been expecting. The room was perfect, complete with a clawfoot bathtub and a standing waterfall shower. The vanity and sink had been updated, and the tile flooring, now that it was finished, was clean and beautiful. The walls were made of a similar tile that the kitchen backsplash was made of, but a bit brighter. A large mirror hung on the wall, replacing the small square one that had been there. I smiled, grateful for Dave and his workers. They had done everything perfectly.

I returned to the bedroom, rubbing my eyes. I still felt exhausted, even after having taken the nap that was who knows how long. I went downstairs and made myself a cup of chamomile tea, letting the warmth from the cup soak into my hands and calm me. I made my way back upstairs, settling into the bedcovers with my tea and my book. I couldn't really remember where I'd last stopped, but I didn't feel that it mattered since I'd already read it several times.

Surprisingly, as tired as I had originally been, the minutes turned into hours until I finally felt my eyes drooping at nearly midnight. I set my book to the side and went to click off the tree lamp but paused. Maybe tonight I would keep it on. If I had a nightmare and then woke up to the light, maybe I would be able to ground myself easier.

So, I nestled deeply into the pillows and closed my eyes, hoping for a peaceful sleep for the first time in a while.

CHAPTER 17

***

I opened my eyes to a room made of black. *Back again*, I thought to myself. I suppose this was what I got for saying these dreams were better. But tonight, I didn't feel fear or anger. Just curiosity. I glanced around, finding the chairs empty. I frowned, turning further. The dim lighting reflected against the floors and walls, but there was no sign of the demon that usually presided here.

"Looking for me, Little Eve?" A velvet voice whispered against my ear. I jumped, heart pounding. I turned around quickly, but no one was there. I felt a hint of fear trickle in.

"Where are you?" I asked into the darkness.

"Right here," his voice whispered again, right behind me. I whirled my body around again, seeing nothing.

I closed my eyes, letting my senses take over. He wanted to play hide and seek? Fine. I took a breath, searching for the source of the lavender and mint that flowed through the room. I kept my eyes closed, wandering around, trying to find the man I had been running from since I first saw him. My nose followed the scent as it grew stronger, and when I knew I must be inches from the source, I reached my hand out and felt a firm, muscular surface.

I opened my eyes to see Daemon towering above me, an eerie grin on his face. "That's a first," he whispered. His silver eyes gleamed in the darkness.

"You know what they say about the lesser evil, and all that," I whispered back. The tension between us was nearly palpable, and I wasn't sure I wanted to shy away anymore. After I made myself orgasm just by thinking of him, why not just give in?

Confusion flitted across his face. "Lesser evil?" He asked.

"Nothing. But this is better than...than that."

For a moment, it almost looked like concern flashed across his eyes, but it was quickly replaced with mischief. "Would you like me to make it worse?" He leaned in to whisper in my ear. My stomach tightened in anticipation, fear, and something darker. "I can be your worst nightmare, Little Eve."

"No." It sounded like an answer to his question, but it wasn't. Daemon couldn't be my worst nightmare because I had far too many others. Between the last three nights and the other memories from my past, he couldn't be worse. The last three nights had cemented that fact. I had begun to miss him being there after the worst of the nightmare.

"No?" He asked. "So strange. Normally you pretend to hate me," he grinned. His head dipped as his nose skimmed the column of my neck, and I stiffened. Was I really going to do this? Let this happen? A part of me still wanted to fight, but another part of me wanted satisfaction, a sense of completion.

"Where is your fire? You look so tired," he murmured. His nose skimmed lower, between the peaks of my breasts, then my stomach. He knelt in front of me, letting his nose trail towards the apex of my thighs. My long t-shirt was the only thing between the wetness between my thighs and his eyes. He inhaled, and suddenly his eyes snapped to mine. For a moment, it seemed like his entire eye had turned silver, but it was gone in an instant. "You came," he said. I knew he didn't mean that in the general sense. The way his eyes darkened, the way his hands moved to grip my hips almost painfully, the way he seemed to be fighting for control; those told me a different story.

"And? I'm pretty sure that's a normal thing to do as a single adult," I replied. It was meant to sound snarky, but it came out breathless instead.

He suddenly stood, faster than I could process, and pushed me backwards, forcing me to stumble back until my spine hit the wall. Then, his hands clasped my wrists, bringing them over my head as he leaned his face in, gazing into my eyes with a dark expression. "And what did you come to?" He asked. I tried swallowing around the giant lump that had somehow found its way into my throat. He snapped his teeth at me impatiently. That's when I noticed his teeth seemed sharper, his canines slightly elongated.

"N-nothing," I choked out.

He tilted his head back and laughed darkly. His head turned back down to look at me. His gaze was primal, almost wild, his eyes burning like silver flames. He moved and placed my wrists in a single hand, then brought the other down to my throat, squeezing in threat. "No one comes to '*nothing*,'" he hissed. "Tell me the truth, Little Eve. Or do you only know how to lie?"

Fire raged inside me suddenly, the accusation turning my blood into pure acid. I spit in his face, the only thing I could really do with his hands holding mine and his body pressed tightly to my front. "*Fuck. You,*" I hissed.

An evil grin tilted his lips. "Did I hit a nerve, *Evalyn*?" His voice was sarcastic, but the words sent my heart to my throat and a metallic taste to my mouth.

I shook away the fear, instead choosing to spit in his face again. He continued to grin. His hand left my throat, reaching down to his black slacks, flicking the button open and pulling the zipper down. I refused to look as he released his cock, not wanting to show my curiosity and lust. But not looking didn't stop me from feeling it heavily rest against my stomach.

"I do not consent, motherfucker." My words came in a snarl, but heat had pooled in my belly, and I couldn't deny the feeling of wetness dripping down my thighs.

"This one is for me, Little Eve. You came, it's only fair that I get to, too." Then, to my shock, he wiped the spit from his cheek and lowered his hand to his cock, lubing it. My mouth dropped open. "Wouldn't want to waste good resources," he said sardonically. Then, he sighed and clicked his tongue. "Well, that's not nearly enough. What a shame." He glanced down, and I couldn't help but follow his gaze.

My eyes nearly fell out of my head. He was *huge*. And was that a piercing? Surely my imagination wouldn't create something like that. I practically choked, whipping my eyes back up, realizing he was watching me. My face burned. His hand released my wrists, but as I tried to yank my arms down, I realized they couldn't move. I glanced up, seeing leather restraints fastening them to the wall. The hand that had been holding my face reached down to grip my jaw, forcing my gaze away from my wrists and onto his face.

"Open," he said. I snarled at him. No fucking way was I going to do whatever he was trying. But his fingers began tightening on my jaw, pressing into my cheeks painfully. He was trying to force my mouth open like a *fucking* dog. "I said *open*, Little Eve. Cooperate, and I might just decide to reward you when I'm done," he growled.

Before I could even try to fight him anymore, his fingers finally made my jaw unlatch. "Good girl," he said sarcastically. "Now, was that so hard?"

I tried speaking, but before I could get a word out, his other hand came up to my face, and two fingers dove into my mouth. I went to bite down but ended up biting my cheek instead, tasting blood on my tongue. His fingers reached the back of my mouth, causing me to choke and gag, though I fought it, not wanting to give him the satisfaction. But his fingers kept pushing, moving down my throat and causing me to choke against them. "I'm not sure how you'll ever handle my cock in your mouth if you can barely handle my fingers," Daemon said darkly.

He was finger fucking my mouth. Embarrassment washed through me, and I felt my eyes beginning to water, both from the choking and the shame. Finally, when the spit began to drip down his arm, he relented, pulling his hand away and bringing it down to his cock. "There, that's better." His voice was low, filled with wild lust. His spit-covered hand began to pump up and down on himself, and I couldn't stop myself from glancing down. This was the most erotic thing I had ever experienced, ever *seen*, even. His other hand moved from my jaw, down to my throat, squeezing harder than before.

He growled low as he slid his hand faster, and I could only watch, mesmerized, as his dick glistened with the spit stolen from my mouth, Daemon unabashedly pleasuring himself. "You could have just been honest, Little Eve," he bit out.

I refused to respond, anger and lust creating a beautiful drug in my system. With each stroke, my pussy became wetter and wetter, and it was clear he knew exactly what he was doing to me. "This would feel so much better if it was your mouth," he groaned. "But you had to lie to me. Now we're both being punished."

He removed his hand from my neck and slapped my cheek, but rather than anger me, I just felt hotter. His hand returned to my neck. "You like that, don't you? You like being pushed around. You love pissing me off because it means you get this side of me, don't you?" He stared at me, waiting for an answer.

His fist pumped faster, and I could tell he was nearing the edge. His eyes were pure silver, his teeth sharp, his muscles rippling with each movement. "*Don't you?*" He yelled, leaning forward to snap his teeth next to my cheek. He was a pure animal in this moment, a true demon, living up to his name. And I had never been more turned on.

"Yes," I whispered, feeling defeated. A tear slipped down my cheek, and his tongue flicked out and tasted it.

"Your honesty tastes *so fucking good*," he groaned. Suddenly, his hand left my throat, sliding up under my shirt and back up, bare breasts and soaking pussy on full display. "Look at that gorgeous cunt. Soaking wet, just for me." His movements became harsher, choppier, as he stared at my body. Suddenly, a loud growl tore from his chest as he came, the white spurts of his come landing on my chest, stomach, and the top of my pussy.

I heard my own moan slipping from my lips as I watched this, heat and ecstasy roiling through me. My hips subconsciously tilted towards him, begging for attention. His gaze came to rest back on mine, and he tilted his head at me. "Now. You have one more chance. What did you come to the other night, Evalyn?" His breathing was still rough and his eyes and face were still wild, as if he was far from satiated.

His tall frame loomed over me, making me feel small. His dark hair slipped over his eyes, his gaze piercing straight through to my soul. He knew the answer. I could see it clearly on his face. He just wanted me to say it. To admit, finally, that I was vulnerable to him. That he had some level of power over me. My heart thundered in my chest, fear snaking its way through me. Then, the word slipped past my lips. "You," I whispered, so soft it was nearly impossible to hear.

His hand that was on my throat released my neck, lifting my shirt higher past my head and then let it slide behind my neck. Then, he brought his hand to my face, gently stroked my cheek. The touch was so gentle compared to what I had expected. His face leaned closer to mine, and he kissed my cheekbones, then the corners of my lips, then my forehead. "Such a good girl," he whispered.

At the words, my heart melted. I didn't want to fight anymore; it was as though it had been sucked from my body. My muscles went limp, my mind waring between shame and pleasure. His hands moved to my sides, one still sticky with spit and come, and slid down over my ass. Before I could even blink, my hips had been wrenched forward, legs spread wide. He hooked his arms beneath my knees, lifting my pussy to his face. My body was bent at a strange angle, but the fire in his eyes made nothing else matter.

His tongue darted out, licking the wetness that had slid down my thighs. He cleaned every drop, teeth nipping at the skin intermittently. When he was satisfied with cleaning my inner thighs, his gaze returned to mine. "What a beautiful sight. Covered in my come and waiting to be feasted on," his rich velvet voice whispered. Then, without waiting for a response, he dove into my pussy as though he had been starving for a millennium. A shriek of surprise left my lips, followed by breathy moans. His tongue and teeth played with my sensitive clit, balancing precariously on the edge between pain and pleasure. Then he dipped down further, plunging his tongue into me, expertly twisting and pressing his tongue into all the right places.

He returned to my clit, this time biting it hard enough I screamed out before soothing it with his tongue. My body was on fire, my whole existence belonging to this moment, this feeling, his mouth and his control. The pain mixed with the pleasure, the pleasure spreading through my veins. A hand reached up, toying with my nipple, spreading his come on my breast. Daemon's fingers expertly pinched and twisted, sending fiery pleasure down to my aching pussy.

"How much pain can you take?" I felt my pussy somehow getting even wetter at the thought. "We'll have to find out someday," he growled. Everything about him in this moment was primal, but somehow controlled. He was pure animal as he feasted, but hyper-cognizant of my body's reactions, driving me higher before pulling me back down, drawing this moment out.

My body was taut, tension winding through every nerve, waiting to explode. But each time I reached the edge, he would slow, torture me in another way before building me up all over again. My moans became whimpers, and before I realized what I was doing, I felt a word slip from my lips. "Please," I begged.

"Good fucking girl," he groaned. He went back to torturing me in full force, sucking, biting, twisting. Every sensation built up, up, up. "Come for me," he growled, somehow managing words while his mouth was still moving against my pussy. I didn't have a moment to wonder about that before my whole body was struck by lightning, a scream ripping from my throat, hips thrashing against his hold. The pleasure was almost painful, the force of the orgasm drowning me in its waves. It seemed to go on forever, and Daemon seemed determined to make it last even longer. As the orgasm faded, my head remained in the clouds. The world around me was fuzzy; I was floating, practically high on the pleasure.

I felt Daemon gently set my legs down, disappear for a moment before returning with a warm, wet rag. He cleaned me gently, wiping his come from my chest and stomach, and mine from my thighs. When he reached my pussy, I shuddered at how sensitive it was. Soon, he was done, and he slipped my shirt back over my head and picked me up. My arms dropped to my sides, shoulders aching. But still, I floated.

I registered him sitting down, cradling me in his lap, tucking me into his chest. My eyes were half closed, but I had never felt more content or happy than I was in this moment. His hands reached around me to gently massage my aching shoulders, soothing them.

I wasn't sure how long we laid there, wrapped in a blanket of pleasure, but I had no desire to move. Even as my head floated down from the clouds, I didn't fight this moment. I just accepted that this was finally a good dream. I felt more at peace than I had in so long, and I didn't want to change that.

I knew I was dreaming, but in the dream, I was resting. No terror, no fear. I didn't need to wake up. I wasn't even sure I wanted to, at this point. A tear slipped from my eye at that thought. I was happier with the man from my nightmares than I had ever been with any other man in the waking world. In some sense, I wanted this to be real, but in another, I knew that would be a bad idea.

Noticing my tears, Daemon gently wiped them away, not asking anything, just being there to comfort. I realized we were wrapped in a real blanket, though I wasn't sure where it had come from, and the softness of it was welcome, soothing away all the thoughts and fears.

"Little Eve," Daemon whispered, breaking the silence softly. "It's time for you to wake up, my love."

My heart clenched. I had so much I wanted to say, but I had been vulnerable enough for one night. I glanced at him, seeing a hint of his own vulnerability on his face. Why he seemed sad, I wasn't sure. Instead of asking, I just nodded. "Okay," I replied. His hand brushed my cheek one last time as the world faded around me.

CHAPTER 18

***

I woke to the sun peeking through the windows, feeling more rested than I had in weeks. The lamp was still on next to me, and I clicked it off. I stretched, shoulders feeling stiff. I rolled them, realizing they probably hurting in the dream because I was sleeping on them wrong. I laid in bed for a bit, sending a quick message to Elly about having actually slept through the night. I left out the details of the dream, instead chalking up the good night's rest to finally hitting my sleep deprivation limit.

It was a bit after 8 in the morning, and it felt good to be in my "new" house. While a part of me still flinched looking at the closet and in the direction of the bathroom, I knew it would fade with time. After donning some leggings and a long sleeve shirt, I made my way downstairs to the kitchen, making myself a cup of coffee and staring at the empty fridge. I supposed I needed to make a trip to the store soon. With my coffee in hand, I stepped outside onto the porch. My feet moving on their own accord, I stepped around to the side of the house, seeing the stone pathway that wound around to the back. There were flower beds along the path that would need to be fixed come springtime.

I stepped off the porch onto the stone path, the icy surface biting into my feet. I rubbed the hot mug between my palms, trying to chase away the cold. I continued on my way down the path, glancing over to the trees not far off to the right. An idea sparked in my head, knowing the trees went on for a while. It could be a place for the photoshoot with Elly next weekend. Because I wasn't looking, I stepped on a stick that had made its way onto the path. I stumbled, my burning hot coffee splashing my fingers.

"Fuck," I hissed, shaking my hand and hopping on one foot. Losing my balance, I dipped away from the path and onto the grass, trying to save my coffee from spilling even more. That's when I noticed the spikes. They were exactly the same as when I had dreamed of them a few nights ago. My stomach roiled, but not having eaten anything since the popcorn yesterday at Elly's, there was nothing to heave. I knew I had seen them before when I had originally looked at the house prior to purchasing, but it was still an unexpected reminder that I wasn't prepared for.

Unable to turn my icy feet in the other direction, I moved towards the ominous fence, glancing up the back of the house, seeing the window I had seen in my dream. I blew out a careful breath, trying to hold myself together.

"Uh, Ms. Evalyn Wright?" A voice called from the front of the house.

Startled, I realized it must be the security company. "One moment!" I yelled back. I glanced down at my hand covered in coffee, now cold from the chilly morning. Sighing, I walked towards the front, truly regretting my decision to walk all the way out here without shoes. I finally reached the porch again, seeing a middle-aged man standing awkwardly, presumably waiting for me to arrive. I cleared my throat awkwardly, feeling painfully naked without my shoes. I glanced at his uniform, seeing the security company's logo. "Um, sorry about that. Just checking things out at the back of the house."

"No problem. I'm Jim, by the way. I have everything for setup in my van over there, but first, we'll go through a rundown of how it works. Is that alright with you?"

"Sure, yeah, sure. Uh, come on in," I said as I opened the door to the house. He entered and instantly started discussing how the security would work. He showed where the control panel would go, followed by the descriptions of how the security worked not only on the outside, but also the inside.

"You wanted full coverage security, so you'll have five cameras outside the house. Now, inside, we won't have cameras, but you're going to have motion sensors in every single room. The motion sensors will activate with movement once the alarm is set, but pets and mice aren't included in that. There is an alarm setting for being 'away' and another for at night. The motion sensors won't be noticeable, so you won't have to worry about them affecting how the house looks. Uh...I think that about explains it all. Any questions?" He asked.

While I wished it all wasn't necessary, everything he said made sense. I may not have ever had a security system personally, but I knew how they worked. Over the next few hours, I watched the worker, Jim, as he installed the cameras outside, followed by setting up the sensors on the inside of the house. He did the rooms downstairs, followed by the rooms upstairs.

"Alright, last one will go in the attic, if you want to lead the way," Jim said as he grabbed the next two sensors.

My heart thumped a little harder in my chest hearing that. But I remembered the steps upstairs the other night, and decided it was better now when I had someone with me than when I was alone. Even still, I couldn't bring myself to yank the cord down myself. "Could you, maybe-" I trailed off, gesturing to the cord handing from the ceiling.

He nodded, looking confused but pulling on it anyways. The stairs to the attic came down with a loud creaking, the hinges locking into place. He made his way up the stairs, boots landing heavily on each plank. I followed behind, trying to ignore the urge to run the opposite direction. As my head reached above the platform, my chest constricted. It was identical to my dream. I shoved the thoughts away, however, hoping it was from seeing some photo somewhere. An uneasy voice whispered in my mind, telling me that there was no way I had seen a picture of this attic.

As he set up the sensor, I wandered around, surprised at the cleanliness of it. I had expected it to be cluttered and messy, the way the spare room had been before it was cleaned. All that remained was a few pieces of random furniture, covered in sheets, looking the same way every creepy horror movie did. However, even without the excess clutter, there was a thick coating of dust over everything. I sneezed a few times, but Jim seemed used to this kind of atmosphere as he got to work. I wandered around, plucking the sheets off the furniture while covering my face against the swirling dust.

As I approached what appeared to be a chair, I pulled on the sheet, finding resistance. I yanked on it with more force, the sheet finally freeing. After sneezing a few more times, I glanced over to see that there was a wooden box tucked beneath the chair, which I imagined was what the sheet must have been caught on. Curiosity and fear wormed through me. I tugged the box towards me, about to open it when I heard a throat clear behind me.

"Well, I'm all done here, Ms. Wright. I just have to go downstairs to make sure everything is properly connected to the panel and then you'll be set to go."

"Oh, thank you so much." I grabbed the box, which was surprisingly heavier than I imagined, and followed him back down the steps. I set the box on the bed in my room before meeting him back at the newly installed panel by the front door.

He showed me how to use the panel to set it at night or when I left for the day. I thanked him as he finished up and left. Feeling safer already with the cameras and sensors, I felt my shoulders relax a little. After last night's sleep and the security I could now feel in my own home, things felt like they were finally getting better.

Elly called, interrupting my train of thought. "Hey, Elly, what's up?" I said into the phone.

"Hey! Sorry to bother, I was just checking up on you. Is all the security installed now?" She quipped.

"Yeah, everything is set up. I have cameras outside, sensors inside. Someone would have to think twice before coming in here." I replied.

"Good. And you said you slept fine last night. Did you actually have no nightmares? You weren't just saying that so I didn't worry, were you?" Her questions ran into each other, and I could tell she'd been having them swirling in her head all morning.

"Yes, actually. I'm feeling...good. Really good. I know it's crazy, but I actually slept through the night. I think maybe I just hit my wall of exhaustion. I'm not sure. Whatever it was, I just woke up feeling more rested than I have in a while," I replied. I blew out a breath, readying myself to share the whole truth.

"What's wrong? Why are you sighing?" Elly asked.

"Well. You know the demon guy from my nightmares?" I asked.

"Yeah, why?"

"Well, he was in my dream last night. But somehow in a really, *really* good way." I held my breath, readying myself for the response.

"Oh, I see. Did you finally let yourself give in to your kinky side?" She asked.

I rolled my shoulders, still feeling the discomfort. "Yeah, I did. And I don't know how it's possible, but I think I had the best orgasm of my entire life while I was asleep."

Elly giggled over the phone. "Ooh. That good, huh? Poor Ethan, he's going to have so much to live up to, now."

"Oh my god," I practically whispered to myself. "*Anyways*," I said pointedly.

"Well, I was also calling because I wanted to see if you wanted to come with me to the pumpkin patch. I totally meant to ask if you wanted to go yesterday, but we both needed sleep. I don't want to carve them up yet, but everyone knows you need to go in early to get the really good pumpkins. We're honestly probably running a little late anyways. We have like two weeks until Halloween which means most of the demon spawn have taken the best ones."

I laughed, knowing she meant children. Elly was one of the few women I'd met that was whole, completely, and entirely uninterested in having a child of her own. While she already called herself "Auntie Elly" for my unborn child and didn't particularly hate children, she knew motherhood just wasn't for her. "Yes, I'd be happy to go and steal the best pumpkins from the little gremlins."

"Yay! Can you meet at my house in like 30 minutes? I have some last-minute stuff I have to do for work to prepare for Saturday, but it shouldn't take me long."

"Sure babes, I'll be there." We ended the call after saying quick good-byes and I ran upstairs to get ready. That's when I remembered the box from the attic. Curiosity nipped at my senses, but I knew I didn't have time for that right now. I hadn't showered in a few days. I didn't truly count the showers I took at Elly's because I hadn't really *washed*. My hair was a greasy mess after getting it wet so many times and not washing it.

I turned away from the box and made my way into the new bathroom, excited to use the stand-in shower for the first time. I quickly grabbed my toiletries and jumped in, standing under the waterfall faucet. The heat from the water turned my skin pink as I scrubbed my hair, washing it twice followed by a hefty amount of conditioner. My still sore shoulders welcomed the heat, soothing them. My skin was a bright red by the time I finished scrubbing my body and rinsing my hair, but it felt so good to feel fully clean.

Easing out of the shower, I grabbed a giant fluffy towel and my hair wrap, drying myself off as quickly as possible. I was running late already, and I wasn't even dressed. Quickly, I went to the boxes of clothes and chose some skinny jeans and a black sweater, followed by some chunky black boots. As soon as I had everything on, I let my hair free from the wrap and decided to let it airdry.

As I rushed to leave, I almost forgot the alarm panel, but quickly backtracked and activated the "away" system. I locked up, rushing to my car and making my way to Elly's. I arrived about ten minutes late, but knew Elly wasn't going to mind. I pulled into the driveway, parking, and honked the horn.

Elly came out with a huge smile on her face, clearly excited for our little trip. I had a mini-SUV, so it was easier for us to use my car rather than her tiny one when it came to pumpkin hunting. We chatted on the way there, talking mostly about the haunted house we were looking forward to tomorrow night. It was just another way I felt like my life was settling back into all the right places, even if that did mean giving into a hot ass demon from my nightmares. I shrugged the thought away, knowing I should be looking externally for pleasure rather than in my dreams. But now that things felt like they were getting better (even if it was on a one-day streak), maybe I *could* look outwards.

We arrived at the pumpkin patch, seeing the hayrides and the children running around a tiny corn maze. We parked, making our way into the field and started hunting for pumpkins.

"We could use these in the photoshoot, too, Ev," Elly mentioned.

"I figured we probably would. Oh! I completely forgot. This morning, I was walking by the house and realized we might be able to do the photoshoot in the woods next to my house. They aren't super thick, by any means, but maybe with your editing it will be enough," I said.

"Ooh, I like this idea! We can scope it out tomorrow and see what we think." Noticing a giant pumpkin, Elly darted off in that direction. "I might have found *the* pumpkin, Ev. Better catch up!" She cackled. Her laughter died as she realized the pumpkin had a very flat, very sticky side.

I spotted a large, upright pumpkin a few yards away. Quickly walking over to inspect it, I grabbed it and showed its perfection to Elly. "Now who has to catch up, again?"

She sent a mocking face my way, but we both laughed. Of course, finding the best pumpkin first meant that you had to carry the pumpkin around until the other found *their* pumpkin. I followed Elly through the fields, arms starting to ache from the weight of my "perfect" pumpkin. She grinned, knowing my arms had to be screaming at this point, but still taking her sweet time to find her pumpkin.

Finally, about 20 minutes later, arms numb and feeling as though they were about to fall off, she found a pumpkin. We made our way back out of the field and quickly paid for our pumpkins, barely making it to the car before our arms gave out. I really needed to start doing my morning yoga again. We drove back, screaming to the music coming from the speakers, laughing and teasing each other. I might be 29 and Elly 32, but we could still act like children.

I dropped her off at her house, leaving both pumpkins in the car since we would likely carve them before the photoshoot and use them at my house. I groaned, thinking about hauling the pumpkins back in. Finally, I made it home, grabbing one soon-to-be jack-o-lantern at a time and gently setting them on the porch.

I entered the house and turned the alarm panel off and made my way upstairs. As I entered my bedroom, the wooden box loomed in front of me. I wasn't sure why, but it gave me a bad feeling. Maybe that was the real reason I had avoided opening it today, rather than using the excuse of time.

I spun the ring on my finger, blowing out a deep breath. *Maybe you should leave the box alone, Evalyn. There could be some weird shit in there from a previous owner,* I thought to myself. But my fingers itched to open it. The attic hadn't had anything fancy in it aside from a few chairs and such, which is why this intrigued me as much as it did. I reached my fingers out, brushing them against the polished wood surface. It was a beautiful box, made of a dark wood, cut with beautiful designs on the lid. The designs were made to look like flames, creating a fun ridged pattern against my fingertips.

A silver latch was on the front, a small padlock on it, one I hadn't noticed before. I ran my hand through my hair, trying to remember if I still had the small bolt-cutters I had used in my old rental. I dug around in some boxes, finally finding it in the box with some gardening tools I had saved. I quickly walked back to the room, ignoring the tightening in my gut for whatever was inside. I sat on the bed next to the box. A bad feeling crawled up my spine, but I moved to clip the small padlock anyways.

Hands shaking, I started to open the lid. It slipped from my shaking fingers before slamming shut again. "Get your shit together, Evalyn," I hissed at myself. I gripped the lid again, wrenching it open before I could lose my nerve. I glanced at the contents, suddenly knowing why I'd had such a terrible feeling.

Inside were four items. Each item making me feel like the beautiful relaxation from today was a sandcastle being smashed by a powerful wave. My stomach churned as I took in the blue scarf, the pearl necklace, the knife, and the *fucking* fedora.

CHAPTER 19

I had seen each of these items before. All of which were in my night-mares. Without lifting the knife from the box, I could feel its ridges as the handle bit into my skin. I remembered how it had felt to unlatch the pearl necklace from the column of our throat, that moment of freedom before we were lost again. I remembered the texture of the scarf in the hands that were not my hands and the neck that was not my neck.

And, beyond all that, I could never forget that fedora. The one from my first dream, the one I hated so much but still felt fear while seeing Daemon wear it. He hadn't worn it since, but I knew who it belonged to. So, I sat, frozen, staring at the contents that were staring back at me, telling me a story that I didn't want to believe.

My dreams hadn't been dreams. My nightmares were real. A shudder-ing breath left my lungs, my stomach clenching in blatant fear. The puz-zle pieces began sliding into place. Daemon, able to reside in nightmares, generating nightmares for his victims. The women, the last of which I knew was Suzanne Elliot, fighting for control as they were forced to exact cruel torture upon themselves.

I recalled the article from before about Suzanne. I wondered if I would be able to find the names of the other women. Up until that moment, I think I had been choosing to go with the most logical explanation for the nightmares – they were just nightmares. But this morning I had woken with my shoulders sore after....

Ice crawled down my spine with piercing fingers as the realization hit me. Humiliation paralyzed me, and I felt lightheaded, like I was about to faint. I had let this demon *touch* me. *Pleasure* me. I had let him pleasure *himself*, and while I had acted like I was fighting the whole time, my body screamed the truth. Revulsion coiled inside me, spreading like a sickness to the rest of my limbs. I was *sick*. Absolutely fucked in the head. I yanked on my hair, wanting to scream.

Elly had been wrong. This wasn't just some psychological kink deprivation leading to these dreams. This was a monster. A monster I had finally given into last night. Would I be next? Would he take over my mind and force me to do what I had vowed to never try again? Would I be able to fight it?

I scoffed at the idea. I remembered how hard the other women had fought, and how it wasn't enough, not in the end. When would he strike? I had to find a way to fight whatever this was. I didn't believe in exorcisms, but maybe that was what the house needed. A fucking purge.

Why had Daemon been so gentle with me after everything last night? Was it to lure me in? But if he could control my mind, why would he go through all that effort to get me to give in to him? Perhaps it was for his own gain – before he went in for the kill, he drew the women in, convince them to fight their baser instincts, only to prove them right, in the end. But why would he have shown me the women dying? Did he do that to each of them?

I needed to tell Elly, but I couldn't move. I could only stare at this open box, the items within. My thoughts swirled and pounded inside my head. How could I fight him? What strength did I have against him? I wasn't stupid enough to believe I could be one of those heroines that was magically special enough to beat the monster. I wasn't special. I was a basic human. But I didn't want to *die*.

These questions and thoughts controlled me as my body stayed frozen on the bed, the loudest thought being *I don't want to die*. Over and over the thoughts tumbled and rolled inside my skull; minutes passed, and hours ticked by. I hadn't moved. I wasn't even sure I had taken a real breath since I had opened the box. My limbs were numb, but my body ached.

I couldn't put enough cohesive thoughts together to truly plan, and, even now, I struggled to grasp that all this was real. That it wasn't a bad dream. As I sat there, I felt another emotion slowly rising up, surpassing the fear. The emotion began to fill my veins, boiling me from the inside out. *Rage.* The same rage I had felt when I fought my father's control. When I realized I didn't want him to control who I was. The same rage that had swallowed me whole time and time again when someone tried to control me, to set a fixed outcome in *my* life.

If I couldn't do anything to stop this, I could at least let him know I wasn't going to go down without a fight. Maybe he had a weakness. Maybe, in the same way he controlled the dream world, maybe I could control it back.

But in order to do any of this, I had to go to sleep. My heart leapt to my throat at the thought, but I knew there was no avoiding this. Finally, with fire in my veins, I was able to move. I glanced at the time, seeing it was shortly after 9pm. I yanked out my laptop and began searching.

I typed in my street address, followed by what I thought might lead me to the right thing. Using "suicide" as a search made my blood boil, but I knew that was how it would be perceived. Finally, when I typed in "woman jumps from attic in the 1980s," I found something. It was a small article, and perhaps not the highest quality. But I would take what I could get. It was labeled *"String of Bad Luck, or Suicide House Curse?"*

"While it may seem a stretch to some, the number of suicides in the house off of Pyke Street seems like a strange, awful reoccurrence in the past century. Since the house was built in 1942, three women have committed suicide. In the year the house was built, Elaine Pallenski was found dead in her bedroom closet. years later, in 1983, Jayda Mance jumped from the attic window. And, finally, Suzanne Elliot, in 2016, was discovered in her bathroom.

These cases are all many years apart, but that doesn't make the situation any less obscure. Perhaps this is simply a string of bad luck – or perhaps it is something more. Perhaps it is a paranormal force drawing these women to do terrible things. It is important to note that there have been many residents who have lived on the property without any disturbances. But three dead in less than a century? Local residents may soon be calling it the 'Suicide House.'"

After finishing the article, I searched "Jayda Mance," followed by "Elaine Pallenski." Instantly, I found more articles. It was clear that these articles had been copied from physical newspapers, but they all held similar information. All three women had died of apparent suicide. No one could argue anything else. The thought made my stomach turn and my anger burn hotter.

After getting the information I needed, I went downstairs to make tea, knowing that falling asleep without it would be nearly impossible. It was now closer to 11pm, and I decided to meditate after finishing my tea. It was a useful tool for me, slowing my thoughts down, emptying out the emotions, drawing me into a place of peaceful nothingness. I slipped a few times from the calm, but eventually fell back into the space of nothingness again. I hadn't meditated in a while, and it was seemingly obvious.

In, out. In, out. I counted my breaths, feeling as though each of my limbs were floating and my heart was beating slower and slower, my breathing becoming nearly invisible as I floated among the nothingness. This was the moment I knew I was fully submerged in my subconscious – where thoughts and words and problems were big and small all at once, nothing and something at the same time. I stayed there, peacefully, letting my mind relax and rest.

Finally, I began to bring myself down from the nothingness, waking up each limb and muscle, feeling each nerve come back alive, my breaths returning to a normal rate. I opened my eyes, back in my room, feeling languid and sleepy. While I had come back down from the nothingness, a part of me still felt lighter, freer. I didn't feel caged or dragged down by the weight of emotions and decisions. Instead, I moved to burrow into the covers and let myself fall asleep.

***

I opened my eyes, not finding myself in the black room as I had expected. No, I was somewhere worse, or, perhaps, just as equally bad. My childhood home caged me, cutting open old scars with its vicious nails. I could almost feel the blood running down the walls, the sins of this room bubbling up from the floorboards. My heart was frozen, my limbs screaming in agony, my mind drowning in an ocean of fear.

My lower back down to my upper thighs was aching, pain pulsing with each flow of blood through me. I felt a warm wetness dripping slowly down my back, down my bottom, down my legs. Blood. I was bleeding. I didn't move. I knew what happened if I moved. My legs were locked in place, the only thing holding me up. I forced my frame to not shake, to stay still. To not cry out. I stared at the dim bulb swinging above my head, trying to keep my eyes from leaking the tears that were threatening to roll down my cheeks.

I felt a hand grasp the back of my neck, and vomit threatened to come up. *He's here.* The hand squeezed, tighter and tighter, until it took everything not to scream and cry in pain.

"You disobeyed me," a voice came from behind me. It was distorted, muffled. I realized it was the blood rushing to my head. He shook me violently by my neck, my body begging me to make it stop, but I ignored it. My eyes screwed shut, and I felt him coming to stand in front of me. He knocked his head against my own, my skull ringing. "*You disobeyed me!*" He hissed. His hand wrapped around the front of my neck, and he lifted, my feet leaving the floor, my toes dangling uselessly. My arms were lead at my side. There was no point in fighting back. No point in running. No point in anything. Blackness took over.

I opened my eyes, a blurry face in front of me. It was *her*. "It won't happen again, baby. I won't let it happen again," she whispered, her voice like a balm to my wounds and shattered heart.

"Why did you leave me?" I asked her. The world dissolved around me.

This time, when I opened my eyes, I was in the black room. The lights were dim, the glow bouncing softly off the walls and floor. The black furniture was in the same spot as usual, but Daemon wasn't seated there. I looked around the room, steeling my spine. I couldn't let the memories eat me, swallow me whole, affect how I chose to hold control in this situation.

There, in the corner, shrouded in shadows, was Daemon. I could see nothing except his shining silver eyes, piercing the darkness. He stood there, watching me, and I fought the feeling of unease pushing against my walls. I approached him, each step slow and sure. I could feel the fire building in my veins, the rage for those women making me feel like I could burn him down with a single glance.

"You're real." My words came out between my latched teeth, my gaze just as unwavering as his.

"I've never said different," he replied, velvety voice falling over my ears; the softness masking the monster.

"I didn't believe you until today. Until what I found." My words were a lashing whip of accusation.

His head tilted gently; his eyes still glued to mine. It was a battle of wills. "And what did you find?" He asked, voice dangerously soft.

"I found your fedora. Among other things." I took a steadying breath, but the rage was uncontrollable. "*How could you?*" I hissed, venom flying from my tongue.

I was a volcano, about to erupt.

"How could I what?" He asked. His voice was as soft as ever, but something in it sounded like he was preparing for a blow.

This was the moment I tested whether or not I could control the dreams, too. The moment I wanted to believe was possible. I held my hand out in front of me, closing my eyes and seeing the items in perfect clarity, one by one. I built them, piece by piece in my head. I opened my eyes, surprised to find the items in my hand.

I grabbed the blue scarf, the familiar texture brushing against my fingers. "Elaine," I hissed. I grabbed the pearl necklace, feeling the cool pearls against my fingertips, remembering how they had felt against my throat. "Jayda." My fingers wrapped around the knife, the handle biting into my palm the way it had before. "Suzanne." I watched every inch of his face, still shrouded in darkness, and watched his eyes twitch with each name. I clutched the knife in my fist, the blade already out. I took a careful step closer, until I was so close I could smell the mint and lavender, feel the heat from his skin, and see the tightness around his eyes. "They died because of *you*, didn't they?" I roared in his face.

His eyes closed, finally breaking contact, ending the battle of wills. "Yes," he whispered.

"How could you?" I asked again, voice loud, ricocheting off the walls of the room. Before he could answer, my fist holding the knife whipped up, tip pointing right for his heart. My hand moved with lightning speed, the blade touching his flesh, pushing in. But before I could slide the blade into his heart, his hand grabbed my wrist, his iron grip unforgiving.

"Don't do this," he whispered. His eyes were pleading, looking as if he held more pain than anyone could ever imagine. For a moment, I stuttered, but remembered that he was a mind-fucking demon. He could say whatever he wanted, make me believe whatever he wanted.

"I'll find a way to stop you," I snarled, hand still frozen in his grasp. "For them. You're a fucking *monster*." He flinched violently this time, looking for all the world like each word had struck a blow. "Now, I want to wake the fuck up, *Daemon*," I bit out.

His head hung, defeat coating him like the darkness around him. The darkness swallowed me whole, world dissolving around me. Right as he was disappearing, I saw something flash across his gaze – fury. My hesitations disappeared. It was an act, like everything else that had occurred between us.

CHAPTER 20

***

I woke up, fire still burning in my veins. But there was a part of me that wanted to believe that emotional side of him, the side that looked broken upon hearing my words. It didn't add up. But how many mind demons were waltzing around making people kill themselves? And, in this house, no less. I felt trapped, no idea what to do or where to turn.

In the few interactions I'd had with him, he's already completely wormed his way into my head. I'd gone from a high of finally accepting whatever he was straight down to hell, where I had become the embodiment of rage. I wanted vengeance for those women, all of whom were in their young to mid-twenties. Their lives had been cut so short, the way they were perceived after death so wrong. None of them had wanted that. None of them had desired to die, each of them had a future ahead of them that was extinguished.

And then, there were the memories. Why did my father have to be there? Why did I have to reexperience it all over again? Was it Daemon, forcing that from me? Or was it the fact I was so out of control in my life right now that caused me to remember those horrible things?

Once again, the thoughts roiled and tumbled around in my head, drowning me in emotions too big for my body. I was exhausted but my mind was racing, and I knew I needed to calm down. So, rather than returning to sleep, I sat up and returned to meditating. While I wasn't certain, this felt like a place where he couldn't reach my mind, a place where I drifted somewhere between sleep and consciousness, maybe even life and death.

This place was a place I controlled, a place I was free. It was a place I had learned to find after the events of my childhood. A place I had forgotten for a short while, in the way that someone might forget a language that they hadn't needed to use for a long while. Things had been upright in my life for so long, I forgot that it was important to find this place consistently. I sat there, feeling like I was floating, drifting in the ocean tides. I was no longer in my body, and that was okay. I drifted and drifted, until finally the nothingness urged me to sleep, promising to keep the darkness at bay.

I woke to the sunlight stinging my tired eyes, and I decided I needed to get some blackout curtains. While the morning sun was beautiful and all, I couldn't sleep in if there was a giant ball of light burning through my eyelids. I exhaled a deep breath and rolled out of bed, groggily making my way to the bathroom. After relieving myself and splashing my face with cold water, I remembered that tonight was Purgatory House, which also meant Elly coming over.

My chest tightened, thinking about what she might say when I told her what I had found out. How had yesterday started out so perfect and ended up so...horrendous? Once again, I felt as though my life was crumbling around me. A single day of hope that things were going to get better was all that was needed to make me feel the real impact of how fucked everything was.

I sleepily stumbled down the kitchen and made some coffee, leaning against the island for support as my hand embraced the hot mug. I was tired, physically and mentally, my head pounding with exhaustion. I twisted my ring around, trying to make things make sense while battling the urge to pretend it didn't exist at all. How would I fight him when it came down to it? Last night, I had barely nicked him, if I had even done that.

If he could push me, control me, force me to do those things to myself, what chance did I have in a mind game with a demon? I thought about exorcisms and laughed. It wasn't that I didn't believe that there *were* people out there that existed that could see more than the normal human, but how would I know who to trust and who not to trust? All I could think of was how so many of them were just people that could sell something that wasn't even real to their customers.

I felt like the only person I could trust to understand this situation and the impact it carried was myself. Not that I didn't think Elly would understand, but the sensations, the experiences, the *nightmares* – all of those belonged to me. It was like the famous quote by Renés Descartes, "I think, therefore I am." While I wanted it to be as easy as the horror movies made it seem, everyone always having an experienced professional practically on speed dial for these kinds of situations was on the same level of some mystery movies, where someone just "happens" to find the key to solving a thousand-year-old mystery after thousands of others had tried before them.

A ping from my phone pulled my eyes out of their glazed state towards the glowing screen. It was a message from Elly, saying she was going to be at the house in thirty minutes, whether I was ready or not. It might

seem presumptuous, but Elly and I had always had an open-door policy
– literally. She could come and go as she pleased and vice versa, unless we
said we had something specific going on.

Elly arrived in twenty minutes, rather than thirty, carrying an armful
of clothes and makeup. "Are you planning to stay for a while?" I asked
her jokingly.

She rolled her eyes at me. "*No*, but I couldn't figure out what vibe
I wanted to go with tonight, so I brought a few options. And if I *was*
staying for a while, you'd better suck it up, bitch," she cackled, clearly
high on caffeine.

I replied with a roll of my own eyes as I helped her inside. I grabbed
the large makeup box while she fought the strap of her camera bag from
falling off her shoulder with one hand and clutched a mound of clothes
in the other. When we finally made it inside, she set everything down on
the new couch, and I placed the makeup box on the floor. She turned,
taking in the new décor, furniture, and floors.

"This is a completely different house, Ev," she breathed.

"Come look at the kitchen – I guarantee you'll cream your pants."

We both giggled, making our way over to the new kitchen. The fear
still lurked in the back of my mind, but I didn't want to spoil this mood,
not yet. I wanted a little more time to feel like I was normal, like the
world was normal. To pretend to go back to a time when I believed in
the supernatural but only recognized it from afar. So, instead of diving
into the danger that lurked in the shadows, I gave a tour of the renewed
home.

Elly gushed over the kitchen, squealing in excitement over the tiles,
counterspace, and appliances. She commented on the wallpaper and
paint in each room, claiming she was going to go home and demand
that Tyler update their walls. When we reached the bedroom, she went

straight towards the bathroom, practically jumping up and down at how perfect it all was.

I smiled and nodded, happy to see my friend in my house finally. While she had been there before renovations, it was different having her there now that the renovations were done. But even though I tried focusing on the positives, the excitement of my friend being there, anxiety pinched my nerves. I couldn't escape the feeling, the constant fear that I was rolling towards an inevitable end, facing a wall of death that no one would believe was anything other than me giving up on life.

A sudden thought occurred, snapping me out of the cycle of thoughts I'd been drowning in all morning. What if by bringing Elly here, she became the next target? Could Daemon have more than one target? What made him choose the victims? Did they have to live in the house, or did they just have to pique his interest? Did someone have to sleep in the house?

"Elly, I have to talk to you about something, *right now*," I snapped, cutting off her current excited chatter about the bathroom.

She blinked at me, concern flashing across her features. "Ev, what's wrong?" To her, it likely looked like I had made a complete one-eighty on my mood, but I couldn't stop the fear now pulsing through my veins for her safety.

"Let's go outside," I said, rushing her towards the hallway and down the stairs. She followed confusedly as I quickly snatched the box of proof I had hidden under the bed. We made it outside onto the porch, and while it made me feel slightly better, I couldn't help but wonder how far the reach went.

I sat on the steps, fingers trembling against the wood of the box. I felt crazy, especially now that I was outside, in broad daylight, about to tell my best friend that the house was being haunted by a demon. That *I* might die soon because of it.

Elly snapped her fingers in front of my face. "Ev, talk to me. What's going on?"

"Elly, I know you never judge me, and you never think of me as crazy, but this time might be different," I rushed out. She started to protest, but I cut her off, forcing the words to come out. Each syllable felt like it was snagging in my throat. "No, listen. You were right about the house being the problem with my nightmares. But it's more than that. The dreams I had while I was staying with you – they weren't just *dreams*, Elly. It sounds fucking *insane*, but I promise you I'm not making this up.

"The first night, I was residing in someone's body, and it felt more like I was watching the situation occur." Elly stared at me, eyes wide and confused. "But I remember it vividly. I felt everything. The girl, she hung herself with a blue scarf." I choked, a war in my body raging. I didn't want to keep going, but I knew I had to. "The-the second night. I still recognized that the girl was not me, but I felt like it was our body, not the way I had the first night. It was more intimate, somehow." My breathing shook. "We walked to the attic and took off a pearl necklace and then jumped. We landed on the fence," I whispered.

Elly's face was paling rapidly, hand halfway raised to her mouth. "Then, the last dream, I *was* the girl. There was no realization of it being someone else. I was the one that took the knife from the drawer. *I* was the one walking to the bathroom and getting in the tub. *I* was the one..." My words cut off, unable to say the rest. Elly knew.

"I just assumed they were dreams. I mean why would I think anything different?" I ran a hand through my hair, tugging on the strands. "Then I found this box. It was when the guy was putting security in the house, and this was in the attic," I whispered. Elly's gaze dipped to the box. All excitement and happiness gone from her face, only trepidation and fear remaining. A tear slipped down my cheek.

"In each of the dreams, the women were fighting against their deaths. I didn't think much of it in the first one due to the disconnect, but I felt it in the second, and *heard* it in the third. A voice. Commanding me to do...to do those *things*." Tears were now pouring, and my hands shook violently as I wiped the tears away.

"Anyways, um. The box." Slowly, I opened the lid, heart thundering in my chest, forcing myself to look at the contents, to prove it was all real one more time. Elly flinched, a single tear streaking down her cheek from her bright blue eyes. "I don't remember if I mentioned the fedora or not. But *he* was wearing it in the first dream, Elly. He's real. These women are *real. He did this to them*," I hissed angrily.

"Their names were Elaine, Jayda, and Suzanne. I found an article last night." I wiped at my face angrily. "And now he's latched onto me. I don't know what to do," I whispered.

Elly grabbed the box and set it aside, pulling me in for a tight hug. I cried, wanting to fight but not knowing how. Feeling powerless. Hopeless. It was like my past was coming back to haunt me, to make me do what I didn't finish before. "Ev, I don't give a shit what it takes," Elly said over my shoulder as she rubbed my back, "we *are* going to figure this out. I'm not going to let this fucker take my twin flame."

I nodded, wanting to believe it was possible. I pulled back some to look Elly in the eyes. "That's not all I'm worried about. I didn't think of it until you were here, but now I'm terrified. I don't know what makes him claim a victim. What if you get claimed now, too? Now that you've been in the house?" I rushed out, more tears flowing. If she died, it would be all my fault.

"No, no, Ev. Listen to me. I've been here before, remember? And I haven't been affected at all. I visited when you first moved in. If all it took was stepping in the house, then I think a lot more people would be dead by now. Don't you dare worry about me," Elly said with utter confidence, pulling me back into the hug forcefully, as though she needed it as much as I did.

Unsurprisingly, she didn't question my story. Even before I finished, she had been looking at me with concern rather than disbelief. For me, that meant more than anything in the world in this moment. It made me feel like I wasn't just losing my mind, like I wasn't alone in this fight. While Elly had always been this way, this situation was far above anything either of us had experienced. It probably helped that she had believed the house was part of the problem in the first place, but it was more than that. It was her ultimate trust in me, in my mind, even though there were a million and one reasons why she could just label me as certifiably insane and send me away.

"So, here's what we are going to do. We're going to spend the day researching and trying to find a solution to this problem – maybe we'll get lucky and find some real advice. And we will keep researching until we find an answer," Elly said. I could tell she was forcing confidence into her voice, both of us drowning in this sea of unknowns. And, to my immense relief, she failed to bring up how I had not only orgasmed with this demon, but practically handed myself over to him.

"Okay," I agreed. "But we're still going to the haunted house. I don't care if the world is burning around me, I'm going to take the happiness where I can get it," I sniffled, wondering silently if this would be my last year celebrating my favorite holiday.

Elly looked at me hesitantly but nodded. "Okay, if that's really what you want, we can still go. If you change your mind later, that's fine, too."

Her arms unwound from my shoulders, sending chills skittering over me. I blew out a breath, determined to at the very least try until my very last breath to fight something I couldn't see or feel outside of my nightmares.

CHAPTER 21

I wasn't sure what Elly hoped to find on the internet about how to resist mind control from a demon, but she searched and clicked through what seemed to be hundreds of articles and websites. She shook her head and rolled her eyes at most of what she saw, and I couldn't help it when my eyes glazed over as she searched.

"I'm no expert, and I don't honestly know how to tell the difference between what is real and what is just some made up bullshit, but a few things seem to stand out. There's the typical house cleansing, through multiple different religious sources. We could use some sage if you think that might help. But as far as the mind? Most of what I found online was some 'repent and shun the devil, look to God' stuff." A laugh burst from my chest, cutting her off.

It wasn't that I judged people for having their own beliefs, or even that I didn't have beliefs of my own. However, I did find it funny that the only hope for salvation in some people's eyes was blindly screaming out for help to something they couldn't see, rather than standing up and doing it for themselves.

"I know, I know," Elly said. "I started focusing on like, shielding the mind – and some say to wear certain stones, which I'm not opposed to trying, and others say that mindful activities such as meditation, Thai Chi and yoga are all some things that can help solidify the boundaries of the mind."

"Well, I picked up meditation again the other day, but I can't do that 24/7, and I'm not certain how that would allow me to prevent a sudden mental attack," I said, twisting my ring while gnawing on my lip. "Like, sure, maybe it would help if I was already meditating and he tried to force me to do that, but I don't see it working otherwise. It's moments like these that I wish life was like the movies – poof, someone is at your door to help." I laughed, but the sound was dry and void of any real humor.

"That would be nice right about now," Elly agreed. She rubbed her eyes, weariness setting in. She'd been staring at a screen of rolling words for a couple hours now, which would hurt anyone's eyes. I shut the laptop in front of her, and as she began to protest, I cut her off.

"No, Elly. You've looked through a ridiculous number of sites and articles and you need a break. I'm here, I'm not dying right at this moment, so let's just spend a little time enjoying the day, okay?" We still had more than enough time before Purgatory House, but I didn't want to keep looking at information that might or might not be valid. How could someone tell the difference between real and fake? Did it come down to true belief or did it come down to a science?

I dragged Elly with me to a box of Halloween decorations I had in one of the few boxes I had brought along with me into the house. Some decorations were homemade, and others were the type of decoration that would have had to be made by someone much more talented than I. I played some music, grabbing Elly's hands and dragging her away from her bad mood and into a good one.

My old therapist would confidently tell me I was 'avoidance coping.' Not a healthy way to handle problems, but when things were too much, too intense, too hard, it was all I could do to hold myself together. Move on and hope the problem didn't throw itself back in my face.

So, fully accepting the fact that I was avoiding the elephant in the room – or house, in this case – Elly and I decorated and sang along to songs. We hung lights and pictures, placed lounging skeletons against the porch, and decorated the surfaces with potion brews and creepy dolls. We used the old sheets that had come from the attic to create disturbing shapes that may or may not have been covered in some of the fake blood we had purchased the other day.

After a few hours, the house was properly ready for Halloween season, and I couldn't help but feel a sense of pride at the new house, new renovations, and all in perfect time for decorations. Halloween was a little less than two weeks away now, falling on a Thursday this year. While I didn't imagine there would be anyone coming trick or treating down my long driveway, I could still enjoy the night with some drinks and horror movies. As we wrapped up, I helped her choose her outfit, finally deciding on something hot and confident, rather than the cute, innocent look she usually pulled off so well.

I myself wore a pair of black skinny jeans, black boots, a dark graphic cropped tee with a cozy leather jacket over the top. We threw on makeup, going for dark and bold, something uncommon for the both of us. We both preferred simplicity – which most of the time did *not* include gobs of makeup. I twisted my long dark hair into a braid, and she let her soft red curls flow freely. After a final few looks in the mirror, we grabbed our things and stepped out to the car, me arming the house and locking the doors behind us.

On the drive there, we focused on nothing but the music and the road flowing under us. I knew we both had the thought in our minds of what could happen if we didn't find a solution, but what neither of us wanted to mention was that it would be nearly impossible to truly know a specific way to fight this thing. Not unless we found someone who had already been through it. And the only people I knew that had been through it...well, they hadn't survived to tell their stories.

We arrived at the Purgatory House; darkness having descended an hour ago. The lights and smoke filtered through the line of people waiting their turn to enter the place between life and death. We purchased tickets, waiting in a line about a mile long – but we knew every minute was worth it. We weren't sure what the inside would look like this year, or what the actors had been hired to do. But Elly and I had been going to this for several years now, and each time was a rush.

We heard distant screams and shrieks, all coming from inside the giant building before us. It was, quite literally, a mansion. Tall, dark spires twisted from the roof, the building made of grey brick and made to look as terrifying as possible. Vines had grown up the sides, and untamed gardens wove throughout the yard. Every part of this place was artfully curated to look abandoned, yet full of life. I wasn't sure what the owners of the property did in the off seasons, but I imagined a large chunk of it had to be dedicated to revamping the inside to make it different each year.

We edged closer towards the massive double doors, watching them open and close with each set of guests. Tall, cloaked figures stood at each side, each carrying what appeared to be a scythe, gesturing the customers in as though welcoming them into the arms of Death herself. I found it ironic, really, that I was going into a haunted house meant to create the sense of the journey between life and death when death loomed so close to me in real life. I shoved those thoughts forcefully away, packing them into a tight little box that I could open after tonight. Tonight was about enjoying life.

Finally, we made it to the doors, the cloaked guards watching us eerily, no eyes to be seen beneath the hoods. They grabbed the handles to the doors and pulled as one, both in perfect synchronicity. A wall of smoke poured out, blinding us as we made tentative steps inside the mansion, seeing nothing but smoke and darkness. As we made our way further, a single flickering bulb swung back and forth from a chain, a haunting melody twisting around us.

Elly and I hooked our hands together, peering anxiously around, waiting for a jump scare. The best part about this place was that the jump scares were entirely unpredictable. Tension wound its way around each fiber of each muscle as we passed beneath the dull bulb, the melody twisting its way into our ears. Wood creaked around us, sending our eyes swinging back and forth, trying to see through the mist by the dim light of the flickering bulb.

We continued on, both of us seemingly holding our breath, squeezing each other's hands in white-knuckled grips. The wood continued creaking around us, the creepy music still lacing the air, but the faint sound of chains dragging could now be heard. Low, continuous groaning caused the hair on my arms to rise up – it was a sound of pain and loneliness. Chains clinked nearer and nearer to us, as though the creature that was bound by them was mere feet away. But the only source of light was the flickering bulb, now too far behind us to make a difference.

Suddenly, a blinding fluorescent bulb flashed on, highlighting the emaciated figure in front of us. Chains hung from his hands and ankles, and his head was tilted at an awkward angle. I wasn't sure how they used makeup to create that look, but it was nothing less than horrifying. A hammer dangled from his hand, clothes torn and bloody. He stepped closer and closer, each one stilted, as though his legs weren't functioning right. His jaw was open and twisted to the side, a deranged look in his eyes. He raised the hand with the hammer, as though to swing it at us, a guttural groan coming from his throat.

It was so utterly realistic that Elly and I both screamed and darted away, trying to give him a wide berth as we passed him in the entry. Purgatory House was no joke when it came to their actors. The moment we were past him, the fluorescent light clicked off, the chains halting their noises. Darkness flooded around once again, the scent of the fog tickling our noses.

Within a few more blind steps, a motion sensor light flashed on as we reached a bright blue door. It creaked open slowly, beckoning us forwards. Elly and I were both silent, nearly holding our breaths as we stepped over the threshold. As we passed through, an eerie sight lay ahead of us. Barely illuminated by blue lights against the ceiling was a sea of bodies, swaying slowly, the mist curling around the legs and arms as though sucking the life out of the standing corpses.

There was no direct path through the throng of bodies, so Elly and I gripped each other's hands tightly, grinned at each other in both fear and excitement and made our way forwards. When we stepped into the field of people, those we passed seem to gravitate towards us, limbs reaching out weakly and sighs of longing slipping past their lips. Chills raked down my spine at their dead stares. There were so many bodies that as Elly and I trudged through, we couldn't prevent bumping into a few of them.

This wasn't a jump scare type of fear, this was simply creepy and psychologically terrifying. Every time I brushed against one of the lost souls around me, I shuddered, feeling as though I truly was walking through a field of the dead. Finally, we made it to the front, seeing a staircase leading upwards, spiraling higher into unknown territory. Elly and I made our way up the steps, both of us wound tight in anticipation for what was to come.

The top of the stairs came into view, a red door blocking the room beyond. The same as the previous door, it creaked open, inviting us forward. We entered the room, and suddenly everything was flooded in blood red lights, alarms blaring. My heart shot up to my throat and I screamed, hearing Elly cry out next to me. Three figures emerged from the opposite end of the room, carrying whips and menacing grins.

"You're not supposed to be here," the first one said.

"The living aren't allowed," the second followed.

"We should *cut you open and eat your hearts*!" Screeched the third. We both screamed again, backing away from them, looking for an exit. The only way was forward, as the door behind us had shut.

"Sister, I'm quite full from the trespassers before."

"Perhaps they should meet the other one instead."

The third one cackled, cracking her whip against the floor. "Then continue to your demise, and we shall see your return when you are dead."

The three sisters circled us before parting to let us through, whips cracking against the floor, their laughter rising around us, setting all my senses on high alert. When we were sure the coast was clear, we sprinted the last few steps to the next door, a poisonous green, the wood looking as though it had been burned through by acid. The laughter grew behind us as we continued forward, the door in front of us opening as the women behind us urged us on, leather tips snapping against the floor with each flick of their wrists.

The alarms stopped and the lights flashed off as soon as our toes dipped past the threshold. The door slammed shut behind us, loud in the sudden silence. Sickly green lights came on, one by one down the room, highlighting the horrors within. Faces, melted like wax, skin dripping and revealing muscle and bone beneath, turned towards us.

"The pit," someone whispered.

"Throw them in the pit," another said, voices sliding through the air like smoke.

More voices rose in agreement, the sound becoming louder, a cacophony of hissed words promising our doom. The melted creatures shuffled towards us, pointing as they whispered the words. There was no way to see between the line of reality and illusion at this point, the worlds blurring together and sucking me down into this fantastical horror world. Fog seeped up from the floor from a grate, the green lights making it look like poisonous smoke. The grate was then thrown open, hands nudging us towards the hole.

Some logical part of me knew there wouldn't be anything dangerous about this hole, but the other part of me was shaking in fear, heart ready to burst from my chest. Fingers poked, not hard or forceful, but demanding all the same. We neared the hole, and I saw it appeared to be a metal slide, but beyond that it was hard to tell from the smoke. Elly and I weren't going to both fit side by side, and neither of us seemed inclined to go first.

"I'll go," I said to her, the adrenaline pumping through my veins, the fear melding with excitement. I dropped down, sliding into the hole, a screech crawling up my throat at not knowing what to expect next. Within seconds, I landed on my ass with a soft umph, a landing cushion beneath me. I lurched to my feet, trying to get my bearings in the dark room while also getting out of Elly's way. As I stumbled in the blackness,

I bumped into a body. A scream wormed its way up my throat, but before it could escape, a leather gloved hand clamped around my mouth and nose.

Fear laced through me, real fear – not the same as before. I couldn't breathe and my lungs were screaming for air. I hadn't been ready for someone to cut off my breath so suddenly. Instinct took over. I bucked in the person's arms, struggling to free myself. I slammed my boot down where I thought their foot should be, the sole of my shoe coming in contact with something, a grunt coming from my captor. They jerked me backwards, my back hitting a large chest. Suddenly, something cold and sharp rested against my jugular.

This wasn't a part of the haunted house. This was more than that. My lungs were screaming, chest spasming in an effort to pull in oxygen that wasn't available. Blood pulsed in my ears; stars danced in my eyes. I felt lips brush against the shell of my ear. "I'm going to let you breathe, but you aren't allowed to scream. If your friend hears you, you won't be the only one getting hurt tonight." I knew that voice, and all I could do was nod, my head feeling light and my heart heavy. With the fears of what resided in the house, I'd nearly forgotten the other horrors in my life. Luke.

He released my nose but kept his hand over my mouth, and I took in as much air as I could, as quietly as I could. I heard Elly's cry as she slipped down the slide, heard her soft thump as she landed on the mat. "Ev?" She whispered.

I felt tears gather in my eyes, wishing more than anything that I could say something, ask her what to do. But I stayed silent, keeping my breaths as soft as possible. Elly couldn't help me now. I heard her steps moving further away as she whispered my name, searching for the person that she had already passed. Another door lay ahead, slowly opening for her, and with another glance around, looking for me, she went through. At the sound of the door slamming shut, I flinched, tears squeezed from my eyes.

Luke pulled me backwards, through a curtain and into what was presumably the actors' hallway. Dim lights lined the floor, providing enough light to walk with but keeping enough light out to prevent ruining the atmosphere of the world beyond the curtained wall. With the blade still pressed to my neck, I closed my eyes to think. Luke had the advantage – he had the physical advantage even without the knife. But my hands weren't restrained, and it was dark enough that I might be able to get away with moving them. If I could get the knife away from my neck, I might be able to twist around and try to go for the weak spots.

"This was almost too easy, Evalyn," Luke whispered in my ear, the smell of alcohol on his breath. Another advantage for me, depending on how much he'd drank. He caressed my neck with the edge of the blade, taunting me. "I really expected a bit more...something." He chucked a little. My hands slowly slid up, and I kept them as close to my body as I could without making noise. "More fight, I think," he continued. "You seemed so feisty, so fiery. I thought you'd fight harder." His words snaked across my skin, making my stomach lurch.

My fingers were nearly high enough, and I itched to move them faster to just get it over with. But I reminded myself that patience was key. I had to choose the right moment. Suddenly, I let my body sag against his, creating just enough space between the knife and my throat for my fingers to slip through. I shoved as hard as I could, pushing the blade away from me. He hissed in fury, but the alcohol seemed to be on my side.

I twisted, fighting the hand against my mouth as I moved, trying to evade the knife but get in a position where I could hurt him. Just as I got a knee in place to knock him in the balls, his hand holding the blade slipped under my jacket and sliced across my right collarbone. I screamed, a new rush of adrenaline and fear spiking through me. I wasn't going to die, not like this. I slammed my knee up as hard as I could.

"Fucking *bitch*," he roared. No more being quiet, I supposed. He wore a mask, but his blond hair was still visible. He relaxed his hold enough for me to lurch back, and as he cupped his bruised dick, I threw my knuckles against his windpipe. *Your turn to be silent, asshole,* I thought. The sound of his gasping sent a roil of satisfaction through me, but I knew I didn't have time to waste. I lurched away, back through the curtain, sprinting past someone who had just made it down the slide themselves. They screamed, but I kept running. The black door opened, and I sprinted through without hesitation.

"Elly!" I screamed, hoping she wasn't too far off. I barely saw the room around me, the inky water in the middle with floating corpses. The bodies chained to the wall passed in a blur as I kept running, looking for the exit. "Elly!" I cried again, hoping she was close and safe. Hoping that Luke hadn't magically found her.

This appeared to be the final room, and screams were echoing, people being chased as actors were tortured. Finally, I found the exit door, leading outside to the starry night. A small body slammed against mine, and a glint of red hair was all I needed to see before I broke down into sobs. "We have to go, Elly. Right now," I said, tugging her along the path that led to the parking lot. She threw questions at me, but I just kept pulling her along until I reached the car. We climbed inside and I locked the doors, looking around at the parking lot, making sure Luke wasn't in sight.

I started the car, peeling out, tears flowing freely from my eyes. As we left the parking lot jam packed with vehicles, I finally thought to look for the SUV and get the license plate, but there was no SUV – at least not one that triggered a memory. Instead, I saw a sports car, strikingly like the one Luke had driven the first night we met.

CHAPTER 22

A s I drove, Elly kept asking me questions, but her words were barely heard as I fell into a shocked state. All I could think was *drive*, because I didn't have the capacity to process all of the fucked-up puzzle pieces that were my current state of existence.

"Ev, you have to talk to me – what *happened*?" She asked.

"Elly, just...just stop. I can't fucking think right now. I can't-" I gasped, choking on the sobs wanting to escape. If I started talking right now, I wouldn't be able to hold it together. I'd lose it, probably dive straight down into a panic attack.

Elly's teeth snapped together, her struggle to remain quiet saturating the small space with tension. For the remaining car ride, she stayed silent, tapping her fingers against her faux red leather pants or tugging at her cream sweater. By the time we pulled into my driveway, the tightness in my chest had barely loosened, my muscles aching from how tense I was and my heart still pounding rapidly in my chest.

My fingers were numb from how hard I'd been gripping the wheel. I blew out a breath. "He was there," was all I got out. I swallowed the sobs trying to break through and forced myself to breathe through my nose and out through my mouth.

Elly blanched in the seat beside me. "Daemon? I thought he only appeared while you're sleeping. He can come out now?"

"No...Elly. Not Daemon," I said. I struggled to keep my breathing steady, my chest convulsing as I tried to keep from hyperventilating. Nothing in my life made sense right now. I felt like I was freefalling just the same as I had been when I was eleven. There was no ground beneath my feet, no edge to cling to.

"*Luke*?" She hissed. All I could do was nod. Robotically, I stepped out of the car, making my way inside the house. The world was grey around me, color sapped from everything as I receded into myself. I almost died. Again.

Elly followed me, seeming to understand that getting me to talk right now wasn't the best idea. I shut off the alarm, making my way to my room and stripping the leather jacket from my shoulders. As my arms moved to pull out of the sleeves, I suddenly remembered the wound on my collarbone. The pain throbbed through my shoulder, and my shirt was wet with blood.

Elly gasped, apparently noticing my wound. "What the fuck happened in there?" She said as she tugged me to the bathroom, turning the water on and grabbing a washcloth from the towel rack. I peeled off my shirt, flinching at the pain. Now that I was aware of it, the intensity had grown exponentially. Shivers began wracking through me even though I wasn't cold – the shock was wearing off.

I took a steadying breath as Elly turned to dab at the wound, glancing down. The bleeding had slowed to nearly a stop on the near thirty-minute drive, but the movement seemed to be preventing it from fully stopping. It was about four inches long, the slice clean and deep. Deep enough that if it had been a half an inch higher, my collarbone would be visible. I wasn't sure I'd be able to handle that.

I hissed when Elly placed the warm rag against my flesh, gently wiping away the drying blood and dabbing at the wound. "Ev, we should go the hospital – I think you need stitches." Her voice was hesitant and quiet.

"*No*, Elly. You know I won't do that. I'll handle it." I gently grabbed the rag from her hand, applying pressure to my collarbone. It stung like a bitch, but I needed it clean before I bandaged it. I grabbed some isopropyl alcohol from under the sink that I'd thrown in there after coming back home. I grit my teeth in preparation for the pain, soaking a new rag that Elly had outstretched in her hand with the alcohol. "*Fuck*," I hissed as I pressed it against my open flesh, handing the old rag back to Elly.

After cleaning it and patting the skin dry, I grabbed the first aid kit I'd had with me for as long as I could remember. Well, for as long as I'd known I would never go into another hospital. I grabbed the tape strips and pulled the skin together, quickly bandaging it and then covering it with gauze. Elly stood and watched the whole time, tears gathering in her eyes.

"Can you at least tell me what happened?" She asked.

I swallowed. "After the slide, he grabbed me. I couldn't breathe be-cause he had-" I choked, remembering his grip on my face, keeping me from breathing. "He covered my face. He had a knife. He said that if I said anything...I wouldn't be the only one hurting. Then he pulled me back into the actors' area." I felt wetness on my cheek and realized I was crying. Quickly wiping the tears I said, "I think he was drunk, and it made it easier for me to get away, but he sliced me in the process."

"We need to call the police." There was no question in Elly's voice on the matter.

"And say what? I don't even know his last name. They'll make me go to the hospital, and they may just not even believe me."

"Why the hell wouldn't they believe you? You have a fucking *knife* wound for fucks' sake, Ev!" Elly's voice had risen to a shout, her frustration at my stubbornness blazing in her eyes.

My own anger rose up to tangle with hers. "You know damn well why I won't fucking do it, *Elleanor*. He can't do shit while I'm here, so it doesn't fucking matter anyways." Each word that left my lips felt like something I would regret later, but I was too angry and terrified to care right now.

"*Fine*," she hissed. Her eyes were narrowed at me, her red hair a swirl of flames floating around her, making her the perfect embodiment of fury. "Don't call them. You're Evalyn, the master of avoiding her problems, after all. But one of these days you're going to have to stop letting your past control you like this. You're in *fucking* danger, in case you hadn't noticed, Evalyn. Not only do you have some mind-fucking monster waiting to make you fucking *kill yourself*, but you also have a psycho stalker walking around trying to kill you. I love you, so fucking much, but you're in over your fucking head." Her hand shook as she pointed a finger in my face. "I have been here for everything. I haven't questioned any of your choices and I've let you do things your way. But tonight showed me that things aren't 'fine' with the way you've been handling them. But clearly, you don't want my help, so I'll just see myself out. Call me when you're ready to face this shit like an adult." With the last words, she tossed the bloody rag into the sink and stormed out, tears glistening in her eyes.

Moments later, I heard the front door slam shut. I knew she was right in most of what she said. But just as I had sworn to never go to a hospital again, I had sworn to stay as far from the police as I could. Tears poured freely down my cheeks, and I felt more alone than I had in a long time. A keening wail began to slip past my lips, growing in volume and intensity. I sank to the floor of the bathroom, a hand over my mouth to muffle the cries even though no one was there to hear me. I didn't know what to do. I understood why Elly was upset, but that didn't make her act of leaving me any less painful.

I tilted my head back, slamming it against the tile wall, an old ache rising in me. The throb in my head soothed the agony of loneliness, so I did it again. And again. Screaming sobs poured from my lips, and I knew I was spiraling. Too many emotions, too many things out of my control. I threw my fist against my thigh, hating myself for everything that I'd done to lead to this point.

Again and again, I hit myself, until my thighs were red and aching. My throat ached from screaming, my nose dripping snot and saliva hanging from my lips. My shoulder was screaming, and I felt wetness there once more. There wasn't enough oxygen; I couldn't breathe. My breath came faster and faster, my head light as I clutched my chest, trying to hold the pieces together while simultaneously fighting the tightness wrapping around my ribs.

I laid myself down on the floor, curling into a ball of tears and agony. I couldn't bring myself back up from this, I was too far gone. I didn't know how to slow my breathing or to stop the tears, and I hated myself even more for it. As I stared through the door of the bathroom into my room, I watched the lamp flick on. The sight startled me, distracting me from the pain on the inside. Suddenly, I felt less alone. I blinked, the sounds coming from my lips stuttering to a halt. My breathing came down to a normal pace, and my sobs turned into sniffles.

I wiped at my eyes, feeling disgusted by all the different liquids covering my face. I sat up and reached for some tissues, keeping my eyes on the lamp, taking comfort in its light. I cleaned my face as best as I could and made my way into the room, snapping the rest of the lights off as I went. I reached my bed, laying down on my side, still facing the lamp. I gently tapped one of the red apples, making it sway on the branch.

"Thank you for showing me I'm not alone," I whispered to whatever spirit had heard my pain and dragged me from the hole I was drowning in. I left the lamp on, simply letting the light wash over me and ground me. The pain was still there, and I couldn't help but feel like an idiot for being thankful for a ghost being friendly to me, but at least it was something. I hugged a pillow to my chest as I stared, hoping that things would turn out okay soon. I wasn't sure how much more of this I could take. At that wish, my eyes drifted shut and I fell into the waiting arms of sleep.

CHAPTER 23

***

I sat up in bed, glancing around. Horror coiled in my chest as I realized this was my childhood bedroom. The purple sheets, the quilt at the end of my bed that I had dubbed my "horsey blanket," the small, jeweled box that held nothing that would mean anything to anyone except for me. Small, colorful stuffed animals sat neatly in a box across the room, beneath the hanging clothes that had no closet. The window to my left blazed with sunlight, burning my eyes.

I slid out of bed, knowing I was in my too small, twelve-year-old body. My frame shook in my purple pajamas as I made my way out of the bedroom. As I passed the window of the cluttered dining room towards the living room, I realized it was now early evening, and no longer morning. I was still in my pajamas, but my hair was wet from a shower.

I knew what was coming, and I only shook harder as my steps stilled in the middle of the dining room, facing the wall that had a large hole in it from a fist I was all too familiar with. I heard the door slam open, and nausea turned in my gut. I didn't know what I'd done, but I'd done something wrong. I could always tell by the way he would come in.

It took every ounce of energy I had to stay still and not sprint back to the bedroom. That wouldn't keep me safe, that would only make it worse. I heard him stop in the living room. "Evalyn, come here." His voice was level, but I knew that this wasn't going to lead to a pleasant conversation.

Still shaking, I made my feet move towards the living room. It was more cluttered and messier than the dining room had been, the same as always. There he stood. A tall, lean frame, thick grey hair, and a bushy beard. I could hardly look at him. My fear was acid on my insides, terror owning every breath.

"Yes?" My twelve-year-old self asked.

"I got a call today," he said. My heart thundered in my chest. What had I done this time? I couldn't think. I could never think while near him. Thoughts just flew in violent tornados around my skull, fearful of the wrong answer and horrified of the right one. "Do you want to tell me?" He asked, voice still low. But I could see the tension in his jaw, how it twitched with frustration.

"I don't know," I whispered, a tear falling down my cheek. I *wanted* to know. I wanted to know the right answer so badly, because maybe it would save me this time. Maybe the right answer would mean my punishment wouldn't be as bad.

"You don't know?"

I shook my head, trying so hard to remember what it could have been. What had I done?

"You're lying, trying to get out of your punishment."

More tears fell. "No, I just really don't remember," I cried.

He lunged forward, grabbing the back of my neck painfully and shoving his face close to mine, his teeth gritted together. "You're *lying*," he said. Somehow, his voice was still level, but danger screamed through each syllable. He stepped back. "Don't move from that spot."

I felt frozen, each cell in my body turning into ice. His steps led away from me, towards the cluttered table in the dining room behind me. I didn't dare look backwards, scared of what would happen. Tears kept pouring, but I tried to keep quiet. Finally, he came back around, two tools in his hand.

"Do you remember when I told you about what happens to liars?" He asked. His lips were a thin line of anger, and I did my best not to flinch. "If you don't answer me honestly, confess to what you did, then I'll remind you."

I wanted to scream, to shout. I wanted to share my thoughts with him *so he could just see that I wasn't lying*. I tried turning off the fear so I could think, really think about why he would have gotten a call. A call from who? The school? The babysitter from the weekend? My mom? Someone else? Nothing stood out to me, the thoughts were racing too fast. "I really don't know, I promise," I sobbed. I knew what was coming, terror spiking through me. My father didn't make idle threats. I knew he believed I was lying, and I knew there was no way to show him that I wasn't. It was a losing game.

"Fine. I warned you." He reached for my face, prying my jaw open wider as sobs wracked my body. He reached a hand up with a pair of pliers, shoving them in my mouth, slamming them down on my wriggling tongue. The metal clicked harshly against my teeth, and all I could do was sob harder. I was nearly screaming.

Suddenly, the front door opened, and my mother appeared. She took in the scene before her and gasped. "Stop!" She screamed. She fumbled in her purse. "Matthew, stop it."

My father turned his head towards her. "She's lying to me, and I need to show her what happens to liars," he said.

"I said *stop*," my mother screeched, pulling out a gun. The pliers gripping my tongue clamped harder, causing me to squeal and lurch onto my toes. "You will *not* do this. This is too far, Matthew." Her chest was heaving, hands shaking around the handle of the gun. She stepped closer, now standing only feet away, adjacent to my father, pistol pointed to his head.

"She has to learn, Diane." He gritted his teeth, raising the second tool, a pair of pruning shears gripped in his hand.

Tears leaked from my mother's eyes. "Please, Matthew," she whispered.

Suddenly, he dropped both tools and lunged at my mother, grappling for the gun. I leapt out of the way as they tumbled right where we had been standing, my father straddling my mother. He ripped the gun from her fingers, slinging it away. "Were you going to kill me?" He asked.

"I'm sorry," was all she said as tears leaked from her eyes. Rage filled his eyes, and he wrapped his hands around her throat. She convulsed, face turning red instantly and trying to rip his hands away futilely. He lifted her up a few inches by her neck only to slam her back down, a dazed look entering her eyes.

I stood in the corner, sobbing, not knowing what to do. To me, my father was invincible. He held my life on a string. But he was killing my mother. I watched as her hands flopped around on the floor, no longer trying to pull his hands from her throat. Was she searching for something? Her chest continued to convulse, and she looked as though she wouldn't last another moment.

Then the scene changed. Suddenly, his hands flew from her neck to his own, red rivulets of blood pouring from his hands and down her arms as she gripped the tool in her clenched fist. The shears he had been planning to use to cut out my tongue were now lodged in his throat. He choked as my mother gasped large breaths of air, his pale blue eyes wide and grey beard turning crimson. He fell backwards, still clutching his neck, his efforts doing nothing to stop the inevitable.

I stared in shock as I watched, his death taking longer than what seemed possible. His blood soaked the carpet as he lay, dying, choking on his own blood. My legs crumpled beneath me, my world upside down. My mother sat in shock, staring at the lifeless form of my father. I couldn't understand why, but she, too, looked as though she had died along with him. While I watched her breathe, stare, and move – she was dead.

Her hand, covered in blood, reached into her purse numbly, grabbing her phone. My ears rang, not hearing her speak as she made a call. Minutes later, flashing lights poured through the windows of the house. I sat still, frozen in place, hiding in the corner against the ground. Nothing made sense. My father lying there without life, my mother being taken in handcuffs, a stranger approaching me with an odd look of pain in their eyes.

The only thing I registered was a single word, uttered from my mother's lips. "*Evalyn*," she screamed as she was pushed into the back of a police car. The world faded around me.

When color returned, I felt myself sitting numbly on a piece of black furniture, staring down at a black marble floor, barely lit by flickering yellow lights. I still wore my jeans and boots, by my chest was only covered by my bra. The cut, wrapped in the bandage, ached. I heard someone approach and watched as they knelt before me. Worried silver eyes gazed into mine, and warm hands reached up to cup my face.

"Evalyn," I heard in a whisper. Fingers caressed my cheeks, a hand moving to brush through my hair. I was tugged forward; my face pressed against a neck that smelled of lavender and mint. Whispered words floated past my ears, not quite making sense. One hand continued to run over my hair, the other falling to gently rub my back.

Slowly, I felt myself peeling away from that memory, the horrors that yearned to keep me there. Even more slowly, I realized where I was and who was soothing me. But in that moment, I couldn't bring myself to care if it was some cruel ploy to fuck my mind even more. Even with that thought, I knew I had to pull away. Even if it was comfort, it was coming from another nightmare. And that wasn't okay.

I pulled back slowly, peering into those bright silver eyes, black hair rumpled and messy. Worry and rage filled his eyes, but I wasn't sure for what. His hands slipped from my hair and back to rest on my arms. I ignored the feeling of loss that panged in my chest. If I could stay, resting in his arms for the rest of my life, I wouldn't complain. But that wasn't what he wanted, wasn't what he was there for. So, I built a fortress, brick by heavy brick, trying to hold in the well of emotions that even I couldn't understand.

"I'm so sorry," he whispered, thumbs rubbing my forearms gently.

I just shook my head, words sticking in my throat.

"Stay with me," he said. "Just...don't leave."

I shook my head again, pain stabbing my heart as I spoke. "I want to wake up," I whispered.

He dropped his head down in defeat, but not before I saw agony flash through his eyes. He nodded subtly, reaching to gently grab my hand and peering back up at me. "I understand. But don't give up. Please, *please* don't give up. Please," he whispered, the final plea seeming to be meant more for himself than me.

I nodded, not understanding why he would want me to *not* give up when his goal was to make me end it all anyways, but agreeing, nonetheless.

"If you go back to sleep after waking, I can make sure you sleep undisturbed. Do you want that?"

Doubt covered my features, again confused by his actions. But dreamless sleep was exactly what I craved, so I nodded. He squeezed my hand again before the world around me faded once more.

CHAPTER 24

***

I woke to a room coated in a soft yellow light, cast from the lamp beside my bed. My eyes were heavy, nose stuffy, and head pounding. I rubbed my face, tears still leaking slowly from my eyes. When I thought I couldn't feel any more exhausted than I was, something came to prove me wrong. My shoulder ached; my bra strap close enough to the cut on my collarbone that it pulled. The blood that had seeped through from earlier had dried, causing the gauze to stick and an itch to form. That's when I realized I hadn't even undressed before laying down.

I stripped out of my remaining clothes, dropping them to the floor carelessly. I couldn't even bring myself to pull on my favorite sleep shirt. Instead, I checked that the bandages were still secure and climbed beneath the covers. I lay on my back, chest feeling hollow and tight all at once. My best friend was pissed at me for reasons even I couldn't blame her for. My stalker had attacked me in one of my favorite places – would I be able to go back? And of course, when I slept, all that greeted me were my nightmares. It was as though someone had ripped up the very memories I'd tried so hard to shove down and stuffed them in my face. And then Daemon. Gentle, soft, caring. He'd wanted me to stay. He wanted me to not give up. In fact, he'd said as much before – he'd said that no matter what happened or what was done to me that I wasn't allowed to give up.

So many pieces just didn't seem to fit. Between Luke's obsession with me and Daemon's complexities, nothing made sense. Why was Luke stalking me? Was it simply the run in at the store that had been enough to garner his attention? Or, perhaps, the rejection afterwards – was that what had caused the start of all this? And for Daemon, I couldn't match what I knew with who I saw in my dreams. He told me to not give up, to keep going, yet murdered three other women. While he had started out as a complete asshole, something in him had changed.

It was almost like Daemon was showing his worst side at the start and was now revealing his softer side. But, again, it didn't add up. If he was trying to lead me to the grave, why would he try to tell me to never give up? I reminded myself that it could all be a mind game, something to convince me to relax, to let him in, to fall for his tricks even when I knew the inevitable.

My mind drifted to Elly, my best friend of over ten years. I'd opened up to her about everything – at least what I was capable of sharing in words. But there were some things that couldn't be shared, at least not completely. Memories that not only attacked thoughts, but reality as well. When I was younger, I had moments where I'd be lost entirely to my memories, all five senses tied to the young child that didn't exist anymore. Elly had known where I'd been, what I'd been through. She'd even been there to support me when I was struggling.

I wondered if tonight was her last straw. I knew all of her frustration came from worries and fears, but I didn't know what all I could do. I didn't know Luke's last name, let alone his address or phone number. I had a security system in place for when I was home. My injuries were mild enough to take care of at home, at least for me. I was hyperconscious and careful when I had an injury. And for Daemon? No police would help. What hospital would I go to if I started hearing voices that wouldn't just admit me into the psych ward?

Thinking of a psych ward made my stomach clench, guts turning violently. *No,* I thought to myself. I would never go back. Never. I pushed my hair out of my face, running my fingers through the tresses. I would text Elly tomorrow and try to fix things. It was these moments when I wished I could take my brain and plop it into someone else's body, just to show them exactly how I was feeling in that very moment.

I knew I wasn't going to change my mind – but that didn't mean I wasn't wrong, though. I rolled over, head pounding and eyes weary, knowing I wouldn't have an answer to any of my problems tonight. I let my eyes drift shut, shutting out the soft glow around me. As my mind slid into the darkness, I just hoped Daemon would keep his promise of holding my nightmares at bay.

When I woke the next morning, I was relieved to realize not only had I not had nightmares, but my dreams had been peaceful. I remembered soft, cool light touching my skin, beams of moonlight shining from above. Other than that, I couldn't really grasp anything. I just knew I had slept more peacefully than I should have after the night I'd had – previous nightmares included.

The images from my nightmare came back in full force, pounding around my skull and torturing me with the same memory over and over. It had been so long since I'd relived that day, so long since I had been back in my twelve-year-old body. Of course, I could never forget, but there were ways to let the thoughts come and go, ways to not get sucked into the vortex of emotions that came with those dreams.

My life seemed to be turning into one chaos after another, and while I knew things always seemed to right themselves, I wasn't certain how this series of issues was going to pan out. I knew I had to reach out to Elly, to mend that bridge. I'd lost too many people in my life – I refused to lose her, too.

Grabbing my phone, I made my way to the restroom to clean and redo my bandages. I peeled the wrap off, dried blood sticking to the gauze. After cleaning and reapplying fresh gauze, I blew out a breath and dialed Elly. I closed my eyes, waiting for the rejection, for the phone to go to voicemail or for her to answer and tell me to leave her alone. When the line picked up, I felt myself flinch.

"Ev, hi, I wanted to call you sooner, but I didn't know if you'd be awake and I'm so glad you called I'm so sorry I left like that I never should have done that and *fuck* I'm so, so sorry," Elly said, each word bumping and shoving into the next, making it hard to understand.

I blinked in shock. Of all the conversations I had prepared myself for, this wasn't one of them. "Elly, hi," I whispered, relief melting my stiff bones. I could hear her sniffling over the phone, clearly having been crying. "I'm sorry, too," I said. "I know you only said those things because you care and I'm sorry I'm a complicated friend – I don't mean to be," I choked out.

"I'm just so glad you called me. I know we've fought before, but this time was different. I was so worried that you would shut down and think I'd abandoned you. And I wasn't, fuck Ev, I promise I wasn't. I just got *so* frustrated because even though I know why you won't go to the police or the hospital, seeing you struggle and having absolutely *nothing* I can do to help *kills* me. I just wish I could fix all your problems. Like whoever this Luke dude is, I swear he's gonna end up dead if he tries anything again. And then with the supernatural shit? My brain just can't handle it. I don't know how you're even functioning at all right now." Elly's voice drifted off, her rambling a good indication of how stressed she was.

"Elly, as long as I have you, that makes the problems in my life seem smaller." I paused, swallowing tears. "Thank you for not giving up on me," I whispered.

"Never," she said firmly. And I believed her. "I can cancel my session today if you want. I can come over and we can just, I don't know, relax?"

Before she could get much further, I cut her off. "No, don't. Go to your shoot and get some editing done. I'm going to do more research and just try and take care of myself today. I'll be okay. Plus, I need to work on my own work. We'll hang out soon, I promise." As much as a day with her sounded nice, I knew that there were some things I needed to do today. I needed to pick myself up and start mending the areas I could. Sitting around and hiding from the stressful aspects of my life wasn't going to get anything done. And, as much as I loved Elly, half of my problems were all in my head, literally. I knew I needed to, at the very least, try to take care of that on my own.

I heard Elly sigh. "Okay, but I'm going to be messaging you all day. It'll make me feel better just knowing you're okay," she said. After trading goodbyes, we hung up and I began planning my day out.

I knew I needed to work on my headspace, and not just in preparation for the fight against potential forced suicide. It was more than that – I hadn't been so low in such a long time, and that thought scared me. While I'd had several ups and downs over the years, they hadn't been this bad in over a decade. To settle my mind again, I knew I needed to bring back certain habits I'd let slip over the past year.

I used to meditate, practice yoga, and write for myself each day. As time went on and life got better, I'd let the habits slip more and more. Today, I would do each of those things.

As I finished my mental checklist of the things I wanted to complete for the day, I began digging around for my old journal. There was something different in writing out the dark thoughts, feelings, and memories than in typing them. After locating it, I spent some time reading some old entries and writing new ones. I preferred doing this before meditation in order to be able to go into the meditation with a lighter heart.

After writing for nearly an hour, dumping my pain and agony onto the page, I stopped, wiping stray tears from my cheeks. I sighed, feeling better than when I had started. I glanced back at the page, reading a piece of what I'd written.

In my worst moments, my lips feel sealed, and my body feels leaden, and my heart feels heavy. My brain though, is like a sandstorm – chaotic, damaging. Each thought slices into another and opens old wounds and tears my mind to shreds. And in the eye of the storm, the one that causes this whirlwind of sand and glass, is a girl. She's angry at me for keeping her locked away, furious with me for trying to silence her, hide her from the world. She screams and screams in agony, fury, and resentment.

But on the outside, I'm calm, if not with a frown on my face. But the sandstorm grows with power and force with every second. It moves from my head to my chest, cutting my heart and tearing my lungs, making it hard to breathe. I feel her agony, I feel the knife-like pain in her throat from screaming so loud. I feel her rage, this bottomless chasm of hatred and bitterness. This scares me the most. She feels uncontrollable, and my hands shake trying to hold her back. She hates me, yet she is a part of me. I feel as though I am trying to push the two sides of the gaping chasm of hatred together with my weak hands alone.

It has been a long time since I released her from her dark prison, since she has fought her way to the surface and ran rampant among the people of the real world. But even when she does escape, the pain and anger never abate. It does nothing to set her free, except fuel her fire of hatred for me when I stuff her back in her dark corner of the untouched memories on dusty shelves in my mind. I try to forget her, but she refuses to be forgotten.

She may be stuffed in a dark corner of my mind, but she is always whispering in my ear, threatening her escape from the cage I put her in. Her pain alone is enough to tear apart the bars of her cage, her anger enough to break the iron.

One might think of her as a fiery creature, but I know better. She is water. She seeps in quietly, trickling through my veins, and once she knows she has a hold on me, she creates a hurricane of inescapable memories and brings her pain to life in me. She drowns me in her sorrows, chokes me with her hate. Her dark emotions are far from heat and fire, they are cold and dark and deadly. She finds joy in her chaos.

She screams her everlasting scream, and I feel it crawling up my own throat. But I bite it down. The world outside does not understand her and would not accept her. I am terrified of her, horrified at the thought of her taking complete control. The destruction she would bring, the loneliness she would incur. Her cold seeps through at these thoughts, reveling in my fear. She wants me to be alone, just as I have made her alone. But she is always there, hiding beneath the surface, the Screaming Girl.

There was more, but I knew I'd read enough. I knew this reflected exactly how I'd been feeling over the past week. And, although last night I had reverted to this other version of myself, I could still feel the endless well of pain and sorrow that sat inside me. I was quiet on the outside, but there was a hurricane of memories, agony, and anger raging inside me.

I breathed, accepting that my pain was there, but focusing on not letting it define me, the way I'd been taught. With that thought, I settled into my meditation. I felt my fears, my bottomless well of emotions bubbling up, but I focused on my breath – each exhale meant letting those pent-up feelings leave my body. With each inhale, I imagined new, clean energy entering me to replace all of the bad. I settled into my body, letting my muscles grow heavy, letting myself feel as though I was falling straight through the floor, down, down, down, until I was rooted into the soil.

With each breath I fell further and further, until I was met with the perfect nothingness that I had a renewed appreciation for. In this moment, I felt free and untouchable. It was like a membranous wall of energy had shaped itself around me, removing the pressure and emptiness from my chest, covering me in safety. I felt calm. Peaceful.

I floated like that for a while, not aware of the time, day, or anything having to do with the physical world. I was free but grounded, and that was all I knew. When I felt ready, I slowly returned to my body, bit by bit. As I opened my eyes and stretched my languid body, I glanced at the time. It was nearly eleven, meaning I'd been meditating for over an hour. My mind felt relaxed, almost sluggish, but not in a bad way. It was as though because I didn't feel stress right now, my head wasn't bothered to work faster.

I rose, going downstairs and making breakfast and a coffee, trying to keep my mind clean of worries and stressors. I kept reminding myself that being anxious and stressed about my problems wasn't going to make them easier to solve. Still, a trickle of fear slipped through the cracks, the question of when the attack might come whispering through my mind. Ignoring that line of thought, I moved on to yoga.

After finishing my exercise, I felt a wetness at my shoulder and realized I must have opened the cut during the workout. I shook my head. I'd let myself get so in the zone I'd forgotten about the cut entirely.

Marching back up the stairs, I went to the bathroom and tugged off my shirt, revealing the bloody gauze beneath. How I hadn't felt the cut while doing yoga, I wasn't sure. I pealed back the gauze, flinching at the trickle of blood. If Elly was here, she'd be pissed all over again. It looked like two of the strips of tape had come loose, so I tugged them off with a hiss and began the process of cleaning and replacing all the bandages.

As I cleaned, I thought about going to the police and telling them about Luke, but I couldn't stop going back to the fact I didn't have nearly enough information to offer to the police about this man. And it would mean breaking a promise to myself. I didn't have his last name and to be honest, I'd briefly wondered if Luke was even his real name. I didn't know where he lived or even what kind of car he drove. Aside from it being a sporty vehicle, I didn't know much. Now, I wished I'd stopped to get the license plate number from the car before I'd driven like a fury out of hell away from the haunted house. But I hadn't. All of these reasons were why Luke was currently an uncontrollable factor in my life.

And then there was Daemon. A complex puzzle with pieces that didn't fit right, parts jumbled and shaken together in a confusing spiral of dissonances. I wasn't sure anyone had ever been through what I was likely to experience soon and lived to talk about it. That fact alone made it harder to know the real way to keep the literal monster at bay, to keep the demon from forcing me to destroy myself.

However, after the events from the last twenty-four hours, I decided I would control what I could control – how I responded to the situation. As for facing Luke, I'd already installed a security system on the house. I should likely be carrying a weapon of some sort on me when I went out, such as pepper spray or a knife. A gun would be an option, as well, if it wasn't for the fact I would likely fuck up while trying to use it, or worse, have the demon use it against me.

I wasn't worried about the pepper spray as it was a non-lethal defense weapon. I also wasn't worried about the knife, seeing as I had plenty of knives downstairs in the kitchen, and even the cursed knife from Elizabeth. Thinking about the box that lay across the hall in the office room where I'd put it after telling Elly everything, I shuddered. Remembering my goal for the day, I paused to focus on my breathing, letting the fears related to those items go.

I felt my phone vibrate and glanced down, seeing a message from Elly.

> Honestly, that sounds amazing. And then we have the shoot next weekend!

My heart cracked a little, knowing Elly was willing to still do the shoot even with everything else that was actively stealing energy from our lives.

> That sounds great ☺ What day do you want to do it?

> Why don't we shoot for Wednesday? I should have most of my edits done by then.

We agreed on where to go and what time to meet, and with the plans set in place, I felt my heart lift a little higher. Elly was still there, still part of my life, and she wasn't gone. There were two routes of thinking – in the simplest terms – logic and emotion. I found myself constantly at war with myself, torn between the logical scenario and the emotional one my mind had driven me towards. Logically, I knew Elly's and my bond was too strong to be broken, no matter the situation. Emotionally, the feelings of abandonment and broken trust would well up, saying,

"Remember what happens when you get comfortable. Remember what happens when you believe you're safe with someone."

These thoughts came from years of trauma and pain, and it had always been a constant battle to fight against the protective instincts my mind tried to throw up. After the death of my father, things had been messy, to say the least. Between the immediate aftermath and bouncing between foster homes, there had been no stability, no sense of security, no sense of self-worth.

I kept seeing my mother's face as she was pushed into the police cruiser, kept hearing her scream my name as she disappeared behind the door of the car. I remembered the sound of her scream being muffled with the slam of the door, silence following. I saw the taillights as the car pulled away, the last familiar thing in my life disappearing over the hill.

Blinking, I pulled myself back into the present. It had been so long since I had relived those memories, so long since I had dreamt of them. I twisted the ring on my finger, another reminder of the long-lost past. Silver twisted together to look like a vine wrapped around my forefinger, a small green gem rested in the center. It was simple, but beautiful, and I would likely wear it until the day I died.

I sighed, combing my hair with my fingers. *Gross*, I thought. My hair was matted and dirty, knots catching my fingers. While I'd cleaned my wound more than once, the sweat from last night and today was more than enough to urge me into the shower. After stripping from my clothes, I twisted the handle to the far left, steam almost instantly filling the room. Stepping under the scalding water, I hissed, carefully keeping my bandaged wound from under the spray. I'd replace it again after the shower, but I wanted to avoid additional irritation right now.

I let the water run over me as I carefully cleaned myself, avoiding pulling on my cut but also enjoying the feeling of the scalding water beating against my skin rhythmically. When I was finished, I stepped out, noticing the screen on my phone lit up. Curious, I wrapped myself in a towel and dried my hands before grabbing the phone.

It was a camera notification, having picked up something. I bit my lip as I opened the app, hoping to find nothing but also hoping to find something so I could be done with this all and call the police. But, when I pulled up the camera, I saw nothing near the house, only something at the end of the driveway. The same SUV, once more. I was surprised the cameras had reached such a distance, but the worker that had installed the security had promised it should.

Before I could even move to dial 911, the SUV slipped onto the road and drove away. Frustration boiled through me. Saving the clip, I tossed my phone onto the counter and finished drying off and getting ready to settle in and read for the night. Maybe later I could pick up the license plate or at least some defining feature. But right now, my goal was to stay calm. Already, the moment of fear had dissipated, my worry slipping away and my mind drifting towards a night of reading.

CHAPTER 25

The remaining hours of my Saturday melted away with the pages of my book. Before I knew it, the final page was read. Shutting the book, I glanced at the time on my phone, unsurprised at the late hour. Still, I got up and checked the bandage once more before crawling beneath the covers and letting my eyes drift shut.

Sleep was peaceful that night. I wondered if it was Daemon, or if it was the mindfulness I had practiced throughout the day. I felt that the former was the answer, even as I hated to admit it. Once again, he felt like a puzzle that had missing pieces, and the ones that were there hadn't found their correct places yet. I couldn't help but want to figure him out, to feel the desire to dissect him and understand *why*.

Why did Daemon kill? And why hadn't I felt even a whisper of his voice in my head during my waking hours? And, if he knew that I was aware of what he'd done, why hadn't he done it already? It could be for the sense of suspense, but nothing felt correct. The more I thought about it, the more my head couldn't wrap around it. It felt like I didn't have the whole picture.

Sunday passed in a haze of yoga, meditation, and writing. Elly and I sent a few messages back and forth, the messages reminding me once again that I hadn't lost my friend. However, throughout the day I couldn't stop the whispers in the back of my mind. *Will he come to my dreams tonight? What should I expect?* Around and around the thoughts swirled, trying to break through my wall of calm I had built around myself.

Shame coated my insides the more I thought of Daemon. I wasn't supposed to think of him, but I continued to turn to pieces around in my head, trying to make them fit together. *He admitted to being the reason they died. What the fuck else do you need, Evalyn?* I chastised myself over and over, trying to beat the thoughts out of my head.

I didn't want to admit it to myself, but a part of me felt like I was trying to make the pieces not fit, because if I didn't, that would mean I had given my body and my pleasure to a true monster. The worst of it was that I had never felt such powerful pleasure as I had with him. These thoughts only added to the shame I felt, but I continued to practice breathing the negative feelings out as I pulled in the positive ones. I hadn't known anything when I had given myself over. Otherwise, I know I never would have.

However, when I fell asleep after drinking my tea, Daemon wasn't there waiting. I thought I felt his presence, but I wasn't sure. My dreams drifted without meaning, hollow and empty, neither peaceful nor chaotic. When I woke the next morning, I rubbed my chest, wondering why my chest ached the way it did. I refused to admit that it could be anything to do with Daemon. How could I even think that when I knew what he'd done?

Yet I still felt a phantom part of myself missing the battle of wills that was a constant in our conversations, his voice and even his smell. I continued to shove those thoughts and feelings down as Monday wore on. My wound still ached, but less than it had before. Things seemed too quiet. While I wasn't complaining, I felt like there was a ticking time bomb waiting to go off – this nothingness couldn't last forever.

It was sad, really, that two days of nothing happening felt suspicious. My days used to be much like this before I purchased the house. Perhaps even the first week of it. I thought back on the early days of me buying the house and moving in. I picked through my mind, wondering what I could have missed, or what I hadn't noticed, because I didn't know what I know now. I thought of the first dream, the first one I'd had. I remembered it was similar to the dreams I'd had every time I had moved, except that this time it was slightly different.

It started out identical, but the end was what had changed. I remember I had been tossed to the forest floor, and someone had sat on my back, pulled my hair, and whispered devilish words in my ear. Was that the first time Daemon had entered my nightmares? It didn't feel quite the same. I couldn't remember any other dreams where it had started in the middle of the action. But the more I wondered, the more I felt it had to have been him. I could almost hear the words again, whispering about being in *his* world. The only thing that was missing was my nickname.

It was another piece of information that I wasn't sure what to do with. I remembered that for the following week, I hadn't had another dream like that. And, until recently, each night had consisted of Daemon invading my dreams, or, at the very least, having nightmares. The patterns seemed odd, and perhaps the dreams were all on his whim. Perhaps the nights I had been left alone were the nights he'd been too bored to bother me. Or maybe it was just another way he was playing with his food.

But, even with all the questions I had, Monday and Tuesday night passed dreamlessly. With each morning, I found myself lost in feelings of confusion and emptiness. I spent the days practicing mindfulness and making progress on my work, but by Wednesday morning, I felt more uneasy than I had been in the last two days. When would he strike? Was it like this for the others? Had they been lulled into a sense of safety because he had gone silent for a few nights? Perhaps he was waiting for me to feel safe before he knocked me down.

I messaged Elly and asked what time she wanted to meet before we went to our spa day together. I wanted to talk to Elly about my fears, but at the same time wanted to avoid that conversation as much as possible. While Elly and I were back to being normal, I knew we still didn't see eye to eye on how I responded to my current myriad of problems. I decided I would keep the questions to myself, not wanting to strain our relationship more than necessary.

Elly messaged back, saying we could meet at any time. I responded, asking where she wanted to meet and if she wanted to do anything before our appointments.

> Can we meet at your place? I totally forgot that we were supposed to look around your property and find a spot for the shoot. If you aren't comfortable with that anymore, I completely understand!

> No, I'm completely fine with that. Come over at any time, I'll be here.

With that settled, I pulled on some comfortable clothes, knowing I would be removing them for the massage. As soon as I had finished getting ready and had started the coffee machine up, Elly knocked on the door. I went and unlocked it, letting her inside.

"Coffee?" I asked.

"Yes, please," she replied, fighting a yawn.

"So how did the photo shoot and edits go?"

"Oh, they went fine. I'm still working on the edits, but I should have them done by the end of the week. Are you excited for the photo shoot?" Elly smiled expectantly at me.

While I was excited for the shoot, the fear that things were going to fall apart soon kept lurking in the back of my head. Ignoring those thoughts, I said, "Of course I am." I returned her smile as I poured our coffee and slid the creamer across the counter to her. As we sipped our coffee, the drink warm and satisfying, Elly chatted excitedly about the coming shoot. Elly loved all things photography. Lighting, color saturation, something to do with different lenses. I smiled and pitched in when I could but let her steer the conversation.

When we finished our coffee, we wandered outside into the brisk autumn morning. Well, late morning, at least. I guided her towards the woods and pointed out some spots that might be good for the photo shoot. She made comments on where we could place the props and how we could use the natural landscape to enhance the photos.

After Elly found a space between several thicker trees that she said would allow for the right lighting and provide enough room for movement, we wandered back to the house. We briefly got lost, giggling at how even in such small woods we could still get turned around. After making it back to the house, we still had some time before needing to leave for our massages.

"So..." Elly started hesitantly. "How are things going? Are you doing okay?"

I blew out a breath, twisting my ring. "Yeah, I've been really working on getting my headspace right, and I feel like it's going well." I left out the part where I'd had a vivid retelling of my father's death the night she left. I also refrained from sharing that I'd had a moment of weakness after, leading to so many more questions about Daemon. And, most importantly, I left out the fact I had been feeling like something was missing from my dreams the past few days.

Elly looked at me like she knew I had more to say. "Well, that's good, then." She chewed on her lower lip, looking for all the world like she wanted to say more, too.

That's when I realized that while I still had my friend, something had shifted. Neither of us knew what was taboo or what was still okay to say. Both of us knew that we wouldn't agree on certain topics, meaning we didn't want to talk about them. The conversation stalled, awkwardness growing. I'd never felt this way around her. Spending time with each other had always been as easy as breathing. Silence was never uncomfortable.

Clearing my throat, I glanced at her. "I'm sorry, for the other day."

Her greyish blue eyes wet wide. "No, no. Please don't apologize. I got emotional and left when I shouldn't have."

I nodded at her, and silence fell once more. I stood, doing some mindless cleaning as I waited until it was time to leave. Finally, after watching the long minutes had dragged on, it was finally time.

We both jumped up at the same time. "Looks like it's time to go," I laughed, cringing internally at what this had turned into.

We got in the car, and I immediately turned the music on. Thankfully, the drive was short and there wasn't any need to fill the silence with the music playing. After getting there, we busied ourselves with signing in before separating to our different rooms. It pained me that we were where we were, but I knew that things would go back to normal – eventually.

After a glorious massage where I drifted through the space between sleep and not-sleep followed by a soothing facial, the spa day was over.

Elly came out within five minutes of me being finished. After paying, we made it outside.

"You're glowing," I said. I meant it genuinely. Her face was glowing, and she looked at peace.

"Thanks." She smiled at me, wide and happy. "You, too."

I felt some tension leave my chest at seeing her smile. "I'm super excited for the photo shoot this weekend," I said. I wanted the conversation to feel comfortable again. I wanted things to go back to the way they were.

"Same! I should have some edits done by Halloween. I can't believe it's next Thursday."

"Oh, shit," I said, realizing she was right. "I didn't even remember that until you said that. Guess we should carve the pumpkins this weekend, too."

"Do you want to do that Saturday morning? If we get an early start, we should be able to carve them up and still have plenty of time to do the shoot."

"Yeah, that sounds good. I don't have much planned." We got in the car, driving off with small talk and music playing in the background. Finally, I felt the same comfort from before that I had always felt in her presence. After getting home, she left, leaving me to my own devices for the rest of the day. I breathed, deciding I was going to work on my script – I wanted to try and get back into the swing of my work.

Surprisingly, the words flowed out of me with ease, fingers speeding over the keyboard and the story taking shape as I typed. A different kind of calm settled over me as I lost myself in my work, the feeling of creativity pouring out almost more satisfying than the massage earlier. A twinge in my shoulder was the only thing that threatened to pull me from my reverie. The massage therapist had been kind when she saw my bandage, not asking questions, just telling me to let her know if I was in any pain. It hadn't bothered me, but now, at home, it had begun to itch.

Still, I wrote, ignoring the burning itch trying to distract me. I wrote until the itch had turned into a throb and finally broke away from my work to take some ibuprofen. I briefly looked at the wound, glad that it looked like it was beyond the point of reopening on its own. I replaced the bandage and then made my way to the kitchen, deciding I should make dinner. The protein bar and coffee from earlier was now fading, hunger causing my stomach to growl loudly.

As I cooked dinner with the groceries I had finally purchased on Monday, I heard my phone go off, and I glanced down. It was the camera. I quickly opened the app, seeing nothing at first. It was so dark that the end of my driveway was hard to make out. That was, at least, until the lights on a familiar SUV flashed on. My heart pounded in my chest, fear and frustration a redundant sensation in my gut. I watched as the SUV quickly pulled away, leaving before the thought to call the police had even entered my mind.

The hairs on my neck rose, a chill racing down my spine. Would this ever end? Vaguely, I remembered I had told myself I would save the camera footage to look at later. As I went to save the clip, I suddenly smelled something burning. "*Fuck*," I hissed, running to the stove where my veggies were burning. Removing them from the heat and stirring them, any thought of the SUV and saving the clip faded from my mind.

CHAPTER 26

I should have thought it was strange how easily I seemed to forget anything about the SUV, but that's the funny thing about forgetting something. I didn't think it was strange because the original thought itself was gone. I spent the rest of the evening relaxing and reading before bed. I made a cup of chamomile tea and sipped it as I wound down for the night. Even though Daemon hadn't made an appearance the last four nights, I felt myself wondering, once more, if he would be there.

Dread sank its heavy weight in my gut at the thought. Not only at fear of being the in the presence of the monster that seemed to be the ultimate definition of an oxymoron, but also because I was scared that when I woke tomorrow morning, I would realize I felt less empty than I had the last few mornings. I don't know how I would handle that knowledge; the understanding that I did, in fact, somehow want to feel his presence. My chest ached at the thought. It felt like betraying the women who had come before me, and I didn't understand why my emotions were so conflicting.

I wanted to lay their spirits to rest by getting revenge on the man who had caused their deaths, but I didn't know how, and I was terrified that I would lose myself before getting to do so. I began to drift off, feeling the soft glow of the lamp next to me, providing warm comfort against what might lay ahead. I had left it on the past few nights, ever since it had saved me from myself. It made me feel a little bit safer, a little less alone. Even if it couldn't save me, at least I could embrace the solace it provided as I slipped into the dream world.

***

I opened my eyes to a glass ceiling above me and watched the gentle *tap, tap, tap* of the rain as it slid down the panes. I felt peaceful, the sound lulling me into a relaxed state. Plants grew around me, lush and green. So vividly green that the whole room seemed to glow in this verdant light. I seemed to be laying on a fluffy outdoor lounge chair. A blanket, made of the softest material, wrapped around me snuggly. I relaxed further as I took in what I assumed to be the greenhouse around me.

Earthy smells of wet dirt and plants tickled my nose. But even as those smells seemingly overpowered the room, I picked up the scents of lavender, mint, and shadows. I felt my muscles stiffening. I glanced around, searching for the culprit. I knew he was here. I sat up, my serenity slipping away from me as I rose. My fists clenched tightly, nails against flesh dragging me into reality. It didn't matter how peaceful this setting was, how relaxed I had been the moment I opened my eyes – a nightmare was still a nightmare.

My eyes latched onto a particularly dense area of shadows, picking out the figure within. Always impeccable, he wore black slacks and a black button up shirt. His hands were tucked into his pockets, tension lining the muscles beneath the fabric of his sleeves. Again, I saw a hint of a tattoo at his neck and noticed a splotch of ink on his wrists. Curiosity nipped at me, my urge to take this demon apart and understand every facet of him warring with my efforts to search for revenge.

Daemon stepped forward and the shadows seemed to follow, clinging to his darkness. I knew I should say the five simple words that would free me from this place, but I had so many questions. Questions not just for me, but also for the women who had come before me. Why? That one-word question seemed to be the only one I needed answers too, yet I felt that if I asked, I wouldn't get the answers I wanted.

I stood up from the seat as he approached, apprehension coiling tightly around my muscles. He may be taller than me, but I would face him standing.

"So much fire in those green eyes," he whispered. Any words I may have had dropped away like they never existed. "So much venom on those beautiful lips." He was mere feet away from me now, silver eyes piercing into mine. "Tell me, Little Eve. What pain should I expect tonight?"

So many words wanted to come out that none came out at all. I was confused, lost. What the fuck was happening? Why was I stumbling? "What?" I asked stupidly.

A small grin twisted his lips. His face dipped closer, a hand slipping from his pocket and rising to brush his fingers across my cheekbones. I barely flinched, but it was enough for him to drop his hand. A tick started in his jaw, frustration coating his features. His silver eyes flicked down to my shoulder, the bandage visible beneath the oversized shirt. For a moment, his face morphed into the face of a monster, the true demon he was. Eyes entirely silver, fangs barred. As soon as the look came, it was gone, and he was back to his calm self.

"Who did this to you?" he asked softly, the sound of the rain against the roof filling the air. His words were a threat, a promise of death to whoever I named. "Who dared to touch what was mine?" I could see his control slipping again with each word, a tremor shaking his frame, his face slowly morphing back into the one of the monster. He closed his eyes and leaned forward, drawing in a deep breath. His tension faded. "Tell me," he whispered, breath tickling my ear.

Luke's face flashed across my mind. "You aren't the only nightmare in my life," I replied.

Apparently, it was the wrong thing to say. He lunged closer, wrapping a hand around my neck and pulling me in until we were nose to nose. "*No one* is allowed to hurt you while I'm playing." His fingers tightened slightly on my neck, causing blood to rush to my face. "And *no one* else is allowed to be considered a nightmare in your life," he hissed.

"Too late," I choked out.

As fast as he had angered, he stepped back. He shoved his hands back into his pockets, fury snapping around him violently. He hissed and turned his head away from me. "I have never had someone test my patience as much as you have, Little Eve. You make me want to ruin you." His eyes burned brighter for a moment. "Make no mistake, I will kill whoever did that to you," he said, nodding to my bandage. "I will fucking rip them apart," he snarled. Why did that viscousness call to a tiny part of my soul?

"Is it just because someone else is doing it? And what if *you* hurt me?" I knew I should stop antagonizing the beast, but I couldn't stop myself. He was painfully contradictory. Could he really be so mad that someone else had attempted to do what he was going to do? Was a death not a death? Perhaps not – maybe he needed the high of doing it himself. Like a kid in the sandbox, screaming at anyone who touched his toys.

His eyes narrowed at me. "I don't share," he said, snapping his teeth together. Once again, they seemed sharper, glinting in the light. He seemed to be holding himself back, but I didn't know why. When had he ever done that?

"Why, Daemon?" I asked, finally releasing the burning question I'd wanted to from the start before he had disarmed me with his words.

"Why, what, Evalyn?" A sardonic smile touched his mouth. "Why do I not share? Why would I kill someone over touching you? Why am I here? Why, why, why? Little Eve, I don't think you want to know the answers to those questions." A dark laugh slipped through his lips.

"And if I do?" I whispered. I told myself it was for the others. It was for the ones who he had hurt, killed. But the curiosity to understand him burned, too.

He glanced at me, stepped closer, shadows curling around him, darkening the world around us. "Are you sure?" He whispered.

"Yes," I said with more strength than I felt. I needed to know.

"I'll make a deal, then. Tell me his name, and I'll tell you all that you want to know." My anger bubbled. "Come on, then. If you share, then I will." He lifted his hand, placing his fingers beneath my chin and gently tilting my head.

This wasn't how it was supposed to go. I wanted to handle one monster at a time, and I wanted to do it my way. Killing Luke wasn't my way. I wasn't sure what was my way, but I knew my way didn't involve me handing my problem to someone else. Especially someone like Daemon. "Promise you won't kill him then," I said.

His eyes narrowed. "Do you want him, then? Is that it?"

I rolled my eyes. "I never said that. But I don't want anyone dead. Not on my behalf," I said, whispering the last words. "Just promise me."

"No," he said simply. "He deserves nothing less than death."

"Fine. I want to wake up," I said. He shook his head, the silver glow of his eyes remaining even as the rest of world around us dissolved.

***

I opened my eyes to the soft glow of the lamp. A thought struck me – was Daemon the one turning the lamp on and off? I shook off the thought. No. Rather than getting up, I simply laid there. I was frustrated that I hadn't learned anything more about the enigma that was Daemon. Taking the deal sounded so simple, so easy. I mean, how would Daemon even get the chance to kill Luke? Surely, he couldn't find him just from his name. Even so, I couldn't bear the thought of someone dying because they threatened me. Not again.

I shook those violent thoughts away. But I couldn't stop the frustration I felt towards myself. I was too stubborn to do anything about Luke such as go to the police, so what was I left to do? Hide and wait and hope that maybe, just maybe, he would forget about me? Still, handing that particular problem to the other problem in my life seemed like the wrong answer. Two wrongs don't make a right. Did that apply for demons? I laid in bed, running through the endless circle of thoughts. My ring spun round and round my finger as I thought. I hadn't felt helpless or out of control in a long time. But there was no other way to describe the way I felt now.

Elly's words from the other night seemed to replay on a constant loop in my head. "Evalyn, the master of avoiding her problems". *That's what they'll write on my gravestone*, I thought morbidly. Was this how I would face all of my problems? Fighting on the ledge until the moment one of them swallowed me whole? I continued to spin my ring. I was suppressing the violence within myself, fighting the tide of anger I felt from a lack of control. I wanted to fight. To punch something, to scream.

My mind froze as I realized the only person I had ever acted out my violent thoughts on was Daemon. I had always kept those urges deep within myself, preferring the logic that violence wouldn't solve anything. But Daemon was an exception. Probably because, at first, I believed he wasn't real. But, when I found out he was real, I tried to stab him. Why was that? Why did Daemon crack down my walls of logic and bring out the wildest part of myself? And why did that feel like freedom?

Of course, that was only made more frustrating by the fact that he had never been affected by anything I had done. Aside from tonight, at least. Although that was more directed towards the wound I'd incurred rather than me specifically. These thoughts added another layer of complexity over Daemon. His anger was always in regard to my safety, albeit also out of possessiveness. But then what about the times he had asked, no, *begged* me to not give up, to keep fighting? He seemed worried for my safety, which was entirely contradicting to everything I knew about him.

I slammed the door against that line of thought. He lurked in my dreams, forced himself into my subconscious, and I was still giving him my thoughts and energy outside of those things. No. He didn't deserve this constant attention in my mind. He was a monster, and that was that. He didn't seem to be planning on killing me within the next twenty-four hours, so I would think of other things. I would clear my mind of the curiosity I held for him. It was all I could do, for now. So, before drifting back into sleep, I meditated, letting my mind slip from my body and float in the beautiful nothingness that allowed for a different form of rest. I let each and every question float away, like falling leaves caught in a breeze.

With each breath, I felt lighter and lighter, the weight of the questions and problems and fears and anger falling away like a chain that had weighed me down for too, too long. I stayed like that for a while, floating, experiencing the beauty of nothingness, my own haven of serenity.

CHAPTER 27

T he next morning, I woke, feeling more refreshed than I had expected. But, to my despair, the emptiness I had felt over the last
few days seemed to be...missing. I felt better. And the only difference was
Daemon. Guilt clawed my insides, violently ripping me apart. I felt as
though I had betrayed the others. The ones whose deaths I had not only
watched but *experienced* on a personal level. How could I know what I
know and still feel anything less than loathing towards this monster?

Perhaps I was the no better than the girls who always find men they
want to "fix." Maybe my desire to understand him was, in turn, my desire
to fix this demon. As I thought this, I realized I was, once again, allowing
him to invade my waking thoughts. I threw my pillow over my face and
groaned, angry at the person I was. I was turning into an oxymoron,
myself.

I blew out a breath and rose out of bed, snagging my phone from
the dresser. After showering, I made my way to the kitchen and threw
breakfast together. As I sipped on my coffee, I pulled out my phone.
I pulled up the browser and began typing in the search bar "Luke,
accountant." It was likely going to pull up a million options, but it might

get me somewhere. I was surprised this thought hadn't crossed my mind earlier. As expected, countless results populated. I narrowed them down with the "near me" option. I scrolled through, looking for anything that might lead to his identity. I looked at photos, searching for his blond hair and cocky smile, but found nothing. The only thought I had in my mind was that he had given me either a fake name or maybe even his middle name.

Frustrated, I slammed my phone down on the counter, abandoning the hopeless search. I didn't imagine he had lied about his accounting job, or his wealth and the family business. But a name is easy to fake. I wasn't sure why I felt so confident that all the other information he had given me was accurate, but I trusted my gut on this one. Thinking back on that night spurred another memory I hadn't pieced together until now. What if the reason he had been so cocky about me liking the bruschetta was because he had watched me eat it before? Elly and I went there frequently. And if that's the case, our "accidental" bump in the store wasn't an accident at all.

I had been so busy with everything else going on in my life, so focused on the man from my nightmares that I had spent too long avoiding this issue entirely. Avoidance. That's what I was good at. Push things away until they eventually disappear. But I knew that in these two problems in my life, ones that were life or death, that wasn't going to work. Dread filled my stomach at the thought. I knew I had to do something, but the only other thing I could do was something that would break the vow I had made a long time ago.

Biting my lip, I called Elly. She picked up on the second ring. "Hey, Ev. What's up?" She asked, tone light and relaxed.

I blew out a shaky breath. "Elly, I decided to take you up on your advice from the other night. You were right about me avoiding all my problems, and I can't in this situation, and I hate that more than any-thing else. I don't want to break the vow I made to myself, but I don't think I have a choice if I want to end up alive the next time Luke comes after me." I left out Daemon's threat. It was ironic, really, that a threat on Luke's life, the same Luke who had presumably tried to kill me, was the thing that had made me decide to break my vow. How fucking sick was that?

Elly stayed silent for a moment. "Ev, I want you to know that I am so, so proud of you for making that choice. That's a huge step for you and I'm proud. Do you want me to come with you?" She asked.

I felt my eyes sting with tears. "I'd love that, but only if you can. Don't mess up your schedule for me," I said, hating how my voice cracked.

"There is no schedule to mess up. When do you want to go?"

"I feel like I should just rip this particular band aid off before I change my mind and chicken out. I'll get dressed and ready to go, and I can either drive to your house or we can meet at mine." I spun the ring on my finger anxiously.

"I'm already dressed, so why don't I head over, and I'll drive the both of us to the station. Deal?"

The final word shoved an unbidden thought into my mind about the nightmare last night. Letting it go, I said, "Let's do it."

After hanging up, I went upstairs and grabbed some clothes, tossing them on. As the minutes passed, my hands began to shake. I breathed deeply, trying to calm myself and let go of the negative thoughts. "This is a life-or-death situation, Evalyn. Just get it over with."

Elly arrived and we immediately got in the car and made our way to the local police station. As we pulled in, a violent wave of nausea hit me. I closed my eyes, blowing out a deep breath, trying to settle myself. My shaky hands reached for the door handle, but Elly's hand on my arm made me pause. I looked at her, meeting her wide, worried eyes.

"Ev, I know this isn't easy, but you're making the right decision. And I am going to be here for you the whole way, okay? I'm here," she said softly.

All I could muster up in response was a stiff nod before opening the door and stepping out of the car. My body trembled as I walked into the building and up to the front desk. The female officer behind the desk looked at me expectantly.

"Hi, um," I started, voice shaking violently. I cleared my throat. "Um, I need to report a stalker."

The officer's eyebrows rose. "Alright. Are you trying to get a restraining order?" She asked in a brisk, no-nonsense tone.

"Um, I'm not sure. Yes, I suppose?"

The officer sighed, clearly not a fan of my indecisiveness. "Well, if you're looking to get a restraining order, that paperwork is processed at the courthouse, not here, unfortunately," she said.

My heart sank. I came here for nothing, then. "Okay, well. Thank you," I said quietly, turning to leave.

Elly grabbed my arm, bringing me to a halt. "Ma'am, I'm sorry. My friend just has a hard time in police stations. She forgot to mention that the stalker actually attacked her Friday night," she said, her voice even and clear.

The officer looked at me, concern in her eyes. "Well, honey, that's something we can help with. We can file a police report and get started from there," she said.

"Thank you," Elly said for me.

The officer spoke to someone on her radio, and a minute later, another officer approached. He smiled at Elly and I, gesturing for us to follow him. "Hi, my name is Officer Brant. We'll go sit down in a quiet area and figure out what's going on," he said. He seemed friendly but professional, putting me more at ease. We reached his desk and took the seats opposite from him. "So, why don't you guys tell me a little bit about what happened? And I'll need you to state your names for record purposes." He held a notepad and pen in his hand, the seemingly ever well-prepared Boy Scout.

Elly looked at me, offering an encouraging squeeze on my hand. I sighed, wishing for all the world that I wasn't here. "My name is Evalyn Wright, and she's Elleanor Tenet. Well, Friday night, Elly and I went to a haunted house. Purgatory House, I mean." I was stumbling over my words, but Officer Brant was taking notes dutifully. "We went through most of the house, but when I went down this, um, slide, I got separated from Elly. Then, he dragged me off the mat and held a knife to my throat and threatened me. If I made any noise, he wouldn't just hurt me, but Elly, too." I felt my chest constrict. "He had his hand covering my nose and mouth, and I couldn't breathe. After Elly stepped away, thinking I had moved on, he-he pulled me into the actors' area." I paused, trying to gather my composure. I didn't want to tell a complete stranger about this. I reminded myself that this was me taking action, no longer sitting and waiting for the storm to pass. "I think he was drunk, and it was dark enough that I could move my hands without him noticing. I was able to catch him off guard and get the knife away from my neck and incapacitate him for a few seconds, but in the process, he sliced my collarbone." I looked down at my hands, fingers white as I squeezed them together.

"Okay," Officer Brant said, glancing at me with concern. "Now, you said this was Friday night. How come you didn't report this sooner?" He asked.

I flinched. "I just, um. I told myself I would never go to a police station again." I didn't have the courage to explain why.

His eyes filled with confusion and a hint of suspicion. "Okay. That's alright. Some people don't have good experiences." He rubbed his temple. "Now, it sounds like he may have known you, is that right?"

"Yes. We had gone on a date a bit ago and since then I've been seeing him around. But I think he was stalking me before the date, even." I felt like I was curling in on myself, my vulnerability making me feel exposed.

"And when was this first date?" He asked.

"Um...It was a Tuesday, I think. Two weeks ago, now." The officer nodded.

"Alright. And did you go to the hospital after this incident?" He asked.

I shook my head. "No, sir."

"So, you weren't concerned about the wound and felt it could be treated at home, is that correct?"

"Yes, sir. Although Elly wanted me to go to the hospital. I said no." My voice lowered to a near whisper on the last sentence.

The officer's eyebrows rose. "I see. Can you describe the specifics of the wound? How long the cut is as well as its specific placement."

"I think it's about four inches long. It's just beneath my collarbone on my left shoulder."

The officer nodded, still writing down notes. "Alright. Now, do you know his name?"

"His name is Luke. That's the name he gave me at least. He's an accountant somewhere. I don't know his last name, I'm sorry. I'm not even sure his first name is Luke." I said weakly.

The officer rubbed his temple again. "Any other descriptive factors?"

"He's blonde. Tall. Blue eyes. He drives a sports car. Black, I think."

"What kind of car?" He asked.

Shame colored my cheeks. "I-I don't know."

The officer made a noise of frustration. "Well. I truly hate to say this, ladies. But I'm not sure what all I can do here. I can make a report, put it on file, of course. But without a full name, address, or anything, finding him is going to be next to impossible. I of course recommend that if you see him, you stay far away. And, if you don't have one already, look into a security system. Preferably with cameras."

"I had one installed last week," I said.

"Good. Now, if you do see his car or are able to find any other information about him, please let us know. If any other incidents occur, again, please let us know. The more we can get on him, the easier it will be to find him."

Elly spoke up. "Can't you guys look at the footage from the haunted house? Or maybe they have cameras in the parking lot and Ev could point out his car."

"Sadly, most haunted houses don't have cameras installed inside. Second, if they had cameras on the lot, the likelihood of finding the vehicle would be challenging, to say the least. However, I can try to pull footage from that night and if I can, I'll bring you back in to see if you're able to identify the vehicle." He paused. "Now, for record keeping purposes, we typically take photos of injuries from these kinds of altercations to ensure we have all of our bases covered. Is that alright with you?"

My stomach clenched at the thought of having a picture taken of my wound and put on a case file. But still, I nodded. Within a few minutes, another officer came in with a camera. After snapping a few photos while I gripped Elly's hand in what must have been a painful grip, we were finished. I practically ran out of the building, thankful that the ordeal was over.

In the parking lot, next to her car, Elly opened her arms to me. "De-compression hug?" She asked. I nodded, falling into her embrace and holding on for dear life. I wouldn't have made it through this without her – I knew that. After a long hug, we got in the car and she drove me back to the house.

"Are you okay? Do you want me to stay a bit?" She offered.

"I'm alright, I promise. Thank you so much for coming with me. It made everything...more bearable." I smiled tightly at her; glad we were back to feeling balanced.

She pursed her lips but nodded. "Alright. Well, if you need me, just call. I'll be right here," she said. I nodded. With that, I stepped out the car and watched her drive away.

CHAPTER 28

The rest of the day, I tried to turn my mind back to a calm state, accepting that I had done what I could in regard to Luke. I had to admit that it was mildly frustrating that I had gone through the painful experience of going there for what felt like almost nothing. As I had predicted, without his real name or any other substantial information, they wouldn't be able to do much. I doubted they would even be able to pull anything from the cameras. But, hey, if I wound up dead, they would know who to look for, I guess.

Rolling my eyes at my dark line of thoughts, I shoved myself away from them. Pulling out my laptop, I played some music while I started a new book, trying to lose myself in the fantasy world that had been beautifully described. But my mind refused – and to no fault of the author's. I wasn't sure when it had started, but the feeling of...*something* happening soon was building in my chest. I wasn't sure how to explain it, but it felt like the fragile bubble I had built around myself since last Friday was nearing a breaking point. I had been holding myself together since that awful night, and was still doing so, but I felt as though it was all bound to snap soon.

I knew my mind wasn't going to fix itself overnight. Especially when the nightmares lurked nearby, still very much alive. Meditation helped to alleviate the weight of my issues, as well as yoga, but all the mindfulness in the world wouldn't make everything right when I'm living in the same space as one tormentor and being followed outside by the other.

In the past several days, I had practiced letting go of the negative thoughts, letting them flow through and out of my mind. But at the same time, I was trying to practice confronting my problems, rather than avoiding them. So, in that sense, mindfulness would give me strength, but constant meditation didn't help me puzzle out my issues.

Why couldn't Daemon just tell me the answers? Maybe I had been asking the wrong ones. Instead of "why?" perhaps I should instead ask "how?" How do I survive? How do I get rid of you? I ignored the pang in my chest at the thought. But the likelihood of him answering those without providing a riddle was almost nothing.

I stood, walking across the hall and into the office room. Spinning my ring, I approached the box that held the four items that confirmed my dreams, my nightmares, were real. Not figments of my imagination. I blew out a shaky breath and opened the box. The items lay within, immediately sending nausea to my gut. Swallowing it down, I grabbed each item, inspecting it carefully. Perhaps there was something I could glean from them.

I ran my fingers over the blue scarf, my agony for the soul it had taken igniting. *I'm so sorry, Elaine,* I thought. I traced the smooth pearls, feeling the same agony for Jayda. The knife gleamed in the light of the room, bringing back fresh memories of exactly how that knife felt, of how the voice had made me, *her*, carve into herself and rip out her soul. Tears sprung in my eyes.

"What do I do?" I whispered to them as if they could hear me. Perhaps they could, perhaps they were the ones who turned on the lamp for me. I wanted answers and I wanted to get vengeance for them. But at what cost? He wanted the name in exchange. Trading Luke's life for the possibility of killing their killer...well it seemed like a worthy bargain, even as my gut twisted violently at the thought.

No, I thought. *Not again.* I couldn't do it. I couldn't watch another person die because someone was trying to protect me. It didn't matter if they were a monster. It didn't matter if they were the worst human alive – but watching someone die simply because they tried to hurt me? I refused. Tears slipped beneath my eyelids, and I couldn't bring myself to accept the only potential solution in front of me. Not after I had already ripped apart a vow to myself once today.

I carefully replaced the items, brushing my fingers against the fedora in the process. Curiosity pulled at me, and I carefully picked it up and flipped it, looking inside the hat. Nothing stood out to me. It seemed like an expensive, well-made hat. But I also knew nothing about hats, so maybe it wasn't. Running my fingers around the brim, I suddenly felt something.

Frowning, I looked closer. A small clip of paper was shoved between the fabric band wrapping around the hat and the brim. I pulled at it carefully, making sure not to rip it. It appeared to be a note, folded over and over to make it small enough to fit in the hat. I began unfolding it, careful to not tear it. It seemed old, the white paper slightly yellowed. Finally, it opened.

Truly, Your Woman Scorned.

~L

Confusion slid through me. Why was this in his hat? And who was L? A sick hope rose in me, hoping that somehow, he was being forced to do these things. I squashed it down. Another thought occurred to me that I hadn't connected before. Clearly, if this hat was here, that meant that Daemon had a physical body. Or did. If so, why wasn't he using it? I realized that with the chaos I had been drowning in, so many clues had been left untouched, forgotten in the hordes of choices and decisions and fears. I kept telling myself that I had all the puzzle pieces, but did I?

So, I did what any writer would do. I began writing. I pulled out a piece of paper and a pen and began jotting down "what I know about Daemon," "what I don't know about Daemon," and "what I think I know about Daemon."

Under the "What I know" column, I was able to put several things:

Controls nightmares

Real

Caused deaths of three women

Comes up with bad nicknames

~~Devilishly hot~~

After writing those last two words, I violently scribbled them out until they were wholly illegible. *What is wrong with you, Evalyn?* I asked myself.

Then, under the "What I don't know," was a much longer list:

Why he kills?

How does he speak in the mind while awake?

Where did he come from?

If he has a corporeal form, why doesn't he use it?

If he can't use his corporeal form, how were the items saved?

Why does he encourage me to push through?

Why is he possessive of me?

What is his endgame, if not killing me?

Who is 'L.' and what do they have to do with Daemon?

And, lastly, for "What I think I know," was only two items:

He might be cursed

He cares

I laid the pen down, feeling like I was only repeating what I knew. While it was nice to see each of the things I knew written out in a what that I could visibly piece together, I wasn't sure what else I could add to the list. I twisted the ring around on my finger and worried my lip as I thought. There was more. Rather than focusing on Daemon entirely, though, I decided I should instead think about the nightmares from the time I moved in until now. Perhaps that would lead to some kind of pattern.

Dreams:

Running through forest

Meet Daemon, he's in my bedroom

First memory dream, in living room. No father. Visit "Daemon's room" for the first time. Tries to seduce me.

Coffin Dream. When Daemon pulled me from that dream, was he upset that I was in shock?

Ties me to the chair and...yeah.

Elaine's Forced Suicide.

Jayda's Forced Suicide.

Suzanne's Forced Suicide.

I give into Daemon.

Confront Daemon, try to stab him.

Father's death memory, Daemon tries to comfort.

Greenhouse dream, Daemon refuses to answer questions, threatens to kill Luke

As I wrote, I realized how deeply impacting these dreams had been. For me to be able to recall them, in vivid detail, and in order (or what I thought was in order), showed how the dreams had managed to etch themselves onto my soul. But, in writing the dreams down, something became immediately apparent that I hadn't put much stock into before – the dreams I'd had involving Elaine, Jayda, and Suzanne had, for one, not been in this house. That part was unsurprising. However, what snagged my attention was that in each of the other dreams, it seemed that Daemon had made it his mission to show up in them. In all of them, he showed up. But for those three? He wasn't there. Not even a hint of him.

CHAPTER 29

I tried to twist my mind around why this could be. He had known what women I was talking about, so surely, he had caused those dreams. But, then again, perhaps not. But who would have shown me the dreams if not the dream demon himself? Could it be the women? Perhaps they took the chance while I wasn't in Daemon's circle of control to show me the truth. But, if that were the case, how did they follow me? Why were they not stuck to the property as this theory would indicate Daemon was?

Day turned into night, and I fell asleep to find no Daemon waiting for me. When I woke the next morning, I felt the question rise against my will. Why did it seem that I was seeing Daemon less and less? Did it mean something? Was he ignoring me? Thursday drifted by with no new answers, as well as Friday. I was restless, frustrated that the one person who could provide answers was seemingly avoiding me. If he was so obsessed with me, why the fuck had he begun to pull away from me?

I realized how terrible that thought was – I should be thankful that I wasn't being terrorized by a monster. But gratitude wasn't on my mind. Saturday morning, I rose once more from a restless night of Daemon-free dreams. I was unnaturally angry, pissed off that I wasn't in control of these visitations. I stormed down to the kitchen and began brewing coffee, texting Elly that she could head over whenever she was ready.

She came shortly after, bringing everything that we needed for the shoot with her. "Hey," she said. "Everything okay?"

I spun the ring on my finger. "Yeah, I'm fine." I didn't know how else to elaborate.

Elly raised her brow at me. "Nothing new?" She pushed.

"I haven't had as many dreams lately. I don't know what to think of it. I should be happy, but I just feel like things aren't adding up. Like, two plus two should equal four, but right now it equals twelve. I've been running it through my mind over and over and over, Elly. What we know about him doesn't add up with what I see with him."

"I mean, he's specifically talented in turning brains into soup, isn't he? Do you think it's just him being contradictory because that's what he wants? To confuse you?" I appreciated that Elly didn't hold an accusatory note in her voice as she spoke, the way that I felt I deserved.

"No. It's not that. I can *feel* that it's not that. And maybe I'm crazy for believing it but I've been thinking. I made some lists the other day to try and organize my mind, or something." I ran over and grabbed the lists, showing them to her. "Now, I genuinely don't know how I'm able to remember all of them, but the three I had when I was at your house stand out to me the most. I've lived in this house for almost a month now, Elly. And in each nightmare I've had while in the house, Daemon shows up. The time I'm at yours, he's absent."

I chewed my lip as I let her read the lists and process. "You think he might be cursed?" Elly looked at me suspiciously.

I fumbled for words. "Well, I don't know. But if he used to have a physical body, why doesn't he use it now? And what does he gain from attaching himself to this specific house? I know this might seem like some paranormal, twisted version of Stockholm Syndrome, but it's not." I took a breath. "Elly, please believe me when I say that my gut is saying there are some giant chunks of this story missing."

Elly didn't seem overwhelmingly convinced, but she pursed her lips and nodded. The dissonances that seemed to be occurring more and more often in our friendship grated me the wrong way. But I knew that when I got the proof, if I got it, then she would understand.

"Ev," she started. "If you think he's tied to this house, then wouldn't the solution just be to...well...leave the house? He can't force his way into your head if you're gone, right? So come stay with me. Can you resell the house? You just had all these renovations done, maybe that could help?"

I felt like I'd been slapped in the face. I realized that in my thought process of trying to untie the complex knots of Daemon, I had let my concern for my life slip to the side. Yes, I remained focused on wanting revenge for the women before me, but more than anything, I wanted *understanding*. But Elly was right. If staying here was the issue, leaving would solve it. If he wasn't the cause for the nightmares of the three women the way I had originally presumed, that meant he didn't have control beyond this property.

I nodded. "You're right. I hadn't thought of that. But I'm not selling the house, Elly. I can't. I mean, I just got it. I'll just stay with you a couple nights, maybe prove my theory, and then we can go from there, okay?"

Elly nodded. "Deal. And if we're right, we can try to find another solution." She blew out a breath. "Now, how about some pumpkins?" The abrupt conversation change was exactly what I needed. For the next hour, we cut into our pumpkins, tossing slimy seeds at each other and trying to make art with a steak knife. Luckily, the results were at least decent. Far from fancy, but definitely usable in our photo shoot. With late morning slowly passing by, we cleaned and changed into our clothes. Grabbing the camera and props, we made our way around the back of the house and into the woods, stumbling around to find the spot we had chosen the first time.

Finally, we found it again, laughing about how neither of us were directionally gifted. I didn't even want to think of what getting out of the woods was going to look like, either. It wasn't like I was living in a national park, by any means, but around the back of the house, the trees were thick enough to get scrambled around. Add onto the fact that there was no path, either, making everything much more complex than it needed to be. Around the front of the house, the trees were spaced out enough that the road could be seen.

When purchasing the house, I had just been happy that I had some level of privacy. Though, with all the stalking going on, both in and out of my dreams, it felt almost as though my privacy had been taken. But staying a few nights at Elly's again might help separate me from the situation. But the last time I had stayed there, I had the worst of all of my dreams. I couldn't help but feel a hint of reluctance even though I had promised Elly.

We moved to set up everything, hanging torn cloth from the tree branches and placing skulls and bones around. We had even brought a small bin for burning with us so Elly would have an easier time editing flames into some of the pictures. Before we'd left, we had put on our initial costumes, but the other dress we hung nearby, waiting until we were ready for it.

Once the props were in place, Elly set up her tripod and placed the camera, looking at the screen and then making adjustments to its position. She grinned up at me and gave me a thumbs up, indicating that it was time. With that, I dropped away all thoughts of the problems plaguing my life, choosing to embrace this moment, this specific point in time that I was sharing with my best friend at my favorite time of year in one of my favorite kinds of settings – spooky and quiet.

Pose after pose and shot after shot passed by, sometimes swapping props and adjusting the camera as the light moved. A hefty amount of fake blood was involved, the sticky crimson substance drippling from our clothes and skin. In a typical photoshoot, it was common to move things around, even find a new area to start photographing in, but Elly and I had agreed that we didn't want to change and redo our décor a bunch of times, especially with the fake blood involved. Getting props dirty wasn't a big deal, but Elly was already flustered enough trying to clean her hands each time she reset the camera. Instead, we focused on finding new angles. Changing the view, even by a few steps, made more of a difference than you'd imagine in photography.

Briefly, we took a break and snacked on some chips and peanut butter and jelly sandwiches we had brought along with us while we waited for the sun to get in the right spot for Elly. "I want to get a few pictures after it gets a little dark," she said.

"We can stay out here as long as you like," I replied. "It's so nice out, and it feels great outside." I was surprised that it was already nearing sunset. What mattered was that we were having fun, and I hadn't thought about the lurking problems in my life...much.

"Well, I'd love to stay out until midnight, but even I don't have the energy for that. Or the battery. I've already swapped it once." She glanced in the direction of her camera that she refused to have to close to our cheese powder covered fingers. "I think that if we get another hour or so in, we should be able to get the lighting I need for what's in my head. When we finish eating, you can go ahead and swap into the fancy gown and tiara. I'll make sure the makeup is good and then we can kick it back off," she said with a smile.

I stepped back over towards the set where my dress was hanging. Pulling some wet wipes out of my backpack I brought along, I went through and wiped the red residue off as best as I could. Since parts of my current dress were already saturated in the blood, I picked a dry spot to help the cleanup go smoother. After what felt like a thousand wipes, I was clean enough to slide the other dress on. Briefly, I wondered if attempting the trek back through the woods to my house would have been worth it. I shook my head – definitely not.

"Elly, I'm just going to change over here really quick, and then we can get going again," I said. I heard her grunt of approval as she cleaned her hands once more before looking at the camera. While I had no shame and wasn't worried about Elly seeing me naked, I felt a little less exposed tucking myself behind a tree.

After removing my dirty dress, I slid the zipper down on the black gown so I could put it on. A sudden snapping twig caught my attention, and I jumped. "Jesus, Evalyn," I whispered to myself. I was acting like a little girl watching a horror movie. Still, even knowing it had to be Elly, the hair on my neck was raised. Shaking my head, I slipped the dress over my skin. The plunging neckline and corseted waist accentuated my figure, and the skirt tumbled down to the earthy floor without much flair but swayed with each movement from my body. The mesh top was black but hinted at the skin beneath, and the silver charms tinkled at my waist, the near musical chime making me grin.

I had just finished zipping the back of the dress when I heard another noise, something that sounded strange, like a shuffling of...something across the ground. "Elly?" I called. Even though the dress had long sleeves, they hardly did anything to soothe the goosebumps flaring across my arms.

My heart thudded in my chest for one beat. Two. Three. Silence. I released the zipper from my fingertips and grabbed the skirt, lifting it up to move easier as I made my way back to our set up, mere feet from where I'd changed. The sight that met my eyes shot fear through my system, so potent that my head felt light, and the color faded from my vision.

Elly laid unnaturally on the ground. Her arm was awkwardly twisted beside her and her feet were bent at strange angles. Her body was covered in red, and I wasn't sure if it was from the fake blood or if it was her own. With each beat of my heart, a pulse of black crowded my vision. Lunging over, I reached for my friend, whispering her name over and over. Nothing outside of her mattered right now. I heard a tearing noise in the background, but the dress didn't matter. Nothing mattered except Elly.

I rolled her onto her back, careful of her arm. I laid my fingers on her neck and felt the pulse there, strong and steady. Relief hammered through me. I quickly checked over her, glancing to see if any of the blood-colored liquid came from wounds, hands turning sticky and red in the process. Nothing seemed amiss. Once the immediate worry for her life was lessened, I whipped my head around, trying to figure out what happened. Had she fainted? It didn't feel right.

My eyes picked up a glint of a needle sitting a few feet from where Elly lay. My breath stuttered to a stop as the reality of the situation came slamming down. Luke was here.

CHAPTER 30

"*W*here *the fuck are you?*" I screamed. The words tore from my throat without a second of hesitation. Elly's unconscious body lay partially on my lap as I knelt on the ground, guarding her from any more harm. My eyes flicked in every direction, head twisting and turning as I tried to find the monster who haunted me outside of my dreams. For a brief moment, I almost wished I had given Daemon permission to kill Luke, if only to save Elly from this mess.

I didn't have any pepper spray or a knife on me, and all the props were too far away to reach. Even if they were in reach, I had no idea if there was even one that could be of use. My hands desperately felt along the ground searching for any source of weapon. My only function in that moment was to protect Elly. I found nothing. It seemed that it would have to be with my own body.

"*I said where the fuck are you, motherfucker?*" Rage and fear electrocuted my muscles, boiled in my veins, and scraped along my skin.

"Right here, *bitch*," Luke's voice said from behind me. Before I could react, something hard hit the right side of my skull, sending my body flying to the side, ears ringing and vision blurring. My face smacked into the dirt; my body ripped away from Elly's. I choked on the dust flying into my throat, dazedly trying to lift myself up.

Before I got too far into that, however, a heavy foot smashed down against my spine. "Evalyn, Evalyn, *Evalyn*. Stay put like a good little girl and your precious little Elly here won't get more than a nice dose of sleepy time medicine." His words were muffled through my still ringing ears, and it felt as though my right eardrum had burst. I blinked away the spots in my vision, trying to get a grip on the situation.

But, as he grabbed me by my hair and dragged me towards a tree, I realized the whole situation was a sinkhole with nothing to hold on to. My hands instinctively went to clutch my hair, but I forced myself to not fight. For Elly's sake. My dress dragged across the ground, catching on sticks and rocks. Finally, he dragged me against the tree, my head pounding and scalp aching. "Stay," he said as he stepped towards Elly. And, just like that, all thoughts of staying compliant disappeared.

I tried lunging up, instincts screaming to protect her, but he turned in a flash, whipping out a knife from the waist of his jeans. "Uh, uh, uh," he said, waving the knife in Elly's direction. "You sit your ass right there while I tie her up, so she doesn't try to come interrupt our fun. You move, she joins the game, got it?"

My body fell back against the tree, despair sinking through me. I watched him carefully, checking for any sudden moves against my best friend. I noticed a log lying next to her and wondered if that was what he had hit me on the side of my head with. I felt blood dripping down my ear and cheek. All I could do was watch as he tied her hands behind her back and roped her ankles together. I wanted to cry so badly, but I refused to do anything that would make Luke feel that he had more power.

The ringing had only faded in my left ear, and I still felt like my equilibrium was off, but adrenaline was also pumping through me. Right now, I had no clear exit that included me being able to save Elly, as well. Frustration mixed with the fear and anger at how I hadn't been able to protect the best person in my life from this monster. Luke stalked back towards me, his skintight blue shirt smeared with dirt and fake blood. His muddy blonde hair was messy, and his jeans were dirty. He stopped at the camera set, chuckling before picking something up. As he turned, I saw it was the tiara that Elly had found and had wanted me to wear.

He squatted in front of me, knife clutched in one palm, and slammed the tiara down on my head. My head screamed in protest, hairs catching on the metal as he shoved it farther down than it was meant to go. "I have to make sure my special girl feels like a princess, don't I?" He said, laughing darkly. "It's just you and me now, baby. Why don't we go for a walk, hm?" He gripped me by my arm, yanking me to my feet as he rose. The headpiece jostled but didn't fall. Before I could react, he twisted my arms behind my back and jabbed the point of the blade against my jugular. "See, you taught me something last time. And I appreciate that. I'm always excited to learn new things," he said casually as he forced me to walk with him.

"I wasn't really planning on doing much last Friday other than give you a pretty good scare, if I'm being honest. Too crowded, too public. Plus, I wouldn't have the time and space to do all of the *amazing* things I have planned for us. But you were supposed to go on my terms, not yours. And you just had to go and ruin that.

So now," he continued, jerking my hands tighter behind my back for emphasis, "you get to keep your hands behind your back and I don't get to have a drop of alcohol in my system. Such a spoilsport." My shoulder was screaming, the scabs threatening to reopen. I stumbled over a fallen branch, causing the knife to nick the skin. I winced, feeling as though I was a mere breath from dying. At least Elly was far back in the trees now. If I had even a moment to get out of this hold, maybe I had a chance of doing *something* that wouldn't end in Elly or me dying.

"Honestly, Evalyn, you might be the dumbest bitch I've ever met. You waited five *days* before going to the police? Are you kidding me?" He shoved me forward, laughing under his breath. "Not that it helped, but you really have no sense of self preservation. I mean, the security system wasn't a bad idea. But see..." he inhaled happily. "That only works at the house. And no one can stay inside forever."

Suddenly, he tossed me to the ground, kicking me in the ribs to roll me over. I was back to the choking mess I had been earlier. At least my head felt less fuzzy. "Here we are. What do you think?" He asked. The tiara rolled away with clumps of my hair attached as I took in my surroundings.

A duffel bag sat to the side and a camera stood angled towards me. There were no weapons aside from the knife still in his palm, but the most disturbing part of the scene were the photos. Countless photos stapled to the trees surrounding us. All photos of me. I rose up on my palms slowly, feeling his presence on my back. He crouched behind me, lips at my ear and knife jabbing my ribs.

"You were so fun to watch, you know? You have no schedule and no set time for anything – and yet somehow you seem like a creature of habit. It was easy knowing where to look for you, easy knowing the best spot for you to see me. So easy to scare and make nervous. But you still didn't do anything about it, did you?" He slung the arm holding the knife over my shoulder.

"Now, you see that picture?" He asked while pointing the knife in the direction of one of the trees. My heart thudded in my chest, and I wished

I wasn't so paralyzed by the situation. I didn't want to be helpless, for fuck's sake. A shaky breath left my lips as I followed the point of the knife to a picture. It was me and Elly, sitting at the Italian restaurant off of Poppy Street. We were crunching on bruschetta while laughing, wine glasses in our hands. Elly and I hadn't been there since well before I bumped into Luke. "That's how I knew you *loved* bruschetta." His free hand stroked my cheek gently.

"When I decided to bump into you in the store, I *wanted* to unnerve you, to see if you'd agree to going out with me. And even though you were clearly uncomfortable, you *did*. You've got to work on saying no, you know that, Evalyn?" His fingers harshly tapped against my temple. "Then, at the restaurant, I wanted to make you squirm, so I played my role." He laughed. "The cocky, rich, know-it-all misogynist. And that's when I got to see your little temper. Has anyone told you how cute it is?" He leaned into my ear, biting the lobe. I flinched, jerking away and feeling nausea churn in my gut.

"Uh, uh, uh," he said, gripping my face in his free hand painfully. I was powerless. "It was my own little experiment. I wanted to see how far I could take it before you finally shut me down."

"Why?" I whispered.

"Why?" He repeated. "Well, we have to go back a bit in time for that one, dear Evalyn. You don't remember me, but you caught my attention many years ago." He swung the knife to another photo. It was me, much younger, wearing long sleeves and a drawn expression. The blood drained from my face. His hand let go of my face and grabbed my forearm twisting it upright. He brought the knife down to my wrist, and I began struggling out of instinct. *No, no, no!* He ignored how I bucked against him and screamed. My free arm pushed at his knife hand. He struggled against my hold, but it wasn't enough. The knife came down, slipping under the sleeve of the dress, slicing the fabric away and drawing a thin line of blood.

Then he lifted the knife away from my arm and yanked his hand out of my grip, then grabbed it and twisted it agonizingly behind my back. It was my right arm, and the pull reminded me of the last time I had been sliced with the knife. I felt a tear run down my cheek, knowing that I was in the worst possible situation I could be in right now. My eyes went back to the picture, and I remembered the pain I'd felt back then. The agony of being alone, of being abandoned. Of everything being *my fault*. Of course, everyone told me it *wasn't* my fault. I was the victim. I was just a *kid*. Still, he held my wrist up in a steel like grip.

"I remember seeing you in the hospital for the first time. I was there, too. See, Mommy and Daddy didn't like how I was a little too attracted to death. So, they shoved me somewhere they hoped would fix me. And it was dreadfully boring – until *you* showed up. Long dark hair, wide green eyes. I could just tell you'd seen some shit. But, at the same time, you had seen nothing of the world. And the bandages wrapped around your wrist? At first, I thought the expression on your face didn't match the attitude of someone who wanted to kill themselves. Maybe it was an attention grab, you know?" He stroked the thick white scar running down the length of my forearm. "There were more than enough of those in there.

"It was a little exciting conundrum, and I wanted the answer. So, I watched you. And I realized that you weren't looking for attention. Who would you be trying to get the attention of? Your mommy and daddy were gone. No. You were angry at yourself. So much anger and hatred turned in on yourself that there was too little room for sadness. You didn't want to just kill yourself. You wanted to *annihilate* yourself.

"I'd asked the doctors about you, but they didn't share much. When I asked if I could be moved to the same therapy classes as you, they said I was 'too old.' So, I dealt with my curiosity by watching from a distance.

"But, like everyone else in there, the meds made you slow. Made you numb. And after some time, I realized I needed to see what would happen outside of that hospital. I wanted to see you away from the constant monitoring, the watching eyes, and the increased dosages when you showed any slight change in demeanor. So, I made sure to start slowly saying all the right things, showing remorse, regret, and a sense of empathy. And when you left, I made sure I left." He leered at me, proud that he'd duped the system. He'd learned to blend in, all so he could follow me.

I remembered the hospital vividly. How he said I'd hated myself so much I wanted to do more than just kill myself. It was true. "You were only twelve when I met you, and I was only fifteen. But I found my favorite hobby afterwards. Watching you. And I watched as you got older, and realized how badly I wanted to watch you bleed. I wanted to see what you had looked like when you first made these scars, covered in blood and all alone." He sighed. "But I was waiting for something special. And things kept getting in my way. You, in foster care, me, with my family breathing down my neck – I could only get so close." He nodded his head at all the photos. "These were my collectibles. I savored each one and the older you got, the more I began imagining how beautiful you would look on the brink of death." He licked the side of my neck. I flinched again, but he merely twisted my arm tighter, causing me to hiss. I glanced at the photos, eyes flicking through my history, the moments stolen by the monster behind me.

A picture from when I was thirteen, walking to school, clutching a giant book to my chest. A shot from when I was sixteen, sobbing, alone in my room. Another from when I was nineteen, holding hands with Elly as we danced at some college party. Then I was twenty-one, doing the first annual photoshoot with her. Twenty-four on a date with one of the guys I had a longer fling with. On and on the photos went, some from younger days and others much more recent. Some photos where I was happy, and some where the world seemed to be cracking beneath my feet. I couldn't count how many there were, and I couldn't even see some of them in the darkness that was rapidly falling.

He pointed to a photo. It was me pressed against a wall with a man's hand on my throat and my legs wrapped around his waist. "That one is one of my favorites. See, this was a bit of a pivotal point for me. It made me realize how sexual violence can be. I started getting off on these visions of you, painted red by your own blood, begging for air you couldn't get. It awakened a whole new fantasy in me. One that you'll get to participate in tonight." My body trembled, a new level of fear coursing through me.

"After a forced marriage with some bitch whose parents ran in the same circle with my parents, I got restless. Impatient. The years had chipped away at the excitement brought from watching you. I needed more. So, I started planning. I tossed out my wife like the piece of trash that she was in a way that no one would suspect foul play. Then, I played my role of a grieving husband marvelously.

"Luckily for me, you never went far. You drifted through a few different towns, but they were all close by. And then you bought this house." He paused, releasing my arm and suddenly yanking me down to the ground, slamming my head against the cold dirt, dazing me, then moving to sit on my chest and stomach faster than I could blink. The breath whooshed out of me and more tears sprang to my eyes. My arms had ended up beneath his thighs, useless. "And how lucky was I that I didn't have to go looking for a secluded setting just like this one?" He leered down at me, casually tapping my cheek with the flat of the blade.

"It's getting a little dark, but don't worry. I brought some mood lighting and a way to commemorate this moment." He reached over to his left, relieving enough weight from my chest that I could breathe a little. His hands came back into view, the knife and some rope in one hand and a giant flashlight in the other, a polaroid camera slung around his neck. My mind whirled, trying to come up with a solution to this problem. My legs were free but useless, and I wasn't strong enough to roll him off me with all of his weight on me. Too late, I realized I missed my chance to knock him off balance. But he had a weapon, I didn't. And I was about to be tied up.

The old feelings of being powerless in the hands of someone else rushed to the surface, and angry tears began coursing down my cheeks. I had told myself I would never again feel this way. I wished this was like the dream where I could just scream and the world that I didn't like would dissolve around me, and then Daemon would be waiting. But this wasn't a nightmare. Not one that I could wake up from, at least. A part of me wished that I could sleep through this, let Daemon show me something other than the world around me.

Thinking of Daemon in the midst of the danger I was in jarred me. When had he become my safe space? More and more I believed that he hadn't directly killed those women. I realized that the fear he caused was surface level. And he wore it like a mask, letting me see him in that light. But then there were the moments where he told me not to give up. Not to let the fear get to me. The moments where he held me after a particularly bad nightmare. He clearly had taken no pleasure in seeing how they slowly killed me.

But he was the easy excuse. He was the most obvious answer to all the problems. But he'd never been obvious – he had always been a puzzle, a thousand piece, 3-D puzzle. Not a book you could read by looking at the cover. And in this moment, I wish I had a chance to say something to him. I was tired of questioning why I felt such a pull to him, why I couldn't fight my base instincts – it didn't matter. I'd only ever spit venom at him, and yet he still wanted to kill the man who'd left a mark on me. So no, Daemon wasn't the monster in my life. The real monster was the one who had lurked behind my shoulder my whole life. The one who was a literal weight on my chest right now.

The flashlight flicked on, blinding me as he pointed it in my face. "It just wouldn't be fun if I couldn't see your pretty blood, now, would it?" The anger built more and more, and I felt my fingers reaching for anything I could use. Just dirt met my fingers, and I wanted to scream. And then I realized that he wouldn't be able to tie me up without moving somehow, and so I focused on that tiny pinprick of hope that crawled into my chest. I slowly bent my knees upwards, hoping I could do this right. He set the flashlight down, letting it shine over us. The light cast an eerie glow across his features, but I ignored it. I focused on each change in his body, any twitch of a muscle to get an idea of when he would move. He watched me closely as he set the knife to the side, far out of my reach.

He placed a hand on my neck and squeezed until I saw stars in my eyes, a quick flash from his camera blinding me before his other hand drifted down my torso, stroking my cleavage. His touch was slimy, disgusting. When his hand slipped beneath the edge of the dress to cup my breast, a gurgled cry left my throat. *Hold on, Evalyn. Just hold on*, I chanted in my head. His rough fingers found my nipple and twisted and pulled, sending a burning pain across my chest. There was nothing sexual about this. I had accused Daemon of touching without consent, but subconsciously

I had *wanted* those things, even if I denied myself over and over. This was nothing like that.

Luke grinned down at me. "I can't wait to make you scream, bitch. I've been waiting so long for this and I'm going to make sure it lasts. I'm going to lick the blood from your chest after I cut you. And then I'll fuck you while you bleed out – and right when the life leaves your eyes is when I'll fill that pussy with my come." His hand left my nipple to stroke himself through his jeans. I felt acid trying to crawl up my throat, and the pressure of his hand on my neck was the only thing that held it down. I was sick – everywhere he touched me, my body was decaying. Every word from his mouth was poison, paralyzing me in fear.

"Please, please, *don't give up,"* I remembered Daemon saying. *"You're not allowed to give up yet."* I held on to those words, wishing that I had stayed with him like he'd asked me to that night. Wishing I had just asked him to tell me the truth about what happened to those women. *It takes just one second, Evalyn. You can do this,* I promised myself. Still holding a death grip on my throat, he raised off my chest while reaching for my right hand. *Now!* I screamed in my head.

With every ounce of strength I had in my body, I thrust my hips upward, using my hands to shove his body away from mine. His balance was knocked off, just enough for me to roll him off of me. His hand left my throat in an attempt to catch himself as he thudded to the ground. I gasped for air as I lunged away as fast as I could. He would recover, which meant I had only milliseconds to spare.

"Fucking bitch," he roared. I finally rose to my feet, head still fuzzy from the hit earlier but the adrenaline enough to keep me moving. I was only three feet away when he made it to his feet but earned a few more seconds as he scrambled for the knife. It was dark beneath the trees, and in a few more minutes it would be entirely black. It didn't matter. I was

lost with or without the light, I just had to avoid tripping, and I would be fine. *I'll be fine.* The flats I wore on my feet threatened to slip off, but I couldn't stop.

I heard him crashing through the trees behind me, cursing as he went. The skirts of my dress were clutched tightly in my fist so I wouldn't trip on them and to allow my legs more movement. My chest was heaving for oxygen, having been deprived of consistent air for too long. My blood pulsed violently through my veins, driving me to run, run, *run*. I would make it to my house. I hoped that Luke would be so focused on me that he wouldn't spare a second thought for Elly, and then, if I somehow beat Luke, I could go back to save her.

"Stay with me..." I heard in my head. I kept running, pushing my legs to go as fast as they could. One of the flats flew off my foot, but I refused to stop. A second of hesitation could mean my life. I just had to get back to the house, I could find weapons there. And then, like the universe had heard my pleas, I saw thinning in the trees and a glimmer of lights ahead. The crashing behind me was closing in, but I was so close. My legs and lungs were burning as though acid had been poured on them. Still, I shoved myself forward, finally breaking through the line of trees behind my house. Just as I made it a few feet outside the trees, I felt a sharp slice on my back, and lurched forward.

I stumbled but forced my feet to keep going. But before I could go a step further, Luke's hand fisted my hair and yanked me backwards, causing a sharp shriek to pass through my lips. He flung me to the ground, and I scrambled away, but he grabbed my ankle and yanked me back, dress scrunching up, exposing my thighs. Flipping onto my back, I slammed my foot as hard as I could into his groin. He stumbled backwards, yelling, "I will fucking *kill* you, bitch!" I crawled away and scrambled back to my feet, closing the short distance to the house. As I stared at the approaching door, I had a grim realization. The doors were locked. I wouldn't have time to break in before Luke caught me and dragged me back to rape, torture, then kill me.

I didn't have my phone to call the police, and the nearest neighbor was farther than I would make it. I shook the thoughts off. I'd figure something out. Just as I was about to leap the black spiked fence to try and find a way into the house anyways, his hand clamped around my upper arm, yanking me backwards and tossing me on my back on the ground. I scrambled backwards as he approached, wishing I had been able to make it just a few more steps.

His knife glistened with my blood, clutched in his fist. "See, that fight is such a turn on, but it only makes your ending that much worse. I am going to make you wish you had never existed, you *fucking* bitch. So, go ahead, fight harder. I'll enjoy it." A sick smile twisted his lips. But just when I thought it was over, his steps halted. Confusion crossed his features, and he squinted at something behind me. Horror flashed in his eyes and his arms flew up, as though to shield his face. He stumbled backwards, and then, as though in slow motion, tripped and began to fall backwards. A hoarse cry left his lips before a black spike lodged in his throat, cutting off any noise aside from a wet gurgling.

I screamed, hands flying to cover my mouth in horror and disgust. Slowly, Luke's body stopped twitching, the life leaving him the way he promised it would leave me. And, with complete certainty, I knew Luke hadn't tripped. Daemon had killed him.

CHAPTER 31

A s my screams faded, numbness crowded in. Memories of my father's blood dripping from his neck flashed through my eyes, his death much too parallel to Luke's. Luke was a threat to my life, so someone killed him for me. My father was the same. Guilt clawed through me, tearing at the membranes of my memories, reminding me of the damage I continued to cause. It hadn't stopped at my father. My mother followed him into death, also caused by her own hand. The last time I had seen her was when she cried my name as she was shoved into the police car.

For a while, I stared at his large form, bent backwards over the fence. I didn't understand how him simply falling a few feet would make the fence drive so deeply into his flesh, but I knew it wasn't as simple as him just tripping. It looked like a spike had just missed his spine, instead slicing through the meat of the neck, pushing through the front of his throat. Blood dripped onto the soil of the empty garden. *Fertilizer*, I thought morbidly. I glanced at his hand. The knife was still clutched there loosely, my own blood shining brightly in the moonlight. I knew I had wounds, but I couldn't feel them.

Finally, I turned away, letting my feet drift towards the house, my hand reaching for the doorknob of the back door. I felt nothing at realizing it was unlocked. As the door opened, the alarm panel beeped, but I did nothing. I let it go until a piercing siren tore through the air, beating through my skull. The ache from my head didn't exist, even though I knew I should be hurting. My right ear tingled, the siren sounding muffled through that side. Letting the numbness take over, I sat at the kitchen table until the flashing lights of a cop car poured through the windows.

As the officers walked to the house, I robotically opened the door. Before they could speak, I said, "My friend is tied up in the woods somewhere behind my house," was all I said. Concerned glances passed between the two cops, and one of them split away to talk on his radio.

"Ma'am, can you tell me what happened?"

"Please find my friend," was my only reply. I turned, leaving the door open for the men to come in and went to the alarm panel, deactivating it. Then I made my way back to the table and resumed sitting. I was exhausted, and I knew I could only hold onto the numbness for so long. Soon, the shakes would start, and everything would come back. Memories from my childhood clashing with those of tonight. I wanted to hold on to the numbness for just a little longer.

The police officer that had originally spoken to me walked in and took the seat across from me, pulling out a notepad and pen. "Miss, can you tell me why you're bleeding?" I didn't want to answer. It meant leaving the nothingness.

I took a slow breath. "I had a stalker," I whispered. The officer jotted it down.

"Had?" He asked. I nodded stiffly. Just then, the other police officer ran into the house, a panicked look in his eyes.

"Bailey, there's a body in the back," he said breathlessly.

The officer in front of me, Bailey, snapped his gaze back to me. "Let's get some extra eyes here," he said to the other officer before he turned back to me. "Ma'am, we're going to have some paramedics come and check you out, and then I think we should head up to the station afterwards."

I looked at him, knowing I looked empty inside. "I won't leave until I know my friend is okay. He drugged her and tied her," I said, voice monotone. "Please," I added. Officer Bailey was older, seemingly well-seasoned. He was in good shape for his age, but his age showed in other ways – his hairline, wrinkles, and eyes.

Confusion melded with concern on Officer Bailey's face, and I knew he couldn't decide whether to forcefully drag me in or to trust that I was the victim. I was alive, Luke was dead. Would I be like my mother? Dragged away and thrown in a cell, only to die because there was nothing else to live for? I clenched my hands together in my lap, shoving the thoughts away. *Stay numb, just for a little longer.*

More lights flashed, along with sirens. Within minutes, three squad cars had pulled in, an ambulance, a firetruck, and a black coroner's vehicle. I felt the first of the shivers coming in, but I fought to go back to the numbness. The paramedics came in, squatting next to me like a child, Officer Bailey still looking at me as though he wasn't sure what to do.

"Ma'am, can you tell us if you're hurt anywhere other than your ear?" I only managed to blink slowly at them.

"Her back. She has a slice on her back," the officer said, eyes glued to me, a frown covering his face.

The paramedics glanced sharply at the officer. "Ma'am, can you tell us your name?"

"Evalyn," I said.

"What about your last name, Evalyn?" They were trying to get me talking. But more talking meant more reality.

"Wright," I said, voice beginning to tremble.

"And how old are you, Evalyn?"

"Twenty-nine," I said, the shakes beginning. The tremors started small but grew exponentially until my teeth were chattering and the pain came back. So much pain. My ear – throbbing, screaming, burning. My back had a line of fire from my shoulder blade to my spine. There was too much pressure in the front of my skull, making it feel as though my head might explode entirely. And emotionally? My stomach felt as though a nest of vipers had settled there, their poison sinking into my veins at the memories of the hands that had done this damage, at the realization that my best friend was alone in the woods, at the knowledge that this was all my fault.

"My name is Leah, and this is Alex," the paramedic that had been speaking to me the whole time said.

My teeth chattered as I nodded. "Evalyn, we need to look at your wounds. But I want you to talk to me the whole time, okay?" Leah laid her hand on my right shoulder, and I flinched. She frowned. "Is something wrong with your shoulder?" She asked softly.

"It's from last week," I whispered.

"Would it be alright if I took a peek at it?" I glanced at the men around us, wishing I felt less disgusting with their eyes on me, even if they were all filled with concern. I looked back to Leah and jerkily nodded.

Carefully, she pulled the dress away from my shoulder, and I winced. I could feel that in the struggle, the scabs must have opened. "You didn't get stitches for this?" I shook my head. "How did this happen?" I saw her eyes involuntarily flick down to the scars on my wrists.

"Luke," I said hoarsely. She nodded. Leah moved to look at my back, gently peeling the fabric away from the wound. Alex moved to dig through the duffel bag they had brought inside with them, pulling out medical supplies and letting Leah get to work. I was thankful that Leah was doing everything, rather than everyone else trying to step in. I continued shaking as she worked, asking me questions even though my answered remained monosyllabic.

Even as she flashed the pen light over my eyes and confirmed I likely had a concussion, my mind was focused on Elly. All I could remember was how I had last seen her, unconscious and tied up. She was left in the cold, alone, and here I was, getting taken care of. The only reason she was even in this mess was because of me. Everything was my fault. Almost as soon as Leah had wrapped my ear in a soft bandage, telling me it would "have to do for now," I heard chatter on the radio.

"Looks like we found the girl. We'll head back to the house so the paramedics can check on her."

Relief slammed into me – she was alive if the medics were going to look at her. But what condition was she in? The little voice in my head was screaming that just because she wasn't dead didn't mean she was fine, either. Time dragged as I waited impatiently to see Elly, and even Leah couldn't get a response from me. Still shaking, I clenched my fists together so hard that I felt them turning white.

Leah stepped away to speak with Officer Bailey, both of whom kept their eyes on me as they spoke. The other officer from earlier came from around the back of the house, a grim look on his face. I watched as a gurney rolled past, a black body bag on it, just like in a horror movie. The officer went over to speak quietly with Leah and Officer Bailey. The coroner left, and a few moments later I saw two firefighters emerge from the trees with my friend, untied but unconscious.

I leapt from my chair, desperate to see her, but Leah, Officer Bailey, and whoever the fuck the other officer was stepped in my way. Desperation tore through my chest, forcing a single word to rush past my lips. "Please!" I screeched.

A panicked look entered Leah's eyes. "Evalyn, breathe. I will personally take a look at her and make sure she's okay, but Officer Bailey needs you to tell him exactly what happened. For that, you need to go with him to the station. I've explained your injuries to him so that he knows how to best take care of you and keep you safe.

I shook my head violently, the world swaying as I came back to a halt. "I need to see her. You don't understand. It's my fault! It's all my fault!" I sobbed, tears pouring down my cheeks.

Leah rested her hand on my arm. "Honey, I know. And you will. But you have to go to the station first." She and the other officer split off from us, heading in the direction of my friend.

Officer Bailey stepped towards me. "Evalyn Wright, you're under arrest for murder. You have the right to remain silent..." his words continued, but a buzzing had started in my skull, and not from the concussion or the damage in my right ear. This was really happening. History was repeating itself and I was going to end just like my mother, hanging in her cell. He cuffed my wrists together in front of me and guided me to the squad car, ensuring I didn't hit my head as I got in. We pulled away, and while the emergency vehicle's lights were blinding, my eyes only sought the comfort of the lamp that I knew would be on in my room on the second floor.

Keep Elly safe, I thought to whoever would listen.

CHAPTER 32

T he ride to the police station was a blur, and by the time we arrived, my whole body felt crushed by pain, physical and emotional. They pulled me into a room with blinding fluorescent lights and a simple table and chairs. My cuffed hands sat limply in my lap, my mind trying to come to terms with where I was and why I was there. I spun my ring around my finger over and over, twisting and twisting and twisting. I stared down into my lap, my dress ruined, covered in rips and dirt and blood, one shoe missing.

Officer Bailey came in with a cup of water, setting it down on the table in front of me. He leaned over to uncuff me, tucking the metal restraints into his belt. I watched as he pulled out a chair, making a horrible screeching noise that scraped against my damaged ear. Once he was seated, he flipped out one of those stupid notebooks that I was getting really tired of.

Ignoring the cup of water, I continued to spin my ring as I waited for him to speak. The silence that fell was thicker than syrup.

Officer Bailey cleared his throat. "Ms. Wright," he began. "I want to go over a few things, and I'd prefer if we just kept this simple as possible. All

I want is a better understanding of what happened." He paused, waiting for a response. I dipped my chin in response. This felt too familiar, too similar to what I had experienced as a child. I felt the familiar screams pushing up my throat, the ones I had once repressed. A silence I had paid dearly for. "I see here that you came in a few days ago to make a report about a stalker that had attacked you, is that correct?"

"Yes." I replied, throat dry and voice raspy.

Officer Bailey's eyebrows drew in, and he nudged the water closer to me. Still, I ignored it. "Alright. Now, the man from tonight – was he the same stalker you were speaking of?"

"Yes."

"And in the report, it shows that you knew this man as Luke, is that correct?"

"Yes." I wanted to go home, to make sure Elly was really okay, to sleep peacefully and never experience another nightmare again.

"Alright. And can you tell me what events occurred this evening to lead to Luke's death?"

I bit my lip, hoping that the officer would believe me, hoping that he would see the truth and not just what he wanted to see. I nodded and took a deep breath, fat teardrops streaking down my cheeks. "Every year, Elly and I do a Halloween photo shoot. She's a photographer and she uses the photos on her website. I just bought the house and the property, so I thought the woods would be a good place to do it." More tears trickled past my lids. *My fault.* "Um," my voice trembled, barely contained sobs lodging in my throat. "I had stepped a few feet away to change my outfit into this dress, and when I walked back, she was laying on the ground. I panicked. I knew it had to be him and I didn't have a weapon so...so I just tried protecting her with my body," I said, my words coming in choked sobs. I tried pulling myself together. Swallowing another sob down, I began again. "But he hit me upside the head with something. A log, I think.

"I was disoriented. When he told me to stay still so he could restrain her, it was the only thing I knew to do." I took another shaky breath. *My fault.* "Then he took me to a different spot in the woods and showed me these...these photos he'd been taking of me since I was just a kid. He was talking about wanting to kill me and-" I choked, not wanting to say the rest. "But I slipped away before he could restrain me. And then I started running. I ran and he sliced my back at one point. But he didn't catch me until we got to the house.

"And then I'm not sure what happened. He saw something, I think, and tripped and fell backwards. It wasn't me, I promise," I ended on a shaky whisper. I felt cold. So, so cold – dead inside. I felt like I was back in my childhood home, trying to convince my father that I wasn't lying.

Officer Bailey rubbed his eyes and sighed. "See, everything makes sense except for the little tidbit in the end. After all that trouble, he gets spooked somehow and *trips* backwards? Ms. Wright," he said tiredly, "I believe that he attacked you and your friend. I believe that he stalked you – when the men went looking for your friend, they found the little spot you were talking about." He sat forward in his seat, resting his forearms on the table. "But that man would have had to have fallen from a much higher place to impale himself the way he did." He paused again. "*Or* you shoved him backwards to try and get him off of you and ended up killing him, intentionally or accidentally, it doesn't matter. If it was self-defense, I can help you with that. Which, based on your appearance and the state your friend was found in, I would say it was."

I shook my head violently. "Officer Bailey, I *promise* you that I didn't do it. I was laying on the ground." My mind scrambled, looking for a way to prove it when only I had been there. Then, a light flicked on in my brain. How had the police even arrived at the house? My alarm system. And I had cameras. Coverage for all angles. Surely, it would pick up the whole scene. "Wait!" I cried. Relief flooded through me. "The cameras!" Tears of relief stung my eyes.

Officer Bailey blinked at me. "You have a camera that would have caught that?" He asked.

I nodded rapidly. "When I realized he was stalking me, I got a security system installed. With cameras that are supposed to catch everything, even in the dark."

He nodded before standing up, reaching to talk into the radio at his shoulder. "Travis, is there a camera in the back that could have caught the footage of the incident?"

Heartbeats passed before the crackle of static came out of the speaker. "Looks like it. I wouldn't have seen it if you hadn't asked. It's too dark."

The breath whooshed out of my lungs, finally feeling something positive coming out of tonight. The system might save me, after all. "I have access on my phone, but I don't know where it is," I whispered.

Officer Bailey's eyes met mine. His eyes still showed he didn't believe me. "Can you log into the system on a computer?"

I blinked. "I think so."

He nodded. "Let me see what we can do. Sit tight," he said before walking out of the room.

Nearly an hour later, he walked in with a laptop. He set it in front of me, and I immediately scrambled to go to the security website where videos were saved. Once I was logged in, I turned the computer to Officer Bailey and let him look at the clips. I didn't want to relive it again, not yet. Instead, I studied Officer Bailey's face as he looked through the footage, particularly noticing when his brows shot up to his receding hairline and his lips parted. I watched as he clicked some buttons, likely rewinding it, and then playing it again and again.

"I told you I didn't do it," I whispered, tears still trickling down my cheeks.

Officer Bailey looked at me. "I see that. You're on the ground when it happens..." his voice trailed off. "It doesn't make sense."

I spun the ring on my finger some more. "I'm just worried about my friend," I said.

He nodded, rubbing his eyes. "I understand. Let me finish up this report paperwork and then I can drive you to the hospital where she is right now. She's fine, but the doctors want to be able to monitor her reactions to the drugs in her system. But so far, she's doing fine."

More relieving news. I sat, impatiently waiting to be transported to see my friend. I stared down at the ring, the one thing I had left of my old life. I wore it out of habit, out of memory. When the police handed me the items she'd had when going into prison, I'd slipped the ring on and had never taken it off. Well, not willingly. At first, it was a punishment. Then, it turned into a token of survival. Right now, though, the two feelings were fighting each other. *My fault.*

My body screamed louder the longer I sat, each cell in my body reminding me of what had happened tonight. The patch-up that the paramedic had done was great, but I didn't have any pain relievers with me. I wondered how many more scars I would accrue in this lifetime. I had already had some on my back, and it seemed old wounds were reopening. Would I finally have peace after this whole ordeal? I felt as though I deserved it. And then I remembered the other problem in my life. Tears welled up, knowing that while my hands hadn't done the killing, Luke's death was my fault. *You don't deserve peace.*

I'm sure a lot of people would say that the world was better off without a man like Luke in it. After all, he was a stalker, alleged murderer, and kidnapper. And, logically, I agreed. But I kept seeing the same thing over and over and over. My father's death, bleeding into my mother's.

***

17 Years Ago

I watched the blood pour in rivulets from my father's neck. The pruning shears were lodged deeply beneath the skin, and his eyes stared out lifelessly at me. I blinked, and the scene was gone. I was in a police station, a blanket around my shoulders and a cup of water resting in front of me. The fluorescent lights combined with the grey concrete and linoleum flooring made me feel ill. Everything made me feel ill right now, though.

"Evalyn, honey, can you tell us what happened?" Someone sat across from me, a woman dressed in a pantsuit. Her face was gentle, her tone soft. Her black hair was straight and ended at her chin. Her brown eyes searched for mine, but mine were nowhere to be found. My eyes belonged to the silver table.

Silver was my favorite color. Not pink, like most girls my age. Not grey, either. Silver. Metallic, shiny, gleaming silver. I knew silver was my favorite color when I saw a comic book character clothed in pure silver, blades at her hips, with white hair. The silver of the table in front of me wasn't pretty, though. It was scratched and old. Dirty.

"Evalyn?" The woman prompted again.

I couldn't open my mouth. If I opened it, it would never close again. I'd scream and scream – scream until there was nothing left of me but the echo of my cries. I hadn't said anything when my mother called out my name as she was taken away, either. There wasn't a single sound that had slipped past my lips since I watched my father's life drain from his body. So, I stared. Even if this silver wasn't pretty, it was still my favorite color. On the outside, I probably looked as dead as my father had. I had to hold back the screams. Maybe they would put me in jail, too.

Afterall, it was my fault, wasn't it? My mother would have never done what she did if I wasn't a part of the equation. It was my fault. The screams I held back turned against me, hatred boiling from keeping them locked away. Hatred at myself for existing. If I didn't exist, this would never have happened. *My fault.*

The woman in front of me shook her head, sighing. "Why don't we come back to this tomorrow after a good night's sleep, okay?" She stood up, walking out of the room. I stared at the silver table.

***

No matter how many nights passed, the woman couldn't get me to speak. Sometimes, she would change rooms, the bright colors of stuffed animals and toys making me hate the fakeness of it all. She put me in here as if I deserved comfort and softness. I didn't. I kept holding the screams back at each question. I deserved to be locked away for life for what I had caused, but I couldn't share my thoughts without releasing the screaming monster inside me.

They would sometimes tell me things related to that night, but I didn't remember most of them. I hadn't seen my mother again. Instead, they had put me in something called a foster home. There was a woman who fed me and bought me new clothes, but nothing helped. She couldn't get me to speak, either. They tried making me write or draw out my feelings, too, but I was scared that the monster inside me would show on the page as well. So, I stared at the paper and pen they laid in front of me, swallowing down the screams. And time ticked on.

Then, one night, I had a nightmare. Not uncommon for me, but this one was different. It was real, or it had felt real. I had seen my mother again, her eyes as dead as the night she killed my father. My view was a close up of her face, lips blue, eyes milky, and skin pale. The view widened, and I noticed her neck was twisted at a strange angle. Wider still my view spread, and I saw her in orange clothing. I began to reach out to her, but before my small fingers could touch her skin, she dropped through the bed she laid on into a pool of glossy black. Gone.

The next day, I sat in the colorful room. The woman held a bag in her hands, knuckles white as they gripped the plastic. Her face was grim, exhaustion pouring from her in waves. "Evalyn," she started. I simply blinked at her the way I always had.

She scooted closer to me. "Evalyn, I have some news." She paused, always waiting for a response. I said nothing. She soldiered on. "I'm so sorry I have to tell you this, but-" her words broke off for a moment. "Your...mother passed away." I blinked and took a breath. And another. Black pulsed in my vision. *Ba-bump. Ba-bump.* My heart thudded in my chest, the screams trying to shove their way up my throat. I held them down. I trembled and shook, but I held them down. She was saying things, but none of her words reached my ears. I heard nothing but the thud of my own poisonous heart in my chest.

I was vile. I was evil. I caused this. I was everything my father had ever called me. Everything was my fault. But I must have looked normal on the outside, because eventually the woman shook her head. Before sending me away, she pressed the bag in her hands into my own, leaving me to return to the foster home. Unrolling the bag with shaky hands, I saw my mother's silver ring with a single, small green stone tucked into the metal. Shaking harder, I slid the ring on my pointer finger, where it sat loosely, but not so loose that it would slip off. I clenched my fist until my nails bit my palm as I stood and made my way out to my foster mother who stood with a tight expression on her face.

That night, the hatred reached an apex – every breath felt like a heinous crime. I felt unworthy of each heartbeat while my parents had none of their own. *I* should have been the one in that cell. *I* should have been the one to die there. It wasn't my mother's fault. It was *mine.* Could I have saved her if I'd just opened my mouth and told them it was *all my fault?* Would my mother, the woman who had sacrificed her life for me, still be alive? *Ba-bump. Ba-bump.* The feeling of my own heartbeat was sickening, toxic – just like me. My silence had been selfish. My silence had cost a life.

My eyes latched onto something silver on the kitchen counter. A blade. A short one, made for small fruits. I snatched it, tucking it away while the woman who took care of me wasn't looking. After dinner, I went to the bathroom, locking the door behind me. I turned on the shower, leaving the water icy cold as I stepped below the punishing spray. I was instantly wracked with shivers, but the blade was steady in my hand.

Small whimpers began passing through my lips, and those turned into keening wails, which turned into the screams I had shoved down for ten months. I screamed and screamed and screamed as the crimson of my sins, the poison in my veins, mingled with the water and slipped down the drain. I heard pounding on the door, but all I could do was scream. An eternal, never-ending chasm of hatred had been opened, and it was all directed at myself. Even as I felt my body getting colder from more than just the water, I screamed. I screamed until the door was kicked open and the woman burst through, ripping the knife from my frozen fingers and tossing it into the sink.

She grabbed me, locking me in a tight hold as she wrapped my arms tightly with a towel, but still, I screamed. I had barely a voice left, but it didn't matter. I fought, but my struggles were useless. I grew weaker, vision turning grey and pale. I closed my eyes, embracing my punishment.

CHAPTER 33
Present

***

I felt each of those raw emotions over again, like a sick deja-vu. I felt the scream itching to burst from my throat, but I held it back. The dark side of me felt I had come full circle. The irony of the situation wasn't lost on me – my father's death leading to my mother's and then my own attempt. Followed closely by my institutionalization where Luke had found his obsession with me. And now, his death. Would this end they cycle of death?

Thoughts pounded through my head. How Luke had watched me for so many years without my knowledge. The way he had toyed with me the way a cat toys with a mouse, keeping me on edge from the moment he revealed himself. How I hadn't recognized him in some way only made everything that much more confusing. But, then again, I had locked those memories down so deeply that it took the world burning around me just so I would face them again.

I sighed, staring at the silver table in front of me, much too similar to the one from my childhood, complete with the cup of water. What was with the cups of water? Staring at the silver table, my mind drifted towards a different, more hypnotizing silver that plagued my nightmares. I blinked hard, erasing that train of thought. Elly was in the hospital, and I didn't have time for anything else. My knee bounced rapidly as I stared at the ring I hadn't removed since being released from the hospital as a child.

The last time I had been to a hospital was also the last time I had tried to kill myself. I was nervous, the foggy memories of cold, sterile rooms and drugs so strong that I couldn't keep my eyes open during therapy sessions coiling in my gut. And I was going back there, tonight. For Elly. And of all the insane, crazy, awful things that had occurred tonight, this was the one thing that felt right. Being there for Elly tonight to make up for the infinite times she had been there for me.

After what felt like hours, Officer Bailey came back in and had me read and sign some paperwork. I was so anxious to see my friend that I practically sprinted from the room as soon as he said he could take me to the hospital. By this time, it was past midnight, but I didn't feel tired. The pain in my back and head was more than enough to keep my body awake, and my mind was wound in an infinite number of knots, each more tangled than the last.

As soon as we reached the hospital, I ran in, asking the nurse at the desk where I could find my friend. Officer Bailey just nodded in my direction in goodbye before walking back to his squad car. The nurse looked at me with deeply concerned eyes, glancing over my disheveled form.

"Do you need checked in as well, ma'am?" She asked softly. The nurse had brown hair pulled into a tight bun, streaks of grey showing a bit of age. Her eyes were blue and kind, and the lines in her face showed that she smiled frequently. But she wasn't smiling right now.

"No, thank you. I was already checked on. I just need to see my friend. Elly – I mean Elleanor Briggs? She was admitted tonight." I was trying my hardest to not sound impatient, but, in that moment, I would have leapt out of my own skin if it meant getting to Elly faster.

The nurse shook her head in defeat and searched for the right room. "Room 408. She's perfectly fine. It looks like she has another visitor right now." I could tell the nurse was trying to imply I should clean up and then go check on her, but I knew that wasn't going to happen.

Instead, I said, "Thanks," and made my way to the elevator, where I received lots of odd looks and worried glances. *Pretty great Halloween costume, right?* I wanted to say. I didn't think they would appreciate my humor, so I chose to keep my mouth shut tightly.

When I finally reached her room, the door was ajar, so I knocked softly before entering. Tyler's head turned in my direction, but that was the only acknowledgement he gave for my entry. Behind the thin curtain was my friend, looking tinier than she'd ever looked on the hospital bed. Her red hair fanned out on the too white pillow, and while the nurses had done their best to clean her up, her hair and face still had smudges of dirt from the woods. My eyes stung as a tear streaked down my cheek, the ache of seeing her like this nearly too much. *My fault.*

However, aside from the grime, my friend looked like she was simply sleeping. Her breaths were even and measured, and she had an IV attached to her hand along with a device that pinched her finger. The silence in the room was heavy, my own guilt amplified with each moment of silence from Tyler. I knew what he must think. And I knew he was right.

"Have they said anything about her?" My voice shattered the silence into a thousand cutting pieces.

Tyler's jaw was clenched tightly, and all I could think of was the last time I had seen him – when he carried me to the shower after my nightmare. "She's fine. That fucker gave her too much, but the doctor's said she'll be fine." He took a steadying breath and turned to face me for the first time. "And you? Did you really kill him?"

I shook my head slowly. "No. H-he fell."

Tyler looked at me with suspicion. "Well, if you had, I'd say good job." I felt like I'd just been electrocuted. That was the last response I'd been expecting.

"I have cameras up. He just fell," I whispered.

"I heard that the only thing you cared about was making sure she was found," he said, gesturing to Elly.

"I was worried about her." My voice came out strangled. I was waiting for the damning words I deserved.

"Thank you," he whispered, holding Elly's hand a little tighter.

It felt like I'd been slapped. How could he say that, when this was all because of me? I couldn't take it. "But it was my fault," I choked out as fat tears began rolling down my cheeks.

Tyler turned to face me fully. His brown hair was disheveled, and he looked more tired than I'd ever seen him. Brown eyes stared into mine, pain and worry evident there. "See, a part of me feels like it's your fault. If she wasn't with you then she wouldn't be in the hospital right now." He sighed as his words sliced into my chest. He was right. I didn't even deserve to be here. "But I also know you didn't ask for some sick fuck to stalk you and try to kill you. And I may not know everything, but I know you've been through more than enough in your life and I think of you like a little sister. So, I'm glad he's dead and I'm glad you're okay. Who knows when she would have been found if you hadn't been there to make sure they looked for her." His words sank in, one by one. I wanted to scream at him, tell him that I'm a poison, that it *is* my fault, that he *should* blame me.

His forgiveness was crippling. More knots twisted in my head, and without uttering another word, I walked to the bathroom, one shoe still missing from my foot. Once inside, I collapsed to the floor, bringing my knees to my chest. I tried crying silently, covering my mouth with my palm as I released some of the overwhelming emotions that were choking me from the inside. My back felt as though it was on fire and my head felt like it would explode as I tried holding in the screams.

I realized that I had been really good at pretending I was normal again. I had pretended so long that it's what I thought to be true. And now, being forced to face my worst experiences all over again, I was crumbling. I felt like my life was a game of Jenga, and I had moved into the house as a tall tower, but each problem was another hole in the structure. Easy to ignore at first, but the weak foundations ultimately collapsed.

I was so *sick* of whining, crying, and being scared. I thought of myself as strong – this wasn't strong. How had I spent so many years pushing away my problems? I'd had an "aha" moment after Luke's first attack at the haunted mansion. But a few days of meditation and yoga weren't going to fix this. Anger, my familiar friend, ignited a small flame. Quickly wiping the tears from my cheeks and sniffling to pull myself together, I stood, straightening my dress as if it would fix the current condition it was in.

I tugged the plunging neckline together, shoving away the thoughts of the hands that had violated me. In that moment, I knew what I wanted more than anything. A hot shower. While this wasn't some nightmare I'd just woken from, I felt like the hot shower would purge some of the negative emotions that were still wreaking havoc on my mind. I stepped out of the bathroom and glanced at Elly and Tyler. He nodded at me before turning his head back towards his wife, resting his head on the edge of the bed.

"I'm going to see if they'll let me shower," I said.

"I'll be here with Elly, don't worry."

I nodded in thanks even though he couldn't see it. Walking out of the room, I went to the nurses' station and snagged the attention of a grey-haired nurse with deep circles beneath her eyes. "I'm sorry to bother," I started. "Is there any way I could shower? I can't leave my friend right now," I practically begged.

She pursed her lips at me disapprovingly. "What you need is someone to look at your wounds," she said, no nonsense in her tone.

I swallowed. "It's alright, really. One of the paramedics patched me up." My eyes trailed down to my shoeless foot.

I felt her silent disapproval as she watched me. "One moment, then." I glanced back up as the nurse walked away from the desk and into a 'staff only' room. A few painful minutes later, the woman emerged with clothes in her hand. She walked back in front of me. "We had a blood drive a couple weeks ago and have some leftover shirts. I only had the extra big ones left over, but I brought you that and a pair of pants and some socks. You can shower in your friend's room." Tears crept back into my eyes as I stared at this firm but kind woman. The pants were the really thin hospital gown material, and the shirt was giant – just the way I liked it. The socks were the classic hospital edition, but they looked warm for my cold, sore feet.

"Thank you, so, *so* much," I stumbled out. I wanted to hug her even though hugging strangers wasn't exactly my thing. But I could feel myself stepping back from the ledge with each kind word and action directed towards me. I gently grabbed the clothes from the woman, thankful for such a luxury after how the night had gone.

The nurse patted me on the arm before turning away to return to her duties. I turned quickly towards Elly's room before I started crying again. I slipped back into the room quietly and ran to the bathroom, thankful for access to a shower. I peeled myself slowly out of the soiled dress, being extra cautious while tugging the material from the drying blood on my skin. Now I didn't simply have a slice on my shoulder, but one on my back and head. The cuts felt hot and throbbed with each heartbeat. Finally removing the single shoe that had made it through the night, I turned on the shower and stepped beneath the spray.

I winced, feeling different aches and pains I hadn't noticed yet, but relieved to watch the grime from the night swirl down the drain. Gently, I washed my hair with the cheap shampoo and conditioner the hospital provided. I moved on to washing my body, fighting the urge to scrub my skin violently until each pore was purged of any trace of Luke.

I didn't know what I would return to at home. Would there be parts of him left on the fence? Would they clean it? I wasn't certain I could handle that. Turning of the water, I snagged the towel next to the sink and pat my skin dry, avoiding any cuts in case they were bleeding again. After drying off and sliding on the clothes provided, I felt like a new person.

I stepped out of the bathroom and towards Elly's bed. She still looked the same, as did Tyler. I sat in the corner chair, curling my knees up to my chest and watching my friend. Luke may not be coming back, but I couldn't turn off the protective instincts to make sure nothing else happened to her. But even as I watched, I felt my eyes getting heavy, exhaustion winning the battle over my body.

It may have been minutes or hours later when I reopened my eyes. It was still fairly dark outside, meaning it wasn't morning yet. Tyler was asleep, head next to Elly's hand. I blinked my eyes open, fighting to stay awake, wishing I hadn't fallen asleep at all, but thankful it had been dreamless. I assumed it had been the pounding headache that had led to waking me back up. After grabbing a disposable plastic cup and filling it repeatedly with water until I couldn't drink anymore, I sat back down on the chair and reclined my head back, accepting that a few more minutes of sleep couldn't hurt, especially if I was tired enough to sleep through this throbbing headache.

When I woke again, it was fully morning. The sun slanted through the curtains, burning my retinas with its brightness. I glanced around the room, noticing Elly still fast asleep in bed and Tyler at the door, the nurse in front of him saying a few more whispered words before smiling and walking away.

Tyler slowly turned his head back towards me. "Elly should be released later today. She woke up for a few minutes a little bit ago. Seems she's sleeping off the drugs fine, and the nurses said she won't have any lasting effects."

"She woke up? I'm sorry I was asleep," I whispered.

"She told me to let you sleep. You were pretty out of it, anyways." He sighed, returning to his seat next to Elly's bed. "She's lucky, you know? They don't know where that bastard got the medicine, but it was professional level. Professional enough that it should need an anesthesiologist to use. If it had been much more than what he gave her, who knows what could have happened?"

I felt fresh tears spring into my eyes. *Fuck,* I was tired of crying. "I'm sorry," was all I thought to say.

Tyler's gaze moved from Elly's face to mine. "When Elly is released later today, why don't you come home with us? Stay for a couple days? I think it would make the both of you feel better." I blinked at him. It was like he'd completely ignored my apology, instead choosing to bypass it as though it wasn't worth responding to. He had already forgiven me.

I felt a burning in my throat as I tried to swallow the lump that had shoved itself there. Instead of speaking, I just nodded. Tyler nodded back, then returned to the seat next to Elly. I was lucky to not only have Elly, but also that she was married to a man like Tyler. Tyler may not understand everything about me or what I'd been through, but he understood enough that he clearly wasn't judging me for the everything that had occurred.

A little under an hour later, Elly finally woke up. Her light blue-grey eyes looked tired, but she seemed fine. I stood up slowly. "Elly, I'm so, so glad that you're okay," I said quietly.

She looked at me, blinking slowly. "If he wasn't already dead, I'd kill him." She shook her head slightly. "I literally don't know where he came from, just that he blocked my airways so I couldn't scream and then shoved that fucking needle in my arm."

I wanted to laugh hearing her voice, so fiery and passionate after just having woken up from a drug induced stupor. How she managed it, I wasn't sure. But I was relieved. Any sign of her being back to normalcy was one more weight off my chest.

"I'm sorry you were involved in my mess." I felt my eyes starting to burn and fought to keep the tears at bay.

"I'm your best friend. Your messes are my messes. Besides, you didn't invite the creep into your life." Her words were almost identical to

Tyler's. How she was so casual about everything was unnerving. Because of me, her life had been put at risk. And here she was, acting like nothing had ever happened.

"Elly – you're in the hospital because of me," I said. A bubble of frustration crept up.

"And I'm fine," she said, narrowing her eyes at me. I twisted the ring on my finger. "I heard he died."

I swallowed. While I doubted that she knew the whole story, it wasn't surprising that Tyler would have snuck that little tidbit in while she was awake and I was asleep.

"When we get out of here, we'll go home and talk about everything." It wasn't a request.

After a few more hours in the hospital with plenty of nurses trying to look at my wounds and Elly saying she was more than fine and ready to go home, the paperwork was finally done and we loaded into Tyler's car and headed home. Somehow, the police had apparently managed to snag Elly's beloved camera, and she was already scrolling through the photos in the front seat.

When we finally got to Elly's house, she dragged me into the bathroom, Tyler separating from us, knowing Elly wanted me alone. "I know you're worried about me. Don't be," she said, eyes gentle. "I slept through the worst of it. I was more worried about you than anything." She turned her attention to my matted hair. While I'd been able to shower, I hadn't really had access to a hairbrush, so my hair was a bit of a lost cause. Plus, the pain radiating through my skull was enough of a deterrent that I hadn't tried messing with it. Still, Elly grabbed a brush and began gently removing the knots from my hair one by one.

"I wasn't awake for too long, but it was long enough that Tyler told me what he knew. Luke died and you got arrested but then managed to convince them to let you come to the hospital?"

I moved to shake my head at the poor retelling of events before wincing and deciding it was a better idea to just hold still. "That's not even half of it," I whispered, wishing I didn't have to retell this nightmare again.

Elly paused her brushing and glanced at me. "You don't have to tell me. But I want you to know that whatever occurred last night, it doesn't mean you're at fault for murdering him. He chose to do what he did, and you survived. And thank fuck you did, or I'd have to go grab your soul from the Underworld or whatever." She resumed brushing.

I swallowed a lump in my throat. It *was* my fault, wasn't it? "No, you deserve to know. But I really didn't kill him. Not directly, at least." I took a breath, readying myself for the story. Elly quirked an eyebrow but stayed silent, waiting. "I saw you on the ground and freaked out. And then he smacked me across the head and dragged me away." The copse of trees covered in photos flashed through my head. "Elly, he's been watching me for years," I said. With that, I dove into the story, stumbling through the fresh memories crowding my mind. Elly's hands stilled and her eyes widened the more I spoke.

I described the scene where any hope I'd had of getting away was gone, followed by Luke's death, and Elly cut me off. "Wait. I thought *you* killed him." Her eyes swirled with concern and confusion.

"No. That's just it, Elly. I didn't do anything. I was...I was done for." I felt, once again, the fear that she wouldn't believe me.

"Daemon?" She asked quietly.

I nodded. "I don't know what else it could have been." I took a deep breath. "Elly, it feels like I'm a kid all over again. It feels like when everything happened – when my dad died." I swallowed down the lump in my throat. "I feel like history is repeating itself, and it feels like I'm just a...a magnet for all of this crazy bullshit. That anyone who comes near me has their life at risk. Like, yeah, Luke was a bad guy. A really bad guy. But did he deserve to die like that? He died because of *me.* At the end of the day, it was me. But then part of me knows that logically I'm being ridiculous, because I wanted to murder him myself when you were put at risk." My chest felt like it was caving in, the words pouring out of my mouth felt like vomit. "I was so scared for you, Elly." I grabbed her hand, squeezing it tightly.

She squeezed it right back. "I was scared for *you.* When I woke up, my first thought was whether or not you were okay. And then when I saw you in the room, sleeping, everything was suddenly okay. No, last night should have never happened. But the fact that you made it out alive is the most important thing to me, and that fact alone is why I feel like I can act even remotely normal. So, I'm holding onto that feeling right now, and when the other stuff hits me, it hits." She looked at me as though she desperately needed me to understand what she was saying.

I nodded, wanting to believe that everything was going to be okay, trying to feel her optimism. "I just feel like I poison everything around me," I said, choking on a sob as my eyes stung with tears. Without a second of hesitation, Elly pulled me into a careful hug, avoiding the cut on my back and pulling my head against her left shoulder, keeping my bandaged ear safe.

And, once again, the damn broke. But this time, the tears didn't feel like they were endless. I felt lighter as I purged myself of the feelings that had been drowning me, accepting that I was still loved, could still be loved, even after everything. I wasn't alone, and because of that, the tears had an end.

CHAPTER 34

For the remainder of the day, Elly and I laid around. I knew there was a lot more to unpack, but I was already exhausted from the emotional rollercoaster I had been on in the last twenty-four hours – scratch that – the last month. But as the day waned and the moon rose in the sky, I said what had been on my mind on and off all day.

"I don't think Daemon killed those girls. Not directly, at least."

Elly paused the cartoon that had been playing. "What?" She asked disbelievingly.

"It doesn't add up. Think about it Elly," I started, sitting upright on the couch. "Remember my lists? How I said I thought he was cursed? He's like, trapped to the house or something." I sighed, knowing how I sounded but also knowing how I felt. "If it's possible for him to exist, then why is it *impossible* for another kind of monster to exist? And, sure, I could just stay away from the house, but that's not a solution. That's a band-aid. I bought the house – that's that. It's my responsibility now. I can't just run from it like I've run from everything else."

"What if it *is* just him, Ev?" Elly asked quietly.

"It's not. I know it isn't." My voice came out steady and sure, something that took me by surprise.

"Okay," she said. "But, what *if?*"

"Then...I don't know. But I can't live like this – live without knowing the full story; live in hiding from my own home." My fingers twisted the ring around and around.

"You can stay here," Elly said, practically whispering.

"Not forever, Elly. We both know that. And ignoring the problem doesn't solve it. I think Luke is the perfect example of that. For fuck's sake, he's been around since before I even met you," I choked out.

Elly nodded, eyes watering. "I could come with you."

I shook my head. "I know you don't believe me, but I'll be fine. I don't know why, but I just *know*. He won't kill me." And I did know. I felt like I'd been trying to put together the wrong puzzle this whole time, looking at the wrong picture and trying to match pieces. First, I refused to believe he was real, then I fought him, then I ran. And after all that, he had saved my life. I wasn't sure what he had shown Luke, but it had ended up keeping me alive.

Elly sniffled. "Fine. So, Daemon isn't the killer, but someone else is. What if they show up?"

I had to admit, I hadn't thought that far. "I don't think it will happen, but if it does, I'll figure it out." I sounded crazy, but I was resolute.

"Ev, I can't lose you. Please, just stay with me," she cried, her small hand squeezing mine.

"You won't lose me, Elly."

She turned her face away but nodded. She sniffled, then turned back to me. "Okay. I can't make choices for you. I know that." She blew out a shaky breath. "When are you leaving?"

The truth was, I wasn't sure. Did I stay another night and risk losing my nerve? Would I even be able to sleep? Since knowing and seeing that Elly was fine, I had been restless. I still had so many questions that needed answers. "Maybe tonight. I haven't decided yet." It was only a bit after six, so I felt like I had time to think about it.

She nodded again. As she opened her mouth to speak, her phone rang. "Hello?" She said into the phone confusedly.

"Mrs. Briggs?" A man's voice came through the speaker.

"This is she."

"Mrs. Briggs, this is Officer Bailey. Do you have Ms. Wright with you?" We glanced at each other.

"I'm here," I said.

"Good. Ms. Wright, I wanted to let you know that your attacker was Lucas Finley. Now, I know you had a rough night last night, but I'd like you to come into the station tomorrow to provide statements and maybe we can get this case closed up clean. Could you ladies do that?"

I nodded, then realized Officer Bailey wouldn't be able to see me. Elly stepped in, immediately agreeing to arrive at the station tomorrow. "Of course we'll be there." After hanging up the phone, Elly turned to me. "So, what do you want to do?"

I deliberated for a moment. Either way, I needed to go home before I went to the station tomorrow. I needed clothes. Elly was smaller than me, and so nothing of hers fit. And if I was going to go home, I wasn't leaving until I got the answers I so desperately needed. "I guess I'm going to go back home tonight. I need clothes. And a real shower. And answers."

Elly's eyes closed, but not before I saw the sadness in her eyes. Maybe I was a bad friend for leaving her, making her worry. But it was going to happen sooner or later – I wasn't going to just sit around and wait for answers that I had to actively go get. "Okay," she whispered.

She stood up and grabbed her keys and purse. "What are you doing?" I asked.

"Well, you're not walking home. I'll drive you. Maybe I can convince you to change your mind on the way."

"Are you even okay to drive? After the drugs, I mean?" I asked it gently, not wanting to push her away, but falling, once again, into concern for her wellbeing.

She snapped her head towards me. "I'm more okay to drive than you are, Ev. I'm not the one with the head injury. Plus, the drugs are pretty much out of my system completely. Plus, if you're so adamant on going home, at least I can drop you off and make sure you're okay. And then I'll pick you up tomorrow."

I wanted to argue, but she had a point. "Alright," I acquiesced.

After telling Tyler what she was dropping me off at home, he had offered to drive me instead, but Elly cut him off and firmly told him no. On the way home, she continued to ask if I was sure about what I was doing. While I was nervous, I kept nodding in agreement.

Her knuckles were white from the tight grip on the steering wheel when we finally pulled onto the long driveway. "Is your laptop inside?" She asked.

"Yeah, why?"

"Good. You are going to go inside and immediately FaceTime me from your laptop, and then I'll know you have a way of communicating with me in case something happens." Realization dawned as I remembered that my phone had been in the woods and had either not been found or hadn't been returned to me.

"Of course." My hand rested on the door handle. "Elly, I love you. I'll be okay. I promise."

She shook her head at me. "Don't make promises you can't keep."

"I'm not," I said firmly before opening the door and stepping out into the brisk night. Urgency was running through me like currents of electricity. Curiosity mixed with something else twisted in my gut as I glanced up at the house.

"I love you, too," she said. I smiled gently at her, closing the door and turning my attention towards the house, not even allowing myself to think about the back yard at the moment.

I had barely taken two steps when I heard the car door open. "Evalyn, wait!" Elly rushed up to me. "I can't let you do this. I don't know why I even drove you here. Come back with me, please."

I looked at her and shook my head slowly. I felt like a horrible friend, but something was dragging me back to the house. The need for answers, the desire to confront Daemon since I knew he had been the one to kill Luke. "I'm sorry, but I have to do this," I said.

"You're fucking *crazy*, Ev!" Elly was trembling, her eyes filled with tears. "You don't 'have' to do anything. You keep throwing yourself into these dangerous situations and expect me to be okay with it! I have *always* let you make your own decisions, but this is your *life*. And not your life against some regular person, but against some supernatural bullshit." She breathed heavily, frustration and worry plain on her face.

"Elly, I do have to do this. Whether it's tonight, tomorrow, or a month from now, it doesn't matter. If I don't get the answers I want tonight, I'm gone. Okay?"

"*Fuck!*" Elly yelled, angrily swiping tears from her cheeks. "Why are you so fucking stubborn?" More fat tears dripped down her cheeks.

"I have to do this," I whispered.

"Fine," she said, fingers angrily running through her hair. She crossed her arms and stared at me. "But I'm staying, too."

"No, Elly. Tyler needs you. He'd probably kill me if I let you stay."

She turned away. "Fine," she said again. "But I expect you to FaceTime me immediately."

"Okay, I will." I paused. "Decompression hug?" I stepped towards her.

She turned and opened her arms. Stepping into the hug and squeezing tightly, I held on until she finally loosened her grip, several moments later. "I'm going to be fine," I said.

"You're not allowed to be anything less," she replied. She turned and stood by her open door. "I'm not leaving until I get that call."

I nodded and turned back to the house. Blowing out a breath, I marched up the steps to the porch and entered my home. Silence greeted me, along with a seemingly tangible darkness. I quickly made my way up the stairs into the office and snagged my laptop from the desk. I rushed into my room, noting the light was off. I frowned but flicked it on and sat on the bed. Opening my laptop, I saw the battery was low, so I plugged it in before making the call to Elly.

She answered immediately. "You sure I can't convince you to just grab some clothes and come back out?"

"It's going to be okay, Elly. I'll be fine. You'll be the first person I call if anything goes weird," I said.

"Okay. Alright." She moved to sit in her car and started the engine. "I'll be back first thing in the morning."

"Okay. I'll see you, then."

"I love you. Be safe, Ev."

"I love you, too. I'll be okay." I felt like I had said that a million times since the moment I brought up coming back here. But it was true. Maybe I was crazy, but I felt it was true.

She hung up the phone and the heavy silence descended once more. I made my way to the bathroom and turned the water on. Shedding my clothes, I turned to look at the cut on my back. Thankfully, it didn't look as bad as it felt. It was relatively shallow but long. It would likely scar, right along the others that had been left from my father. The worst part would be trying to clean it and bandage it. Turning to look at my face, there was a horizontal cut on my face that dove into my hairline, just above my ear. It also wasn't a deep cut. It would probably heal without scarring if I was careful.

I stepped under the warm spray, wetting my hair to wash it. I longed for the hot water I typically used, but I was trying to be careful of my cuts. Even the lukewarm water stung, so I couldn't imagine how the hot water would feel. After showering and carefully drying off, I tried to bandage myself as well as I could with my limited reach.

It wasn't perfect, but it was clean enough that I wasn't worried about an infection. I knew it was too early for sleep, but I wanted to sleep now, my impatience for the answers overwhelming. So, instead of sleeping, I picked up my book and stared at the page, hardly registering any words. I felt restless and irritable. I wanted to get it over with. It was hardly eight when I finally snapped my book shut and slid under the covers, leaving the lamp on and closing my eyes.

My mind whirled, questions flying around my head. Of course, when I wanted to sleep, I couldn't. I forced myself to relax, winding down into the black emptiness that was a welcome change to my screaming thoughts. It took longer than I expected, but finally I felt reality slipping away as I sank into the river of dreams.

CHAPTER 35

I opened my eyes to a world of grey. My eyes widened as I looked around. There were no textures, no ground and no sky. I wasn't floating, I was simply existing. Panic crept through me. This wasn't right. Something was wrong. I turned, trying to find something other than this endless grey that held no shape or form. Finally, my eyes caught onto a spot of darkness, nearly blinding in its potency compared to the rest of the landscape.

"Daemon?" I called out. My voice sounded muffled and muted. I knew it wouldn't carry to him. I began dragging myself through the space, fighting to move. There was no traction to hold on to, to make myself move faster. Everything here felt heavy, lethargic. My body quickly wore down, but I kept doing. Something was very, very wrong. Worry for Daemon slipped through me, and confusion at the worry followed close behind.

I felt like I was moving mere inches with each stride rather than feet. Still, I pressed on. His dark form felt so far away. The closer I got, the weaker I felt. After what felt like hours, I finally reached him. "Daemon," I said again, my voice still nearly silent. I glanced at his sprawled form, fear trickling in. He looked dead. I dropped down to his level and grabbed his shirt. "No!" Then, I felt the faint beat of his heart and saw the miniscule rise and fall of his chest.

I needed to get him out of here. But where was there to go? A forbidden thought entered my mind – what if Elly had been right? What if he was a risk to my life? I'd been looking for a way to destroy him, hadn't I? Now, he was weakened, or at least it seemed that way. Could I leave? My stomach churned at the sick thoughts. *No*, I told the pessimistic voice in my head. There was more to Daemon than met the eye.

I looked again at his unconscious form. Everything was both so close and far, Daemon and I the only life in existence here. It was clear that he was dying, the world leeching the life from him. Or, perhaps, his life was pouring out of him into the world. I looked around, desperate for something, anything. And then I remembered the one dream where I had brought in objects with my mind. Could I change the landscape?

With a death grip on his shirt, I closed my eyes and built the first scene that came to my mind. I felt the air chill, a firm, cold ground building itself beneath my knees. I heard branches rustling above me, the heaviness of the grey world lifting as I willed my own world into existence. Finally, I opened my eyes to a forest of trees, branches barren from the approaching winter. Daemon laid in front of me, his form still unmoving, face still pale. Standing on my knees to look over him better, I pressed on his chest.

"Wake up, Daemon." My voice now carried through the quiet air. Frustration curled through me when he didn't move. Moving to straddle him, I grabbed his shoulders and shook him roughly. "Wake up!"

His head lolled to the side, black strands of hair falling into his face. I shook his shoulders again, not knowing what else to do. I was new to these things, and I didn't exactly have a manual for it. Anger bubbled up, the world seemingly mocking me. I shook his shoulders roughly. "You aren't allowed to fucking die before I get my answers. You got to kill Luke, so now it's my turn to get what I want!" I punched his chest lightly. "Wake. The fuck. *Up*!" I began hitting his chest repeatedly, desperate for any form of change in his countenance. My eyes burned as tears pooled up, blurring the world around me. I punched out my frustration, anger, and fear. Maybe it was cruel of me to punch someone on the verge of death, but he wasn't going to get off that easily.

Suddenly, the world tilted around me, my back slamming into the frozen ground, breath whooshing out of my lungs. A heavy, dark form laid on top of me, and my wrists were locked in a tight grip above my head. My back screamed in protest, but I ignored it.

"It's not nice to hit people, you know," a velvety voice purred from above me. I nearly cried out in relief.

"I just wanted you to wake up," I said, trying to put venom in my voice that wasn't there.

"I heard," Daemon said dryly.

"What's wrong with you?" I blinked away the tears and looked up at him. He still looked pale – far from his normal self. His eyes were dull silver rather than the glowing inferno they usually were.

Daemon sighed, sitting back on his knees and releasing my hands. He glanced down, raising an eyebrow at the position we were in. "No underwear? Naughty," he said with a small grin on his face. Heat flushed through me, and I quickly scrambled back and tugged my oversized shirt down to cover me. He rolled his eyes, but didn't move to stop me.

"You didn't answer my question," I said firmly, ignoring the way my cheeks burned.

He rolled his shoulder as though trying to remove an ache. "No, I didn't. Let's just say I broke a rule last night, and it took a lot of energy to do so."

Guilt smacked me in the face. He meant whatever he did to Luke. Meaning that he had almost died protecting me. Old memories surged up from the recesses of my mind. "Why?" I asked, a slight tremble to my voice.

His tired eyes met mine. "I couldn't just watch it happen. Not again. Not like that."

"You looked like you were going to die," I whispered.

"I probably would have soon if you hadn't started beating me up." His fingers gently brushed against my calf. I tensed, not knowing what to expect. His hand pulled away.

"Is it really beating you up if it saved your life?"

His face twisted in a grin. "A bad deed is a bad deed, no matter the outcome."

I huffed in annoyance. "I should have left you in the grey." As soon as the words left my lips, I regretted them. I opened my mouth to apologize, but loud laughter exploded in the silence.

Daemon had a wide smile on his face, teeth flashing in the light. "There's that lovely fire." He moved to sit against a tree, arms resting on his knees. He was wearing his black jeans and long sleeve shirt, along with combat boots. His toned muscles showed beneath the fabric, and, as always, a hint of tattoos peaked from beneath the clothing.

My large t-shirt felt thin against the cold. Why had I chosen this place? I felt my nipples hardening against the cotton and tried to ignore the urge to cover my breasts. "I have questions," I said simply.

"I might have answers. What's in it for me?" The devil's grin fell on his lips. While he looked tired, color was returning rapidly to Daemon's face, a shine returning to his eyes.

I shook my head at the audacity of his question. "I saved your life!"

He nodded thoughtfully. "Hm. And I saved yours, if I recall." His eyes sliced into mine. I flinched, realizing that I wouldn't have had to save his life if he hadn't saved mine.

"What do you want?" I asked, feeling my chest tighten.

"To play," he said simply.

My brows furrowed, wondering what that meant in Daemon's dictionary. "Play how?"

"It would ruin the fun if I told you, wouldn't it?" His dark laugh raised the hair on my neck.

"Does it involve my death?"

Daemon rolled his eyes. "No, Little Eve. I think we're past that, aren't we?"

I hated that I agreed with him. "I don't know. But if you can promise that this 'playing' doesn't involve my death or anyone else's, then fine." I needed answers, and I was willing to do just about anything to get them. Electricity snapped through the air.

Daemon's grin widened. "Deal."

The look on his face was unnerving, but I soldiered on. "Tell me how those girls died."

The grin dropped from his face instantly. Silence filled the air for a few moments before he finally spoke. "I drove them to it. Not...intentionally," he whispered. "But it was still my fault. Their fear of me pushed them over the edge." He peered up at me through his dark lashes. "You're the first one that has let me give you anything less than a nightmare."

My brows furrowed. "You're lying. They didn't just kill themselves because they went loopy," I hissed. So, maybe I was wrong. Maybe he really did kill them.

He flinched, confusion and shock washing over his face. "What did you say?" He said quietly.

"You heard me. I know you're lying. I experienced every single one of their deaths. I heard their *thoughts* as they were forced to do those horrible things." My chest was heaving in anger. "Either tell me who did it, or I'll have no choice but to believe it was you." He stared at me. Giving up, I lunged to my feet, ready to walk away.

His hand gripped my wrist, stopping me. I turned to say the words that would free me, but his other hand slapped over my mouth. "No, you're not going anywhere. Not yet. You're going to tell me exactly what you mean when you say you heard their thoughts. What you mean when you say they were forced."

I wanted to slap him. Rage whipped through me as I stared at him, the monster I had wanted to believe wasn't really a monster. Slowly, he pulled his hand away from my lips. I glared at him furiously, debating whether or not I should play along and tell him exactly what I knew or whether I should just leave.

No. I wasn't leaving or running away this time. "When I was away from the house while the workers renovated my room and bathroom, I had a dream each night. The first one was of Elaine. I was in her body, but I was conscious that it wasn't mine. I heard her telling herself to shut up. And then she killed herself.

"Then, Jayda. I felt a little more connected to Jayda, like we were doing everything together. She was fighting her movements, trying to stop herself. But she couldn't stop. And she jumped." I took a shaky breath. "Then, Suzanne. I thought it was me. I thought I was doing it. And there was a voice screaming in my head, forcing me to grab a knife and walk to the bathroom. I fought so hard. *She* fought so hard." A traitorous tear slipped from my eye. "The voice didn't stop until Suzanne was dead."

I glared at him, wishing I hadn't saved him. Why did I want to understand him so badly? Why couldn't I just let it go? I could have stayed with Elly. "If I was bound to die anyways, why did you save me?" I snarled. "Were you even dying? Or was this some kind of mind-fuck?"

Daemon jerked backwards, horror in his eyes. "It wasn't me, Evalyn. I swear." His voice was low, but confident.

"Then who was it? Where's the other mind-fucking demon around here? I didn't want to believe it, but maybe I'm just delusional. Who else can enter someone's mind and make them do something like that?" I refused to let him sway my resolve. I wouldn't fall for the monster this time.

Daemon shook his head in disbelief. "I can't enter anyone's mind outside of this fucking hellhole I'm in!" His voice rose in frustration. "Sometimes you humans are so narrow minded." Venom coated his words. "You just assume the worst because it's easy to pin the blame on me. I thought you were different."

"If it wasn't you, then who did it?" My teeth ground together in frustration.

"If I had to guess, probably the witch who put me here." He turned away from me, arms crossed and muscles tense.

I blinked at him. "What?" I asked stupidly.

A humorless laugh escaped him. "You think I choose to stay here?" He asked, turning back towards me. "In here, I can't hardly feel anything. In here, I only get to actually live when someone falls asleep in this house. In here, either someone goes crazy and dies, or I stay here forever, lost in a whole lot of nothingness." His eyes were nearly wild, gaze burning like that of a monster who'd been trapped in a cage for too long.

My mouth moved, but no words came out. Everything he said confirmed what I had believed before this dream. But was he lying? I thought about the fedora that was in the box with the rest of the items. Clearly, he'd had a physical body at one point. "If you're telling the truth, then why did you get trapped here?"

He slid back down to the ground, elbows on his knees and forehead resting against his arms. "I was summoned, and I broke the rules. This witch – she wanted me to terrorize Elaine's family. It had something to do with Elaine's father. He had dirt on the witch, and she was hungry to not only find out what, but find some dirt on him, too. Or plant some." He sighed tiredly. "When you're summoned, you do what you're told. If you do, you get to go home and go back to your normal life. So, when she sent me in to slip into their dreams and drive them mad, specifically the daughter, I tried to get the job done.

"But I found out that the witch wasn't planning on sending me home. She wanted to keep me, enslave me. She wanted to use me for more than one job. She wanted to use me for her own pleasure and gain. I'm a demon, and we don't respond well to entrapment. I was furious. It goes against our very nature. So, I confronted her. I demanded she let me return home. Her response to my disobedience was to trap me in this house and force me to do exactly what I had refused to do. Drive people mad.

"She said that if I wanted freedom, I had to find someone that wasn't afraid of me. But she made sure it wouldn't be easy. She made it so that my first impression on everyone was irrational fear. I was fighting an uphill battle. Until you." He raised his head, glowing silver eyes clashing with mine. A dry grin touched his lips. "You were scared, but not in the same way everyone else had been. You were angry that you were scared. And then I realized that some level of you saw through the fear and was attracted to me. I felt like you might actually be the one to free me.

"But then you realized I was the reason for the death of each of those women. And, rightfully, you fought me. Turned against me. And I nearly gave up again. But through all that, when I saw the cut, all I felt was rage towards whoever had done that to you. It was the first time in years that I had felt rage towards anyone that wasn't the witch. I wanted his name so that maybe, if I ever got out of here, I could hunt him down and gut him for touching you.

"And then, last night I felt your fear through the wall that I sit behind when you don't sleep. I felt its potency – I felt you calling out to me. I don't know how I did it, but I shoved through the wall and killed him. I wanted to do more than that, but I could only do so much before I was snapped back into 'the grey,' as you called it. It had taken all of my energy. If I'm being honest, I thought I was going to die, but I felt okay with that since I knew I had saved a life this time. Your life.

"But you came. Crawling through the grey to reach me. Your desperation, fear, and anger dragged me from the edge of death. And you not only created this world, but pulled me into it, as well. And you wanted me to be alive." Wonder gleamed in his eyes as he stared at me. As he finished, silence filled the air once again. His words connected the pieces together in a way they hadn't before.

Like I'd told Elly, it wasn't unreasonable to think there was another monster in play. I mulled over each part of the story, wondering if I was stupid for believing it. "So, where is the witch now?" I asked.

He shrugged. "Probably dead. She would be old by now."

"And if she's not?"

He frowned. "Then she's almost there. She can't live forever."

"If she can force people to kill themselves, why didn't she take care of the family on her own?" I asked.

"Why do rich people hire maids? Plus, she had other plans for me. It wasn't as simple as just that one job."

I nodded slowly. "So, if I'm not scared of you anymore, why are you still trapped here?"

His smile turned dark. "Why do you think it was only women who died? Single women, too." Confusion flitted through me. He shook his head in mock sympathy. "Sweet, innocent, naïve Little Eve. I can only be free when someone gives themselves over to me."

My mouth dropped open in shock. No. Fucking. *Way.* This was a majorly fucked up Beauty and the Beast story. "This is turning into a rated-R fairytale." My tone was clipped, but I felt the heat in my face.

His laughter echoed around us. "I suppose there is some irony in that." His face turned serious. "Evalyn, I never wanted those women to die. In fact, I stopped haunting their dreams. But they always died shortly after. Up until now, I thought it was because I had driven them to insanity."

Every word was sincere, and his eyes were pleading. And maybe I was crazy, but I believed him.

CHAPTER 36

We sat in silence for a moment. "So, to free yourself, someone has to sleep with you?" I practically choked on the words. I wasn't a prude, by any means, but nothing about this was normal.

"In basic terms, yes. I can't force it. They have to choose to. And they can't be afraid." His silver eyes glowed brighter.

"That's it?"

A grin tilted his lips. "Are you thinking of freeing me, Little Eve?"

I rolled my eyes. "I just want to understand. There are other things, too. You said that you felt my fear. You said my emotions were what drew you away from death. I don't understand that."

"I feed on emotions. The fear, anger, sadness, hate, joy – it sustains me. It's how I've stayed alive this whole time. Well. That and I'm not really supposed to be easy to kill. But in here, I have a limited supply. So, after I used all of my energy to kill the creep, I had nothing to...recharge me. Until you walked in like a tornado of emotions. As far as feeling your fear last night, I've never really felt emotions outside of our nighttime cage fights. So, when I felt it, I fought to get to you." His gaze dropped, some unrecognizable emotion flitting across his face.

"Why did you kill him?" I asked. The question had been burning below the surface for a while now. Memories of how my mother had killed my father and how, in turn, she had died were rising up like angry waves, trying to shove me below the surface and drag me down to the depths of the sea. Once again, it was all my fault.

He looked at me. "He was trying to kill you, Evalyn." His eyes darkened and the shadows seemed to crowd around him.

"And? The other women died, too. *You* could have died. Why would you risk your own life for mine? Now his fucking death is *my* fault." Anger and panic whorled viciously around my chest.

Daemon slowly rose to his feet and stalked towards me, a dangerous look gleaming in his eyes. Heat flashed through me, straight to my core. Why was I so excited by fear? He looked angry. He stopped in front of me, staring down into my eyes as I tried to prepare myself for whatever was coming next. I shoved my shirt further down my legs that were folded beneath me. He dropped down to a squat, head tilted and arms resting on his knees.

His face was inches from mine. "Your fault? Because I chose to kill someone? Maybe, Little Eve, I have somehow made it unclear that you are mine." I dropped my chin, both wanting to be stubborn and fight back and also not wanting to egg on the monster further. But the choice was taken as my jaw was squeezed in a tight grip and my face was lifted against my will. Liquid silver swirled in Daemon's eyes, the whites disappearing slowly. He grinned at me, but his teeth were sharp. "Let me tell you a little secret, Evalyn. I didn't care about anyone but myself until you waltzed in. No, that's not right. I hadn't had a true *obsession* until I met you.

"I had never seen anyone as fiery as you. You fought even when you didn't want to fight, simply because you refused to be wrong. And your fear was burned alive by the rage inside you. You've turned the pain in your life into anger. And any time you feel fear, sadness, or loss, you turn it into fury."

The same fury that he spoke of was bubbling up right now. "I prefer anger," I said through my teeth.

His thumb stroked my cheek, and he grinned at me. "Oh, I know. But what you don't know is how deep that anger goes. I think it's time for you to face the root of your anger, don't you?"

My brows furrowed, apprehension stiffening my muscles. "What are you talking about?"

"The reason you're sitting there, blaming yourself because I killed someone that you knew was going to kill you. You blame yourself, you're angry at me – have you considered being angry at the source? The person who chose to inflict the pain that you'd never asked for?" I tried to jerk my chin out of his hand, but he shook his head. "Uh, uh, uh. And here I thought you wanted to get over your avoidance tendencies." His face turned serious.

"Something that I've learned over the years is that just because you ignore something, that doesn't mean something doesn't exist. A burning house, for example. Imagine you're standing in front of this house, and you choose to close your eyes. Is the house still burning? Yes. Now, let's say you choose to keep your eyes closed and live your life there, ignoring the house on fire. Does that change the fact that the house is burning? No.

"Now, you closed your eyes, so you can't really go anywhere. You're either rooted to the spot or you risk stepping into the flames or some other potentially disastrous outcome. But you're not moving on. So, what if, instead of closing them, you opened your eyes? What if you opened your eyes, saw the burning house for what it was, and walked away? You've accepted the house is gone. It hurts, but you know it's true, and then you go on with your life. Eventually, the house on fire is only a speck in the distance." His silver eyes burned into mine. "In the second scenario, you give yourself a chance to say goodbye."

His words hit their mark – I'd carried the weight of my parents' deaths for all these years. And I'd addressed it as pain, but I also felt anger, so much anger. I had never allowed myself to think about how it could be directed towards my parents. My father, for all he had put my mother and I through. My mother, for abandoning me right when the world turned upside down, turning the world sideways.

I gritted my teeth together. "Who are you, my therapist?"

His eyes flashed, but his smile stayed the same. "Therapy can be fun. Have you heard of sex therapy?" He was goading me on, and it was working.

I slammed my palms against his chest and shoved him backwards, making him fall onto his hands. Lurching to my feet, I glared down at him. "You could have left their memories alone," I snarled. "But no. You had to dredge them up. Were you just trying to fix me?"

"You don't need fixing. And, for the record, I didn't dredge up those memories. You did."

I flinched. "What are you talking about?"

"You made yourself remember. The first one was triggered because of your fear of me, so I suppose you could blame that on me. But I never made you remember those things. In fact, I wasn't sure of what those dreams would drive you towards, and I wanted to stop them because of it."

I felt speechless. I had just assumed it was him. "What about my other nightmares?" I asked.

"The first time I tried giving you a good dream, you turned it into a nightmare." He shook his head. "It's my fault – I shouldn't have tried so soon."

My head was swimming. "I...don't understand," I whispered.

"Isn't it so easy to blame the bad guy, Little Eve?" Daemon bared his teeth up at me in a feral grin, the silver swirling endlessly in his eyes. "I can only set the scenes of dreams. What people do with them afterwards is entirely up to them. Well, nearly."

"What do you mean, nearly? That doesn't make sense."

"In my prime state, I can create any dream. In here, I'm fighting an uphill battle against fear. I've been made into a monster, a violent, horrifying monster. See, I can set the stage, but the influence of fear is poisonous. The initial emotion can affect the outcome of the dreams, whether I was here or free. In here, everyone was just afraid of me – except you. But before this cage, I was whatever I wanted to be. People didn't have to be afraid of me."

Silence fell around us gently. He had taken every perception I'd had of him and twisted it around. I was the one who had broken down the walls built around my memories. I had forced myself to relive it all in all of its horrific glory. I felt sick. He wasn't the predator here – he was the victim. He didn't deserve to be here.

And that thought opened another well of questions. If he was freed, would he return to his home? I knew he would. And while I should be relieved, I couldn't help but feel a pang in my chest. The emotions I had for him were far from love, but there was a level of affection there that I didn't quite understand. Perhaps it was the times he had tried to save me, body and mind. Or maybe it was a sadness for what he had been through.

What had he done to me? A twisted thought flew in. What if I didn't free him? I could take the time to break down these conflicting emotions inside. My stomach lurched violently. Was I any better than the witch if I did that?

"So, you'd probably go home if you got out, wouldn't you?" I tried to sound casual, but my heart thumping around my chest violently screamed otherwise.

"Eventually, yes. But I'm in no rush." His eyes darkened, his face turning into that of a cat that had found a very delicious looking mouse.

"But why not?"

He finally stood, brushing his hands off on his jeans. He took a step towards me, and then another. I stepped backwards as I had done so many times in our other encounters. But my back landed against something solid – a tree. A flash of pain ran through me. He took advantage of my cornered state, pressing his large body into mine, leaving his face mere centimeters from mine. My senses were overloaded; my vision filled with nothing aside from the man made of shadows and steel, my skin on fire where every inch of his body lined up with my own, my mouth tasted the crisp air as I gasped, my ears filled with nothing but the sound of my own heartbeat, and my nose smelling nothing but the lavender, mint, and darkness that was Daemon.

"Because I still want to play," he said, his deep voice running through me, leaving me trembling in its wake.

"Play?" I asked breathlessly.

"We made a deal, didn't we?" His eyes flashed as he stared down at me. I stared at him, vaguely recalling how this encounter began. How did he always send my thoughts flying away so effortlessly?

"What if I'm not done asking questions?" His hands had rested on either side of my face on the tree, making me feel small, but in a delicious way.

"Well, by all means, keep asking. But our play time won't be cut short, if that's your goal." I blinked at him. That thought hadn't even crossed my mind.

I slowly shook my head, heat spreading through me at not knowing what was coming next. I knew he had me right where he wanted me. I didn't care. He had taken the time to melt my worries away until there was nothing left but desire.

He grinned, teeth gleaming. Before I could react, his body was no longer pressed against mine, leaving me cold and bare. He stood back several feet. My head cleared. "What the fuck?" I said stupidly. He'd had me where he wanted me and then just stopped.

He shook his head at me. "Now, now, no need for that. I want this more...exciting," he said. I stared at him. "Run," he said.

I let out a laugh. "What?" I wasn't running. I'd done more than enough of that lately.

His face went cold. "You're going to run, and I'll tell you why. I'll tell you what pisses me off the most," he said, stepping close enough that his face was inches from mine. Unease churned in my gut. His voice had gone as quiet as death. "From the very beginning, I thought you were different. All these years, all I wanted was for someone to not run the fuck away from me when I proved I was *real* to them. But they were all weak. Every fucking last one of them. But it doesn't matter, because their blood is still dripping from *my hands*. It's my fault they died, simply because I *existed* in their lives. If they had just been able to look with more than just their eyes, maybe they would have seen what I could have given them.

Just like I would give *you* everything. But then, earlier, you still tried to run from me."

My heart thudded to a stop in my chest. His words felt so raw. My mouth opened and closed, but no sound escaped.

His eyes darkened, stare turning even colder. "So, you're going to *run*."

Confusion swirled through me. This wasn't at all what I had been expecting when he'd said "play." What had just happened?

"If you don't start running, I'm going to stop playing nice. You don't want to see what happens, I can promise you that," he growled. His eyes turned to pure silver, his teeth elongating into sharp points once more. Shadows slipped around his body, sucking all the light from this world. Fear trickled through me finally, realizing he wasn't just be messing around.

I stumbled away, staring at him in shock. Was he going to kill me? *No*, I thought. *It's just a game*. But what kind of game? I thought he'd meant something sexual. My heart throbbed in my chest, and I began moving faster as I saw him slowly stalk towards me. His face had somehow turned more nightmarish, and I decided that I didn't want anything to do with whatever creature Daemon had decided to be in this moment. I ran.

CHAPTER 37

My feet hit the frozen ground as I began running from the demon that was slowly walking towards me as though he had all the time in the world. I felt like I was in a classic slasher movie – the killer walks, the victim runs. Absolutely ridiculous. But my body didn't care. I ran faster, the muscles in my legs already beginning to ache. The shirt I wore did nothing to protect me from the cold, and certainly did nothing to support my chest. I dodged sticks and rocks that were littered across the ground, my feet already remembering the pain they had gone through last night.

Faster still I ran, not having any idea what was waiting for me when it came to this hot and cold monster that was Daemon. My breath rasped in my lungs, my hair flying in my face. Why was he doing this? I heard a branch nearby snap, and my heart picked up faster. I stopped caring about dodging sticks and rocks, I just ran. Surprisingly, the pain in my feet faded as I did, but nothing stopped the burning cold.

Déjà vu hit me, my mind recalling the many times I had had this dream. Hadn't I created this place out of memory? What was wrong with me? It was like I was fulfilling some creepy prophecy or something. It was too late to change now. Icy fire bit my lungs as the leafless trees seemed to reach for me. I could barely see through the locks of long dark hair that flew into my face. *Faster, faster* was the mantra playing on repeat in my head. I wanted to believe Daemon didn't want to hurt me, especially after our conversation, but I was terrified of testing that theory. Why was he doing this?

I heard another crack of a branch. Anticipation twisted in my stomach, and then slipped lower. He was going to catch me. What would happen when he caught me? I felt my heart slamming against my ribcage, a strange flush creeping over me that had nothing to do with the exercise I was currently getting. My legs were tired, my lungs ready to burst. And that's when I heard his laugh. It was over. I flash of darkness on my left sent me sprawling into the ground. *Run,* I thought. I went to get up, but Daemon's weight pushed me back down. His laughter echoed between the trees as his knee pressed on my spine. His fingers tangled in my hair, and before I could think, my head was yanked back.

"You didn't think you could outrun me, did you?" Daemons velvety voice whispered in my ear. "You're *mine* now, Evalyn. You're in *my* world. There is nowhere for you to run. Now, where shall we begin?"

"You were the one that told me to run, motherfucker."

"I think it's time we took that fiery mouth and put it to a different use, don't you?"

My breasts were pressed against the earth, the icy touch causing my nipples to harden. When I had fallen, my shirt hadn't done much to protect me from view. Slowly, he shifted his weight until his lips were at my ear.

"Your fear tastes so sweet, my love." A shudder went through me at his words. "See, I enjoy unpredictability. I thought you would like this. After all, you like it a little rough, don't you?"

"You're a sick fuck," I bit out, even though I felt like I'd scream if we stopped now.

"You haven't even seen me fuck, baby," he crooned as he ran a finger down my cheek, other hand still in my hair. He stood, releasing me. I heard a button pop, and I felt my thighs clench. *Nope*, I thought, beginning to crawl away. But a hand latched onto my ankle. "Uh, uh, uh. You're going to be a good girl and stay right there." The hand on my ankle moved to grip my hair again. He lifted me effortlessly off the ground, settling me in a kneeling position.

"Might want to rethink that, unless you don't mind not having a dick afterwards," I hissed. Inside, I was screaming at myself for fighting because I knew how bad I wanted this. I glanced up at him, his jeans button undone and cock fighting to be freed. His hand gripped my hair as he stared down at me, no whites left in his eyes.

"Is that why you're drooling, Little Eve? Pretend to fight, but I can feel your desire." I trembled as I stared up at him. He could see through me, but in that I almost felt a shred of relief. I could fight as much as I wanted, but he knew my true needs. "Unzip me, why don't you?"

"You can't manage that yourself?" I grinned at him sarcastically.

His grip tightened on my hair, pain igniting on my scalp and eyes watering. "Pull my cock out. Don't test me," he said in a dangerous purr.

I rolled my eyes for good measure. "Or what?"

Shaking his head, he leaned down and picked me up, pulling me over to a tree. Setting me on my knees with my back to the tree, he grabbed my wrists and pinned them above my head. The bark bit harshly at my wrists, but it only made me feel hotter. This was carnal, violent. My back whined in protest, but I ignored it as I watched him do the job that he'd asked me to do. Slowly, he pulled down the zipper and freed himself.

It looked painfully large so close to my face. And the metal bar going through the head made it look even more daunting.

I felt my mouth watering, my eyes glued to Daemon's cock. "I'll give you an option. Either I can fuck your face against this tree until you can't breathe, or you suck me off and I'll try to remember to play nice." I evaluated my options. On one hand, I could control the situation. On the other, I didn't have control. Not to mention the likelihood of reopening my back wounds. Did he know about them? A flash of pain went through me at the thought.

"Choose, Evalyn." His eyes clashed with mine, a challenge and a promise resting there. He looked like a god from this angle. Black hair dripping down his forehead, glowing silver eyes, fanged teeth, and dick that looked like it could send me to heaven. Or hell, more likely.

I slowly unlatched my jaw, staring into his eyes with intent. A wicked grin painted his face while he waited. He wanted me to make the first move. My arms still pinned above my head, I leaned in and swiped my tongue across the tip, feeling the ball of the piercing as I did so. What would it do to my throat? I shoved the thought away. I licked again, swiping my tongue around the head, gently enough to tease the monster but not enough to do much else.

I heard a low growl emanate from him. Taking the hint, I leaned forward and wrapped my lips around him, not wanting to admit how worried I was about fitting him fully in my mouth. It wasn't something I had ever really had an issue with, but his size combined with the piercing had me nervous. Massaging him with my tongue, I gently tugged on my wrists to indicate him to let go.

"No, you chose to play this way, now we both lose a little something." His eyes watched my every move as I swallowed him deeper, grazing him slightly with my teeth – not because I had to, but because I wanted to. "Fuck," he hissed through his teeth. "More."

So, I gave him more. Moving from the teasing glide of my tongue and lips, I dropped my jaw wider and pulled more of him into my mouth. The tip of his cock brushed the back of my throat before I pulled back, only to go further down again. Eyes watering, I gazed up at him, relishing the way he stared at me, as though he knew he was at my mercy in this moment. I pulled back once, all the way to the tip, and gently tugged on the piercing with my teeth. I had no idea what I was doing, but his reaction was that of a wild man possessed.

His hips jerked uncontrollably, and his fingers tightened painfully on my wrists. Fighting a grin of victory, I swallowed him in one go, feeling the tip of his cock at the back of my throat and pushing further. I gagged, but nothing mattered except for his pleasure. I grazed my teeth across his length as I pulled back only to do it again, deeper this time. Saliva dripped from my mouth, down my chin and onto my thighs. Without the use of my hands, it was more challenging, but I didn't stop. I wanted him to snap.

Again, I tugged gently on his piercing as I pulled back, only to swallow him deeper than I had before. Before I could blink, he pulled himself away. His cock glistened with my spit, and I licked my lips, smiling up at him. "My turn," he said gruffly. With that, he gripped my hair with his other fist and pushed his dick against my parted lips. The moment I opened my mouth, it was all over.

He became a wild animal, thrusting his hips and plunging his cock into my mouth and down my throat. He was pushing further than I had been able to without the use of my hands. I gagged again, the water in my eyes beginning to spill over and roll down my cheeks. He was relentless. My head jerked back, and I knew that his hand was the only thing keeping my skull from banging into the tree as he fucked my face. My body protested, back aching, wrists burning, head throbbing. But my pain didn't matter. He stared not at me, but at my soul as though possessed and enraptured. His pleasure had heat flushing through me, dark whispers of desires pouring through my mind as he fucked my mouth.

My air supply was limited, hardly able to breathe between thrusts. A moan escaped my throat, and he bared his teeth at me. "Yes, baby. Cry for me. You look so beautiful with your tears running down your face and spit dripping from your mouth." All I could do was stare as he said the words between thrusts. "You're going to swallow this fucking come. If any escapes, I'm going to punish you," he threatened.

Not able to respond, I just stared at him, more moans escaping as I felt him grow larger, his thrusts becoming more uneven. Then he thrust once more, deeper than ever, and I felt him release. I swallowed, fighting the urge to gasp for air while he pulsed in my mouth. After what felt like an eternity without oxygen, he pulled away, releasing my arms, chest heaving. I fell forward on my hands, gasping for air. Vaguely, I heard him zip his jeans. Before I could fully recover, the world tilted as he lifted me into his arms and held me against his chest.

"I hope you don't mind a little change in scenery," he said quietly, words rumbling in my ear. I blinked, and the world changed. We were back in the black room, except this time there was a large bed in the center, as well as a door.

He walked us over to the bed and tossed me down. I winced. His eyes narrowed at me; the silver only visible through the slits. "What hurts, Little Eve?" His head tilted in assessment.

I felt a strange relief in knowing he hadn't known before being so rough. I scrambled to sit up. "Nothing, it's alright," I said as calmly as I could with my heart trying to slide up my throat.

"I didn't ask you to tell me some bullshit lie. What. Fucking. Hurts?" His monstrous form was back, making him look like the god of death and fury.

Shaking my head, I backed away. "Can't we just pick up where we left off?" My feet pushed me further away. Suddenly, he gripped my foot – the left one. It was the one I had lost my shoe on. He raised it, looking at the cuts. They were all superficial, hardly more than a scratch but enough to sting. Still, he looked angry.

Dropping my foot, he stared back into my eyes. "What else?"

I didn't want to show him. If he was that upset over a few little scrapes on my foot, what would he do when he saw the cut going down my back? "I don't want to talk about this," I whispered.

"Then I guess it's a good thing you don't have a choice in the matter," he said in a low growl. Yanking me towards him, he grabbed my shirt and ripped it over my head. Instinctively, my hands when to cover my chest. He just shook his head at me. "Turn around."

I looked up at him, knowing I must have a desperate expression on my face. "Please," I said, hardly any sound passing through my lips.

He shook his head again before picking me up and tossing me back down on my stomach. The silence was tainted with the roaring fury coming from him. He didn't speak, but I knew it just as well as if I had heard him yell. Yet, when he touched the inflamed skin next to the wound, his fingers danced across my flesh in a featherlight touch.

"Evalyn, I'm truly sorry." His words came out husky, filled with regret. My brows furrowed.

"For what?"

A humorless chuckle escaped him. I couldn't see his expression, but I knew it was deadly. "I'm sorry I didn't kill him slowly," he said. I blinked down at the black comforter. I was speechless. "However, I can't help but want to beat your ass so red you can't sit for a week. Why didn't you say something?"

My mouth opened, then shut. Opened, shut. Just like a fucking fish tossed on land. I felt a sharp smack on the right side of my ass, causing a small squeal to escape. "Uh," was all I could manage.

Another smack, even harder. "I asked a question. Why would you not say anything and let me anger your wounds further?" He was more than angry – he was livid.

"I-I forgot and then...then I didn't care. I didn't want to stop," I choked out. How fucking embarrassing. I was admitting that I was so desperate for this man that I would ignore my own body's pain just to get a taste.

Three rapid smacks – left, right, left. I groaned at the pain but felt the pain slide right into arousal. "Well, did you consider that *I* might care?" He asked quietly.

I went to flip around so I could look at him, but he shoved me back down. Instead, I craned my neck to look at him, immediately wishing I hadn't. Shadows swirled around his shoulders, pulsing like a living thing. His eyes were bright, but his face was masked in calm rage. "You said you wanted to play," I said hoarsely, feeling as though my voice was disappearing.

Smack. That one was harder than the others, and I cried out. "I suppose I'll have to ask you in the future then, won't I?"

I shook my head violently. "*No*. I'm okay. Really."

He shook his head slowly. "I don't believe you."

I was at a loss for words. This man was upset at me for not telling him that I was in pain, but he was administering *more* pain? Pain that I was enjoying, much to my shame, but still pain. "Why does it fucking matter?" I spit out furiously. "You're upset by the wound but here you are, beating my ass."

A low laugh escaped him. "Oh, sweet, sweet Evalyn. You're right. Perhaps I should simply...stop now. Move on and let you wake up from this little 'nightmare.'" His words were slow and condescending, but I felt my heart lodge in my throat. I wanted to immediately disagree with this conclusion, but I held it back.

"Please," I started, wincing at how needy I sounded. "If you'd wanted me to wake up, you'd have let me already."

"*Let* you?" His laugh echoed around the room. "You can wake up at any time. You know the words. You've used them to run from me, over and over and over. No, you, my venomous girl, are desperate to stay. I can practically see your pussy weeping all over the bed."

He'd caught me. In my lies, in his claws. He had me. I swallowed. "Ungh," was all I managed. He was the first man to leave me without words. What kind of bullshit was this? Had my brain melted?

"Maybe, instead of beating your ass red, your punishment should be me forcing you to wake up." I flinched. "Oh, yes, I think that's probably the best punishment." He paused. "Or, you can stay, but you have to tell me how much you want to. Will you run away again? Or will you finally choose honesty?"

Stubbornness begged me to say I didn't care, to lie to his face. But the ache between my legs was growing into a dangerous need. I knew that I wanted to have sex with him. I had, for a long time. But knowing he would be free afterwards? I wasn't sure how to confront the idea. Some sick, twisted part of me wanted him to stay, if only so I could understand

him better. Understand the man that had wound his way through my
head so flawlessly that I had turned into this salivating mess in front of
him.

I'd gone from fearing him to wanting him but fighting against him
the whole way – denying myself. Then I'd found out about the deaths.
I'd forced this anger towards him, forcing the stupid little pieces to fit
together until I finally broke down and asked him for the truth. And
he'd laid it out for me. And somewhere between the start of this dream
and now, I'd turned into this wanton mess, desperate to sleep with the
monster behind me. Was I strong enough to admit that, though? Was I
strong enough to set him free, not knowing if he would stay or leave?

I took a deep breath. He'd sat in silence, waiting for me to deliberate
over my options. Hesitantly, expecting him to prevent me, I moved to
sit in front of him. My ass burned a little, but I ignored it. My legs
folded under me, I stared at the man before me. He was a god – a tall,
menacing, unearthly god. My mouth suddenly dry, I swallowed. He
waited expectantly, unmoving and unruffled.

I opened my mouth to speak the words that would damn my soul to
hell.

CHAPTER 38

"Daemon, I..." I wasn't sure where to start. My thoughts swirled in pieces around my skull, coherent sentences slipping through my fingers. Maybe I shouldn't have turned around. He was intimidating to look at, and in this moment, he had handed the reigns over to me – leaving him to stare expectantly at me. "*iwantofreeyou*," I said. The words were less than audible, mashed together like potatoes on Thanksgiving.

He simply quirked his eyebrow. I knew he was waiting for me to say more, to speak in words that weren't mumbled. My face heated to a dangerous shade of red. My heart pounding in my chest, I opened my mouth. "I-I want to free you," I choked out, stumbling over the words.

He tilted his head to the side. "I'm not convinced. Try rewording that, hm?"

Fury warred with embarrassment. He was playing with me, like I was dense or something. Why was he doing this? He knew what I wanted. "Little spitfire Eve, cat got your tongue?" He taunted. White hot rage at his provoking burned away the embarrassment.

"You know what I want, mother fucker." My words came out in a snarl.

"Do I? I don't think I do. Maybe you really would rather wake up." His tone was dry, bordering on boredom.

He was egging me on, but I couldn't stop the irritation. "Now you take the time to pretend you're oblivious to my pussy? *Now?*" I hissed. "Fine. You want words? Alright. I want to have sex with you, Daemon. And I know that means your freedom. So, I want to free you. Is that what you wanted? My fucking humiliation?"

A slow grin spread over his beautiful lips. "Was that so hard?" He asked. I shot daggers at him through my eyes. Until he got on the bed and loomed over me, rendering me breathless and stupid. His hand reached out, caressing my cheek. "You're such a good girl – thank you for your honesty." His voice was low and husky. I simply stared into his molten silver eyes, chest warming at his words; no indication other than instinct that he was watching me with more intensity than a dog waiting for their master to give them a treat.

Suddenly, he grabbed my waist and pulled me on top of him, resting my naked pussy against his jean clad cock. His hands encircled my wrists before he yanked me down, pinning my wrists against his firm chest. *It just isn't fair for anyone to be this hot*, I thought to myself. Moving one hand to hold both wrists, his other hand reached up to brush the hair from my face. "I hate to break it to you, darling, but freeing me isn't as simple as fucking me." I blinked at him.

"But, you said," I stumbled on my words. I was so confused. What else was there to it? Did I have to love him? Because that wasn't what this was.

He chuckled at my flustered state. Slowly, he rolled his hips into mine, the rough material of his jeans both uncomfortable and insanely erotic.

"You have to fuck me, yes. But not just me. You have to fuck me in my true form." My forehead creased in confusion.

"I don't get it. This isn't your real look?" Apprehension coiled in my stomach. What if he was just putting on this provocative face to draw me in? Looks weren't overly important, by any means, but if he ended up being an eight-tentacled monster with slimy skin, I was *out*.

He grinned; fangs barred in a feral grin. "My sweet, innocent, Little Eve." His thumb stroked my lower lip, causing my mouth to part instinctively. "No. This is the more...human aspect of my appearance," he said. "It would be terribly unfortunate if you ran from me after seeing what I really look like." He paused, letting his words sink in. It couldn't be that bad, right? "Do you think you can handle seeing the truth?" He rasped.

"Um, does it involve anything slimy?" I asked, voice high in my own ears.

His deep laughter filled the room, rumbling through my body. "I have some cousins that are, but I can assure you, I'm not." He paused. "It's been a long time since anyone has seen the real me," he said quietly. He sounded sad. Gone was the sarcastic monster. I felt his words tug at my heart. What must it have been like, spending the last eighty or so years trapped in a place where people only feared you? Trapped somewhere where no one could stand to see you for who you really were? Being forced to wear a mask because your presence alone was scary enough?

I tugged my wrists from his grip, pulling away. A flash of pain covered his features before being hidden, but he didn't try to prevent me from moving. I moved off of the bed, standing in the spot he had been in when he forced me to remove my own mask. Fear coated my stomach, but I felt resolve strengthening my movements. "Show me," I said without hesitation.

His brows lifted in surprise. "Are you sure?" He asked.

Taking another step away from the bed to give him space, I nodded. "If it's too much, you'll know."

He dipped his chin once in acknowledgement. My back was facing the door, an obvious exit that I somehow didn't feel I would need. Slowly, he moved to stand in front of me. He crouched down and unlaced his boots and pulled them off, kicking them to the side. He moved to stand again. With deliberate movements, he reached for the hem of his shirt, slowly pulling it up and over his head. My heart raced at what could be hiding beneath the fabric. But, when I looked, all that I saw were tattoos. Long, black strokes of ink creating the forms of snakes wrapped around his torso and arms. I blinked at them, feeling some apprehension leave my body.

He was beautiful. The toned planes of his stomach rippled down and formed into a perfect V shape that dipped below the waistline of his jeans. My mouth watered. Slowly, my eyes made their way back up to his face, his glowing eyes watching my every reaction. He waited. I stepped closer, snagging my fingers on the waistline of his pants. Looking into his eyes, I slid my fingers to the front until they brushed across the button and zipper. I popped the button and slowly slid the zipper down. I swallowed, fear and lust pulsing erotically through me.

Gently, I tugged his jeans down over his toned thighs, trying not to spend too much time looking at his fully hardened cock in front of me. His thighs were also littered with tattoos, though these were made of strange symbols and twisting figures. I had no idea what they meant. I slid the jeans past his feet before slowly standing back up, gently running my fingers over his skin as I did so. I saw his length twitch in response. As I stepped back, I let my fingers briefly slide across the velvety skin that covered his hardness. Regret at not doing more slid over me as I resumed my place a few steps back from him.

He looked at me, waiting for any sign of hesitation. When he found none, he clenched his jaw and closed his eyes, the silver glow disappearing. I watched closely, bracing myself for a change. Slowly, the darkness I was so used to seeing shrouded around him began writhing. My heart thumped – what was going to happen? Looking down to his body, I saw the darkness pouring from him, or, more accurately, his tattoos. They seemed to be moving, glowing, and changing. I blinked as I tried to fight off the tricks of my eyes.

The ink seemed to coalesce towards his shoulders, moving from the deep V of his hips up, up, up, until there was only skin. The tattoos on his legs glowed but stayed in place. Even still, I couldn't see much of anything with the smoky air moving around him. Slowly, the inky darkness slipped back into his skin, leaving nothing but the man beneath.

I blinked as I took him in. He looked incredibly different, but also the same. The bone structure of his face was pronounced and sharp enough to cut glass. His eyes remained closed, but the angle seemed different – more menacing. His black hair drifted down his face gently, looking as though it was floating.

The most noticeable difference, however, began at his neck. Scales, like those on a snake, rippled down from the skin just below his jaw down towards his hips. The scales were the texture of a snake's, the same shade of black that his tattoos had been. Where his plain skin met the scales, the design swirled and curved, inky lines dripping down his waist. Subconsciously, I stepped closer, fingers itching to touch his skin.

I felt a whisper of wind and looked to see where it had come from. The sight made me choke. Strange, bony wings trailed behind Daemon, claws on the end brushing against the floor. They were so large I wasn't sure how I had missed them in the first place. The wings were covered in the same black scales as his skin, glinting softly in the dim light. The man before me was beautiful – a god. Not as simple as a man, beast, or even angel. He was more.

I hadn't realized I had walked so close to him until I felt the heat coming from his skin. My fingers shook as my hand reached forward to touch him. My fingers barely grazed the scales, their soft yet firm texture catching me off guard. My fingers trailed slowly down his chest, wandering to the space where scales met flesh. A quick glance down quickly reminded me that we were both very much naked. I stepped back slowly only to peer around his shoulder at the wings coming from just below his shoulders.

Hesitantly, I reached my fingers out to brush against the thin membrane between wing joints. I heard his sharp intake of breath as my fingers pressed against the skin. It was surprisingly strong – not what I thought wings would feel like. I realized my train of thought. What had I thought wings would feel like before now? A giggle slipped through my lips.

"Evalyn?" Daemon whispered next to my ear.

Squealing like a child caught with a hand in the cookie jar, I jumped back. "Sorry! Does that hurt?" I asked.

Daemon tilted his face towards mine, lips peeling back in a smile. "Hurt? No. I'm...surprised," he said. His teeth glinted, pointed fangs longer than I had ever seen them. I swallowed thickly.

"Oh." I stared into his eyes, still a burning silver. "I was expecting something more, I don't know, scary?" It wasn't that his form didn't look lethal, or that he didn't look like something that had come straight out of a dark fairytale. It was that Daemon still looked like...Daemon. I wasn't sure what I had expected, exactly, but I thought maybe his whole face and body would change. Not just some simple alterations to what he already looked like.

His eyebrow lifted. "Disappointed?"

"No, no, I didn't mean it like that," I rushed out. "It's just, you didn't change as much as I expected you to."

His brows furrowed. "Did you expect me to turn into an octopus?"

My words tripped in my mouth. "W-well, n-no," I stumbled. The truth was that it *had* crossed my mind. I shuddered internally, feeling a great sense of relief in the fact that slimy tentacles weren't something I had to get comfortable with.

Daemon chuckled, calling me on my bluff. His hand raised, and I realized his arm was also covered in scales, but they ended in swirls near his hand. His fingers traced my bottom lip, my mouth opening slightly. "You're not afraid?" He asked dangerously.

A bubble of stubbornness rose to the surface. "You wish," I taunted. Before I could blink, his hand was around my throat, squeezing until my vision blurred. His tongue darted out and tasted the air. That's when I realized his tongue was split down the middle. I blinked rapidly, trying to clear my vision. He brought his teeth close to my ear, snapping them together threateningly. A trickle of fear slipped beneath my skin.

"Are you sure?" He whispered, squeezing my neck harder until a little cough escaped. But even with my air supply nearly nonexistent, or perhaps *because* of it, I felt wetness dripping down my thighs. I shook my head as well as I could with a hand limiting my movements, fighting the blackness crowding my vision.

"Of course not." His voice was husky, coated with desire. "You're not afraid because you *like* fucked up. I can practically taste you already." I jerked as I felt his tongue flick out and touch my ear. "In fact, I think I'd like to taste you now." He released my throat, leaving me gasping and coughing. Before I could even recover, he pushed me, facedown, onto the bed, bringing my knees under me and forcing my ass high in the air.

I heard a gasp escape my lips before I felt his teeth digging into the already sensitive flesh of my ass, pointed fangs threatening to break flesh. Just as quickly as he bit down, he released the skin, licking it to soothe the ache. He moved lower, biting and licking as he went, torturing my ass and thighs. I groaned into the comforter with each bite, my breath coming in shallow pants as my skin heated. He was teasing me, dragging out the sensations until I was ready to scream at him for not soothing the nearly painful ache between my thighs.

Finally, *finally*, his tongue swept over my folds, forcing a cry from my lips. It was the only warning I had before he devoured me. His tongue and teeth tortured my flesh, the strange split in his tongue bringing everything to a whole new level. He nipped at my clit, causing a sharp cry to escape before gently soothing it with his tongue. Pain, soothe, pain, soothe became the only thing I understood. I could feel myself rising higher, towards the peak.

Expertly, he pushed me towards the cliff and then pulled me back, building the pressure until it felt explosive. His hands gripped my thighs painfully, and he lifted me up so he could improve his angle. I groaned as his tongue dove between the folds before retreating and biting my clit again. My voice felt hoarse already, and my mind felt like it was a million miles away yet zoned in entirely on each sensation Daemon brought on. I was lost, completely at the mercy of the man behind me who demanded nothing less than the most intense pleasure.

My heart was beating painfully in my chest and a thin sheen of sweat coated my body. He brought me up, then down and back again. How long could he make this go on? Each time he pulled me up, I felt closer to slipping over the edge. Finally, I knew. One more touch and I would be a screaming mess. When he did send me over the edge, it was from biting down on my sensitive clit, causing agony and pleasure to ripple through me. I tumbled and rolled along the waves of my orgasm, feeling, once more, like I had been struck by lightning. I heard my scream as though from a distance as he dragged out the pleasure with continuous strokes of his tongue.

"Please, please, please, please," I cried. I didn't know when I had started saying it, but the word poured out of my mouth on repeat as Daemon pushed me on. I whimpered as he continued to lick, easing me down from the high. My limbs were leaden, my breath coming in gasps as I tried to fight my way back to reality. My heart slammed against my ribcage, making me feel as though the muscle might explode.

Slowly, he pulled away. Without the support of his hands on my thighs, I collapsed to my side, melting into the soft mattress. My hair stuck to my face, but I couldn't bring myself to give a single flying fuck – not when my body had been sent to heaven and then fell right back down into earth. He sat near the headboard, propped against pillows before leaning forward and pulling me on top of him. His wings were spread beneath him, making him look every bit like a fallen god.

"It's not so hard to tame you, after all," he said. I blinked lazily at him, still not quite fully present. He gently slapped my cheek. "We aren't done yet, Little Eve. I have so much more to show you." He leaned up, mouth latching onto my breast. It was slow, languid, and pulled me gently from the shores of nothingness.

The ache began to build again, and with the flesh so sensitive already, it felt like a fire was burning. "I...don't know if I can," I gasped.

He removed his mouth from my chest and looked at me. "You can. And you will. Because I want you to." His tone was firm, demanding. I couldn't deny that I wanted sex, I wanted *him*. I wanted to feel us coming together as one. But somehow, this monstrous demon had sucked the life out of me after just one fucking orgasm.

A sharp slap on my tit had me bolting upright. "Hey!" I cried.

His head tilted. *Slap.* The sting went straight from my breast to my core, adding to the inferno that was already blazing. "Let me show you more," he purred, driving his hips into mine, his cock sliding against my wet folds.

A breathy moan escaped. Slowly, he teased me until my body was reawakened, electricity flowing in my veins as need settled heavily between my thighs. Hands and mouth taunting the sensitive flesh of my breasts and hips shoving the hard ridge of his cock against my clit, I felt like a mess. No, I *was* a mess. My hands moved to grip the headboard for balance. "Are you going to fuck me?" I breathed.

His movements paused. "Is that what you want, Evalyn?"

I nodded. "Yes. Please," I begged.

A dangerous smile danced on his lips.

CHAPTER 39

H is hands moved to my hips, lifting me up. "There's something beautiful about a woman on top," he said huskily. "But don't let this make you feel like you're in control." He guided his cock to my entrance. "I wouldn't want that to go to your pretty little head, now, would I?" At the final word, Daemon impaled me. A hoarse cry poured from my lips. I could feel the head pushing against my cervix, and I felt stretched in a way I never had before. And my *god* the piercing. A year of abstinence surely hadn't done me any favors in this situation, either.

Already swollen and sensitive, my body felt every single ridge and curve. I realized I had clenched my eyes shut and Daemon had gone still. Breathing out, I opened my eyes to stare into his. He looked like he was using every ounce of control he had in this moment. He was holding back, but that wasn't what I had asked for. If it hurt for a moment, I wouldn't protest, simply because I knew I would be flying high immediately after.

But rather than telling him to lose control, I decided to make him. Agonizingly slowly, I rose up while staring into his eyes. Even slower, I lowered myself down, one centimeter at a time. His eyes flashed. "*Fuck,*

Evalyn," he hissed. "You feel so fucking good." The muscles beneath the black scales on his shoulders rippled as he let me play my game. Who would cave first?

His hands rested on my thighs as my own drifted towards my chest, fingers grazing my skin lightly. I settled down onto him fully before raising back up, stroking my nipples teasingly as he watched. I didn't change my pace. His eyes were glued to me, to everything I was doing. *Not in control, huh?* I joked silently. But still, he didn't move. Clearly, I needed to up the stakes.

I reached down and grabbed his hand, holding it so his fingers trailed along my stomach up to my chest and then neck. Finally, I brought his fingers to my mouth, gently kissing them before tracing my tongue down the middle finger only to bring it back up and wrap my lips around it. Not that long ago, he'd shoved his fingers in my mouth as punishment for spitting on him. Not tonight.

I moved slowly, up and down, matching the pace with my mouth and tongue. I dragged my teeth against the flesh, less than gentle, while staring into his eyes. I watched his fangs clench together and felt him twitch inside me. I grinned, teeth digging into his flesh. I moaned around his fingers as I moved, the piercing adding a new level of sensation to the pleasure.

Still, he was in control. *Fine.* Not wanting to take it slow any longer, I rose up to the tip, sliding a hand up his chest, teeth and tongue toying with his fingers. Without warning, I slammed back down, biting his fingers while the other hand went to wrap around his throat. *Get a taste of your own medicine, Daemon,* I thought briefly before losing myself in the moment. While I still kept a teasing pace, I moved on tip of him, grinding and rotating my hips for my own pleasure as I rode him. My hand was still clasped around his neck, his own hand in my mouth, still caught between my teeth.

He growled, eyes blazing. The energy crackled around us, heating my skin and electrifying my blood. Already, I felt close to tipping over the edge again, even with the teasing pace. My spit dripped past my lips and down his hand, my teeth still latched on his fingers. I squeezed his neck harder, the skin surprisingly smooth beneath my fingers. *So close.* I inched towards the edge, my moans becoming more erratic. He grinned evilly. *What?* I thought to myself. Before I could ride the waves of my orgasm, he gripped my hips and lifted me, sliding out of my dripping wet pussy.

I snarled, rage at being deprived when I was so close. He laughed, the vibrations running through my fingers that were still wrapped around the column of his throat. I curved my fingers, nails biting into his skin as I bit his fingers harder, no longer teasing or playful. "Little Eve, I told you that you weren't in control, didn't I? While I was enjoying myself immensely, I didn't give you permission to come."

Fury pulsed through me. I pulled my mouth away from his fingers dripping with saliva. "Last I checked, I didn't need a man to make me come." I reached down with my free hand, drifting it to my aching clit. Eyes glued to his, I slipped my fingers through my folds, determined to steal my pleasure back.

Daemon stared back, unimpressed. "Well, by all means, go ahead. And when you're done, I'll remind you what a real orgasm is. Show me how you play," he taunted.

"I'll be just fine with my own, thanks." I wanted to shove the words back in my mouth. What I really wanted was for him to drive me past all rational thought and send me into a sea of flames, burning away my sanity as I experienced pleasure unlike any I had experienced before. I wanted it because I knew he could.

His twisted grin said he knew it, too. But my pride made me want to prove him wrong. So, I played with my clit, rubbing it in a rhythm that matched my pounding heart. I flew to the clouds, losing myself in this moment while looking down at his silver eyes that were hungrily eating me up. As I inched closer to my orgasm, my fingers tightened on his throat, nails digging in. He growled, but not in anger. Instead, it seemed to have the opposite effect. My moans grew louder, my whole body taut as I waited to tumble over.

My fingers plunged into my pussy as I ground against my palm. The friction only accelerated the flames, though my fingers were much too obvious of a difference from Daemon's cock. But it was enough. With a cry, my orgasm shook through me, easing me down from the manic mess I had been only moment before. My chest heaved as I relaxed my arms, releasing Daemon's neck and pulling my fingers away from my overly sensitive sex.

A grin curled on Daemon's lips. "Is that all you got, Little Eve? I must say, I'm a little disappointed." His hands still gripped my hips, lifting me a few inches above him. My legs shook, aching from how tense I had been all night.

I made a face at him. "Like you can do any better," I snipped. Inside, I knew he could do much better than what I had just done. Sure, it felt great. But even that was nothing like the orgasm I'd had only a few minutes before.

He shook his head in exasperation. He moved me off of him, setting me in the middle of the soft bed as he rose, glittering black wings stretching. "I don't want to make your back bleed again, so while I would love to throw you on your back and pound into your dripping cunt until you didn't know anything other than my name, I think we should stick to a safer position." I rolled my eyes. He moved towards me, picking me up and wrapping my legs around his waist. He knelt on the bed, his muscular legs supporting me. Daemon suddenly yanked my arms above my head, gripping my wrists and holding them tightly.

Confusion swept through me as I felt his fingers trailing back down my arms, but my hands were still fastened. Glancing up, I saw that a rope had somehow found its way around my wrists, the top attached to a beam above the bed frame. Tugging on it, I realized it didn't budge. Arousal coiled through me as I realized the false sense of control I had been clinging to was gone as though it had never existed in the first place.

My breath came in small gasps as I looked back down into his eyes. His fingers lightly traced down my side, tickling the flesh. Daemon grinned viciously before I felt his palm smack my ass, hard. I shrieked. I tugged on the restraints, knowing it was futile but not caring. Again, a slap echoed around the room as I felt blistering pain spread along the skin of my ass. My shrieks slid into moans, the fiery pain dripping into pleasure. I panted, mouth parted and waiting for more. He gave me more.

I threw my head back with the next slaps, hips tilting towards him, both to escape the blows and to satisfy the desperate hunger growing inside me. Less than a moment later, his cock plunged into my folds, already dripping from anticipation. A hoarse cry slipped past my lips as I felt the piercing slide against the sweet spot inside me. Hands gliding back to my thighs, he raised me up an inch.

"Gentle play is over, Little Eve. I'm going to show you the monster I really am." Without waiting for a response, he drove himself into me in a punishing rhythm. A long, guttural moan came out of me as I lost myself in Daemon. My eyes half closed, I saw Daemon not for the monster he claimed to be, but rather the god he was. His eyes glowed as his wings flared behind him, the scales on his skin rippling with each movement. His face was wild, growls rumbling in his chest. He drove into me, pulling another orgasm to the surface, much to quickly.

A surprised cry came from me as the pleasure washed through me, lighting along my skin like fireworks, flooding my head with chemicals that left me feeling high.

He shook his head. "No, no you can do better than that," he growled. "Again, Evalyn."

I shook my head. "I can't," I cried. I meant it, too. Every muscle was shaking like Jello, my pussy so sensitive that each movement was nearly painful.

"That's not an option. You're going to give me all of your pleasure, Evalyn, until there is nothing left of you to give. You're mine, and so I will choose when you have nothing left to give." His devilish grin grew. "But don't worry, Little Eve, I'll make sure I give as much as I take."

I felt my body droop, the weight pulling at my wrist. How could I be so tired when I was dreaming? I felt Daemon's strong arms lifting me up, supporting me. One hand snaked up to wrap around my throat, arm acting as a pillar to lean against, while the other wrapped carefully around my waist. His touch was both firm and gentle, rough and caring. He rolled his hips, the movement sending my eyes rolling into the back of my head and another low moan to spill from my lips.

As he thrust deeper inside me, I felt a warmth stirring in my chest, some foreign sensation that had me feeling as though the world spun and dipped around me. I pushed it away, choosing instead to lose myself in the way Daemon was moving within me. He groaned, pulling out nearly to the head before driving himself deeper. Again and again, he drove himself into me, driving me back up to the edge. His hand slowly tightened around my throat, sending blood rushing to my head.

I felt my body tensing, muscles aching as he moved, angling my body to his. "There you go, baby," he said huskily. "Let me feel you come apart on my cock." My heart stuttered, body warming at his praise.

Suddenly, he paused, raising us up and pressing my naked chest to his. His hand that was wrapped around my throat moved to wrap in my hair, tilting my head back and dragging his fangs across my throat. He rolled his hips against mine, stimulating my clit, sending a cold sweat over my body. Short, rapid thrusts drove the ball of his piercing into the sweet spot within me. I cried weakly, voice breaking and body trembling violently as I was dragged mercilessly back to the ocean of pleasure that I would surely drown in.

His teeth pressed into my skin, the fang points threatening to break through. The sensation sent electricity skittering across my skin in anticipation. "Do it," I said, words slipping past my lips in barely more than a whisper. Why I wanted him to, I wasn't sure. But I needed him to.

His tongue trailed up my neck. "As you wish, my love." With that, his teeth dove into my flesh, a brief rush of agony rippling through me before euphoria crashed down. Lightning travelled down my spine and out to my limbs my orgasm slammed into me. In that moment, Daemon possessed my body, mind, and soul. Pleasure choked me, vision blackening as everything disappeared except for Daemon. Distantly, I heard my own scream echoing around the room. As my orgasm finally began to fade, Daemon growled viciously against my neck before I felt him thrust once more, burying himself within me. His hand fisted tightly in my hair; his arm wrapped around my waist squeezing me closer. His cock pulsed, releasing inside me.

Gently, he released his teeth from my neck, kissing the wound as he lifted me up, his cock slipping out of me, his come mingled with mine dripping down my thighs. His fingers trailed up to my wrists, brushing against them in soft touch before I felt my arms dropping down around his shoulders, hands touching his wings. Carefully, he laid me down on my side, disappearing briefly before returning, warm rag in hand. Gently, he cleaned my skin, starting with my neck and moving down to my thighs.

I winced as the cloth brushed at my sensitive skin, wiping away the mess we both had made. When he finished, he cleaned himself before laying back down and dragging me on top of him. I laid there, too exhausted to do anything. I had never in my entire life been so wholly satisfied. *Why couldn't it have been with a normal man?* I wondered to myself.

"You may have asked for a man, Little Eve, but you were given the devil." A dark chuckle shook the chest that my cheek laid on. *Guess I said that out loud,* I thought. He said nothing else as he ran his fingers through my hair, making me sink further into the bed, wishing I never had to wake up. A blanket was pulled over me, and Daemon and I just laid there, his warmth heating my skin, his heart firm and steady beneath his ribs.

How long we laid there, I wasn't sure. It didn't matter. Nothing mattered, not right now. I was practically in heaven. The wild events from the day before didn't matter, having all faded away to background noise. All that mattered was me, Daemon, and his hand gliding through my hair.

It was when morning light began teasing my eyelids that I realized I was waking up, roused from my dreams that had been anything but restful. Still, I felt Daemon's firm body beneath mine and his hands on my scalp. Perhaps this was part of the dream. Hesitantly, I opened my eyes, not sure what to expect.

There he was, laying in my bed like he had been there this whole time. The morning sun rose behind him, encasing him in light. Real light. Gone were the wings, scales, and fangs. All that remained was his smooth skin covered in snake tattoos. His eyes were shut, but he looked peaceful – normal. Was this real? Or was this just another part of my dream?

"Daemon?" I whispered.

His eyes slid open lazily, the whites having returned. The silver still carried a strange glow. "Yes, Little Eve?"

"Am I, are *we*, awake?" A tremor shook my voice slightly.

A smile stretched across his face. "Yes, we are. Good morning, love."

In that moment, the strange warmth from before rose up, followed by a single question – what now?

ACKNOWLEDGEMENTS

I wanted to share my absolute adoration and love to Kinzy, for being the reason I started this journey and putting up with the absolutely endless pestering for her opinions and ideas. And the book wouldn't be the same without Ally, for being the inspiration for one of my favorite characters. Kaitlynn, you gave me the feedback and advice I needed, and I couldn't love you more for it. And, of course, Brian, for supporting me and my dream always, as well as letting me act out scenes so they felt authentic to me (those moments inspired plenty of laughter). This book would have died before it was done if it hadn't been for all of you and the love you have provided me. I love you.

And, to all of you lovely, wonderful, beautiful readers, *thank you*! Honestly, I wasn't sure I would ever get to the point of publishing my own book. There were so many projects I'd start and then lose track of, but then I started this piece. And the more I wrote, the more I fell in love. But, let's be real. Without trauma, there wouldn't be this book. And without the help of certain social media platforms that showed me what "dark romance" was, there wouldn't be this book.

So, to the people that defined the word "trauma" for me, thank you. And to those of you who taught me what "dark romance" was, thank you even more. Because I have never felt more heard than I do with this community. It's beautiful being able to embrace the darkest parts of me and bring them into the light.

ABOUT THE AUTHOR

V.V. Webb has been weaving stories since she was just a little girl. She grew up in a strict, religious household that meant a lot of moving around and left much of her life unstable. She never knew what the next day would look like, only that she had to keep moving forward. At just seven years old, she had clarity of what she was experiencing and the cunning to continue to find a way out of an abusive home.

Finally, Webb was placed in foster care and went from home to home, using reading to escape the memories that clung to her and writing as her outlet for the experiences she'd had. She would write about things she was interested in for a while, but then set the stories down to gather dust on the pages of the several journals she set aside.

Webb went to college and participated in several creative writing classes where she learned new points of view that helped her improve the quality of her work. Still, she couldn't seem to complete any work she ever started. She was told that her writing and her stories were "too dark," and raised concerns for her mental health. But, she wrote what she knew – and what she knew was dark and rich with emotions that most people tucked away.

After years of trying to find a good way to write a memoir or an autobiography for the freedom she knew it would provide, Webb discovered Dark Romance. After bingeing several novels, she realized that she had found her niche, her safe place to truly express herself. An idea started to form and blossom, turning into her first book. She found herself cutting open old wounds, but allowed her to finally gain the closure she had longed for, for so long. Her writing is more than a few spicy scenes in a book – it's her own form of a majorly, *majorly* dramatized autobiography.

www.ingramcontent.com/pod-product-compliance
Lightning Source LLC
Chambersburg PA
CBHW021956130726
47903CB00014B/1463